Theseus

by

Grayson J. Stevens

Theseus

by

Grayson J. Stevens

© 2013 Grayson J. Stevens

Theseus is a work of literary fiction that draws on certain storylines and characters from Greek mythology and literature. Use of mythological or historical names, events or places is allegorical in nature. Otherwise, names, characters, businesses, places and events are the products of the author's imagination or are used fictitiously. Any resemblance to actual events, locales or persons, living or dead, is purely coincidental.

Cover drawing by Hannah K. Gray

Theseus

Table of Contents

ARETÈ 1

MINOTAUR 53

DYKE 367

MAP 406

GLOSSARY 409

πρώτο μέρος

ARETÈ

With those who identify happiness with virtue or some one virtue our account is in harmony; for to virtue belongs virtuous activity. But it makes, perhaps, no small difference whether we place the chief good in possession or in use, in state of mind or in activity. For the state of mind may exist without producing any good result, as in a man who is asleep or in some other way quite inactive, the activity cannot; for one who has the activity will of necessity be acting, and acting well. And as in the Olympic Games it is not the most beautiful and the strongest that are crowned but those who compete (for it is some of these that are victorious), so those who act win, and rightly win, the noble and good things in life.

Aristotle, *Nicomachean Ethics*.

α

"Winds from the Ionian east and the Peloponnese south swirl over our heads like birds circling a freshly planted field. The poets tell us that the bronze age is behind us and the fourth race of man now walks the earth. The gods favor us. Do not doubt that this is so. Phoebus Apollo guides our reason. Demeter and Artemis reward us with abundant grain and hunting stock. Pallas Athena herself has given us a great city where we find protection. From Prometheus we have innovations that separate us from our forbearers. But there must be justice if we are to prosper. This is commanded by the almighty lawgiver, Zeus himself. The justice I speak of is not merely justice with the gods or among men, but justice between men and the *polis*. For men are mere mortals, cursed with limited days, but the *polis* remains forever."

Antiphon and Enticles sat looking at Theseus as he spoke. Theseus was reciting the argument he had prepared for Enticles. Enticles would soon be called before the council of elders to prosecute his case against Demaratos. Antiphon smiled suggesting he was very pleased. Enticles was nervous and unsure.

"You certainly cannot expect me to say these things before the Areopagus," Enticles said in exasperation. "You may be skilled in the arts of rhetoric and oratory, but I am not. The elders will know these are not my words. They will mock me and toss me out of the council."

"Don't be too quick to judge what Theseus has prepared for you, Enticles," Antiphon replied. "Let us hear the rest of the speech."

The case Enticles was to argue was a difficult one. Enticles was accusing Demaratos of receiving stolen property while on a military tour in the mountain range shared with Boeotia. Demaratos was a popular figure in the city. Skilled in warcraft, he earned numerous victories in the field and was one of Athens' most accomplished generals. A year earlier, Demaratos had been summoned to appear before the council to provide his assessment of a campaign to rid the border with Boeotia of its lawlessness. Demaratos related to the council that Athena had shown herself in a dream and told him he was to lead a force against the thieves that plagued the region. The council trusted in the vision and supported his battle plan. Aegeus, the archon king of Athens and head of the Areopagus, gave Demaratos a well equipped battalion to conduct the expedition.

The mission did not go as planned and the great victory foretold by the goddess never came to pass. Instead, Demaratos encountered numerous ambushes that scattered and frustrated the Athenian forces. After months of fighting, the border remained violent and precarious, and landowners reported mounting losses of herd. Enticles himself sustained a measurable reduction in his fold. Evidence surfaced that Demaratos was accumulating recovered cattle for himself. Facing depleting wealth, Enticles asked Antiphon for help in bringing a case against Demaratos before the Areopagus.

"Let me begin my case by describing my own grievance, and later on I will address the great catastrophe to our city if justice is not done," Theseus went on. "My stock was plentiful and secure until Demaratos arrived with his army. Slowly, but surely, my herd lost its number. The marauders came undeterred upon my cowherds and took what was rightly mine. If that had been the end of the matter, I would not have this complaint against Demaratos. How can I bring a charge against thieves I do not know or who dwell in another place?"

"At this point, Enticles, you are to present your head housekeeper as a witness before the Areopagus," Antiphon explained. "Mention is his name, I think. Remember, Enticles, the good Mention is not to speak, only appear. His presence will be sufficient to corroborate your account. Now, Theseus, continue, if you will."

"Wise judges," Theseus started again, "I present to you my household servant, Mention. He was in Thebes during the time of the fighting. Mention was there to secure supplies of wine for our religious celebrations. Not all of what I had Mention purchase was for my own libations, I promise you.

Do not think me selfish. I frequently buy sufficient wine for those who cannot afford their own and come to the rites empty handed. I try to do what I can for the less fortunate among us. But I digress. While in Thebes, Mention overheard talk that Demaratos had been offered borderland and cattle from the thieves if he pulled back our forces. Now Mention has been in my household for many years. He is a good, loyal servant. He has no interest in this dispute I have with Demaratos. He has never met Demaratos himself or even seen the man.

"I tell you now, and you should consider this evidence of the truth of what I say, that I offered to submit Mention to the torture to test him. This I made very clear to Demaratos and even invited him to question Mention while on the wheel. Demaratos has refused this overture, even though I suggested it on more than one occasion. If Demaratos has the clean hands that he claims, why would he not have Mention subjected to the torture? Because he knows what words Mention would say. This is clear evidence that Mention knows the facts as they happened. It supports my contention that what Mention heard in Thebes can only be the truth."

"This is too much for someone without the skill for speaking to remember clearly much less recite," Enticles lamented.

"My friend," Antiphon replied, "you have already submitted the dispute to the Areopagus. If you withdraw or refuse to pursue it, only harm will come to you. The Areopagus will likely fine you five hundred drachmas for bringing a false claim. So please be quiet and hear the rest of the argument Theseus has prepared."

"Demaratos has caused me great harm and suffering," Theseus declared. "Without my cattle I will be a slave to poverty, the sworn enemy of every fine nobleman. So I ask you that Demaratos be required to return the fifty head he has stolen, or pay me two talents so I can myself replace them."

Theseus looked at Enticles and Antiphon, and then

proceeded.

"Do not hold it against me, great council, if I do not stop there," Theseus said. "I am compelled to ask for something more. Not for myself, mind you, but for our city. Whatever righteous cause led us to attempt to clear our border with Boeotia of these robbers, Demaratos' wayward tale of Athena's instruction has brought disgrace upon us. He told us of his dream and on this we relied. But it was a false dream. Athena did not appear to Demaratos. She did not advise him to take on the endeavor. If she did, then our warriors would have been successful in a fortnight. This supposed vision is beyond belief, gentlemen. How are we to judge Demaratos' claim? Do we not honor Athena in the proper ways? Would the grey-eyed goddess, who favors our city, deceive us? No. Demaratos either lied about the dream and the goddess or was himself mistaken about the origin of the prophesy. In either case, it is Demaratos' burden to bear. Demaratos must be punished for misleading the people. This offense must not go without answer or else many others would predict our future for us and deliver us to ruinous ends. Are we to entertain everyone who claims direction from the gods? Let those whose divine revelations lead us to harm be held responsible or otherwise learn to hold their tongues.

"Some of you are friends of Demaratos and all of us know his reputation as a great general. Our city owes a debt to him, to be sure. But this cannot be a reason he should not be punished. Justice does not allow for this. Bad men who do good things do not escape their fate, and good men who do bad things must suffer the consequences. That is our law. Imagine if you exonerated every man that has a bit of good in him from evil acts. Our law would mean nothing, and justice would never be done. Good men would become bad under this system, because men committing harmful deeds would go on without fear of retribution. We would lose our notions of right and wrong. Our great city would delve into anarchy and chaos unless the law is enforced against the good and bad alike.

"I say to you, great diviners of justice, in addition to what he rightfully must give to me, let Demaratos pay over to the state another two talents. Give one tenth of what is recovered to the temple of Athena so she harbors no ill will toward us, and deposit the rest in the treasury to repay the cost of the army. And so that we are not further polluted by the presence of Demaratos within our walls and again have him blaspheme Athena, have him banished from our land for a year. Let this malfeasance by Demaratos be a lesson for us all."

Antiphon and Enticles sat silent after Theseus finished.

"My friend," Antiphon spoke to Enticles, "you have just heard from the next great legist of our age. Take his argument to heart, and commit it to memory. If you can recall but a third of it, I can assure you will receive the justice you seek from the council."

β

Theseus was born in Troezen to Aethra, the daughter of Pittheus. Pittheus was a decedent of a long line of Troezen kings. He possessed great wealth and authority, but was known for his judiciousness and wisdom. Aethra gave birth to Theseus while she was young and unmarried. Some said Theseus' father was mighty Poseidon, the earth-shaker.

In the absence of the child's true father, Pittheus assumed the paternal role and saw to the rearing of Theseus. By all accounts, Pittheus treated Theseus as if he was his own son and raised the boy with affection and resolve. Pittheus was sure Theseus was fated for a high purpose.

"It is my firm belief, dear boy," Pittheus would often say to Theseus, "that the immortal gods look upon you with favor and your name will be remembered."

Theseus' education started at an early age. Pittheus entrusted Theseus to the care of Connidas as his pedagogue. Connidas had been Pittheus' companion when he was a young man and lived as part of Pittheus' household. Over the years, Connidas assisted Pittheus with his affairs and ventures, and Pittheus had come to rely upon him as a loyal advisor and confidant. When the time came for Theseus to receive formal instruction, Pittheus asked Connidas to undertake the charge.

"Theseus will be a leader in civic affairs, my good friend," Pittheus said to Connidas, "and I want you to prepare him for his vocation. Teach him first respect for the gods and to act with honor. Then proceed with the political arts. He will need to possess skills and knowledge perhaps unnecessary for us, but essential for the generation that follows."

Connidas felt the grave responsibility given to him by Pittheus, and agreed without reservation to see to the education of the boy. From the beginning, Connidas was fastidious in the molding of Theseus' character. In the traditions worthy of his line, Connidas committed Theseus to developing his mind and body while embracing aristocratic ideals.

"There are common qualities possessed by men of nobility," Connidas told Theseus. "These things I must teach you. Learn and master these traits, Theseus, and I will have fulfilled my obligation to Pittheus."

Connidas began Theseus' training with religious instruction. Connidas taught Theseus about how the world came to be, with Chaos, Earth and Tartarus appearing one by one in that order, and of Earth's progeny. Connidas recounted to Theseus the story of Zeus, Poseidon and Hades, the sons of Cronos who divided up the heavens, the earth and the underworld. He explained the Titanomachy, and named the gods who aided Zeus in the terrible war and claimed their rightful place on Mount Olympus. Connidas counted among them Hera, Poseidon, Demeter, Athena, Dionysus, Apollo, Artemis, Ares, Aphrodite, Hephaestus and Hermes.

"You must learn about Nereus," Connidas told Theseus, "for he remembers Truth without fail and knows Mercy and the Law. And take to heart the origins of Order, Peace and Justice, children of Themis, Zeus' second wife. Always praise Hecate, who is forever favored by Zeus, for she can bring wealth and glory to the men she chooses. Above all, lay your sights on Athena, the equal to Zeus in spirit and intelligence. She is patroness of the shrewd. You should also be wary of the lesser deities often forgotten in our times, particularly the more menacing agents. I speak of darkened Night, she who bore many of the afflictions of men. Lawlessness and Ruin, closely aligned, came from her, and Oath, who punishes those who knowingly swear to falsehoods."

Connidas made certain that Theseus learned the religious traditions of his day.

"Religious rites, although often complex and difficult to decipher, exist purely to please the gods," Connidas told Theseus. "It is our task to abide by them lest we incur their wrath."

Theseus was brought to the temples and shrines and exposed to the divine ceremonies performed there. Theseus observed the priests present libations of wine and olive oil and slaughter animals for sacrifice. He witnessed the processions on the public festival days and the parades of sacrificial animals that would be offered at the altars, adorned and purified with water and barley. Theseus viewed the lines of steeds mounted by horsemen dressed in fine tunics and cloaks. He marveled at the dancing troupes and listened to the hymns and prayers sung by the young maiden choruses that recounted the glory of the gods.

Theseus' favorite festivals were the annual rituals for Apollo and Athena, which he attended with Pittheus and Aethra. Theseus was allowed to freely partake of the public feasts prepared during the festivals. He enjoyed the abundant fresh meats, breads, olives and fruits that were on display. Theseus would run off with his friends unescorted and often enough find mischief. During a festival honoring Athena, Theseus and one of his mates found the reserves of wine meant for the temple rites, took a taste and ran off to boast before the other boys. When one of his cohorts called him a temple robber, Theseus grew fearful that Athena would punish him. He was frightened for days by what he had done but soon forgot when there was no reckoning from the goddess.

Connidas allowed Theseus to watch all the major festivals except the ones involving the Eleusinian mysteries or those glorifying Dionysus. Connidas was fearful of cultish sects and the unpredictable effects they could have on the young. He prohibited Theseus from attending these rituals lest he be corrupted. Theseus learned to be forever wary of those that participated in the mysteries.

"Our ceremonies are kept by the priests and religious officials," Connidas lectured Theseus, "those who possess the knowledge of the proper procedures for sacrifice. These observances have been handed down through the generations and most citizens do not know their origins. Nonetheless, on most questions of rites, the proclamations of the priests are not controlling."

Connidas explained to Theseus that the priestly class did not have authority to settle religious issues. If a question of

Theseus

first impression arose or there was a need to deviate from the ancient traditions, members of the Troezen aristocratic families would gather together in assembly to consider the matter. The assembly would often consult with oracles to be sure that the gods would be pleased with their decisions. Connidas related to Theseus that many years before, the priest of the shrine of Pegasus died without an apparent heir. Several of Troezen's noble families expressed an interest in acquiring the position, knowing that Poseidon would bestow favor on the family honoring Pegasus. After some debate, the assembly decided to ask the Pythian oracle whether to fill the vacancy by lot. The oracle responded that the office should be turned over to the one who covets it the most. So the assembly decided to hold an auction and award the post to the highest bidder. A large sum was raised which was divided equally to fund the shrine and the city's treasury.

Connidas also taught Theseus about sacral laws and sacrilege, and entertained his questions on the subjects.

"A polluted person," Connidas once told Theseus, "one who has contact with a corpse or association with a murderer, cannot enter a temple or the marketplace until purified. Destruction of olive trees or violent acts toward priests or others in a sanctuary draw severe penalties. Defacing a shrine or religious figure is also a heinous crime. Wrongdoing during the festivals is to be avoided at all cost. No one is allowed to strike another or seize someone else's money or property, even in satisfaction of a debt, during our ceremonial days. Profaning the gods at festival times is strictly prohibited, as is the use of magical potions or incantations."

"Tell me Connidas," asked Theseus, "what is temple robbing?"

"It involves actual stealing of temple property," Connidas said, "or failure to pay what one owes into a temple fund. A serious crime. Why do you ask, young man? Do you have some notion of this?"

"My friends have made mention of it," was Theseus' reply.

"Let me say a word to you about honesty, young

Theseus," Connidas cautioned Theseus. "Listen to me carefully. It is Truth that binds gods and men and allows for trust without suspicion. Zeus despises all who don't keep it. There is a tale that Zeus sends Iris to bring the *horkos* when it is time for a god to swear an oath. If the oath proves false, the god is stricken without breath or voice for one year. For another nine years after that, the god is banished from his place at the councils of the gods. So it is with Truth. Be honest in all your dealings. Now, what more have you to say about temple robbing?"

"Does one have to attain a certain age before he can be punished?" Theseus wondered.

"I am not aware of exceptions for minors, Theseus," Connidas responded softening his tone. "Perhaps the gods at times overlook the transgressions of youth. Even so, it is wise for the young not to tempt the wrath of the gods. Keep this forever in mind."

γ

Intermixed with his learning of the gods and religion, Theseus was taught of the great heroes. Connidas spent hours with Theseus relating tales of legendary men and their quests for adventure and glory. Theseus cherished these times. Theseus learned of many high-hearted heroes and deeds of bravery and valor. He loved stories of great courage and audacity. Two of his favorite heroes were both aided in their pursuits by Athena and recognized as founders of great cities. They were Perseus, who killed Medusa and founded Mycenae, and Cadmus, who slew Ares' dragon and established Thebes.

Of all the heroic tales, he prized those about Heracles the most. Theseus sensed that Heracles was different from the other heroes. Theseus admired Heracles' early choice to follow Virtue over Pleasure, for it was Virtue who told him that to be blessed by the gods he must honor them, to be loved by friends he must help them, and to be revered by a city he must render it service. He was fascinated by Heracles' great exploits to rid Greece of thieves, wicked men and monsters, beginning with his defeat of the lion at Mount Cithaeron. Theseus was amazed that Athena herself fitted him with armor. At play, Theseus would spend hours in the hills near his home pretending he was Heracles and mimic his countless heroic deeds.

Not all of the stories Theseus heard agreed with him. He was troubled that kings such as Pelias and Eurystheus plotted the destruction of the heroes, and even the gods worked to increase the heroes' labors out of the gods' own jealousies and ambitions. The madness that haunted Heracles from time to time was itself very disturbing to Theseus and not easily understood by him. The tales of great men confronting the Amazon women caused him particular fear and anxiety. These alien creatures lived outside normal society. They were wild and inhabited the edge of the world. The Amazons were fierce warriors on the battlefield and violent toward men. They were sexually active outside marriage, and known to kill or castrate their male children or have them sold into slavery. Theseus often had dark dreams about the Amazons, dreams he never shared with anyone.

The stories of heroic figures were recounted by the great poets, and Theseus developed an affinity for poetry. Connidas used poetry as a teaching tool, knowing it made strong and lasting impressions and conveyed the aristocratic ideals of virtue and noble conduct. Connidas had Theseus commit many of the epic verses to heart. During idle time, Theseus would repeat the lines to himself over and over. Poetry made Theseus feel strong and one with the great heroes of the past.

Connidas was not content that Theseus merely learn names and events from the stories. He wanted Theseus to draw moral themes from them and understand the noble character. Connidas questioned Theseus on why the heroes acted as they did.

"Tell me, Theseus," Connidas asked, "what do you see as common to these men? Why do they stand apart from all others?"

"My answer you already know, Connidas," Theseus responded. "The heroes are men of remarkable strength and courage, and undertake daunting tasks without hesitation."

"But what drives them to pursue these adventures?" Connidas said pressing the inquiry. "Many of the heroes face hardship and die on their quests. What motivates them?"

"They don't fear death, or at least don't admit to it," was Theseus' answer. "They seek glory."

"Why so?" Connidas continued. "Think a little harder on this."

"Well," Theseus said after some thought, "glory is better than death. Without glory, death is sleep without waking. But glory is never forgotten. It is immortal like the gods. So I think the heroes knew that if they achieved glory, they didn't have to be concerned about death."

"Now we are getting somewhere," Connidas said. "Tell me this, how do these heroes achieve their glory?"

"By fulfilling their duty," Theseus responded.

"Duty to whom?" Connidas returned.

"To the gods, their father and family, to their king or people," Theseus said. "There seems always someone they are acting for."

"And what reward does one seek or receive when fulfilling a duty?" Connidas persisted. "Glory is not the answer. Nor money."

"All right," said Theseus, "then it must be what comes before glory. I would say it is honor. Yes, honor. One must be recognized by others before there can be glory. That is honor, I suppose. Connidas, maybe the heroes act honorably so they can be honored, and there is glory in being honored in the right things. Maybe what makes a man noble is doing his duty even in the face of death and expecting to receive honor in return. And also to be willing to give honor freely to those deserving of it."

Connidas smiled, quite impressed with the young Theseus' thinking.

δ

Connidas took Theseus to school to assemble with other children and learn grammar and mathematics.

"Do not take the study of grammar lightly, Theseus," Connidas told him, "even if you think it comes easily to you. Names, syntax, etymology and the rest are the foundation of meaning and ultimately of truth. It is also the basis for the important language arts that are to come. Mathematics is no less vital. Prometheus himself claimed there to be wisdom in numbers and geometrical relations. So devote proper attention to it."

Theseus quickly demonstrated abilities uncommon to his years and mastered his subjects with apparent ease. The instructors were impressed by the boy's profundity.

Connidas also enrolled Theseus in gymnasium to develop his physical skills. Connidas intended that Theseus' body be shaped to carry out the ideals he was being taught.

"Physical strength and agility are preconditions to courage and valor," Connidas taught Theseus. "One must be strong of build before one can hope to be brave."

Theseus immediately distinguished himself in gymnasium. He was swift of foot, strong in boxing and favored in spear throwing. Theseus proved most accurate with the bow. He could throw the pig iron farthest and was feared with the sword. When the time came, Theseus displayed skill with the horse and chariot. Theseus' precocious athletic prowess garnered much attention among his teachers and peers, and soon the community.

At a relatively early age, Connidas began enlisting Theseus in the athletic games held on special festival days. Young men competed in races, wrestling, boxing, distance throwing and horsemanship. The winners were glorified and awarded prizes. Theseus proved superior in many of the athletic events and earned honor for himself and his family.

Connidas considered music essential to Theseus' education. Music imparted rhythm and harmony to the spirit, and made temperate the excessive tendencies of heroism and

Theseus

bravery. Theseus chose to play the lyre, and Connidas saw to it that he practiced fervently. He became known as a gifted musician, and some say the richness of the sounds he created with the lyre were the equal of Orpheus. Theseus performed publicly on occasion and earned recognition for his technique and syncopation.

Connidas also had Theseus attend theatre performances. He watched plays and reenactments of the tales of gods and men. Many playwrights would enter their works in the competitions at the festivals in the hope of winning awards and fame. Theseus was captivated by storylines pitting god against man and the trials of many great people who railed against their destiny. He imagined himself upon the stage addressing the masked chorus with the crowds fixed upon him.

When it was age appropriate, Connidas had Theseus turn his attention to eloquence and debate. For this, he began taking Theseus to hear visiting sophists that frequented Troezen. The sophists traveled from city to city to teach rhetoric and hold polemics on political theory. Citizens met in the marketplace to hear them speak.

"The subjects treated by the sophists are important for public life," Connidas told Theseus. "They claim they know the techniques for effective communication. These skills will prove more valuable to you than your way with the spear. Persuasion in public speech means influence in public affairs. But be wary of these teachers. Rhetoric can be dangerous if used only to advance ordinary or uninspired causes. There is no merit in convincing a mob to act unscrupulously. And beware of the curse of Thersites, hated by the great princes at Troy for his bombastic and rude speech."

Theseus would sit with Connidas and listen intently to the sophists. With proper respect and deference, he often asked questions of them to probe the foundations of their positions.

On one occasion, an acclaimed sophist of the name Leodamas came to expound on methods for winning arguments in the law courts. Theseus attended the lesson with Connidas.

"Be attentive to what I say to you," Leodamas proclaimed. "For what I teach surpasses even the Muses' gift of convincing speech before the assembly."

Leodamas began with describing how to best an opponent in a trial.

"The first thing to keep in mind," Leodamas instructed, "is that every trial is political because it is held in a public forum. Each decision of the lawgiver should be understood as having a political outcome. Do not lose sight of this. Now, all effective arguments are premised on personalizing the issue at hand. This we can manage in a number of ways. First, a litigant who presses charges must display anger or enmity toward one's opponent, and he should work to convince the judges that they too should share those feelings. This necessitates knowing something about the opponent, and portraying his character as socially reprehensible and worthy of condemnation by the community. Once this is established, the litigant should be clear that he is seeking revenge and the opponent should be severely punished for his behavior. The last, and not least important, is to recommend to the lawgiver that they are responsible for deciding the case in a fashion that will be beneficial to the community as a whole, that it will serve to deter others from acts that are undesirable in society or harmful to the city."

The gathered listeners were visibly uncomfortable with the demagoguery espoused by Leodamas.

"I can see from the looks on your faces that you are not convinced by what I teach you," Leodamas observed. "Let me offer you an example. Put yourself in a seat at the council and imagine how you would decide a hypothetical case. Now, you two gentlemen up front here, what are you called by?"

The two men who Leodamas identified gave Pyrrhos and Megistas as their names.

"Suppose that Megistas buys a horse from our friend Pyrrhos and within a month of the purchase the horse dies. Megistas decides to summons Pyrrhos before the council for selling him a diseased horse. Now our rules on landed trade are not complex. The elements of a commercial transaction occur at the time the goods are delivered and paid for. Let's assume the trade occurred in the marketplace, and the law says that no one is allowed to speak a lie there. Megistas brings an action for false representation of the goods sold. Megistas argues before the lawgiver that he paid for a healthy horse, and wants either his money back or a horse that is fit. This is straightforward and seems to be a fair claim. If a horse dies quickly after purchase, the animal must have been sick before, and a buyer would never pay full price for a sick horse. But Megistas is likely to lose. Pyrrhos will argue that he made no statement about the vitality of the horse and our custom in the marketplace does not impose warranties on sellers of goods. We all know this is true. The lawgiver will find in favor of Pyrrhos, even though it is quite likely that Pyrrhos tricked Megistas in the transaction."

The men before Leodamas nodded their agreement that this was the probable verdict.

"Consider now a strategy along the lines I suggest," Leodamas said. "In his argument before the lawgiver, suppose Megistas shows anger toward Pyrrhos for cheating him. The council will likely share this sentiment as no one likes to be cheated. Let's have Megistas also say that Pyrrhos is not a respected member of the community, that he is unmarried without children and cavorts with harlots, that he has not paid his fair share of the military and bribes city officials. Now we have the council hating this man. Megistas does not stop there. He argues that Pyrrhos should be punished for his deceitfulness because it occurred in the marketplace. Megistas asserts that a seller of goods should be required to inform the buyer what he knows about the thing sold. Megistas implores the council to decide the case in order to deter others from engaging in this type of misconduct in our emporium. If everyone acted like Pyrrhos, Megistas claims, commerce would cease because no one could trust each other. Now on top of all this, Megistas asserts that it is the duty of the council to maintain the mores of the city and teach the young people of the community that this type of behavior is intolerable in society. By ruling in his favor, Megistas assures the council that it will be passing on the standards of society to the next generation. Now, tell me how you would vote on the case?"

The men all agreed they would rule in favor of Megistas.

"You now see the power of strategic speech," Leodamas affirmed. "An ordinary dispute is turned into a significant political decision for the council. Simple custom gives way to high minded principles for the community to uphold."

"May I pose a question, master?" Theseus asked Leodamas.

"Please proceed, young man," Leodamas said.

"Who is the greatest speaker you have ever heard?" asked Theseus.

"Well, there are many, I suppose," answered Leodamas. "In each place I travel there are those I have taught who are convincing before the lawgivers."

"Do these men surpass Heracles in influence?" Theseus asked.

"What a question!" Leodamas laughed. "You look highborn, my young friend, so tell me what your name is. Who is your father?"

"I am Theseus and my grandfather is Pittheus," Theseus dutifully replied. "My father I do not know."

"My apologies," Leodamas said, "if what I asked was difficult for you to answer. It is a hard thing for a young man if fate leaves him without a father. But your relation to the great Pittheus explains your astute questioning. He is known to be a wise man."

"My grandfather will be glad to hear of your sentiment," Theseus said. "And be not sad for me, for I am sure I will come to know my father someday. But please, good teacher, what is your view of Heracles? How would he fare against speech makers?"

"No man can doubt the greatness of Heracles," Leodamas said. "But if I must give an answer, I would say that the great orators do indeed have advantages over Heracles."

"But Heracles is the issue of Zeus," Theseus countered. "He has great strength and power."

"That is true, young Theseus," Leodamas responded. "Strength is without question a prized attribute. But someone who does not possess the grand physicality of Heracles can be just as formidable. I say that intellectual ability is an equal measure of character, if not a greater one. And this can be taught, which is why I make my way to many cities. Agility and might can be developed, but not learned. The powers of strategic oration are attainable by most everyone and can be realized by learning rhetoric and reasoning. Lest the great Heracles comes to seek me out and do me harm for what I say, I would claim that persuasion and shrewdness are ultimately greater than physical prowess."

Theseus was not satisfied with Leodamas' reply.

"Heracles' strength was not the only thing that made him noble," Theseus said. "He had virtue. Does rhetoric teach virtue?"

"Civic virtue, certainly," Leodamas rejoined. "Rhetoric and oratory are the virtues of public life."

"But what duty does the study of rhetoric impart?" Theseus continued.

"Duty?" Leodamas said becoming a bit impatient.

"Yes," said Theseus. "Does your subject teach duties to family or friends, or to the people? Does it teach one how to act with honor? Duty and honor made Heracles the hero that he is."

"Duty and honor of the kind held by Heracles are traits of a bygone age, young man," Leodamas said with finality. "Political advantage and cunning define our time. These attributes cannot be secured without an astute mind and a command of language. Now, I think it best we return to the discussion that I am here for."

Many who were in attendance were amazed at Theseus' questioning of the sophist. Connidas in particular was proud of Theseus' pointed debate and his respectful handling of Leodamas. Connidas felt that Theseus' character was taking shape.

3

After Theseus' exchange with Leodamas, Connidas decided it was time Theseus traveled. Connidas wanted Theseus to witness conditions elsewhere. Pittheus agreed that travel would be good for Theseus, and arranged trips for him. Theseus visited neighboring cities such as Argos, Corinth, Mycenae and Sparta. On these sojourns, Theseus learned the history of the great kings of the Peloponnese and developed a sense of unity with all Greeks. He also traveled to some far off provinces like Pontus and Lycia.

Wherever he went, Theseus took account of the differences in language, dress, religious customs and attitudes toward the state. Theseus spent a fair amount of time in Ionia, notably Miletus. He was intrigued by the unique character of the Ionians.

"The Ionians are a free thinking people, but they are not unified together," Theseus mentioned to Connidas. "They value their individual liberty and don't find much in the state to be of interest. How can they expect to prosper and be secure without strong cities to protect them?"

During these travels abroad, Connidas made it a point to expose Theseus to the fabric of commercial life, and had Theseus study the interdependency of agriculture, manufacture and trade. Theseus became aware of the significance of resources and sound business practices. While in Thasos, he was allowed to attend a dispute over the improper dilution of wine before a civil magistrate. Thasos was known for the purity and excellence of its wine, and the product was sold in many places abroad. A merchant was accused by the city's exchequer for selling substandard wine. The merchant was found to have mixed water with the wine to increase his stock. He was required to pay double the cost of the wine, which was collected for deposit into the city treasury. Theseus thought the penalty reasonable for the protection of Thasos' wine trade.

Theseus evinced his astute observation of the ways of commerce while visiting Delos. Connidas was meeting with a shipping magnate named Hyblesios who used Delos as his base. Theseus slipped into the parlor where Connidas and Hyblesios were discussing how Hyblesios could secure rights in foreign harbors. Connidas suggested that Hyblesios have his ships arrive with rare merchandise for the wealthy who resided there. Connidas thought in this way he would always be welcomed by the authorities in the ports he visited.

"But wouldn't it be better," Theseus asked, "if Hyblesios brought basic goods needed by the citizens of the place and sold them at a fair price?"

Hyblesios was somewhat taken aback by the young man's intrusion into the conversation. But Connidas laughed heartily and asked Theseus to explain himself.

"The problem I see with the proposal," Theseus said, "is that the styles of the rich can change rather quickly. And those in high positions may be removed by competing political factions. Hyblesios could be mistaken in his prediction of the tastes of the wealthy or win favor with one group only to lose it with another. Catering to the citizens would be more stable and profitable in the long term. It is unlikely those in authority would act against a merchant popular with the people, especially one that furnished much needed goods for the city."

Hyblesios was duly impressed by Theseus' insight combining commerce and politics. Connidas was particularly pleased that Theseus had devised a course that had the interests of the common people at heart.

On another occasion, Connidas and Theseus were traveling through Aeolis and stayed several days as the guest of a large landowner in Smyrna. The man had his residence near the assembly place in the central part of the city. He lived in a rectangular house that surrounded an open courtyard. Theseus awoke one morning to a loud noise outside his room. He opened the door to a rain of stones pummeling the courtyard. Theseus sought out the tumult and was told by an anxious servant not to leave the house.

"Nonsense," Theseus replied, "I will see what this commotion is about."

He walked out onto the street and fell across an angry crowd moving by the residence toward the assembly. Theseus stopped a man carrying rocks as he hurried by.

"What is this mob scene that you share in?" Theseus demanded to know.

"Unhand me," the man shouted looking hard at Theseus. "From the looks of you, you are not from here. That is good for you. This place is forsaken by the gods. No crops grow here. The land is dry. The king Archelaos has brought a curse upon us, and he refuses to atone."

"What is this curse that you talk of, my good fellow?" Theseus asked.

"Learn the truth, young man, and may the gods protect you," the man said. "The king profanes Demeter because of the famine, refusing her prayers until the harvest returns. We can stand no more of it."

"Theseus!" Connidas screamed coming upon him in the crowd. "Come with me."

Connidas took Theseus back into the residence and out the rear gate.

"I've arranged our escape from here," Connidas said to Theseus.

He led Theseus through winding streets to a stable with horses and a cart with their belongings.

"Letting the people go unrestrained is not a good thing," Connidas said. "The crowd is not easily controlled if inflamed by passion and I think naturally inclined to be resentful of the higher class. Nothing good can come from the mob. Places like this are destined for chaos."

"The king is to be faulted if I am allowed to say it," Theseus stated. "He neglects real measures to aid his people. Without a stable economy, there is little hope for the peace and well being of the community."

ζ

As Theseus grew older, he suffered occasional bouts of melancholy which weighed heavily upon his spirit. These episodes often followed the recurrence of a strange dream. Theseus would see himself in a labyrinth facing a giant that was half man and half beast. The heinous brute breathed fire and had immense strength. Theseus would strike at the monster with his spear and stab him with his sword, but he could not vanquish him. Theseus always awoke just before the creature, bleeding and in wild torment, fell upon him.

But there was more to Theseus' sporadic gloominess. Theseus began to entertain doubts about what he had been taught about the immortal gods. He was both awed and skeptical of their cabalistic manner.

"How is one to carry on with the gods forever interfering with mortal man?" Theseus would brood. "Is it not enough that we are plagued with youth and old age, while the gods are never changing? And who amongst the Olympians sends me the image that repeats while I sleep?"

To clear his thoughts, Theseus would often take to the mountains or the sea and return home when the clouds lifted. Pittheus and Connidas would question him on the reasons for his absence.

"Do not be concerned," Theseus would say, "I am drawn outdoors when my thoughts are troublesome. The solitude I find there gains me peace and perspective."

Theseus did not let on that his times away were not enough to shake the demons whenever he grappled with the metaphysics of divinity and mortality.

While traveling with Connidas to Naupactus in Locris, Theseus befriended a young man named Elpides, who like himself was of noble birth and nurturing. One day Theseus confined in Elpides about his nightmare.

"Theseus," Elpides said, "some god is giving you a message. Maybe Apollo himself is speaking to you. Let us make our way to Delphi and ask the oracle what it means. Connidas and my family would certainly object to this, so we will have to escape without notice."

The two left in darkness one evening and traveled many days. They managed to find shelter and sustenance from strangers they met on their journey. When they reached Delphi, the lads climbed the summit to reach the Temple of Apollo. They found the place deserted and without life. Looking upon the grand temple, they read the inscription "Know Thyself" carved above the entry doors. Storm clouds gathered, and for a whole day and night they sat outside enduring terrible winds, lightening and rain.

A priestess of the temple finally emerged and addressed the young men.

"What business do you have here," the priestess inquired, "and why have you come without gifts or tribute for the temple? Have you not been taught properly of the sacral law? Zeus himself would be angered by your impudence if the silliness of your youth was not a defense. Be gone from this place."

"Great lady," Theseus responded, "do not drive us away so quickly for we have traveled a long distance. We have come only to be told of the meaning of a simple dream. Some god, Apollo it may be, has shown me strange things."

"Young nobles, do you not know that you tempt fate by coming here?" the priestess said.

"We seek only to hear of prophesy that will tell us of our destiny," Theseus said. "Am I to slay the monster that plagues my nights? What glory will be mine?"

"Do not try to learn of your future from the oracle who serves Apollo, for you are too young to hear of it," the high priestess responded back to Theseus in the way a mother rebukes her son. "Knowledge of the future is a heavy burden and not meant to be known by mortal man."

Theseus gathered his courage and stood fast.

"We saw you coming, Theseus," the priestess said, "and we did not come out to greet you in the hopes you and your companion would go away."

Theseus and Elpides looked at each other with surprise and apprehension.

Theseus

"If you know of me," Theseus said, "then tell me what I want to know."

"We know of you, Theseus," said the priestess, "and of your mother Aethra and your true father. You and your friend are brave indeed to have made your journey here, and the gods will be pleased if you honor them with appropriate sacrifices when you return to your homes. But you must go as I say."

Theseus became agitated at the suggestion of his father.

"How can you send me away after speaking as you have of my father?" Theseus implored the priestess. "Tell me if I am the son of Poseidon as some say or some other. I beg of you."

"Why must young men be so impetuous?" the priestess responded remaining calm. "Commit your energies to attaining the ideals for which you were born. Honor you will have if you stay true to the lessons Connidas has taught you, though it will not be of the kind bestowed on Heracles. Yours will be won by your way with the lawgivers, not with the sword and shield. The identity of your father you will learn when Pittheus sends you out from Troezen. This is all you are to hear from me."

Theseus and Elpides scaled back down the mountain. Theseus was downcast after failing to learn of the meaning of his dream and his father's name. When they started back on the road on which they came, they met Connidas who had come in search of them.

"By the grace of Zeus," Connidas cried out in relief, "here you are. What possessed you to leave Naupactus and travel to Delphi? Have you no concern for the families that raised you? What if you were accosted by some thieving highwayman or taken away as slaves to some foreign soil? Speak as if the immortal gods themselves commanded you."

"Connidas," Theseus replied, "do not chastise or throw blame upon us for seeking out wisdom from the oracle. The high priestess has sent us away without telling us what we wanted to know."

"Wisdom is not in the knowing of what awaits you in

your later years," Connidas said. "Did you not see the inscription on the great temple? Alas, you have yet much to learn. Let us leave here and announce your safety to Elpides' family."

Connidas led Theseus and Elpides back to Naupactus, and upon their return sacrifices were made to the gods as the priestess had instructed.

η

As Theseus approached manhood, he grew strong and tall. He developed long sinewy legs and a thin waist, but broad shoulders and muscular arms and torso. His hair was flaxen and curled, and he had deep set eyes, high cheeks and a sturdy chin. Theseus had a commanding, resonant voice and his delivery was deliberate.

Several incidents proved to Pittheus and Connidas Theseus' growing maturation. One day when Theseus was about the Troezen harbor, he took up in conversation with a group of oarsmen. The oarsmen boasted that they were the best rowers in the country and could not be defeated in a race. Theseus accepted the challenge and recruited several of his strongest friends to test the claims of the oarsmen. Pittheus thought the contest was ill fated, as he knew the men were unmatched in their skill and power in all of Troezen.

Theseus arrived with his friends on the appointed day for the race. A crowd had gathered to witness the event. It is said Aphrodite was looking on and she made the young men beautiful. The spectators were amazed at their godlike appearance. For their part, the oarsmen were burly, muscular and intimidating. No one doubted that the older, experienced rowers would prevail.

The two boats left the dock and proceeded to the beginning position out along the coastline but far enough removed from shore where the water was calm. Pittheus called the start of the race from a third boat. The race was to cover a distance of two stadia. The oarsmen started fast and quickly synchronized their strokes. Their boat seemed to glide across the water. The young men struggled to right their direction at the outset, but kept pace over the early going. Suddenly and inexplicably, two of Theseus' crew got their oars stuck in the water right after the catch due to improper feathering. The two rowers lost control and were ejected from the shell by the force of the oars jutting upward. No one present could recall ever seeing a shell lose two of its crew in this manner before.

The oarsmen by this time had opened a healthy lead and were moving ahead. Theseus and his fourth colleague repositioned themselves and rowed feverishly. Soon, Theseus' remaining companion grew exhausted and fell limp in the boat. Undeterred, Theseus took up both oars and rowed with the strength of four men. His pace was furious. The people watching then witnessed something that could only be described as astounding. A heavy mist covered Theseus' boat and it became impossible to see through to his strokes. Some say Athena herself propelled the boat, others that Poseidon had come to share the rowing with Theseus. When the cloud lifted, Theseus' craft had closed the gap with the oarsmen. Grimacing through the pain of his strokes, Theseus was coming on to the oarsmen's boat with great speed. The oarsmen shouted at one another to go faster. The onlookers gathered at the finish roared with excitement. At the end, the race was called for Theseus by half a length.

The oarsmen were so amazed at Theseus' performance they drew his boat near and brought it to shore. They lifted him up onto their shoulders and carried him all the way back to the dock while shouting his name. The spectators cheered when they approached and offered Theseus congratulations. Young girls who were watching made laurel wreaths and placed then on Theseus in honor of his victory. Theseus felt awkward with all the attention, especially the interest shown him by the young girls. He had not had that feeling before.

Word of the day's events spread throughout Troezen, and Pittheus had his household organize a symposium to commemorate Theseus' feat. Because Theseus was not yet of age, he was not allowed to attend.

"Grandfather," Theseus said to Pittheus, "explain why this affair is closed to me and my friends. Did we not defeat the oarsmen in a great victory? We should be given the honor we deserve."

"The young should be elated when their elders commend them," Pittheus replied, "and the old when given homage by the young. Let that be enough for you. The gathering is for the men from the great families. There will be drinking in abundance and likely freedoms taken with women. It is not an appropriate place for young men such as yourself and your school friends. Besides, the men come not to honor you, but to honor me. You see, noteworthy achievements by young people are a source of great pride to their fathers and grandfathers. The men come to congratulate me on my good fortune. We also celebrate that our way of life is being embraced by a new generation. There will be time enough for you and your friends to partake in these things."

Not long after Theseus' victory over the oarsmen, Theseus was called into military service. All young men were required to devote three years to the military and join in the defense of the city's interests. Theseus shunned the navy contrary to the wishes of Pittheus.

"If I were to man the ships," Theseus declared to Pittheus, "I would be coddled by the commanders due to your influence. No, I will join the infantry. There I can make my own way."

Theseus was quickly recognized for his leadership and was appointed captain of a battalion. His men were loyal and showed Theseus great respect. He forever won their admiration when he led an expedition in Argolis and fought in a three day battle against forces from Epidaurus. The Epidaurians were aggressively razing woodlands claimed by Troezen, and Theseus was dispatched with his men to drive the invaders out of the country. Theseus led his men in fierce fighting. Both sides incurred heavy losses and were growing weary of the conflict. After an armistice was agreed for each side to collect their dead, Theseus called upon the Epidaurians to volunteer one of their numbers to a sword duel. A great Epidaurian warrior rose to fight Theseus. In front of both armies, the two men locked in a vicious battle. Eventually, Theseus struck down his foe with a blow to the chest greater than any Ares could have managed. Theseus stood above the fallen man with his sword fixed at the man's throat.

"I do not know your name," the man cried out, "but you are of regal blood from the sight of you. I am Markarios. My father is Nicodromos, and his father was Gelon, who was known as a great leader of Epidaurus in times past. You can bring darkness over my eyes and send me off to Tartarus as is your right. Your way with the sword has bettered me. I am not afraid to die on the battlefield. But do not strip me of my armor, and let my body be taken back to Epidaurus so my wife and mother can give me a proper burial. This is all I ask."

Theseus looked upon the man and vacillated. Theseus' heart was pounding and his breath was heavy as he held the man's life in his grip. The figure of the great Heracles came to his mind. He knew that Heracles would slay the man without compunction.

"You may yet see yellow robed Dawn again, but only if you do as I say," Theseus said. "Get up and take your men from here, and go back to your city. Pray to Paeon, who heals the gods, that you recover from your wounds. Remember the name Theseus, the one raised by Pittheus in Troezen, and say the name to your countrymen as the one who spared your life. Tell those who may wish to return to this place that they would need to face him, and his mercy is not boundless. Away with you."

The man rose and withdrew with his army. Theseus' men cheered upon the sight of the retreat. The Troezen army claimed victory and put up a trophy. Theseus had the men prepare offerings and pour libations to celebrate the victory. The men honored Theseus with song and wine that night and brought the tale home to the people of Troezen.

θ

Pittheus was well pleased with Theseus and knew Connidas had taught him well. He saw in Theseus the cumulative effects of his education. When Pittheus felt it was time, he took Theseus aside to speak to him of his future.

"Theseus, I have raised you as if you are my own son," Pittheus said. "I am proud of you and those things you seem to hold true. The day has come for you to leave my house and your mother, for the gods have work for you. Troezen is no longer your place. You must travel to Attica, where your future begins. Connidas says you show some promise for the law. That may be. In Athens, you will find many great men. Intellectuals and rationalists collect there like no other place. You are to go to Athens."

Theseus listened intently to Pittheus and was saddened that he was to leave Troezen. But his heart was also glad of it. Theseus knew it was time for him to undertake adventure and set out on his own.

Theseus visited Connidas before departing for Athens. Connidas had grown old and now walked with a bent. Theseus felt gratitude toward Connidas for his years of commitment to his education.

"One story I never told you about Heracles, Theseus," Connidas said. "He had a music teacher named Linus, who was a hard task master. Heracles did not like it when Linus hit him, so he caned Linus with his lyre and killed him. I was careful never to drive you in that way."

"My good Connidas," Theseus responded. "I learned of that story long ago, but never myself made mention of it. It is sad to think that a student had fallen his teacher. Heracles was regretful of his recklessness, and I don't aspire to replicate Heracles in all things. Besides, Linus you are not. You never raised a hand against me and were considerate in your instruction to the end. If the gods truly favor me and my name is remembered, yours will be also."

As Theseus made his preparations, Aethra came to him.

"Theseus, my son," she said to him, "are you leaving your

poor mother for some better place? What have I done to drive you away? My heart is heavy with your ingratitude."

"Do not be disconsolate, dear mother," Theseus said to Aethra. "Sons must leave their mothers if they are to become men, and it is my time. I will honor you with those things I achieve. Heralds will visit you with tales of my accomplishments."

"Well, if this is what young men like you must do, then go," Aethra said weeping. "But before you do, I must tell you a story. Years ago, a great king came to Troezen. This king was insecure in his reign because he had no male heir, and he feared the intentions of the many sons of his brother."

Theseus knew that brothers and their male issue held claim to the estate of any man who died without a son.

"The king had every reason to be wary," Aethra sighed gathering herself. "When he visited Troezen, Pittheus showed him the hospitality due a traveling stranger. In his talks with Pittheus, the king complained of his childless state and the fate of his throne. The king admitted that he had thoughts of taking another woman without his wife knowing in order to beget a son. The king told Pittheus that he had visited the oracle at Delphi for direction, but the advice he received mystified him. Pittheus said nothing, but thought of a prophesy of his own. An oracle had told him long ago that his daughter would never wed but nonetheless bear a famous son."

Aethra took hold of Theseus' hands and had him sit down with her.

"Pittheus hosted a great banquet in honor of the king," Aethra recounted, "with abundant wine, food and dancing. The king was pleased with the display and forgot his woes. After he had drunk many cups of wine, Pittheus asked me to attend to him. My father's intentions were clear. Oh, what things a daughter does to please her father! Truth be told, I pitied him and, by the will of Aphrodite, gave him my affection. The king spent the next several days in Troezen with me, but then made plans to leave. He told me if I was ever to have a son, that I was to send him off with a sword and sandals that he left behind with me. These things the king would recognize if he ever saw them again. You are to take these items and have them about you. If the gods allow, it may be you chance upon your father on your travels."

"What words are you speaking to me now, mother?" Theseus said with some vexation. "Do not lay these things on me just as I embark on my journey. The young suffer enough angst when they are to leave their families. I will take these tokens if my rightful father might see and remember them. But whoever he may be, he will know me by my deeds and the great things I do."

ι

Theseus traveled by land to Athens and settled into a residence that had been arranged for him. He decided to devote himself to learning Athenian law and the system of law courts. He had made the acquaintance of a well known logographer named Antiphon during a visit to the Agora and took up with Antiphon as an apprentice. Theseus was eager to learn from him. Antiphon was getting on in years, and he welcomed the overtures of the young man from Troezen.

"I will teach you what I know, Theseus," Antiphon said. "The legal landscape is changing, and it's too much for an old man to keep up with. So I will require you to do more than just listen to me carry on."

"Use me as you will, Antiphon," Theseus said. "I am hoping to do what I can to assist if my talents allow it."

"I have no doubt that you will contribute greatly," Antiphon responded. "Many more persons are seeking advice on how to obtain redress in the courts and what arguments prove most successful."

Antiphon taught Theseus how cases in the law courts were brought and decided. The law in Athens required litigants to argue their own cases. Volunteers or representatives were not allowed, except in public cases where men could bring charges and argue them as a member of the community. Theseus learned that *dike* was the writ for private disputes and *graphe* for public offenses. Antiphon also identified to Theseus which magistrates had jurisdiction for particular offenses and the cases that were reserved to the Areopagus.

Theseus spent months with Antiphon learning the laws of citizenship, marriage, inheritance, property, trade and crimes. For instance, Antiphon taught Theseus the peculiar procedure for homicide cases. Charges for killing another citizen could only be brought by a survivor of the deceased before the Areopagus, and each side was allowed to make two speeches. Theseus learned that at the end of the accuser's first speech, the alleged murderer was free to leave

Theseus

the court and agree to exile. In this way he could avoid death if otherwise found guilty.

Theseus also became versed in the forms of oaths and the nature of oath giving. Oaths were an extremely vital aspect to all types of proceedings, and served to establish the truth of assertions. The giving of an oath, or the refusal to give an oath, was often dispositive of a case. There were various forms of oaths, and in many matters only one party was entitled to give an oath. In others, both sides were required to swear. There were imposed oaths, oaths of denial and action deciding oaths. Oath challenges were employed by litigants to force an issue or achieve settlement. A judge charged with deciding a case often had to swear an oath that his decision was true. If found later to be wrong, the judge could himself be subject to penalty. Understanding oath giving was a critical component of the law. Theseus found the subject intriguing because oath giving was grounded on fear of the gods and not the central authority of the state. He remembered Oath's relation to Night, and that Zeus himself required the *horkos* upon which oaths of the gods were taken.

Not all of the laws learned by Theseus were to his liking. For example, he felt that in adultery cases, a married woman was presumed to have been seduced while a single woman was presumed a seductress even if both held citizen status. One could be fined for speaking ill of a person in a public forum but free to slander another in a comedy performed during the festivals. If a man borrowed money and failed to repay it, he could be taken as a slave of the lender in repayment of the debt. Losing one's freedom because of poverty Theseus thought harsh.

The law of impiety was particularly nettlesome to Theseus. It was ill defined and often punitive in application. The penalties for religious offenses were quite severe and included exile, heavy fines, confiscation of property and even death. Theseus was to learn that politically motivated attacks were often brought on the grounds of impiety. Uncertainty about the scope of the law was a reality of life in the city. Many actions were not necessarily thought of as impious until a charge was brought and the case argued.

Eventually, Antiphon instructed Theseus about constructing effective arguments in the law courts. The lawgivers were not legal professionals, but aristocrats of good standing in the city, and had no written record of prior decisions to guide deliberations. Antiphon explained that moral suasion, political arguments and entreaties based on empathy or equity were often most persuasive. Early on in his training, Antiphon included Theseus when advising citizens seeking justice in the law courts. Theseus learned quickly, and showed great skill in fashioning statements for the citizens who came to Antiphon for assistance in their cases.

There were several early cases that brought Theseus some notoriety as a talented logographer. The first case involved the failure of a magistrate to enforce a law of marriage. Dicaeus was the cousin and only male relative of a widower and heiress named Cymone. The law required that Dicaeus either marry Cymone himself or provide a dowry for her to marry another. If a marriage was to be arranged, the dowry set for her class was two talents. Dicaeus did not fancy the heiress and did not wish to marry her. He also did not want to pay the substantial dowry. The magistrate, whose duty it was to ensure that Dicaeus fulfill his obligation, did nothing which caused Cymone great humiliation.

A man named Appolomedes had an interest in Cymone and the dowry. Appolomedes had come on hard times. He was a large, overweight man, with droopy eyes and a scraggly beard. His father was Nisos, who managed his household poorly and had left his three sons without means to properly support themselves. Appolomedes thought by marrying Cymone he could secure his future. Appolomedes had approached Dicaeus on several occasions on the subject of marrying Cymone, but was rebuked. The magistrate, an elderly man of the name Isagoras, was a good friend of Dicaeus' deceased father, and it was suspected that Dicaeus had bribed Isagoras to avoid enforcement of the law.

Appolomedes had become incensed over Dicaeus' refusal

to allow his marriage to Cymone. He approached Antiphon on what could be done. Antiphon, who had taken ill, asked Theseus if he could assist. Theseus obliged and met with Appolomedes.

"So what is it that you seek to achieve?" Theseus asked Appolomedes.

"I wish to marry Cymone, if it can be arranged," Appolomedes said. "But Dicaeus refuses my overtures and won't marry her himself. Isagoras favors Dicaeus, and avoids his duty as magistrate."

Appolomedes shifted back and forth on his feet with a pained look on his face.

"I came to be advised by Antiphon," Appolomedes said, "but here you are. Do not take offense to what I say since I can see that you are of high birth, but how can I expect any satisfaction from someone without experience with the lawgivers."

"Judge me when we have fully discussed your injury," was Theseus' reply. "I will gladly defer to Antiphon if you are not pleased with what I might suggest you do."

Theseus and Appolomedes met for a long time. They decided that Appolomedes should submit a writ before the Areopagus. The Areopagus met to conduct its affairs on the hill of Ares and citizens came hear the cases brought before it.

On the day of argument, Appolomedes was called to give his statement before the council. He was nervous to speak, but managed to state his grievance and what the law required. He brought witnesses to testify as to his good nature. Dicaeus, for his part, claimed that the law did not compel him to marry or marry off Cymone by any set time. He stated that until the magistrate came to enforce the law, he was not required to do anything. On this he rested his case.

Appolomedes feared that Dicaeus statement was a strong one and that the council would vote against him. Theseus, sitting behind him, motioned Appolomedes over. Theseus spoke to him for several minutes. Appolomedes then asked for time for rebuttal, which was granted. There was discussion among the council because litigants never collaborated with others during the hearing of a case.

"My good lords," Appolomedes began again, "do not let Dicaeus harm me in this way. It has already been one year since Cymone's husband died. Nothing has happened. What good is a law if people are not required to follow it? I may not be as quick with words as Dicaeus, but I don't know how this could be. So I say to you, make Dicaeus pay five hundred drachmas if he doesn't provide marriage for Cymone by the next festival day. And if Isagoras, the magistrate whose duty it is to see that this be done, does not see to it, let him pay double what Dicaeus owes. Have it deposited in the treasury."

A murmur rose from the council following Appolomedes' proposition. Never before had it been suggested that a magistrate be held accountable to enforce the law in this way.

Aegeus, sitting at the head of the council, seemed uncertain as to what to do and looked about the elders as if seeking guidance from their expressions. But before he could make a statement, a citizen rose from his seat and beckoned Aegeus to bring the dispute to a vote. There was a loud clamor from the crowd in agreement. Aegeus raised the scepter to quiet the gathering and then called for a voice vote from the council. He asked for those supporting Dicaeus. There was utter silence. Aegeus then asked to hear from those siding with Appolomedes. As if speaking in a single voice, the elders exclaimed "Aye!"

"Then let it be as decided by the council," Aegeus pronounced. "Dicaeus shall arrange the marriage of the woman by the end of Thargelion. If he neglects his obligation, Dicaeus shall be levied a fine of five hundred drachmas. And Isagoras shall see to it that Dicaeus performs what is required or he himself shall pay double what Dicaeus owes."

The declaration of the council's edict in favor of Appolomedes was a watershed moment. From that day on, magistrates were wont to arbitrarily enforce the laws for fear of penalty.

Theseus

Questions about the young man Appolomedes spoke to during the hearing became fodder in the Agora. Word spread that Antiphon had engaged a clever young man to attend the law courts for him and provide counsel to those wanting to prosecute disputes. Rumor had it that he was a foreign traveler and entertained many strange ideas. Some said that Apollo watched over him and often spoke through him. Others believed that he was a sophist by trade and had conned Antiphon into providing him an introduction to Athenian society.

The next case handled by Theseus brought him greater attention. Calliphon had come upon Neleos during the festival of Athena and a quarrel erupted. It was not clear who started the brawl, but during the confrontation Calliphon swung at Neleos. Neleos staggered and fell backward. His head landed upon a jagged rock, leaving him unconscious and bloodied. Calliphon fled the scene thinking that Neleos was dead.

Calliphon was the son of Polymedes, the head of the Eurestian clan. Neleos was the youngest by Odius, the patriarch of the Mesean tribe. The Eurestian and Mesean *demes* had been feuding for years for reasons no one could remember.

When the lifeless body of Neleos had been carried to Odius' house and he was told of the beating at the hand of Calliphon, Odius gathered up the stronger men of the family and marched to the estate of Polymedes. He demanded that Calliphon be given up. Polymedes refused, having already sent his son away in hiding. In a rage, Odius and his brethren set fire to Polymedes' land and laid waste to Polymedes' crops. Some say the billowing smoke from the blaze could be seen as far away as Mount Parnassus. Odius remained at Polymedes' gate and refused passage to all comers. Isolated clashes ensued, property was further destroyed and men were wounded.

News of the conflict reached the city, and there was concern that the fighting would draw in other families. Citizens were fearful of the violence and the blasphemy in having a murderer in hiding. People became afraid that the pollution would draw punishment from Athena.

The incident was reported to the palace, and an order was issued calling Odius and Polymedes to appear before Aegeus. Reticent about the summons, Polymedes visited Antiphon.

"Tell me, Antiphon," Polymedes started, "how is it I am to avoid losing my son and any more of my property? Calliphon set upon the young Neleos, it is true, but the thoughtlessness of youth was his affliction. Speak skillfully about how to escape a tragedy for Calliphon and my family."

Theseus knew the law. Anyone found to have assaulted or killed another during a religious festival was subject to death or banishment if found guilty by the Areopagus.

Antiphon discussed the punishment for killing and the options open to Calliphon. Neither was pleasing to Polymedes.

"Calliphon claims Neleos started the fight," Polymedes asserted. "He had no intention of killing Neleos."

"The law does not distinguish between intent or not," Antiphon said. "If his blow caused the death, Calliphon can be punished. The people will want the city rid of the contamination. You will not be allowed to continue to conceal your son."

Theseus interrupted and offered his own views.

"It may be best to offer up ten talents to Odius to avoid calamity for your son," Theseus said. "Aegeus I believe is most interested in quelling the conflict among the Eurestian and Mesean families, more so than satisfying Odius' demand for revenge. The feud is causing great upheaval, and the people are concerned that the violence will spread. Offer this when you speak to the king. Agree to send Calliphon away for a time and pay another ten talents for the temple of Athena, and I suspect you will have a reasonable outcome."

"Who is this young man who speaks out of turn?" implored Polymedes. "His words are interesting to the ear, Antiphon, but it is you I wish to advise me here."

"Do not be put off by Theseus, good Polymedes," Antiphon spoke. "He speaks thoughtfully and his words are well considered for someone so young. There may be some merit in what he says."

"How can Aegeus agree to this when death or banishment is the punishment for a killing?" Polymedes argued.

"There is word that Neleos is alive, Polymedes," Theseus responded. "Badly beaten, but alive."

"May the gods be praised!" Polymedes exclaimed. "If Neleos lives, there is hope for my son."

The men continued debating the best plan for their side, and in the end they agreed to Theseus' proposal.

On the appointed day, Odius and Polymedes rode into the city to present their arguments to Aegeus. Each came with an escort of combatants carrying swords, spears and shields. The atmosphere was tense and brittle. Antiphon and Theseus came to observe the proceedings.

The great hall of the king's palace resembled a war summit with the number of heavily armed men. Aegeus sat taciturn on his throne. Next to him was Lysias, one of Aegeus' most trusted advisors. Medea, Aegeus' consort, attended but remained in the background.

Lysias spoke first.

"What is this we see?" Lysias started. "So many men girded for a fight? If any man dares to raise a sword in this house, may Apollo strike him down with his bow and let darkness cover his eyes. Odius and Polymedes, tell your people to lay down their weapons. Aegeus cannot be pleased with this spectacle. Show honor to your king."

When the parties disarmed and took seats, Lysias invited each contestant to speak their case. Odius began first, bemoaning the beating of his son and demanding retribution. Polymedes, for his part, defended Calliphon and pleaded for his son's life. Odius strenuously objected and called for Calliphon' death. The arguments became bitter with scant prospects for a resolution.

"Odius," Lysias said, "you give Polymedes no hope for saving his son. If this is what you want, bring a suit before the Areopagus so the dispute could be resolved in the proper way. Enough of the fighting between the families."

"Let me propose another solution," Polymedes said in response. "Odius' case before the Areopagus, if followed upon with my oath that Calliphon was not responsible for Neleos demise, would win the day for me. But it would do little to lift the anger he feels. Perhaps there is a way out for Odius."

Polymedes then put forth the ideas espoused by Theseus.

"I will send my son Calliphon away for a time, out of Attica," Polymedes submitted. "I will also pay ten talents to Odius to make amends, and another ten talents to the temple of Athena to cleanse the city of whatever pollution was caused. This I am willing to do, if Odius accepts my offer."

Polymedes' proposal aroused Aegeus, who straightened up in his seat.

"Polymedes," Aegeus said, "your ideas are novel and most welcome. This proposal gives honor to Odius and softens the loss he has suffered in losing Neleos. It also carries the promise of quelling further violence."

"This offer from Polymedes is not agreeable to me," Odius said firmly. "I will have honor only if Calliphon is given up. Athena will be angered if Calliphon continues walking the earth."

"Tell us, Odius, on your oath," Polymedes interjected, "is your son alive or dead?"

"By the grace of Zeus," Odius answered, "he breathes. But I demand justice just the same."

"So your son is alive and not killed by Calliphon?" Aegeus asked.

"Yes," Odius replied. "His wounds are severe but he is to live."

"Wonderful news!" proclaimed Aegeus. "My good man, your son's life has been spared. You have no reason now to pursue your vengeance. So let us consider what is proposed here. Punishing Calliphon will only prolong the feud between your families. The hatred will boil and others among your family will likely die in the ensuing bloodshed. No, let us discuss a way to end the hatred and build peace within our great city. What is offered here by Polymedes is recompense

Theseus

enough and punishes the wrong. As for grey-eyed Athena, let us consult the oracle and hear his view. We should know of any curse that might linger from the violence committed during the festival."

Lysias sent word to Sostias the soothsayer. Sostias was a resident in the great house and called on to guide Aegeus by his divinations. Lysias described the proposal to Sostias. He asked him if Athena would accept the ten talents from Polymedes and release the city from the blasphemy.

Sostias listened to Lysias, and then shut his eyes tight. The room was perfectly still.

"My good king," Sostias said opening his eyes after several minutes. "The goddess Athena is the great protector of our city. The offering from Polymedes would please her well enough for her to lift this curse."

"Are you sure of this, Sostias?" Lysias asked. "Would you swear to this at the altar?"

"When I woke today," said Sostias, "outside my window I saw two great hawks fly down to feast upon a water vole. The birds did not clash or fight one with the other. The hawks moved about the quarry but then let the rodent go free against their nature. I was puzzled by the meaning of the vision, until now. This was surely a sign sent from Athena. Calliphon is not to be harmed. Odius is to accept the offering from Polymedes."

Aegeus stood up and let out a cry of delight.

"So let it be done, good nobles!" Aegeus announced. "Odius, can you agree to this?"

Odius stood with a defiant look about him.

"To make the matter more palatable to you Odius," Aegeus decreed, "on top of what is to be given to you by Polymedes, I will add twenty oxen from my own stable and give you a seat on the council of elders. In this way you will have authority over similar crimes and help settle things. Come now, both you and Polymedes agree."

Odius softened his stance, and he consented to the pact as the king wished.

Before Polymedes took his leave, Aegeus approached

him.

"Tell me Polymedes," Aegeus asked, "who among the immortals spoke of the compromise that you proposed today? Was it Apollo who made this clear to you? I found it to be a most worthy resolution."

"No," Polymedes said. "I had no vision from he who strikes from afar. Nor did almighty Zeus who dispenses justice to mortals appear to me with the idea. It was one Theseus who trains under Antiphon. He is a young man from Troezen, of noble stock. The gods favor him with a sharp mind. Some say his father is Poseidon."

x

As he became acclimated to life in the city, Theseus began to spend time in the Agora. He conversed with the merchants and learned about trade in Athens. He also took up with many of the sophists who used the Agora as a forum to lecture and host dialogues. Athens had become a magnet for great minds from across Greece, and Theseus reveled in the confluence of new theories and ideas that were exchanged in the marketplace.

A sophist named Timocrates came to the Agora one morning to preside over a dialectic on the nature of the state. Theseus arrived to hear the discourse on the topic.

"To begin our discussion of the *polis,* is it not best to start with asking who among us shall we call citizens?" Timocrates asked. "That should be our first inquiry."

A debate ensued among those in attendance. Some said that the citizens are those who are recognized by birth as descendants of the first people that sprung from the ground and populated Attica. Others claimed that those with inherited wealth and property were the true citizens. One stated the concept in the negative, that citizens include everyone but aliens and slaves. There was one theory advanced that citizens should be the people who properly honor the gods and participate actively in the religious ceremonies.

After these preliminary observations, Timocrates posed a question.

"What then is the character of the citizen?" he asked.

As before, those in the crowd wrestled with the question and various answers were proffered.

"The citizen is he who can participate in civic life and enjoy the public displays during the festivals," one person exclaimed.

"The ones that are allowed to speak before the assembly are true citizens," another said.

"No," yet another interjected, "a citizen must be capable of bringing a claim in the law courts to protect his rights."

As was his way, Theseus waited for others to speak before he offered up his views.

"Tell me, wise Timocrates," Theseus started, "is the citizen defined by his status in the community or does he have some quality that makes him so? Are the aristocrats the only ones who should be citizens due to their education or property? Is it possible that someone of low birth and meager means could claim citizenship? Please, share your views on this."

"Who is this man that suggests our nobles are not the ones that hold true citizenship," someone shouted indignantly from the crowd.

A young man stood and advanced toward Theseus.

"Come now, explain your thinking," the young man protested. "Otherwise, sit down and let those with more knowledge speak."

Theseus was startled by the outburst but remained calm.

"I am Theseus," he said, "and hail from Troezen although I claim Athens as my home now. I take it, good sir, my words are not to your liking. Perhaps you hold preferences for the wealthy and privileged among us. But answer me this. Do those not blessed with a lineage not have a vested interest in the welfare of the community? Does our state not ask people of less rank to take up arms in her defense or contribute in other ways to her prosperity? Is the tradesman or ship captain any less concerned about our success? What I imply is citizenship may be for all those that have an interest in the business of the city and participate vigorously in her affairs. This is not a trait reserved only to men that have the benefit of an inheritance."

"You are certainly free with your ideas in this place," the young man countered, "but I doubt you would be so bold with your words before Aegeus or the council."

"I would not be afraid to discuss my thoughts before the king or Areopagus if called on," Theseus said. "Let me ask you, sir, are there noble people who take no part in city affairs? You need not answer, because you know that there are. You would agree that these people are not our best citizens. They fail to contribute much to ensuring her well being. A good citizen takes views on what is best for society and works to bring about improvement. I say let all those freemen that contribute to the greatness of the state and participate in deciding and administering her affairs be called citizens. I could go so far as to say that those who do not claim a side on important civic matters should be disenfranchised."

The young man stood glaring at Theseus. He eventually sat down without responding, but was angry. Others in the group took up the debate and the discourse continued for another hour. When the discussion waned, Theseus moved to go. The young man who had interrupted went up to Theseus as he was leaving. The two stood facing each other, and any enmity felt by the young man toward Theseus quickly faded.

"Do not think badly of me," he said. "I was told you speak of wild and confusing things to people in the Agora, so I came to call you out. But I find that you are sincere with what you say and have the interests of our city at heart. Your words have merit as I now can see."

Theseus looked upon the man and was impressed by his sincerity and genuineness.

"Think little of it," Theseus said. "There is no dishonor in debating the nature of citizenship. Tell me, what is your name? I have seen you here many times of late, but you have not spoken before."

"My name is Pirithous," the young man said, "son of Ixion."

Pirithous was a few years younger than Theseus and hailed from a great family outside Attica. Like Theseus, his build was strong and imposing. He had longish black hair that was pushed back over his ears. Pirithous had a serious but agreeable countenance.

"I saw you first, Theseus, when you came to the great hall of Aegeus with Polymedes," Pirithous said. "Aegeus learned that it was you who had counseled Polymedes on what to say. Aegeus was most impressed."

"So you have come to find out more about me, is that it?" Theseus asked. "Aegeus has sent you here to keep a watchful eye on my activities."

"It was not Aegeus that commanded me to this task," Pirithous responded. "After the Polymedes affair, Aegeus asked Lysias about you. Lysias sought out information from those in the house, and what he learned was reported back to Aegeus. Aegeus was told that you were the protégé of Antiphon and conversant in the ways of the law. It was said you were crafty and had peculiar notions about justice."

"So it was Lysias who sent you out?" Theseus asked.

"No," Pirithous said. "Medea, who shares Aegeus' house, had overheard much of the talk. She asked me to follow you. She said that you spoke of things that undermine the *aristos* and side with the commoners in your arguments. You were wily and someone to fear, she said. She asked me to observe your time in the Agora, perhaps detect some fault that could be used against you. She planned for me to ambush you in the Agora. When you stood to speak, I was to engage you in debate and expose you as a true enemy of the social order. All of this for the purpose of undermining your credibility before Aegeus."

"What you say concerns me greatly, Pirithous," Theseus said, "but be assured I intend no harm to Aegeus. My guess is you and I share many things in common. We should be friends and work together for the benefit of the city. It would be best for the two of us."

"Your entreaty strikes me as something we should do," Pirithous responded. "I have a proposal that might interest you, Theseus, if you are willing to listen."

"Most certainly," Theseus said.

"It is evident that your training and skills are ideally suited for the law," Pirithous said. "I myself claim an interest, and perhaps some capacity, in this. What would you say to us making ourselves available to Aegeus? He holds the *aegis* at the council and calls the assembly to order when there are matters to debate. We could volunteer our services and thereby have involvement with the lawgivers. What do you say?"

"To have a position in Aegeus' house as counselor at law would no doubt be an opportunity worth undertaking," Theseus responded. "How could we win his audience?"

"Leave that to me," Pirithous said. "I will arrange for both of us to appear before him."

A noble vocation, thought Theseus, to have a place before Aegeus and the lawgivers. The cloud gatherer Zeus and Pallas Athena herself would most assuredly find it a worthy labor.

Part II

MINOTAUR

When he arrived at Crete, as most of the ancient historians as well as poets tell us, having a clue of a thread given him by Ariadne, who had fallen in love with him, and being instructed by her how to use it so as to conduct himself through the windings of the labyrinth, he escaped out of it and slew the Minotaur, and sailed back, taking along with him Ariadne and the young Athenian captives.

Plutarch, *Plutarch's Lives, Volume I.*

1

The nymphs sauntered into the room single file as if in a procession. They were undeniably attractive, a few quite beautiful. Illyria was known for its striking women and the six did not break the cast. All were elegantly clothed in white linen gowns and several wore headdresses of gold leafed garland. The women stood there sultry and insouciant before Theseus and his associates.

Anaxis, chairman of Aigaion Corporation, was a frequent guest of this social club and liked to entertain here. Not entirely certain of the protocol, Theseus looked to Anaxis for direction. As Anaxis explained, the selection process went according to seniority. Anaxis had the first pick, but he graciously deferred to Theseus. Theseus was uncomfortable but eager not to offend Anaxis. Theseus looked over the lineup and pointed at a slender woman who had an appealing smile. The third woman in the row gracefully moved her way around the large marble table to take her place next to Theseus. Theseus turned toward Anaxis, who nodded with approval and then motioned to Alcaeus to go. Alcaeus was one of Theseus' favorite associates. Alcaeus chose number five, a petite woman with wispy dark hair. Iollas and Nikon, the other young lawyers accompanying Theseus on this trip, were next. There were two women left when Anaxis had his pick. He shouted something indiscernible and waived the girls off. Another four came quickly into the room and Anaxis made his selection.

When all was said and done, each of the men had their woman for the evening. Plates of meats, cheeses and olives were brought in and scattered about the table. One of the women went to the head of the table and lined up pints of a rare local ale. She balanced shot glasses on the rims of the steins and poured jiggers of premium absinthe. The woman then tipped the first shot glass and one after the other splashed down in a perfect chain reaction. The pints were passed among the men. Anaxis raised his hand and welcomed the lawyers in a traditional Illyria toast. The group voiced their approval.

The men drank freely and the women kept the drink flowing. When a glass was empty, it was automatically filled. The men were taught by Anaxis to pour for the women and they obliged without argument. The women proved adept at feeding the men as they drank. Anaxis called for music and players ambled in with flutes and string instruments. Soon the women were singing melodies meant to weaken the better instincts of the men. Iollas and Nikon rose to join in.

After a full repertoire of songs, the group settled back in their seats for more drink and talk with the women. Anaxis looked satisfied with the proceedings. The drink and nymphs were having their effect, and the men, save Theseus, were slowly losing all power to manage. Soon, an old woman appeared without warning and the nymphs vanished as if by some sorcery. Iollas and Nikon loudly voiced their disappointment at the turn of events. The old woman began to speak but Theseus and his crew were unable to understand her. Anaxis stood to explain. The men had three choices. Each could have his pleasure upstairs or take his nymph back to his room for the evening. Or, they could all return home alone. Anaxis looked at Theseus and his men keenly as if to gauge their worth. Iollas and Nikon were noticeably enticed and ready to carry on through the night.

Theseus knew that drink, jetlag and temptation were a combustive mix for associates and a long week lay ahead. There would be time later perhaps for frolic. He told his associates that it was best to wind things up for the evening. Not to appear ungrateful, Theseus took Anaxis aside and expressed his appreciation. Like all Greeks who honored Zeus, Anaxis treated his traveling guests well. Theseus told Anaxis that he was a most gracious host and his hospitality unmatched, but that he needed these young men to have clear minds over the next week. He could scarcely afford to lose them on the first night.

Anaxis understood and seemed content that enough had been accomplished for the evening. To the disappointment of Iollas and Nikon, the revelry was concluded and everyone turned in for the night.

The next several days were spent in Illyria wrapping up a strategic deal for Anaxis and his company. Aigaion was a large telecommunications business and Anaxis was intent on buying the assets of The Cottus Company. Cottus manufactured circuit boards, and Anaxis wanted Cottus' technology for Aigaion's expansion overseas.

Cottus was spun off a year before from a company called Geryon Corp., and Geryon still held a large stake in Cottus. Although Cottus' revenues were meager, its technology was advanced. Geryon originally wanted to form a joint venture with Aigaion, but Anaxis was interested in control. After several days of trying to negotiate the joint venture plan, Geryon capitulated and agreed to an asset sale for cash. Both Geryon and Cottus' management were poised to earn substantial profits from the sale to Aigaion.

Theseus was instrumental in bringing the negotiations to a close and securing the deal Anaxis wanted. Anaxis commended Theseus more than once on his skillful handling of the transaction.

The firm's fees for Aigaion's acquisition of Cottus would be substantial for about four months' work. Theseus was pleased with the firm's performance. At least twenty different lawyers stepped in at different times. Many had worked nonstop for weeks to help get the deal done. The firm was adept at managing and processing large, complex transactions quickly. Clients paid top dollar for the privilege of having the firm as their legal counsel. The firm charged exorbitant hourly rates for lawyer time, even for those associates right out of law school. The firm often demanded and was paid a premium over the high fees after a deal closed if it could be justified. Theseus would ask Anaxis for a premium on the Cottus representation, as the work was completed over a relatively short time.

With his work in Illyria done, Theseus left Alcaeus, Iollas and Nikon in Illyria to finalize the documents and maybe another visit to the salon. Theseus told Alcaeus to monitor

Iollas and Nikon and keep them on the straight and narrow over their remaining stay.

On his flight back to Athens, Theseus settled in for a quick read of the firm's management reports for the next day's partner meeting. Theseus was looking forward to attending the meeting. He had missed the last several, and was feeling a bit removed from firm affairs. Theseus had also learned that there may be some important announcements made at the meeting.

Theseus arrived at his flat in the late evening. He paged through a stack of letters that had accumulated while he was away and then laid down and slept. He woke the next morning and walked across the street to his athletic club knowing there would be no time for exercise later in the day. Theseus began a strenuous work out regime years ago to stay alert and fend off fatigue, which he found critical to performing at a high level.

When he returned to his apartment Ophelia had already laid out his dress for the day, a dark suit, blue shirt and tie. Ophelia had been Theseus' housekeeper ever since he arrived in Attica. She handled all of Theseus' domestic affairs, everything from laundry, cleaning, food and attire. Ophelia knew his favorite groceries, restaurants and clothiers. Theseus rarely saw Ophelia, but her services were essential to his lifestyle and work schedule.

After returning from his exercise, Theseus dressed, ate the breakfast Ophelia had prepared and went downstairs. A driver was waiting to take him directly to the office.

2

"Good you were able to make the meeting, Theseus," Pirithous said when Theseus entered the conference room.

About fifty of the firm's partners were in attendance, a heavy turnout. Normally, these meetings drew far less. It was an unspoken rule that client business always came first and billable hours trumped all firm functions. Partners often talked about who couldn't attend and the reasons why. Absences created by scheduling conflicts due to client affairs were heralded and praised.

"There is something afoot," Pirithous conjectured. "Not sure what it is. Maybe we're to merge with another firm. There have been rumors. Maybe we're increasing associate pay again, or adopting some sort of partner compensation formula. We'll have to wait until Triton and Isocrates are finished with their presentations."

Triton, the firm's business manager, stepped up to give an overview of the firm's finances. The firm had over the years become a money machine, generating huge profits for the partners. The partners earned growing sums each year, driven by the burgeoning number of billable hours logged by the firm's lawyers and the revenues collected from clients. The partners sat atop a massive pyramid of attorneys, paralegals, legal secretaries and back office staff devoted to ever increasing billings and collections. The firm was one of the highest grossing law practices in the country. Triton reported another record year of profits per partner and realizations, and prospects for the coming year were exceeding budget. Triton cautioned, nevertheless, that the legal market was becoming increasingly competitive and the firm needed to stay vigilant. Partners were reminded that the best marketing was unequalled lawyering.

Isocrates then took the podium. He was the firm's general counsel. Most large law firms had one of their own partners devote his time to managing the legal malpractice claims and ethics issues which seemed to grow every year. Isocrates was a big man and always looked like he was about to laugh. Theseus thought that was a good quality for a general counsel. Isocrates oftentimes took up parts of these meetings to lecture the partners on legal ethics and the pitfalls of everyday practice. Today his topic was the risk to the firm from bad clients.

"Times are certainly good," Isocrates began. "We are living in a truly unparalleled era for the law. The amount of money we are making is exceeding our wildest expectations, and we all want this run to continue. The biggest risks facing us are not missed opportunities. We have business in abundance. Firms stumble because of the clients they have. Surprised? You shouldn't be. The number one cause of missteps involving the firm are *bad* clients. You know who they are. Clients that come to us after dismissing their former law firm after claiming mistakes were made. The ones that are months late paying their fees but always need something done overnight. It's the client that wants a steep discount on the first deal but promises to pay full freight on later deals which never come. Or clients that don't take the counsel we give them. That's usually a dead giveaway. These clients cannot be trusted because they are not honest. And we should not have them as clients. They refuse to pay us and sue us for the opportunity. Then there are those clients trying to raise money."

This last category hit a nerve. A large segment of Theseus' practice dealt with companies looking to attract capital. He had for years assisted corporations with raising money in the public markets, representing both issuers and underwriters. In the past, the companies that came to market were seasoned and had established revenues and profits. That was changing. Now companies with little or no revenues or earnings were going public, mostly businesses with new and groundbreaking technologies. The investment banks were pushing these companies aggressively, and investors were not shying away. The market for these issues was surging.

"Companies looking for cash present unique problems," Isocrates continued. "There are two risks with these clients.

Theseus

One, they never want to pay their legal bills until the money comes in. If it doesn't, they will attempt to stiff the firm on the invoices. Second, and perhaps a greater danger, are those clients that are successful in raising equity capital. Law firms are prime targets for shareholder suits if things don't turn out as expected. Bottom line, we can't be too careful in selecting who we take on as clients."

Isocrates finished and Aegeus rose to address the partners. The room became perceptibly quiet in anticipation of what he was to say. Aegeus had headed the firm for as long as anyone could remember, certainly spanning Theseus' tenure with the firm. Aegeus was a large, imposing man with silver hair and thick, bushy eyebrows. He conveyed an impression of the perfect gentleman. Aegeus looked one in the eye when in a discussion and was an attentive listener. He was always impeccably dressed and wore the finest handmade suits from Byzantium. His shirt sleeves were monogrammed and he was never without cufflinks.

Although he had gradually delegated authority over the years to the firm's executive committee and practice group heads, Aegeus was still firmly in control and decisions of any consequence landed on his desk. Theseus often wondered how a man like Aegeus rose to power. Was he like Deioces of Media, a man of ambition and ability, who was selected king by his people based on his reputation for just dealings? Or was he more like Darius, who conspired to oust the sitting king of Persia, convinced his co-conspirators that a monarchy was the best form of government and then through guile managed to secure the throne? Perhaps it was simply an accident of birth common to so many successions. Theseus thought the last the least legitimate claim to leadership.

Aegeus was an attorney from an earlier age. He joined the firm when there were only twenty five lawyers. Everyone back then came from the top law schools. Aegeus was one of three new hires when he started with the firm. He got the job because he was engaged to a girl whose father was a good client. That's the way things worked back then. The pay was meager at the start, and associates did what they were asked.

Young lawyers would go to court to argue a case before a judge, negotiate a contract or draft a will. There were no practice groups, no boundaries. Clients made appointments and waited patiently in reception to be seen. The partners wrote up the bills based upon what they thought the value of the work was to the clients. Clients paid their lawyers without a lot of fuss.

Aegeus' rise to importance in the firm was the stuff of legend. In his second year at the firm, Aegeus was sent out to a small architect's office to review a redevelopment contract. The architect had used another firm for most of its legal work. Aegeus struck up a conversation with the secretary, who told him that her fiancé had inherited some property in Cephallenia. He had never seen the property and didn't have the money to go there and arrange selling it. The secretary said she had called the company's regular counsel, but hadn't heard back in over a week. The secretary wondered if Aegeus could help. Aegeus promised he would see what he could do. When Aegeus returned to the firm the next day, he asked around if anyone knew anything about Cephallenia real estate. No one did. So Aegeus picked up the phone and found the number for the land records office in Cephallenia. He obtained the legal description of the property and was given the name of a local surveyor. The surveyor referred Aegeus to a land appraiser and reputable estate agent. He wrote down the information and conveyed it back to the secretary.

About six months passed when Aegeus got a call from the secretary. She told Aegeus that her fiancé was able to get the property sold through Aegeus' contacts. Her fiancé received a tidy sum of money from the sale, and with it they were able to get married. She now wondered if Aegeus could handle a will for her and her new husband. She added that they now had a few dollars extra to pay him. Aegeus knew nothing about wills, but again agreed to help. He asked for a partner's advice in preparing a simple will and testament, and took it out to give to the secretary. The architect came across Aegeus and the secretary discussing the will, and asked what they were doing. The architect said he didn't have a will

Theseus

either, and asked if Aegeus would do something for him as well. Aegeus obliged, but this time had the partner prepare the will. The architect was very pleased with Aegeus' efforts. From that time on, the architect included Aegeus in all of the company's legal affairs. The company in time grew to become one of the most successful commercial architectural firms in the land, noted particularly for its work on office towers. Aegeus was eventually appointed a director and served on the company's board for over thirty years. That client relationship spun off other work for Aegeus and propelled him in his career at the firm.

"The law and this firm have given me wonderful opportunities," Aegeus addressed the meeting, "and not a few surprises. I hope that is true for you. I look back and can say I would do it all over again. It has been my privilege and honor to be a lawyer and to serve as chairman of this firm. But it is time that I step down."

There was a loud gasp from the partners. The room erupted as the partners all began talking at once. Theseus wondered why there was all the commotion. Aegeus was getting old and didn't have the step he had in earlier years. Theseus thought Aegeus was probably challenged maintaining the energy necessary to head a large law firm.

In his sporadic dealings with Aegeus, Theseus sensed that Aegeus had become obsessive about turning over power. He had no apparent heir. Although there were a few possible candidates with skill in managing practice groups, Theseus saw no one with the mettle to actually lead the firm. Several partners had surfaced to recommend themselves, but Aegeus had not embraced any of them.

"Some of you know that I have struggled with my decision to pick a new chairman," Aegeus said. "I don't deny it. You are all to know that I have not yet chosen a successor. But I can no longer run from the inevitable. No one can escape old age. I have decided I will pick my successor by the end of next year. I cannot promise who it will be. But I will keep to this calendar. This much I can promise."

Aegeus stepped from the podium.

The partners rose amid a groundswell of animated conversation. Theseus remained seated, thinking about which of the partners might be chosen. As he sat there, Lysias approached him with a note. Aegeus wanted to see him as soon as possible after the meeting. Theseus thought it odd, as he was not currently handling matters for any of Aegeus' clients. And Theseus judged himself too young for Aegeus to consider him a contender to be the next chairman.

Theseus went straight away to see Aegeus in his office. Theseus found Aegeus standing by his desk and peering contemplatively out of his window. Aegeus had a large office with its own conference table and bathroom. His desk was a stand up without drawers. It was clear except for the daily law journal which was spread out for reading.

"I created quite a stir, I think," Aegeus said to Theseus. "The vultures will start circling. I'm not eager to face this next year and a half. I wish I was young, as you are, Theseus, and passed my days handling interesting transactions like you. Those were the best times. But I didn't ask you in to have you hear me complaining. Please sit down."

Theseus took a seat.

"I want you to step in on a transaction involving a man named Minos," Aegeus said to Theseus. "Minos runs a company, some technology startup, I think. Tantalus brought it in. Lysias learned about it from the conflicts check Tantalus ran. Minos has some big plans. I have approved the engagement, but I don't think this is the sort of thing Tantalus should be handling. It's got too many moving parts and he's a tax lawyer. Tax lawyers don't know how to run corporate transactions. Go down and talk to Tantalus. I know you are busy with your own clients, but I would like you to take this over. It's important for the firm."

Theseus said he would be happy to do whatever he could, but he sensed there was more to the story. Aegeus seemed to read Theseus' mind.

"Now Minos and I have a bit of a history," Aegeus said. "Not completely pleasant. He had a keen interest in a matter that turned out badly. He thinks that I, our firm, had

Theseus

something to do with it. Let's leave it at that."

Not inquiring any further, Theseus got up to leave.

"By the way, Theseus," Aegeus asked, "do you have any interest in serving on the executive committee? Lysias is recommending you."

Theseus told Aegeus he was flattered, but unsure how other partners would take it. Theseus remarked that there were probably many others who considered themselves ahead of him in line.

"I can see why you might feel that way," Aegeus said. "But think on it some, and get back to me. And go see Tantalus about Minos."

3

That evening Theseus reflected on Aegeus' invitation to join the executive committee. He had mixed feelings. Theseus knew it was an opportunity to assume a formal leadership position in the firm. That appealed to him. Theseus felt bred for the role. At the same time, he enjoyed the work he was doing and was concerned that management would remove him from it. He asked himself why he shouldn't be satisfied with merely developing his practice and enjoying the rewards of being a partner in the firm, which were many. He also was not confident that he had developed a sufficient reputation among his partners to warrant the appointment. He was still building his practice. The natural order was to give the older their due.

Theseus sought out the advice of Pirithous about what he should do. Pirithous had become to Theseus what Pylades had been to Orestes and Peisistratos to Telemachos. These were the loyal friends of men that fate had left with heavy burdens. The honor earned by Pylades and Peisistratos was equal to the men they attended.

"Lysias wants you in management, and he has Aegeus' ear," Pittheus told him. "So I wouldn't procrastinate. He probably wants to bring you in, see how you do. You could be Aegeus' choice to succeed him. That's likely what's going on."

Theseus said that Aegeus didn't really know him well, and questioned whether he would have the support of the other partners. He would have to be voted in.

"You can expect that Aietes and his cohorts at least will challenge you for the spot," Pirithous said. "Aietes has visions of grandeur and operates purely out of self interest. He won't act with the good of the partnership in mind. For the sake of the firm, I think you need to do this. Who knows if you will have the opportunity later on."

Theseus listened to Pirithous, but chose to hold off. He decided that he needed additional client successes to draw the attention and then the support of the partners. With a string

Theseus

of noteworthy client representations, he could earn the respect of his colleagues. Elevation to the executive committee would be easier and he could elude the politicking that would otherwise be necessary. He told Pirithous that he would consider the post but only after managing a series of client representations that would bring him well deserved acclaim. Theseus felt that if he prevailed in this, he would be in the right to accept. If he failed, he would not be worthy of the nomination. Pirithous believed Theseus was being too dramatic, but left him to his decision.

Theseus gave thought to how his plan could be executed. He was not to wait long before the first suitable matter arose. Theseus received a visit from Zosimus, one of the firm's patent lawyers.

"My client Nessus Technologies is being battered by Periphetes Logistics in the market," Zosimus repined. "Periphetes is a big manufacturer of mainframes for scientific applications in Argolis and known for being aggressive. Nessus is a smaller competitor and has lost a host of critical supply contracts. Nessus is certain Periphetes is behind it. Unless something is done quickly, Nessus' market share will likely decay rapidly."

Zosimus asked for Theseus' assistance, and Theseus was quick to oblige. Zosimus arranged a call with Nessus' general counsel for that afternoon. After learning more of the facts, Theseus devised a line of attack. He called Alcaeus and had him look into potential trade violations that could be used against Periphetes. Theseus told Alcaeus to scour any and all court filings, newspapers and trade journals that mentioned Periphetes and to reach out to other companies in the industry to gather intelligence. Time was of the essence. But Alcaeus needed to be discrete. Theseus wanted him to be like Diomedes and Odysseus when they went surreptitiously amidst the Trojans under cover of darkness to ascertain the Trojan's plans for attacking the Danaans.

For his part, Theseus enlisted the help of the firm's antitrust lawyers. Over the next few weeks, with attorneys working around the clock, the firm constructed a chronology evidencing a host of anticompetitive behaviors by Periphetes. There was ample evidence that Periphetes had engaged in below market pricing, bid rigging, control of distribution channels and corruption of suppliers. A clear pattern had emerged that Periphetes' market tactics were intended to give it a virtual monopoly.

Theseus then had Nessus contact Periphetes to arrange a meeting. When that was unsuccessful, Theseus sent Periphetes a letter threatening a lawsuit for tortuous interference of contract and antitrade claims unless Periphetes stopped pressuring Nessus' suppliers. Theseus was certain Periphetes would reject the demand out of hand, but it would serve to put the company on notice. He was correct in his assessment.

Theseus put in a call to a lawyer named Elpidius at the trade authority. He knew that Elpidius was himself looking for a defining case that could propel him up the ladder at the authority. Theseus wanted to serve the case up to Elpidius like a supplicant at the altar of the goddess Nike. Theseus began feeding Elpidius the information Alcaeous uncovered about Periphetes.

Several months after beginning its own investigation, the authority filed a massive case against Periphetes alleging numerous antitrust violations. The financial papers picked up the story. On the same day, the firm went to court seeking an injunction on behalf of Nessus. The complaint asserted multiple counts of unlawful trade practices by Periphetes and asked for damages in an amount that, if awarded, would cripple the company.

At this point, Theseus thought there was a good chance Periphetes would agree to settlement negotiations with Nessus. It didn't. Many companies like Periphetes were confident their sheer market dominance meant they would have no difficulty prevailing before a judge in court. A misguided theory, in Theseus' mind, and one that often resulted in huge costs, time delays and unintended consequences. Theseus never did believe the courtroom was a good forum for resolving business disputes. It took too long and consumed limited resources. Besides, astute businessmen prided themselves on negotiating deals. Why substitute the vagaries of a judge's thought process for their own? If it was absolutely necessary to go outside for dispute resolution, why not adopt the procedure depicted on the great shield of Achilles? There, two disputants placed money before the judges and each judge gave his opinion. The straightest opinion among the judges was adopted, and the money was given to the judge who proffered it. A most sensible approach for business disputes, Theseus thought.

Because Periphetes would not negotiate, Theseus had no choice but to argue Nessus' case in court. The judge assigned to the case was named Paseas, and he was not experienced in antitrust law. On the day of the hearing, Theseus stood before Paseas and calmly asserted that Periphetes was intent on driving its competitors out of the market and employed unlawful means to achieve its goal. If Periphetes was allowed to prevail, Theseus argued, not only would Nessus most likely go out of business, but innovation would be stifled in an industry critical to the economy. Theseus portrayed Periphetes as a corporate oligarch that curried favor with politicians and used government to protect its markets. Free enterprise was undermined by companies like Periphetes and the law required that something be done. Theseus saw the professional irony of the position, knowing as he did the clientele of the firm. But it made a good case for Nessus.

Those in the courtroom saw Paseas swayed by Theseus' arguments. It took two days before Periphetes approached Nessus to discuss settlement. Periphetes evidently did not want to face both an unfavorable opinion from Paseas and a prolonged fight with the authority. Theseus suspected that Periphetes was also concerned about what would be uncovered in discovery if the litigation became protracted.

4

Soon after Nessus prevailed in its antitrust battle with Periphetes, Lysias asked Theseus to attend a firm reception honoring the ambassador from Megara. The gathering was held at Aegeus' residence, a three story palace with a bright white facade and Mediterranean styled roof on five acres of land. The estate was surrounded by a ten foot wall and tight security. Guards with dogs paraded the grounds. The windows in the front were large and grated, overlooking groves of pomegranate, fig and olive trees. Theseus imagined Odysseus gazing upon the orchards of Arete.

The foyer of the great house rose two floors, and in the middle was an opulent fountain. There was an expansive drawing room with doors that opened out to a large pool and guest house.

Aegeus often made his home accessible for special firm events. He housed one of the finest collections of Greek art in the city, and many of the pieces were the purported gifts of Croesus of Lydia to Delphi. Croesus was said to have made some of the most lavish offerings to the temple honoring Apollo in the hope of obtaining favorable prophesies for his invasion of Persia. Numbered among the artifacts were exquisite tripods, bowls, and statutes. The art was discriminately placed throughout the common areas of the residence.

The Megaran ambassador was an important figure in Athens, as Megara was one of Athens's closest neighbors and trading partners. Theseus was aware that tensions between the states had been running high of late. Megara was experiencing increasing internal violence over illicit drug trafficking. Megara blamed Attica for creating demand for the drug production but also for allowing its financial institutions to launder drug money.

When Theseus arrived, he was surprised at the small size of the affair. He saw Lysias when he entered and went over. Lysias was of good height notwithstanding a slight slouch and had gray hair and clear eyes. He eschewed fancy suits and opted for buttoned down shirts and foulard ties. Lysias made his mark at the firm as an astute trial lawyer with good business sense. He was a worldly man famous for his travels, and had a weakness for epic poetry. Theseus regarded Lysias highly. He was like the elder statesmen Nestor, who the Greeks held in high esteem for his sagacity and sound advice. Not all things are given to men at the same time Nestor is remembered saying to Agamemnon. There was no substitute for the acumen won by age, Theseus thought.

"This was actually organized by the government relations group," Lysias said to Theseus. "They wanted to keep it private. Not many really knew about it. Aegeus told me I should attend, so I thought I would invite you."

Theseus considered it odd that the affair was kept secret. That was very unusual for the firm to do, especially since Aegeus was hosting.

Theseus walked into the drawing room and noted that there were several other dignitaries present. The government relations partners obviously had hand selected attendees.

Theseus saw Aegeus off in a far corner, so he made his way over.

"Ah, Theseus," Aegeus said, "Lysias said you might be here. I want you to meet Ambassador Callias. He is here to speak before the council tomorrow. By the way, nice piece of work for Nessus."

Theseus shook the ambassador's hand, and welcomed him to Athens. Aegeus left the two together and walked off. Theseus inquired of the ambassador the subject of his speech.

"Well," Callias said, "Megara has been a good friend and ally of Athens for many, many years. But it is time for Athens to recognize the problems it is creating for our country. Our mutual treaty requires Athens to come to our aid if our security is threatened. That day has come. I am here with a delegation to meet with your people. I will address the council tomorrow and speak candidly of the issues we are facing. Unless Athens recognizes the problem and decides to take remedial action, I'm afraid our long standing relationship may be in jeopardy. Your firm knows people in government and represents many banks, and it is my hope that you can use your influence to benefit our two countries."

Callias and Theseus spoke a little while longer, but broke it off when Lysias approached.

Theseus spent the next hour or so introducing himself to other members of the Megaran delegation. He had visited Megara many times and enjoyed the country, so he was interested to learn of the changes that had been occurring there.

Toward the end of the evening, Lysias told Theseus to stop by and thank Aegeus for hosting.

"He's back in his study off the library," Lysias said. "You should poke your head in before you leave."

Theseus was not eager to appear solicitous of Aegeus, but agreed to see him out of deference to Lysias. As he made his way to the study, he found several of the government lawyers lounging on the library couches, drinking cognacs and puffing away on cigars. Aietes, who headed the lobbying group, looked like he was holding court. Bacis and Tisias sat with him. They made up an odd trio. Aietes had spotty, rough facial skin and was balding. His suit was too tight from excessive dry cleaning, and the white handkerchief in his coat pocket made him look pretentious. Aietes spoke quickly and always looked past his listener. Bacis was obese and couldn't button his coat. His face was flushed and he had a wide nose and enlarged nostrils. Tisias was on the tallish, thin side and looked overly scrubbed. His heavily greased hair accentuated his cowlick.

Theseus asked if Aegeus was in his study.

The men turned to Theseus with a look of indignation. Aietes spoke first.

"What business do you have with Aegeus, Theseus?" Aietes asked. "I'm sure he's engaged and shouldn't be bothered. Besides, I didn't think corporate types were allowed in here tonight. You know, I thought it was to be a classy affair."

The men mocked Theseus with their condescending

laughter. Theseus made an effort not to display his anger.

"Now hold on, Theseus," Aietes remonstrated, "no need to get in a huff. We're just enjoying the evening, you know, having some fun. Come, sit down. Have a drink and cigar. Where is Hagnon, our server? Always disappearing just when we need him. Hagnon! Here, get young Theseus a cognac. And bring a few more of those cigars."

Aietes and his retinue came into the firm from the outside. It was an unusual move for Aegeus to bring in a group from another law firm, but Theseus suspected Aegeus saw something in Aietes that made it worthwhile. Aietes joined the firm with some fanfare. He was touted as a government insider with contacts ranging from high elected officials to bureaucrats. Theseus knew that Aietes' angle wasn't generating legal fees per se. He was a lobbyist and he was paid to make connections. As it turned out, Aietes did not have a large client base when he arrived. But he proceeded quickly to get audiences with the firm's largest clients with Aegeus' help, and managed sufficient early traction with them to generate some sizeable retainers.

Lobbying was a new game for the firm. The firm had built its reputation on its legal prowess. Why Aegeus thought the firm needed to lobby was a puzzle to Theseus. Partners individually supported candidates of their choosing, and there was never any pressure to grease the lawmakers. Theseus thought lobbyists were gladhanders of the highest order, incessant talkers with little if anything of substance to say. They peddled access to government and the courts, buying influence and fixing outcomes. Cynics would say they elevated graft and kickbacks to an art form. For lawyers like Aietes, it was all the more legitimate under the auspices of a law firm. Theseus knew that corruption of the lawgivers was a serious problem in ancient Athens and undermined the early democracy. Measures were adopted to prevent bribes and payoffs, and perpetrators could be put to death or banished. Theseus asked himself if it wasn't time to again impose severe penalties on the persons involved in pay to play practices.

When Aietes joined the firm, he needed some upfront money to work his magic. He managed to convince Aegeus that the firm should have a political action committee to fund campaigns. Aegeus approved establishing a fund, and the firm adopted a policy that every lawyer was expected to donate. Contributions were supposedly voluntary, but it was quickly understood that failing to contribute was viewed negatively. Soon the likes of Bacis and Tisias were on the phones hounding partners for money.

"Aegeus himself is expecting you to participate," Bacis or Tisias would say. "You don't want to disappoint him. Everyone in the firm who contributes will benefit, so you don't want to be left out."

The younger partners felt the greatest pressure to ante up, and most did so. Funds were deducted automatically from paychecks, which made it difficult to opt out. Theseus understood that the only one gaining from the fund was Aietes. Aietes controlled how the money was spent, and he spent it on his own causes. Although the fund was available to all partners, it was difficult to shake money loose if Aietes didn't favor the expenditure.

"So what is it you want to see Aegeus about, Theseus?" Aietes asked.

"I think the great Theseus may be trying to ingratiate himself with Aegeus," Bacis opined.

"Oh, so you have designs on being the next chairman," Aietes said. "Well, I wouldn't put too much effort into that. The firm needs someone more experienced than you. These are troubling times, Theseus, and we can't afford to let the firm slip."

"The next chairman will come out of our group," Tisias chimed in. "Don't you see, Theseus, the firm needs someone who knows politics and the ways of government. Corporate types don't fit that bill. You don't have the skills we do, what's necessary to lead. The art of persuasion, if you know what I mean."

Theseus found Aietes and his crowd feckless and boorish. They were no different than the suitors for Penelope's hand during Odysseus' long absence from home after the battle of Troy. Theseus was tiring of their banter.

"Why don't you let Aegeus be?" Tisias said. "He's a fatigued old man. Go on back to your corporate boards and executives. We'll take care of Aegeus. Now, let us get on with our important matters of state."

"Gentlemen," a woman's voice suddenly came in from behind. "Why are you pestering Theseus in this way?"

Theseus turned to see Medea standing over him.

"Don't be bullied by these impish people, Theseus," Medea said coquettishly. "They are nothing but blowhards."

The lobbyists laughed at Medea's words.

Medea was a real estate lawyer that succeeded in garnering Aegeus' attention as a young partner and managed to have herself appointed the head of the real estate group. Word was she pushed aside more than one partner to get there. Theseus knew that Medea largely took credit for the dramatic growth in profitability of the real estate practice despite the fact that the city was in the midst of a cyclical construction boom. Lawyers like Medea had a tendency to overlook the market factors that accounted for many successful practices. But she had become a favorite of Aegeus, and she was often in his company. So much so that it was rumored their relationship was more than professional.

Medea had sable hair and dark eyes, and was of short height. She was always stylish in her dress, and this night was no exception. Medea sat down on the arm of the chair where Theseus was seated. Her black dress rose up high on her legs as she crossed her thighs and leaned suggestively over him. Theseus tensed up.

"Is it Aegeus you are waiting for?" Medea asked smugly. "He speaks highly of you, you know. He thinks you are one of the most promising talents that we have."

The government lawyers had stopped to listen. Aietes was not pleased.

"Medea," Aietes interrupted, "why lead good Theseus on as you do? Theseus, be careful of this woman. She has a propensity for devilry."

"A sorceress," Bacis added.

"She dabbles in black magic, many say," blurted Tisias.

The three men had a good laugh.

Medea threw a forced smile at Aietes and his men.

"If you're not careful, Theseus," Aietes said, "she will poison you just as she's drugged Aegeus."

Having had enough, Theseus stood up. He bid the government lawyers and Medea good night and started toward Aegeus' study. Medea followed him and grabbed his arm before he got to the door.

"They are fools, those men," Medea said in a low voice. "I think it's good that you are spending some time with Aegeus. But put out of your mind any notions of becoming chairman, Theseus. That's not in the stars for you, I wouldn't think. Let's be sure to talk again soon."

Medea turned away, leaving Theseus somewhat ill at ease.

"Ah, Theseus," Aegeus said greeting him. "Come in, please. Was that Medea I heard? Have you two worked together? If not, you should. She is quite the go getter. Some say a little pushy for her own good, but you need to be aggressive in the big law firms these days. Especially the women. I dare say she has given me a lift in my waning days. A remarkable young woman."

Aegeus offered Theseus a drink, which Theseus declined citing an early client meeting the next day.

"Well, you won't mind if I fix one for myself," Aegeus replied.

Aegeus poured himself a healthy glass of tsipouro.

"A strong young man with a noble bent like Pirithous," Aegeus said. "And a reputation for cleverness and wit with the law. Nothing less would I expect from the grandson of Pittheus, a good friend I have not seen in many years. Now, sit with me a while. What is it you have been working on these days, Theseus?"

Theseus mentioned several things currently on his plate. Aegeus questioned Theseus about the firm's corporate practice and whether anything needed to be done in support of it. Theseus said that the next five or ten years could be good for the corporate group, although he perceived an imminent bubble in the equity markets.

"Yes, we should be careful of that," Aegeus said. "You let me know what we can do for corporate. The practice throws off a great deal of work to the other groups. The more we can grow it the better for the firm."

The conversation drifted toward the prosperity of the firm generally. Aegeus asked Theseus' opinion about expanding the firm overseas. Aegeus had been in talks with a law firm in Sardis and another in Rhegium on a possible combination. Theseus was not completely surprised to hear of it.

"Very preliminary," Aegeus said. "But we need to look at it. Other firms are starting to expand and we don't want to be left behind. Tell me Theseus, what would be your reaction if the firm went that direction?"

Theseus stated that he did not see any downside to having offices in other places. In point of fact, he thought it was inevitable. But he didn't necessarily think that merging with other firms was the right strategy.

"I'm curious to know why you say that," Aegeus said.

Theseus explained that he believed most firms combined with other firms out of weakness. The firm was strong and growing, and it would continue in that fashion in spite of itself, similar to how classical Athens was relentless in its expansion after defeating Xerxes. It was far better to send the firm's lawyers out to found new offices, just as the Greeks colonized Anatolia and the islands off Italy. That way the firm would have strong ties with the foreign offices by blood and culture.

"I must say," Aegeus said, "that certainly is an unconventional way of looking at it."

Theseus went on. It was important to preserve the customs of the firm and inculcate its lawyers with the firm's own standards of professionalism, partnership and mutual benefits. That, thought Theseus, was the bond that not only held the firm together, but also defined its greatness. If the firm's culture was lost, the firm would eventually falter.

"How are we to assure that our expansion meets that criterion?" Aegeus asked Theseus.

Maintaining awareness and commitment to shared values is the most critical thing, Theseus continued. That's hard to achieve when merging with other established firms. Some firms that have already spread overseas found local lawyers and paid them large sums to start offices. These lawyers have proved largely unsuccessful in establishing productive practices and inevitably walk away with handsome severance payments. Theseus thought the firm should start new offices with its own senior people, then hire younger lawyers from those places and have them work in Athens for several years. Once integrated into the firm, they can be better counted on to keep the interests of the firm at heart.

Aegeus was intrigued by what he was hearing.

"Well, you are certainly giving me something to think about, Theseus," Aegeus said with some seriousness.

Aegeus got up to fix himself another drink.

"Have you talked with Tantalus yet?" Aegeus asked changing the subject. "Please do that, if you would. I don't want Minos' transaction moving ahead without your involvement. Tantalus needs your help."

Aegeus bid Theseus a good night.

"Let's talk more about your ideas," Aegeus said. "You may be on to something there."

5

Theseus did not know Tantalus well. Tantalus joined the tax group of the firm right out of law school and managed to secure his place among the partners a few years back. From his intermittent contacts with him, Theseus knew Tantalus had a penchant for self absorbed verbosity.

Tantalus had a corner office with excellent street views. He arranged his furniture so that his desk faced the windows and his back was to the door. Theseus walked in to find Tantalus with an associate named Diocles.

"The whore!" Tantalus shouted.

With great violence, Tantalus threw a large file folder across the room. The file struck a framed diploma that was hanging on the wall, shattering the glass encasement. Paper flew everywhere. Diocles was frozen.

"Oh, Theseus, come on in," Tantalus said when he noticed Theseus at the door. "I just got word that my old secretary is filing a sexual harassment suit against me. What a bitch! I knew she'd be headache when I threw her out of my house, but god almighty! Can you believe this crap?"

Tantalus got himself involved with the woman after she broke up with another lawyer in the office. Tantalus became interested a little later in an executive assistant at a consulting firm named Leda, and promptly gave the secretary the boot.

"Aegeus said you would be coming by," Tantalus said calming down.

Tantalus was short and husky and carried a slightly distended girth. He had an aquiline nose and wide chin that jutted when he frowned or smiled. Titian bangs fell over his forehead which he had a habit of sweeping up with an open palm.

"Hey, Diocles, get the hell out of here!" ordered Tantalus. "Can't you see I'm talking to Theseus?"

Diocles quickly collected his things and scurried from the office.

"That tramp!" Tantalus piped shaking his head.

Theseus wondered aloud if another time might be better.

"No, no," Tantalus answered. "It's got to be now. Have a seat."

Tantalus sat back in his chair and pushed his hair off his face.

"Theseus," Tantalus started, "you and me, we haven't worked together much. There are probably a few things you should know about me."

Tantalus took a deep breath and began with what sounded like a canned declamation.

"I grew up in the mountains of Sipylus in Lydia," Tantalus said. "But don't take me for a backwater country lawyer. My family had money and I went to the best schools, same as you. Graduated *cum laude* from law school. Know how I did it? I ingratiated myself early on with the law professors. I got the outlines for the courses from older students and didn't let on with my classmates. I talked a lot in class and shouted down other students. Probably what you did, too. That was the way to make it. I didn't feel sorry for the suckers who didn't learn the system. The firm was the first to offer me a full time position."

Tantalus leaned toward Theseus and eyed him closely.

"This Minos thing will be a good opportunity for us to get acquainted, really get to know each other," Tantalus said. "I expect to get elevated to management at some point, hopefully soon, so I will be someone you want in your corner. I belong up there, you know, with the gods looking down on the pathetic masses below. I can already hear them laughing. I share the immortals' disdain for the old, the weak and the infirm."

Theseus decided he had heard enough from Tantalus to take the measure of the man.

"I need you to come to dinner tonight with Minos," Tantalus announced. "He's coming over to the house. Leda's watching my pork barbecue right now. Have you ever had pulled pork? Not the way I cook it."

Ducking below his desk, Tantalus came up with a couple of helmets. He tossed Theseus one and said he had his bike downstairs. Theseus said he had a few things to finish up, and would meet Tantalus later at this house.

"That won't work, Theseus," Tantalus protested. "We need to go now. Minos might be there already."

"Just move with me when I turn," Tantalus instructed Theseus when they reached the garage.

Tantalus and Theseus were quickly on the streets maneuvering through stalled traffic. Crossing a bridge, a white van driven by a Persian sped past on the left and then cut back into the lane ahead of the motorcycle. It was a little close for Tantalus' liking.

"Goddamn moron!" he screeched.

Tantalus throttled the engine and pulled up alongside the van. He turned and gave the Persian the finger while shouting profanities. The Persian started yelling back. Before things got uglier, Tantalus slowed and made for the exit. Tantalus and Theseus were soon off the bridge.

"That ass!" screamed Tantalus. "You see what he did? I mean, why should I put up with that?"

When they reached Tantalus' house, he directed Theseus to go inside and said he would be in after parking the motorcycle.

"Pork barbeque," he called out. "I'm telling you!"

As Theseus walked around back to the kitchen door, he noticed someone through the window. Theseus assumed it was Minos. As Theseus looked on, he saw the man half sitting on the kitchen counter. He appeared to be talking to someone. A woman came into view wearing nothing more than a man's dress shirt. The woman was evidently putting the make on, and from the looks of things the man was not putting up much resistance.

Theseus hurriedly rang the doorbell several times. Tantalus came up around the corner.

"Hey, I said go ahead in," Tantalus ordered as he passed by Theseus and opened the door.

Minos was now sitting at the kitchen table. There was no sign of the woman.

"Tantalus! How the hell are you?" Minos greeted him. "About time you got here."

Minos was a middle aged, handsome man. He had large shoulders and big hands. His hair was golden brown and his eyes ocean blue. He had a friendly air and kinetic smile. Minos was casually but impeccably dressed, and wore an expensive watch.

"Minos, I brought you the best damn securities lawyer there is at the firm," Tantalus exclaimed. "Meet Theseus."

"Hello, Theseus," Minos said amicably extending Theseus a weak handshake. "Always good to know a quality lawyer."

As Minos and Theseus began to talk, Tantalus moved back to the kitchen. There was a loud clanking of pots.

"Damn it, Leda!" Tantalus shouted. "Leda! The barbeque isn't cooked! The pork's raw! Leda!"

Theseus heard a door open on the second floor and saw the woman, now fully dressed, coming down the stairs. She walked right in to Tantalus' tirade.

"I told you to keep the meat on low heat all afternoon!" Tantalus hollered. "What the hell!"

Leda said sheepishly that she had to turn the heat off because she was out of the house for several hours. Tantalus blew. He grabbed the cooking pot and hurled the pork right into the garbage. Leda started crying and ran back upstairs. Theseus and Minos just stared at each other, incredulous at the tantrum.

Many minutes passed before Tantalus cooled off. The men decided just to order out. That gave Minos and Theseus some time to talk. Leda came back in when the dinner arrived, but the atmosphere was a bit tense with her there.

Eventually, Leda cleaned up the table, retreated to the den and shut the door. Minos and Theseus withdrew to the living room.

"Here's what I have going, Theseus," Minos said. "I bought this public company in Thessaly. Well, it's not really in Thessaly. It's just incorporated there, right Tantalus?"

Theseus learned that Minos acquired Larissa Minerals through a reverse merger with a private company he owned. Larrisa's business was all but nonexistent. It had long term lease rights to some undeveloped mining property, but little else. The acquisition of Larissa was the beginning of Mino's venture. He renamed the company Asterion, Inc., and began to acquire small storefront computer consulting shops in various locations such as Messene, Argos, Corinth, Pylos and Mantinea. The acquisition currency for these businesses was Asterion stock.

Theseus saw immediate red flags for Asterion, not least of which was the reverse merger. Thessaly was a haven for questionable enterprises, shell corporations and penny stock fraud. Thessaly had lax laws regulating corporate formations which drew all sorts of schemes concocted to make quick money. The typical structure involved a corporation that had hundreds or thousands of stockholders but defunct or no business operations. Larissa fit the pattern perfectly. The stock price of these public shells would be quoted in the over-the-counter trading market for cents on the dollar. A promoter would find a fledging business and merge it into the public shell and acquire control. The promoter would then issue favorable press releases about the company. Investors would soon start buying the stock, driving the price up. When the stock price got high enough, the promoter would start selling. Eventually the stock would fall and the public investors ended up with worthless stock. It was the classic pump and dump scheme.

"Wait, Theseus, I know what you're thinking," Tantalus judged. "This is legit. I've taken a look. Very clean. The business operates out of Crete, nowhere near Thessaly."

As it was, Asterion's stock began to increase in value after Minos reported several quarters of modest but increasing revenues from the business acquisitions. Within nine months, Asterion's stock price had risen tenfold and the company carried a meaningful market capitalization. Minos' own net worth rose dramatically based on the trading value of the stock he owned in Asterion.

"We got a high tech call center in the works outside of Stratus in Arcanania," Minos said. "There's capacity for about a hundred dialers. I'll take you up there and we can ski. But here's the killer. I can get my hands on some software developed by a company in Thebes, of all places. It will revolutionize how small and midsized companies integrate their technology systems. It's unbelievable stuff."

Minos further elaborated on the plan. He would acquire the Theban company and complete a public offering of stock. Minos also had designs on developing a data center in Tegea to host the software.

"Theseus," Minos said, "this venture has huge potential. I hear you are the best damn attorney in the firm. Here's what I want. Collect a whole bunch of your lawyers, whoever you want. I like the young ones, though. They work hard and take orders. Use as many associates as you can. Go to Thebes and get me that software company. With that deal inked, we are going to go out and raise some serious cash. The market is hot. I'm counting on you guys to get this thing done."

"Hey, Minos," Tantalus interrupted. "Theseus will take care of all of that. I've got to show you this speedboat I have been working on. It's out in the garage. Vintage. I'm rehabbing it myself. Bought the wood, electric saw, everything. Will take me about a year. Leda! Minos wants to see the boat!"

6

Upon returning to the office, Theseus set about assembling a team for Mino's project. The work would require lawyers from a variety of practice groups in the firm, including corporate securities, employee benefits, intellectual property, real estate and tax, among others. Theseus wanted designated partners to lead or oversee the efforts in these areas, and delegate specific responsibilities and tasks to associate lawyers. When Theseus put together a group for a deal, he felt like Jason organizing the Argonauts for the voyage to Colchis.

Theseus was successful in getting the coverage he needed from the partners he wanted, and he left it up to the partners to select their own associates. The corporate securities work would be the most complex and time consuming, and this Theseus would handle himself. But given his own work load, he decided he would need some partner backup.

Theseus first gave Xenos a call. Xenos had been with the firm a couple of years, joining as a lateral partner from another firm. Xenos specialized in acquisitions for public companies and had a keen grasp of the intricacies of public company transactions. Theseus worked with Xenos a few times and was impressed. He found Xenos not adverse to rolling up his sleeves and putting time into a deal, even if it wasn't his own.

"Mr. Xenos is no longer with the firm," a secretary told Theseus when he called. "You should speak with Mr. Lysias."

Theseus was naturally surprised. The firm had made a concerted effort to recruit him from his prior firm. Xenos was editor of the law review at his law school and graduated first in his class. He wrote prolifically on public company topics in law journals and was a regular speaker at legal seminars across the country.

"What can I tell you," Lysias said when Theseus reached him in his office. "Xenos resigned yesterday."

Lysias told Theseus that Xenos apparently fabricated his

portable book of business and carried a huge amount of personal debt. He had a few good years at his former firm, and then went on a personal spending spree. Xenos opened a margin trading account at a large brokerage firm and began shorting stocks and writing options. He also bought a large house on Samos. Xenos was deep in debt when he joined the firm.

"We never had any idea the fix he was in," Lysias said. "He was overbilling all of the matters he was on and clients started calling. He began doing things for clients they never asked him to do. We have massive receivables from his work we will probably never collect."

With Xenos gone, Theseus went next to Melesius. Melesius was an old line corporate lawyer who rode the growth of the law over the past four decades and made a veritable fortune in the process. A contemporary of Aegeus, he had an enviable list of clients in his day. As he got older, he started putting in banker's hours and delegated a lot of work to other lawyers. Nowadays, Melesius stayed clear of firm management, never looked for new business and seldom traveled. He could not be found in the office on weekends. But he remained an integral part of the corporate group nonetheless and was one of the best liked and respected partners in the firm. Theseus knew he could count on Melesius to pitch in if needed.

Theseus thought about the associates he should use. Alcaeus, Iollas and Nikon were the logical selections. They performed well on Aigaion, and Theseus liked them. When putting a team together, it was often necessary to do some juggling and a little selling to other partners to get the right group of associates. Associate lawyers in the firm were required to bill an enormous number of hours in a year. That was in addition to administrative, training and pro bono time requirements. It was not uncommon for an associate to spend nearly every waking hour for weeks on end in the office or traveling on client business. A career in big law was not for the slothful. To keep up with the hour requirements, associates generally had to work for several partners at once and manage the competing demands placed on them. Many partners did not tolerate less than a full commitment, and were possessive of associates' time. Theseus made some calls to make sure that Alcaeus, Iollas and Nikon were sufficiently freed up to devote a large amount of time to Asterion.

Alcaeus was a senior corporate associate seven years out of law school with an impressive acquisition and finance deal list under his belt. He was from common roots, but managed to secure a spot in a top law school. He was slim and had sandy, thinning hair. Alcaeus was slow to speak as if at pains to select the right words, but was exceedingly analytical and intelligent. He was up for partner this year, so Theseus knew he could be depended upon to do whatever it took. Alcaeus was on pace for an ungodly number of hours, and he had come off of two recent, successful public offerings. He logged thousands of travel miles from coast to coast to get his deals completed. Theseus wondered when Alcaeus last took time off. He was married, but with no kids. Theseus was curious how the marriage was faring given the hours Alcaeus was putting in at the office. Alcaeus once mentioned that his wife spent a great deal of time with her parents at their country residence when Alcaeus was on the road. Not a good sign. Theseus speculated whether the wife would hold out for him to make partner. Theseus guessed that she wanted him to fail. Many spouses did.

Iollas had not committed to anything new since Aigaion and so was available for the project. Iollas joined the firm about three years ago out of law school. Iollas was a little on the short side and had neatly cut hair with a perfect left side part. He always wore crisp shirts with loud ties. Theseus thought him competent to the extent that was possible for a third year attorney. But Theseus wasn't sure if Iollas was long for the firm. While in Illyria working on Aigaion, Iollas spoke of his designs on one day developing a practice in entertainment law. This type of work was generally handled by small, boutique firms located on the coasts and was frowned upon by the established firms. Entertainment lawyers were seen more as sports agents than practicing lawyers, and the clients were egotistic and slow to pay their legal fees. Theseus told Iollas not to be too conspicuous with his ideas. Undeterred, Iollas wrote up a practice development plan detailing how he would go about setting up an entertainment practice. He intended to present it to Lysias. He wanted to join trade organizations and attend the film festival in Thespia to identify potential clients. Theseus tried to dissuade Iollas from taking his ideas any further in the firm. The plan had absolutely no chance of success. Not only would the entertainment law proposal be flatly rejected, but the firm really had very little interest in any client development efforts by younger associates. Junior associates were generally expected to work on partner matters and nothing else. Any indication that an associate was not fully committed to serving the interests of the partners was grounds for termination.

Nikon had just finished his first year. He was cerebral in appearance and wore thick stemmed glasses. Nikon always looked tense, lost and uncertain. He was from a prominent family in Athens whose affairs were handled by the firm. Theseus guessed that the family patriarch put pressure on the firm to bring him on as an associate. There were a couple of client induced hires in every associate class. Nikon seemed to accept the work load a little grudgingly but performed adequately in spite of it.

Theseus also looked to Calliope to round out the associate group. She had been with the firm less than a year. Calliope arrived from one of the better law schools in Miletus and earned a master's in creative writing before getting her law degree. Calliope had round eyes and face, her skin was white and her cheeks dimpled. Her red hair was always in a ponytail fixed atop her head. She never wore lipstick, but had brightly painted fingernails that changed colors from time to time. Theseus liked her for her spirited and sunny disposition. He respected her initiative and work ethic, and wanted her involved to counter any problems that might arise with Nikon.

The only complication arose when Tantalus called to ask

that Theseus get Diocles involved as the midlevel associate instead of Iollas. Diocles had been with the firm about four and a half years and was a reasonably solid performer. Theseus knew him as personable and somewhat raffish. He was a favorite among the paralegals and secretaries given his tendencies for good natured but irreverent antics. Diocles had a tall athletic frame, dark curly hair amassed atop his head and longish sideburns. Although Theseus couldn't attest to it, Diocles did have a reputation for disappearing late in the evenings when projects were in full swing. That was usually the end of the line for an associate. Many partners demanded that associates be at the firm well into the night and became livid when a late call to an associate's office went unanswered. Partners would often reach associates at home and have them return to the office to report on current work or to be given new assignments. Janos was a commercial finance lawyer who was notorious for calling associates at two or three in the morning. She would often tell associates she wanted to meet late in the afternoon but then not be accessible until after midnight. Uninformed associates would leave the office late only to be woken out of bed.

Theseus wondered if Diocles used the old associate tricks to make partners think they were still around at night. Associates would leave their lights on and hang coats behind their office doors to convey the impression they were about somewhere. If this was indeed his habit, Diocles managed to evade scrutiny for skipping out early.

Theseus wasn't convinced about Diocles, but Tantalus wanted him involved.

"Diocles is the man," Tantalus called Theseus to say. "Use him and Iollas both if you have to. Let Diocles do the diligence, go to a few meetings. I know he'll do fine. He's got the time."

Theseus told Tantalus he would use Diocles on one condition. Theseus was to have complete supervisory authority over Asterion. That meant neither Tantalus nor anyone else would have a role unless Theseus approved of it in advance.

"What are you saying, Theseus?" Tantalus objected. "Asterion is my client. I brought it in."

Theseus said that Tantalus didn't have the experience to manage the Asterion project, and he, Theseus, would not tolerate interference or divided loyalties. If Tantalus insisted on being involved, he would step aside and Tantalus could ask Pirithous.

"Pirithous?" Tantalus shouted out loud. "God no! I've got my hands full with him as it is."

Theseus said those were his terms.

"Oh, what the hell," Tantalus agreed, "you can run it. I don't really know the area. But I want to stick my head in once in a while. You know, just to see what's going on. Other than that, it's your puppy."

Theseus swung by Alcaeus' and Iollas' offices to let them know about the Asterion project. When Theseus looked in on Nikon, Theseus found him at his desk counting bills. Diocles was there, and he had his wallet out and a twenty in his hand. Nikon was surprised to see Theseus.

"Hey, Theseus!" Nikon said as if caught in the act.

Diocles was holding back laughter.

Theseus told the two they should gear up for the Asterion assignment. Nikon saw that Theseus was looking at the pile of money and the spreadsheet of names on his desk.

"Well, sure, no problem," Nikon stammered, plainly embarrassed. "This isn't what it looks like, Theseus. I'm not selling anything and I'm not a bookie."

"The hell you're not," Diocles interjected with a cackle.

"Well, ok, I am, sort of," Nikon admitted. "Let me explain. A bunch of us associates decided to start a running wager on Seculus sightings."

Seculus was a long time pension lawyer with an unmatched mastery of the dense employee retirement statutes. Seculus kept himself holed up in his office and was rarely seen around the firm. Some said he only moved around at night. Others believed that he never went home. Many in the firm didn't even know he existed or what he looked like.

"Every week we add to the pot," Nikon said. "No one has spotted Seculus for about two months, so the take is getting large. The rules are simple. Seculus must be seen out of his office and there must be at least two witnesses. There's a bonus if Seculus is actually caught talking to someone."

Nikon moved the money to his top drawer.

"Do you want in, Theseus?" he asked.

7

Minos wanted to meet the deal team and asked Tantalus to arrange a meeting with Theseus and his group. Theseus arrived in Crete with Alcaeus, Diocles and Calliope. Iollas and Nikon had scheduling conflicts and couldn't make the trip. Asterion's offices were not extravagant. The reception area was small and not well appointed. Behind reception was a large space with cubicles for about ten people. Circling the cubicles were glassed-in offices, many of which looked vacant. Off to the left was a single large conference room with a glass wall facing the office entrance. The outside view was blocked by the weathered brick facade of the building next door.

The receptionist greeted the attorneys and led them into the conference room. Theseus took note of the collection of adjoining scuffed rectangular tables and the pictures of Minos with various politicos and Olympic athletes. Theseus thought the picture display a bit vulgar. A portable video screen was positioned in one of the corners.

Minos entered the room with a confident gait and unbridled grin. His clothes were casual but sharp like when Theseus first met him. The dullness of the place dissipated upon Mino's presence.

"Welcome, everyone," Minos said with some enthusiasm. "Great that you are here."

Minos introduced Thrasycles as Asterion's vice president of corporate development. Thrasycles wore a tie and blue striped suit which was a couple sizes too large. He was small in height and build, and stuck Theseus as quite young. He had light hair that stood up on his head from a heavy application of tonic. Otherwise he was a fairly nondescript fellow, the type easily overlooked in a crowd. Thrasycles reminded Theseus of someone, but he couldn't put his finger on whom.

Minos also had at the meeting a young looking woman named Ariadne. Minos introduced her as his personal attorney and let everyone know she would be intimately

Theseus

involved in all aspects of Asterion. Ariadne was tall with long flowing dark hair. She had sparkling hazel green eyes and pure white skin. Her complexion was radiant. Ariadne had on a smart navy suit that hugged her chest and thighs. She wore a string of fine pearls above a white blouse.

Theseus went to greet her and was struck by her elegance. He thought her exquisite. Ariadne was likewise captivated by the sight of Theseus. She was taken by his well proportioned frame and handsome features. Ariadne blushed as she extended her hand to Theseus. The moment was not lost on others in the room.

"Ok," Minos said smiling at Theseus and glancing at Ariadne. "Now that we're acquainted, let's get down to business. No time to waste. We have great plans for Asterion that we want to share with you."

Minos had everyone take a chair. Theseus kept his glaze on Ariadne. She looked more beautiful to him than the goddess Aphrodite. Ariadne's cheeks were flushed, making her look ever more resplendent.

Minos went straight into his plans for Asterion. He called on Thrasycles to give a brief overview of the company's structure. Thrasycles explained how Asterion started with the Larissa merger, and then completed the acquisition of four consulting businesses. Asterion now had about thirty employees and offices in five cities.

"We are starting negotiations with a software company in Thebes, as you probably know," Thrasycles said. "If we can get that done, we will have the platform we need to expand rapidly."

Minos had Thrasycles go over Asterion's finance plan. The goal was to build some revenues quickly and do a large public offering for cash. Asterion's systems chief came in to talk about the company's technology. His name was Ucalegon. Ucalegon had long unwashed hair and wore large horn rimmed glasses. He was certainly animated if not eccentric in his manner. Ucalegon projected flow charts and timelines on the video screen from his computer. The plan was to create integrated software packages attractive to the middle market and operate free standing hosting centers.

Theseus gathered himself and questioned the presenters on points he felt were not addressed and offered his suggestions as to how to attack the legal obstacles Asterion was likely to face. Theseus noted that Alcaeus and Calliope were completely absorbed by the discussion. Diocles has his eyes on Ariadne.

After the meeting, Minos and Theseus met in a private office.

"What's Thrasycles' role going to be, ultimately?" Theseus asked.

"You go right to the heart of things, don't you Theseus?" Minos responded. "I like that. I met Thrasycles a while ago. He wanted to get out of his accounting firm and, you know, hit it big. He's inexperienced, thinks he knows more than he does. But he got his father and some of his friends to put some early cash in the company. I needed the money, so here he is. He acts sometimes as if he owns the place. Listen, I know we don't have the right people yet to do an offering, Theseus, but I'm not concerned about it. We'll find the people we need."

Minos shifted in his chair and arched his shoulders as if stretching.

"Now Ariadne's law firm has done work for me going back a few years," Minos said slowly, trying to choose his words carefully. "They have some good people, but they can't handle this. Ariadne works on a lot of my personal affairs. It is important to me, Theseus, that you keep her involved. She will sort of be my eyes and ears. Treat her decently. Give her a few things to do here and there. Who knows, maybe she will have an important part to play."

Theseus felt oddly covetous upon hearing this. He was not altogether enamored by the thought that Minos had this kind of relationship with Ariadne.

"She's a beautiful woman," Minos continued. "Not attached, I'm pretty sure, which I don't understand to be honest. Maybe her beauty and good graces intimidate potential suitors."

Minos tried to read Theseus.

"I know you'll look out for her," Minos said with a furtive smile.

Theseus wasn't sure what Minos was insinuating.

"I also need you to keep Tantalus in check," Minos continued. "I got to your firm through him. I don't expect him to be involved day to day. The guy can be a royal pain and I don't want him sticking his nose into everything. Aegeus and I go back some too, you should know."

When the meeting broke up, Theseus made a point to seek out Ariadne before leaving.

"Feel free to call whenever, Theseus," Ariadne said to him. "I can give you a little more background on the company."

She slipped Theseus a business card and smiled shyly.

Over the next couple of weeks, Theseus several times thought about ringing Ariadne. He tried to convince himself that it was reasonable to call her about Asterion, but he knew his interest had nothing to do with the company. He debated what to do for days. Finally, he picked up the phone and dialed her office number. The phone rang just once before Ariadne answered.

"Hello," Ariadne said. "I was actually hoping you would call, Theseus."

After some awkward small talk, Theseus nervously suggested they get together for dinner. Ariadne readily agreed. Theseus came up with a reason to be in Crete over the upcoming week, and the two settled on a date.

Almost right away, Theseus had second thoughts. He wasn't sure why he had proposed dinner. They could discuss Asterion just as easily over the phone. Theseus decided more than once that he should cancel, but couldn't bring himself to do it.

Theseus and Ariadne met at one of Theseus' favorite Cretan restaurants. He arrived early and Ariadne came before long. Theseus was uncertain of himself when he saw her. He found himself tongue tied, like a smitten schoolboy.

"We have your table ready, Mr. Theseus," the maître d'

said directing the two to follow.

Ariadne seemed favorably impressed that Theseus was a recognized patron of the restaurant.

When they were shown their table, Theseus held Ariadne's chair. He felt embarrassed at once that he showed her that courtesy. She sat gracefully and smiled up to him.

"Minos has been very complimentary of you, Theseus," Ariadne said pleasantly. "He was certain you were the right one to lead Asterion the moment he first met you. And from the meeting at his offices, I can see why."

Theseus, not easily flattered, was glad of the impression made on Ariadne.

Ariadne graduated from a well regarded law school and earned top grades. Her firm did some legal work on a couple of Minos' earlier ventures. This was not Minos' first attempt to build a business, Ariadne told Theseus. She ended up being assigned to a few of his projects, and Minos started sending work directly to her.

Theseus felt a mix of animus and jealousy toward Minos as he listened. Ariadne sensed it and responded.

"Minos treats me as if I was his daughter," Ariadne said. "He's fond of me for some reason. But he's turned out to be a decent client of our firm, and my partners have encouraged me to cultivate the relationship. It is not without benefits."

Over the course of dinner, Theseus learned that Ariadne had two sisters, both of whom started off with impressive career opportunities. In their turn, the sisters traded their careers to raise families.

"They don't understand why I'm not married," Ariadne explained. "It does bother me sometimes, what they say. They make me feel I've chosen something peculiar, you know, unnatural for a woman. Having a career of my own. It's put a bit of a wedge among us. I don't talk to them as much anymore."

Theseus sensed a sadness about Ariadne, which made her vulnerable.

"I was surprised when I heard your firm would be involved with Asterion," Ariadne said changing the subject.

"Maybe a bit unorthodox for your firm to take on a client like Minos."

Theseus agreed that Asterion was not the firm's typical client. Theseus explained that the firm didn't take on clients that had a lot of risk to their business. When the firm did, it was usually because of the management group. The success of most companies, of whatever size, depended on the quality of management. Enterprises run by experienced managers with degrees from the top graduate business schools tended to pay off. They were generally successful in attracting capital and resources. Asterion was an exception. Minos was not the quintessential corporate executive.

But, Theseus noted, Tantalus pushed to have the firm involved and Aegeus approved the representation. The partners at the firm were committed to supporting each other. The firm worked hard at not having a collection of silos, with each lawyer going their own direction. The firm felt that policy served it well over its history. Theseus himself had embraced the firm's orientation, feeling that it kept the partners together, made them dependent on each other. The whole is always stronger than the parts, Theseus said. Most lawyers today don't see that. If you are not supportive of the institution, you weaken it.

Theseus also stated that the firm had made a concerted effort to break into early stage technology. Theseus himself had built a reputation in that market, and the focus was beginning to pay dividends. The investment banks were increasingly looking to involve the firm in technology underwritings. It was big business.

"Well, I have to caution you, Theseus," Ariadne said voicing concern, "Asterion may not be everything it seems. Minos is not necessarily committed to the technology or anything other than the money. He'll leverage off your firm's reputation, but won't hesitate to turn on you when the time comes. Despite appearances, you have to understand what Minos is about. His friendly demeanor masks what lies underneath. You should be wary."

Theseus took Ariadne's admonitions at face value.

"There is more I can tell you, Theseus," Ariadne said. "Your firm was not the first to be considered for the work. And there is something between Minos and Tantalus."

Ariadne continued talking, but Theseus stopped listening. His mind drifted away from the conversation. He thought about Aspasia, the hetaera of the most important statesman of her day. Aspasia was beautiful, educated and independent. Not homebound like most Athenian women because of her foreign birth, Aspasia had a public life and was regarded as an astute political advisor and confidant. Under her management, Pericles' household became a center of intellectualism and social discourse in Athens. Pericles loved Aspasia famously.

"Theseus," said Ariadne reprovingly. "Have you heard anything of what I have been saying? I hope so."

The two sat staring at each other over their meals before Ariadne spoke again.

"When I met you, Theseus," Ariadne confessed, "I felt as if we've been together before someplace. It all feels strangely familiar to me. I sense you feel something too."

Ariadne took a few sips from her glass as she looked at Theseus.

"Let me help you with Asterion," Ariadne said.

8

Over the weeks following the Minos meeting, Theseus was presented with a second challenging transaction. Two owners of a large marketing firm called Sinn Consulting Co. in Corinth were warring over the future course of the company. The owners were father and daughter, adding an unusual dimension to the matter. The father, named Sinis, was a colorful figure known for his love of horses and truculent business tactics. In a moment of familial sentimentality, Sinis had given his young daughter, Perigune, an equal share of the business and made her the chief executive. Perigune had worked diligently at the company since college, and Sinis wanted her rewarded. He was also bent on gradually moving himself from the business so he could concentrate on his equestrian interests. Sinis continued on as chairman of the Sinn board.

It was not long before Sinis regretted giving Perigune her stake and letting her run the company. He missed the limelight of heading a leading business in the city and the notoriety that it brought. Sinis no longer had the attention of the bankers, lawyers or the employees. When he went into the office, he sat around bored. Soon, he began meddling in company matters that served to undermine Perigune's authority. Sinis resented his daughter's predominance and became obsessed with regaining control.

Perigune asked Theseus for help in the dispute. Theseus was a little concerned about taking the matter, since the firm had done some work for Sinn when the old man ran it. So he decided to go to Lysias for advice. As he approached Lysias' office, he heard Tantalus' voice. Theseus waited outside.

"I've got a big problem with Pirithous," Tantalus said heatedly. "I want him fired. Now."

"What are you talking about, Tantalus?" Lysias reacted quizzically.

"My client is putting together this fund," Tantalus explained peevishly. "He has raised a ton of money and wants to close. The money is sitting at the escrow bank, and they won't release it until we've delivered our legal opinion. Pirithous won't issue the opinion. Says there hasn't been a valid private placement or some such crap. He should be kicked out of the goddamn firm. I want you to see to it!"

"Not any easy thing to get rid of a partner, Tantalus," Lysias said. "Takes a supermajority vote of the whole partnership."

"I don't care what it takes," Tantalus screamed. "He's not a team player and needs to go!"

"Who is the client?" Lysias asked.

"Phalius is his name," Tantalus said. "This is his second fund. I did all the documents. He's got the money and Pirithous is holding things up."

"How did the first fund do?" Lysias questioned.

"Returns haven't been great," Tantalus said. "There have been some losses, but that's beside the point."

"Why is Pirithous not willing to give the opinion?" Lysias inquired further.

"Something about not having subscription agreements from all the investors," said Tantalus. "Total bull crap move by Pirithous. We can't have lawyers that are finicky and not good businessmen. He should be forced to give the opinion or we should throw the guy out."

"Pirithous is one of our most conscientious securities lawyers, Tantalus," Lysias said. "There must be a problem with the deal."

"Look, the client needs the money," Tantalus said. "He's been on my back for a couple of days now. I want you to call Pirithous and tell him to do it. No more wasting time! I'll call Aegeus if I have to. He'll agree with me, goddamn it."

"Let me call Theseus to see if he knows anything about it," Lysias suggested.

"Don't go to Theseus," Tantalus moaned. "He'll only agree with Pirithous."

Theseus decided that was his cue and walked into Lysias' office.

"Hey, Theseus," Tantalus said in a friendly pitch. "We were just about to call you."

Theseus

Theseus said he had heard about the issue already from Pirithous. Theseus recounted what Pirithous told him. Phalius had gone with an institutional raise for his fund and had come up short. He decided to do a final capital call on investors in his first fund, mostly high net worth individuals, even though the fund had sustained substantial losses from failed investments. Phalius wanted to put the money that came into the old fund to make the minimum on the new one. Phalius didn't inform the investors in the first fund what he was doing with the money they sent in, which was the first problem. The second problem was the new fund had a different, and higher risk, investment strategy.

"Hell," Tantalus exclaimed, "Phalius only wants to earn the money back for his initial investors by putting them in the second fund. He knows what he's doing."

Theseus said that not only was there likely fraud in doing what Phalius wanted, the securities laws didn't allow mixing institutional money with funds from individuals. He was creating major issues for both funds. Pirithous was right in not delivering the firm's legal opinion. The firm would certainly be sued for the losses sustained in either or both funds if what Phalius had planned came to light.

"Well, that settles it," Lysias said.

"You guys are hanging me out to dry here," Tantalus grumbled. "No way Phalius is going to pay our fees if we don't perform. I'll take a hit on compensation, damn it."

"Better to give up the fee than get sued, Tantalus," Lysias said.

Tantalus stormed out of Lysias' office. Both Theseus and Lysias just looked at each other in dismay.

"He's the one who should be booted out," Lysias said to Theseus. "I don't know how Tantalus has managed to stick around here so long. He's a walking liability."

Theseus was beginning to share the sentiment.

"By the way," Lysias asked Theseus, "were you looking to talk to me about something?"

Theseus explained the situation with Sinis. He told Lysias that the firm used to represent the company but the file had been closed for years.

"I don't see a problem with it," Lysias said.

Theseus went ahead and took the engagement. Theseus liked Perigune and thought her accomplishments at Sinn remarkable for someone her age. As for Sinis, Theseus had met him several times at civic functions and considered him a pompous senile bore whose time had passed. Theseus came to the conclusion that the relationship between Sinis and Perigune had devolved into a battle of generations that would eventually tear Sinn apart. Sinis called on the support of his handpicked directors and battle lines were drawn. Overall company morale was deteriorating and the rift was approaching contagion.

Theseus asked Perigune if there was any agreement drawn up when she received her shares in Sinis. Perigune told Theseus a shareholder agreement had in fact been signed. There Theseus hoped to find a solution. The shareholder agreement had terms that were somewhat rare in a family owned business context, but these terms would prove pivotal. The agreement contained a provision giving Sinis and Perigune the right to offer to buy the other out at a stated price. But there was a catch. Once an offer was made, the offeree had the right to buy out the offeror at the same price. This forced the initiating party to make sure the price was high enough to prevent the other from countering, but not too high so to overpay. The amount of money involved was enormous, so the risk of failure was acute. Perigune supplied Theseus with Sinn's financial statements and projections. Theseus turned to an outside valuation company to determine the intrinsic worth of Sinn. Theseus thought that if they could get to a number that could be financed he could rid Sinn of the cantankerous old man.

While the valuation work on Sinn was being completed, Theseus decided he had time to fulfill a law school recruiting obligation he had scheduled months before.

9

Law firms and law schools had an incestuous courtship every fall. The firms came to campus to interview second year law students for their summer programs and the law schools hoped to attract the best law firms for their students. The students submitted their resumes for the firms they wanted to talk to, the schools collected them and sent them on to the recruiting coordinators at the firms. Recruiting coordinators were often winsome legal secretaries who found their way into a firm's administration. Some firms used young lawyers that weren't making it in the practice but related well to the students.

The most prominent firms interviewed only at the best law schools. Theseus' firm was solidly in that group. The firm took resumes from other law schools, but the selection process for those was severe. From the hundreds of additional resumes received each year, perhaps a handful were pulled for review.

For the on campus interviews, a partner would arrive at the law school or a nearby hotel and spend a day or two meeting with students. Each candidate that had passed the initial screening was given a half hour to state his or her case and make an impression. From those interviews, the partner would recommend that a few be invited to visit the firm. The students were invariably in the top quarter of their class and most likely on law review. Once in a while, a less qualified student slipped into the mix. There was usually some non-quantitative reason why someone was chosen. A family history, client connection, attractive appearance, sport or leisure activity was often enough to tip the scales. Theseus thought the process capricious, depending too much on the predilections of the partner that happened to arrive on campus. But the practice stood the test of time.

After the interviews, the students recommended by the partner received call backs. The firm arranged the travel and put the students up at a fine hotel near the office. Each student met with six to eight lawyers and lunched with two or three associates. Everyone at the firm was involved in the interviewing process. With few exceptions, senior partners to first year lawyers were expected to pitch in and offer up time during the interview season. The firm required attorneys to submit evaluations of the candidates within a day of the interviews. The evaluations were collated and reviewed by an associate hiring committee manned by young partners and a couple of senior associates. A single derogatory comment from an interviewer could sink a candidate. Theseus questioned allowing junior lawyers a say on who gets hired, since they had no experience on which to judge. Theseus supposed the reason was they were the ones who would have to practice with the new recruits the longest.

Offers to the fortunate students were made by phone. Rejections were communicated by letter, and the letters were worded carefully. The firm wanted every rejected candidate to feel inferior to the lawyers practicing at the firm under the theory that the firm would forever have the advantage in court and across the negotiating table.

Theseus' first interview in the afternoon was Adrasteia. Adrasteia was of moderate height, wore her ecru tresses long and curly and was nicely dressed. She flashed a confident smile and came across as good natured. Women were increasingly in demand and those that had poise had many opportunities.

"One of the big reasons I wanted to talk to the firm is the pro bono commitment I've read about," Adrasteia said. "It's very important to me that I work for a law firm that takes pro bono seriously and gives back."

The emphasis on pro bono work at a large law firm was misplaced if not naïve, Theseus knew. Most firms adopted pro bono standards for its lawyers out of necessity rather than social consciousness. Local bar associations pressured firms to provide free legal services to the indigent and many large corporate clients required that the firms they used show a commitment to pro bono. So pro bono programs were touted by many firms, but seldom for the right reasons.

At the firm, lawyers were asked to devote fifty hours to

pro bono activities each year, amounting to less than five hours per month. Lawyers could generally choose from a variety of assignments, from filing custody claims to defending mortgage foreclosures. Lawyers at large firms, whether first year associates or partners, usually muddled through these matters trying to figure out what to do. Pro bono clients were always pleased, no matter what the outcome, as they felt honored to be represented by an attorney at a big law firm. Competency was never questioned. Many senior lawyers at the firm soaked up their pro bono hours sitting on charitable boards. They could claim their hours while networking with prominent members of the business community.

The pro bono program at the firm was headed up by a lawyer who devoted all his time to the task. His name was Catalus. Catalus would rather have been at a social service agency serving the poor full time, only he couldn't afford it. He could make better money at the firm. Theseus knew that Catalus despaired of private practice. He was also not particularly good at it.

"I've learned that the firm encourages all new lawyers to take on cases that interest them and then provides the resources," Adrasteia said. "I like that."

Theseus thought Adrasteia's interest in pro bono was admirable, but her value to the firm wouldn't hinge on how many pro bono hours she logged. If she devoted a substantial amount of time to pro bono it meant partners were not using her for billable work.

"I heard about one of your associates who handled an immigration case," Adrasteia said. "He helped a kid get asylum in Athens because of the gang violence in his hometown."

She was referring to an article in the city paper about Straton, a third year who was successful in convincing the immigration service to allow a fifteen year old from Cythera to enter the country and live with his aunt and uncle. He was fleeing the terrible gang wars in his neighborhood that made it impossible for him to go to school there. Straton received accolades for his persistence and novel arguments before the immigration service. Theseus knew Straton's days at the firm were numbered notwithstanding the good publicity. Straton's billable work was dangerously low.

"Don't get me wrong," Adrasteia continued. "I am very interested in the corporate work of the firm. That's what I want to practice."

Adrasteia mentioned that her parents were divorced and her mother was working as a paralegal in the city. She obviously had been through some difficult times but managed to distinguish herself by attending a top law school and performing well there. Theseus presumed she would be a hard worker and diligent. And she could probably handle the difficult partners and demanding hours.

The next candidate was of a whole different ilk. Timais was from a prominent family in Euboea. His father was well connected politically and was a noted philanthropist. The family controlled a conglomerate of industrial companies that were professionally managed, and the firm had represented the family and its commercial interests for decades. The firm did not shy away from hiring associates with family ties to clients. It was good business.

Timais was tall and tanned, probably from having spent the summer at the shore. Sporting a finely tailored suit and the best oxfords money could buy, he was not timid flaunting his social rank. As with many of his extraction, he came across cool and composed.

"I think litigation is where I want to go, you know, big securities cases," Timais explained. "Insider trading would be an area to explore."

Timais didn't have many questions about the firm, associate compensation or what the job entailed. He was more inclined to talk about polo matches, summer parties and travels abroad.

Timais attended Aloadae, an elite boarding school. A fair number of Aloadae students found their way to the city's top investment banks and accounting firms. Many would serve in high government office. Whether Timais understood or not, he would benefit from the Aloadae network throughout his career. His peers would hire him and he would refer matters to them. Back scratching was part of the Aloadae curriculum. The ties that bind translated into deals, billable hours and revenue.

There was no question Timais was a fit for the firm, perhaps even a candidate for partner one day.

Cosmas was one of the last to interview. He had actually clerked at a firm in Mycenae after his first year. He claimed he received an offer to return, but wasn't sold on Mycenae. A student that had an outstanding offer from another firm was usually a step ahead and often guaranteed offers from everywhere else. Law firms were competitive. No one wanted to pass on a candidate someone else wanted. Born in Macedonia, Cosmas was fluent in several languages. His family had fled his native land at a time of civil unrest and found their way to Attica and settled in. He attended college in Athens but spent his summers back in Macedonia.

"I want to be involved in cross border financings and use my language skills," Cosmas said. "I'm not talking to too many laws firms, just the ones that match my interests. One of my law professors said I should talk to your firm. I think trade with Macedonia will become more popular in Attica. That is something I know a lot about."

Cosmas was a heady and determined young man. For all this seriousness, he had a dry sense of humor. Theseus could picture the ease with which Cosmas would one day navigate financial transactions throughout the Aegean.

Cosmas was direct and probing about what the firm could offer him. He quickly turned the interview around and Theseus found himself trying to convince Cosmas why he should join the firm. The firm didn't have a single partner who was from Macedonia, although the firm had many clients that did business there. Theseus knew that times were changing and as the firm grew and expanded, diversity would become critically important.

Adrasteia, Timais and Cosmas would each make the cut. The countless other students that came through were all plausible candidates, but for whatever reason didn't register. Time would tell if this trio would pan out.

When Theseus returned to the office, the valuation report for Sinn was sitting on his desk. With the report in hand, Theseus worked with Perigune to secure bank loans. Her stock in Sinn would prove sufficient collateral and the financing was easily and quickly arranged. An offer was made to buy out Sinis. Sinis was outraged. He had sixty days to respond to the offer. Sinis tried in vain to come up with the money to make a counter offer. A good part of his net worth was tied up in his horses and farms that were not liquid. The banks would not loan him money, and his old friends turned from his pleas for help. Sinis became irrational and his behavior erratic. By the time Perigune completed the buyout, Sinis had gone completely mad. Perigune was saddened by the effect on her father and extended an olive branch to him. But Sinis withdrew from society and soon died a lonely and defeated man. Theseus, who had grown fond of Perigune, introduced her to a longtime friend and client, Eurytus. Eurytus was himself the owner of Hind Scientific Company, a developer of laser instruments. Perigune and Eurytus lived happily together and had many children. The family became well known as one of the great patrons of the arts in Corinth.

10

Theseus woke up just as his plane landed at the airport outside of Thebes. He was groggy and feeling queasy from the short flight. After a relatively easy pass through customs, Theseus walked off the plane with his overnight and briefcase. The hour was late and the airport nearly desolate.

The purpose of the trip to Thebes was to cement the deal Minos was negotiating with Nemean Software Systems, the target Minos wanted Asterion to acquire. Nemean had developed some advanced proprietary business software that integrated disparate information systems quickly and efficiently. Nemean created the technology to link enterprise software pieces from a variety of vendors. The company's technology could rapidly combine accounts receivable, product ordering, distribution and inventory control in a seamless interfaced system, even if the separate functions were run on software produced from different companies or on different operating systems. The software was robust and ideal for small to medium sized businesses that could not afford to hire expensive programmers.

Theseus was staying at the Spartoi Hotel. The hotel recently opened and quickly became one of the most popular in Thebes. Minos insisted that Theseus stay there. The lobby was contemporary with black granite floors and neon lighting. Water seemed omnipresent from enclosed falls and pools. On the guest floors, each room was unique by furnishings, floor plan and hardware. Word had it that a different Theban artist designed each room.

As pleasant a place as the Spartoi was, there would be little time for Theseus to enjoy it. Theseus was expected at the offices of the Theban lawyers for Nemean early the next morning and he knew he would likely find himself there late into the evening. If negotiations are slow, Theseus would have to repeat the exercise the following day until the outlines of an agreement were hammered out.

Theseus had a message waiting for him at the front desk. Minos wanted to meet for breakfast before the meeting.

Theseus checked into his room and found it difficult to sleep. He managed a few hours but did not feel rested when he woke. Minos was already waiting for Theseus when he arrived downstairs in the morning. The breakfast room was small but functional. The serving table had an array of regional staples, including an assortment of colorful fruits, breads, marmalades, grains and dates. The waitress poured Theseus a juice and brought a small pot of coffee with fresh cream. Theseus thought the breakfast food was sensible compared to the sugared fare back home.

Minos sat over his coffee affable as ever. His watch, rings and gold bracelet were glittering.

Minos arrived in Thebes a few days before with his wife Delilah so she could find some antiques for their mansionette under construction. Minos had obtained a sizeable loan from Talos Bank for the house and had to give the bank a pledge of his Asterion stock to secure the loan. Although Asterion had not yet generated much in actual sales, the stock was trading a hundred thousand shares a day and was hitting and exceeding its yearly high. Minos was not only able to start the house with the bank loan, but had purchased a yacht and a spacious condo in Rhodes all based on the stock's market value. Theseus questioned whether Talos had done an adequate credit check of Asterion before making the loans to Minos.

"Theseus," Minos started, "it's a shame I had to bring Delilah along. We could have spent some time in the red light district. That would have been a ball, huh?"

Theseus pictured Minos in front of the windows taking looks from the girls. Ariadne let on about the wild things Minos would do on his trips. Theseus knew Adriane traveled with Minos on occasion and wondered if Ariadne was in on any of it. The image he conjured up in his mind was disconcerting.

"I need you to tie this thing down quick, Theseus," Minos said. "The Thebans don't like to sign anything and they will keep changing their minds and draw you out until you want to scream. But I don't have that kind of time. I need to get back to nail the other parts of the plan, and then we're cooking."

Minos' blueprint for Asterion was a simple one. Nemean would provide the product and Asterion the technical service capability. Minos would then layer on distribution based on telemarketing. He would build out the call center in Stratus and tap the army of educated, low cost workers that lived there to work as sales associates. Young foreigners traveling by backpack found Stratus a satisfying stay with cheap lodging, and many looked for steady work that could help pay for ski trips in the nearby mountains or sailing around the islands off the coast. The call center would identify prospects and leads, and Asterion's technical teams would close sales. The data site planned for Tegea would host the software for customers. A perfect turnkey solution.

That was the grand plan. But first Asterion had to acquire Nemean.

"Look," said Minos, "I don't have any cash. We need to convince Pedocles here that our stock is better that cash. It'll be worth many times what it's valued now. I've seen his technology and it's pretty remarkable, very powerful. It's quick, low cost and installation is easy. Pedocles understands that he doesn't know how to get to market quickly and that if he doesn't, his window of opportunity is lost. That is what we can give him. Fast marketing. Without us he is dead in the water."

Minos was becoming so enthused he couldn't contain himself.

"Damn it, Theseus," Minos said excitedly, "this is what I've been waiting for. I can tell you that combining Asterion and Nemean is as good as gold. I need you to get it done for me."

Minos took an incoming call.

"Yeah," Minos said into the phone, "he's here. So I think we're covered."

Theseus didn't know who Minos was talking to, but didn't ask.

"Theseus," Minos implored as the two got up from the

table, "I need to get back to Crete, so finish this up over here. Offer him a percentage of Asterion for Nemean. Go as high as you have to. He can be president, chief operating officer, director of development, whatever he likes. Give him an apartment in Athens. I've got to get Delilah out of here before she buys a Praxiteles."

Theseus grabbed his briefcase and walked with Minos to the front of the hotel. Minos asked that Theseus give him periodic updates, and they said goodbye.

Theseus decided to walk to the offices of the Theban lawyers where the meeting with Pedocles, Nemean's founder, would be held. The offices were near the central plaza and train station. The city center was small, crowded and centuries old, but had its charm. The law offices were just off the northwest corner of the main square. The building was modern and in stark contrast to the surrounding period structures. It had a concrete foundation and wrap around windows and was the tallest building in sight.

Theseus took the lift up to the top floor, and was greeted by his Theban counterpart of the name Keos. Keos was cordial and from appearances not in much of a hurry. Keos had a receding hairline, squat nose and small mouth. His spectacles were round and made him look more like a bookkeeper than a lawyer. Keos and Theseus chatted briefly about Theseus' travels and the better places to go at night in the city.

Keos led Theseus into a conference room for the meeting. Several of Keos' colleagues were there. Pedocles came in shortly. Pedocles was skinny if not gaunt, had sallow sebaceous hair and a day old beard. His rectangle glasses deflected a taut face and thin mouth. Pedocles wore straight legged khakis, earth shoes and a pager on his belt. His shirt was unironed and he had on a tie but no suit jacket. Pedocles looked like he kept a stiff upper lip.

"Gentlemen," Pedocles beckoned, "let us get on with it. Mr. Theseus, you are most welcome in our city, and I hope you have a pleasant stay. Minos tells me you are entrusted with the authority to discuss our venture and come to agreement. That is most excellent. If we can, I would like to have our terms settled by this evening. I will then have you out to review our site in Leuctra."

Pedocles' Theban lawyers didn't appear all that interested in the deal and seemed ready to take lunch. They had their cell phones with them, and the phones were answered whenever they rang. Whoever was calling was evidently more important than Pedocles and his company.

Everyone sat down around the large meeting table. Theseus was in the middle with Pedocles directly across. The Theban lawyers spread out, and Theseus had to ask them to turn off their phones. Theseus then produced a term sheet for the transaction. Minos and his company would acquire Pedocles' firm for stock in Asterion and Pedocles would have a seat on the board. Pedocles would be given a managing director title and be responsible for developing the combined company's software products.

As Minos suspected, Pedocles was skeptical of an all stock offer.

"I was hoping to get cash for my company," Pedocles complained. "There is too much risk for me in taking Asterion stock. What if the company fails?"

Theseus set out Mino's financing plan. He said that Asterion would not have sufficient cash until it completed a public offering, which would only be feasible after he rolled up Nemean into Asterion. With the combined company going to market, the stock price would easily be worth double what Pedocles would realize in an all cash deal.

Theseus could see Pedocles' mind turning.

"When can I sell the stock?" asked Pedocles. "When would it be registered with the authorities for trading?"

Theseus made clear that Pedocles would most likely have to wait nine months to one year after the public offering.

"Well, that does not please me," Pedocles said sounding as if he had been misled. "Minos said I would have immediate cash."

Theseus was not sure what Minos had promised, but he tried to explain that public offerings of companies followed certain standards set by the market. The investment bankers typically locked up all the company insiders for an extended period following an offering. Early selling was a sign that management did not have confidence in the company's prospects and resulted in a depressed trading price.

"Then I will have more stock if I am to wait," Pedocles responded.

Theseus told Pedocles that Minos could raise the stake, but only by one or two percent.

Pedocles was pensive, mulling over the proposal. The Theban lawyers said nothing. Without committing, Pedocles said he wanted to move to other aspects of the deal.

Over the next several hours, Theseus outlined the remaining terms. Asterion would acquire the exclusive rights to the technology, as well as all trademarks and trade names owned by Pedocles' company or himself individually. Minos would have his auditors review Nemean's books and records and the financial statements going back to the start of the company. Theseus and the firm would perform extensive due diligence on all of Nemean's charter documents, property interests and contracts with its credit providers, vendors and suppliers. The process would take about two months if things went smoothly. By the end of the meeting, Pedocles seemed upbeat and optimistic.

"We accomplished much today," Pedocles said. "I am not unhappy with the proposal. I will stop at your hotel tomorrow at half past nine, and we will drive to our facilities in Leuctra."

Pedocles left the office. The Theban lawyers were obviously satisfied that their client appeared content with how the day went. They decided that the night would require locating a first rate restaurant. Keos extended an invitation to Theseus to join them for dinner, which Theseus accepted.

Upon returning to the hotel, Theseus dialed Minos to give him the news. Minos was at the airport waiting for a plane with Delilah. Minos was surprised the terms were so readily accepted and was immensely thrilled.

"I thought Pedocles had more sense," Minos said. "I

Theseus

would have given him a much larger stake in the company if he demanded it. What he took is a steal. Feel free to offer more if he thinks better of it in the morning."

Theseus suggested that Pedocles was too interested in the back end riches and that his lawyers wouldn't put their phones down long enough to negotiate better terms.

"The Thebans pride themselves on being world wise traders," Minos commented, "but when they want something badly they are easily persuaded."

Theseus made a few calls back to the office, then headed for the restaurant. The Theban lawyers were already there and by the look of it had started out right after the meeting. The place was old, dim and cramped, but lively. It was actually an ancient home that had been gutted and transformed into a bistro.

The Theban lawyers had no burning desire to discuss the Nemean transaction. Politics and good food were the order of the evening.

Theseus and Keos started comparing the differences between Athens and Thebes.

"We failed to embrace true democracy as you," Keos observed. "We never quite let go of our tyrants, and our people don't exhibit the same individualism or enterprise as yours. Perhaps we are insecure and need a strong leader. Maybe it's that Thebes didn't possess the resources to have influence beyond our borders or draw the great thinkers. It is hard to say."

Theseus recalled the hard history of Thebes. It was home to one of the two great tragic families of the Greeks, the other being Argos.

"Ah, yes," Keos followed. "You mean of course Oedipus. Killing your father and marrying your mother is a nasty business. But I blame his son Eteocles and brother-in-law Creon for all the mayhem that was to come. Eteocles refused to share the throne with his brother Polynices. Their fate was to kill each other. Creon took over and had the chance to settle things down, yet refused to take the advice of those loyal to him. Creon condemned sister Antigone to death for trying to bury Polynices according to god's law, and lost his son Haemon in the process. Not a way for a leader to act. The curse of that family has never faded."

Theseus reminded Keos that there were golden moments to Thebe's history. He mentioned the military genius of Epaminondas.

"Epaminondas earned fame by ending the domination of Sparta," Keos acknowledged, "yet he is blamed for weakening Greece as a whole and allowing Macedonia to conquer us. Thebes remains the sad stepchild of Greek history."

As dinner wound down, Theseus' phone rang and it was Ariadne.

"Theseus," Ariadne said excitedly, "I heard you were in Thebes. How is Asterion going?"

Theseus gave her a quick synopsis of the day's negotiations.

"Sounds like it went well," Ariadne said. "So are you up for a brief detour to Chalcis? I just arrived on business and will have a couple of free days after. Maybe I could entice you to come up when you finish in Thebes."

The idea caught Theseus unprepared. Without thinking, Theseus said he had some matters that required urgent attention and he would be in the office all weekend.

"Oh," Ariadne said disappointed. "Work comes first, I guess."

Theseus suggested another time and said goodbye.

Walking back to the hotel, Theseus regretted being so short on the phone. Here was a beautiful woman inviting him to a pleasant weekend in Euboea. He wondered why he could not have been more spontaneous and taken Ariadne up on her offer. Was his practice so all consuming that he couldn't break away for even a day? Theseus never really thought of himself that way, as one of those lawyers wedded to their practice at the expense of all other things. He fought off a strong inclination to call Ariadne back.

Pedocles' personal driver, a strapping man named Endios, arrived at the Spartoi the next morning as arranged. Diocles had arrived in Thebes the night before and would be in

Theseus

charge of the Nemean due diligence. Endios rode both Theseus and Diocles out of Thebes and headed south toward Leuctra. The day was partly cloudy and warm. Pedocles apparently headed to the company's facilities much earlier and sent Endios back to pick up Theseus and Diocles. Theseus would be staying only the day. Diocles was to remain on to review documents and interview company personnel.

Endios drove the highway for a period then exited to take local roads.

"Mr. Pedocles thought you might want to see some of the country," Endios said.

They rode through undulating plains and pastures flanked by assorted mountain peaks. As they drove, Theseus noticed the Leuctrans riding bicycles in every direction. It was a curious spectacle. The bikes were almost all of the black, old fashioned variety complete with baskets on the handlebars. The people rode very upright and flowed easily with the motor traffic.

"We may seem simple to some, riding our bicycles as we do, but it is a trait we are proud of," Endios said as if aware of Theseus' thoughts. "Many of the people you see have no other means of transportation. Trains and buses are used to get to Thebes and other cities, but otherwise we ride our bikes."

Diocles remarked to Endios that it seemed a fun way to get to work or run the daily errands. He said it would be great to have a bicycle to ride during his stay in this part of the country. Endios turned around and gave Diocles an inquisitive look.

They arrived at the company offices and Endios left Theseus and Diocles at the front entry. Right next to the entrance was a rack with some twenty or thirty black bicycles, obviously for the local employees. The building was larger than Theseus was expecting and had a clean high tech look. Theseus and Diocles were ushered up a floor to Pedocles' office. He had his door shut but he could be heard talking in a roused voice. His executive assistant moved the two to a nearby conference room. Within a short time a beverage and pastry cart was wheeled in. Espresso, cappuccino or café au lait were there for the choosing. Teas and juice were also available, as well as an assortment of rolls, cakes and Boeotian chocolate. The service made rounds in the executive quarters of the building almost on the hour throughout the day.

"I see you are already receiving what you need," Pedocles said as he popped in. "We love our coffee so please help yourself when you like. Endios said you were taken by our bicycle culture."

Pedocles was looking at Diocles.

"Most foreigners find it a fascinating aspect of our country," Pedocles offered. "I don't know if our mode of transport is due to our resistance to change or lack of means. We are a dignified people, even if we choose not to have fancy cars like your clients."

Pedocles couldn't hide the disparagement in his voice. Theseus wondered if Pedocles resented Minos because of his ostentatious life style or because he was selling out to a Dorian. No matter, Theseus thought. His time at the company was not to indulge Pedocles in his prejudices.

"I am not entirely pleased with my future stake in Asterion," Pedocles said. "My company is worth a great deal more to Minos it seems to me."

Theseus remembered what Minos had said about the negotiating style of the Thebans. Theseus grew worried that trying to get to terms with Pedocles would be like Neoptolemus trying to wrest Heracles' bow from Philoctetes.

"Let us say that there is more to discuss," Pedocles informed Theseus.

Theseus was somewhat irritated that Pedocles was raising his concerns now without his lawyers present and said so.

"We do not favor our attorneys here with the same regard you enjoy in Attica," Pedocles said. "They are paper pushers, as you say, and not decision makers. I am not too confident with them. You, on the other hand, have Mr. Minos' trust, so I speak to you as I would speak to him."

Theseus explained that Minos had been generous in

offering Pedocles a significant stake in the company, and any more would create valuation issues that may impact the public offering. Investors would take a dim view if Minos was seen to be paying too much for Nemean. Theseus tried to persuade Pedocles that a smaller stockholding at a greater market price would be more lucrative to him.

"You may be right," Pedocles responded. "I will think more on it."

Pedocles, Theseus and Diocles spent the next couple of hours talking about Nemean's operations, its management policies and how the software development was proceeding. Theseus pressed him on whether the date for beta testing the software was firm. It was critical to Minos' timeline. The idea was to introduce the software capabilities at the technology expo in Elis in a couple of months and start taking orders. Minos wanted to post strong sales numbers before the public offering.

Lunch was brought promptly at noon, and the group had their choice of cheeses, breads and meats. Oddly, beer was available if anyone was so inclined. Diocles seemed tempted, but chose a soda. After lunch they headed down to the first floor where the software development team worked. As they descended the stairs to the first floor, Endios was coming up. He and Pedocles exchanged looks. Pedocles smiled.

"I had Endios go out this morning to get you a bicycle," Pedocles said cheerfully to Diocles. "Since you will be with us several days, you can make good use of it."

Diocles looked flummoxed.

"I really wasn't serious when I said I wished I had a bike while here," Diocles said stammering. "I won't have any time to use it. Thanks anyway."

"I see," said Pedocles, taking umbrage at Diocles remark.

Endios stiffened up.

"Let us put you to work then since that is why you are here," Pedocles said flatly.

Diocles wished he had his words back.

Endios departed with a scowl as Pedocles led Theseus and Diocles to the developers. There were about fifteen of them in two rows. They sat side by side and back to back. No partitions divided the space. Each programmer faced two or three computer screens. The floor was linoleum, and the desk chairs had well oiled wheels. The developers were constantly rolling back and forth peering at each other's screens and discussing the software code they were writing.

Most of the software developers had degrees in computer engineering from schools such as Telchines, a local university known for science. They were a little older than Theseus expected and all men. Pedocles explained that he looked for people with some business experience to write the applications.

A unique aspect of the company was its computer laboratory, which was set off from the programmers in a self contained, sterile room. Not only could Nemean write the software programs that would integrate software packages, it could test out its performance on the actual equipment used by customers. Customers were not required to purchase hardware along with the software. Pedocles' company would go out and find matching equipment, set it up in the computer lab and make sure the applications operated correctly. Nemean could test downloading the company's software on client equipment to make sure there were no glitches. In this way, Nemean was able to solve unanticipated problems in its own office and not have its professionals trying to resolve problems at a customer's site. A high level of customer customization could be achieved without a large number of people working out in the field. All the intense work was done without the customers ever knowing it. The customer only saw a brief implementation and testing of the system.

Besides the development team, the computer lab and the executive offices, there wasn't much more to the business. Pedocles obviously ran a lean operation. Pedocles' people didn't know it, but Minos intended to relocate Nemean's business to Athens. It was likely the entire operation would be shut down in Leuctra. A few critical people would be offered positions, but the majority of employees in Athens would be new hires. The Boeotia group would be for the most part let go.

Diocles spent a good part of the day off reviewing contracts and other documents. His job was to make sure there were no third party rights to any of the company's intellectual property, no infringement claims and no approvals or consents belonging to others.

It was getting late when Theseus was set to go. Theseus gathered up his things and sent for Diocles. Pedocles was waiting with Endios in the car to drive them back to Thebes.

"I'll have you look over there, Mr. Diocles," Pedocles said as they pulled away.

Pedocles pointed to the bike rack. The bikes were gone, except for one brand new red bike.

"There's your bike," Pedocles said bluntly.

Endios had a steely expression as he looked at Diocles through the rear view mirror.

11

All in all, Theseus felt things were in good order. He was satisfied with the Sinn outcome and pleased with the effect the transaction had on his partners. The case had received attention in the newspapers, and his representation of Perigune was mentioned several times. A number of partners expressed to Theseus their congratulations, and Theseus even received a call from Aegeus. He also thought Asterion was progressing nicely and on schedule.

Theseus often stayed working at the firm well into the night when the office was quieter. His mind relaxed and he found it a good time to concentrate on client affairs. There was something about working when it was dark that invigorated him. Some of his best and most creative thinking occurred during these hours.

A young female lawyer happened by Theseus' office late one evening while Theseus was reviewing Diocles' due diligence on Nemean.

"Hi," the woman said as she popped her head into Theseus' office.

Her blond mane was neatly clipped at her shoulders, and she wore a tight but fashionable dress that accentuated her shapely figure. Her skin was fair and a pair of designer glasses complimented her soft facial features.

"I hope I'm not disturbing you," the woman said. "I haven't been with the firm long. From your name plate, you must be Theseus. My name is Neaira."

Theseus hadn't seen her before. With the growth of the firm over the years, Theseus couldn't keep up with all the new associate hires. But the woman did not have the look of an associate. Theseus generally knew all new partners. The vetting process for lateral partners involved the entire partnership, so he was bound to have gotten word if someone new was joining.

"Just though I would introduce myself," Neaira said. "Still trying to get my feet wet. I am in the wealth planning group, but mainly handle charitable giving and fiduciary relationships."

Theseus knew that wealth planning was marketing jargon for traditional trusts and estates. Although the work involved complex tax issues, trusts and estates was not a big money maker for the firm. Smaller tax firms with lower fees were capturing the bulk of the business.

"What's your area of practice?" Neaira asked.

Theseus told Neaira that he was a corporate lawyer and did a fair amount of work with technology firms. He asked Neaira when it was she joined the firm. Neaira sensed the reason for Theseus' question.

"I've been here just a couple of weeks," Neaira responded. "I'm not an equity partner. I guess the firm wants to see how things go before committing to me."

Theseus thought that curious. Many other firms had adopted the practice of bringing on more experienced lawyers with insufficient portable business as salaried attorneys. They were paid a set amount and couldn't participate in partnership affairs or in the profits of the firm, and could be terminated on short notice. For want of a better title, these lawyers were called "of counsel." To Theseus, they were little more than highly paid associates. The firm had always shunned the practice of bringing these kinds of lawyers on board, so he was surprised when Neaira explained her situation. Due to his heavy work load, Theseus assumed he must have missed the firm's change in policy.

A week passed when Neaira again appeared at Theseus' door.

"I've been struggling with a couple of issues of the corporate variety," Neaira said. "Can I get your thoughts?"

Without a response from Theseus, Neaira took a seat in one of his office chairs.

"One of my individual clients owns a business and asked me for ideas to help create funding for some employee options," said Neaira. "The employees are restless for some cash, and my client is fretting about losing some key people. But I'm unsure of the securities laws."

Theseus asked who held the company's outstanding stock.

Neaira said it was owned entirely by her client. Theseus suggested that if the company had some extra cash it could do an issuer self tender. The employees that wanted could exercise their options and tender their shares to the company for purchase.

"Why, that's simple, Theseus," Neaira said. "Brilliant! Do you think you could talk to the client and work on it?"

Theseus said he would be glad to discuss it with the client, and probably get an associate to do the work.

"Sounds like a plan," Neaira said excited.

Another evening Neaira came by over an office spat with a partner.

"I've been asked to make a pitch to a charity board to handle a new fund raising campaign," Neaira said. "I learned that Adelpha had done some work for charities. So I called to include her in the pitch."

Theseus knew Adelpha as a young, aggressive corporate lawyer that specialized in board governance.

"I had marketing put some firm materials together, you know, for the presentation," Neaira conveyed. "Adelpha is complaining that I have my business card and resume on top of hers in the marketing book. She's made a real stink over it. I don't really want to get crosswise with her, being new and all. What do you think I should do?"

The late night office visits became more regular. And as they did, Neaira's behavior became more flirtatious and her clothing provocative. Her hair would be down and her blouse opened. Neaira would stand in front of Theseus and bend toward him with some document in hand or entice him with some pose. Theseus was not immune to these seductive overtures by Neaira and began to welcome her evening visits.

One night Neaira mentioned her curiosity about sailing, and, after Theseus spoke of his passion for the sea, she implored him to take her out on the water. Theseus was hesitant, but found it difficult to say no.

When the day for sailing arrived, the sky was clear and there was little wind. Neaira met Theseus on the pier. Theseus told Neaira that proper sailing was not a leisure activity and she should expect to be physically challenged. He recommended she bring appropriate attire. Instead, she appeared in an embroidered sundress and her hair was pinned back by colorful flowers.

"This is not a day for exercise," Neaira said coming toward the slip. "A leisurely sail in pleasant winds is enough for me."

Her smile drew Theseus' undivided attention.

"I have brought grapes, cheese and wine for us, Theseus," she said. "So take us out on the water. Let's enjoy the sun and let go of the day."

Theseus helped Neaira on board, pushed off from the pier and unfurled the sails. A slight breeze propelled the boat out into the open sea. For a long while, the two were content as Theseus maneuvered the cresting waves. The water was crystal blue and the nearby beach presented itself as in a master's painting. Neaira kept her gaze fixed upon Theseus as they cruised.

Neaira began to ask Theseus of his family and early days as a child. She questioned him on his exploits as a youth and his achievements in school. Theseus did not usually speak of himself openly, and was at first terse in his answers. But Neaira's earnestness overcame his better instincts and Theseus began to converse more freely. He moored the boat near shore and Neaira and Theseus sat on deck watching the waves.

"You are a remarkable man," Neaira said to Theseus. "Everyone at the firm holds you in such high esteem, including Aegeus."

Theseus reclined on a couple of life vests.

"The women talk of you incessantly, but you probably know that," Neaira went on with a giggle. "How is it you remain unattached? Tell me, do you have a steady girlfriend? Maybe your work schedule makes that difficult."

Theseus thought of Ariadne and felt uneasy with the conversation. Neaira continued speaking about the firm and the gossip she had heard about many of the partners. Theseus' mind drifted as he spied a sea gull high in the air.

He followed its flight as the bird slowly descended toward the sailboat.

Suddenly, Theseus recoiled as if woken from a deep sleep. He realized he had dozed off. He found Neaira lying next to him with her arm across his chest.

"My dear Theseus," Neaira spoke softly, "I do believe you left me for a moment."

She lifted her head and looked at Theseus.

"So who do you think will be the next chairman?" Neaira asked. "Medea would be a good choice, don't you think? She's the one who brought me into the firm, you know. I've known her a long time. A woman of her caliber doesn't come around very often. Medea could really take the firm to the next level. Maybe you should talk her up with Aegeus, even garner some support for her among the partners. It would mean a lot coming from you."

With a firm hand, Neaira drew Theseus' eyes into hers.

Theseus jumped to his feet. The face Theseus saw looking back at him was Medea's. He was bewildered by what was happening. Somehow, Medea had taken Neaira' place.

"What dark magic is this?" Theseus exclaimed as he broke away.

"This is not what I expected from you, Theseus," Medea's visage answered scornfully. "You act rashly and disappoint me. Aegeus was wrong about you."

"Do you take me for a pawn, Medea?" Theseus demanded to know.

As he spoke the words, Medea's face faded and Neaira's reappeared.

"Medea?" Neaira glared back at Theseus. "Have you lost your senses? Take me to shore. I don't want to be near you."

Theseus quickly upped the sails and maneuvered the boat back to the dock.

"I can't tell what kind of madness made you think I was Medea," Neaira said as she departed, "but you have every reason to fear her."

Neaira made her way to land unescorted, leaving Theseus behind.

When Theseus returned to his flat, he gave Pirithous a call.

"Never heard of the woman," Pirithous said. "If your description of her holds, I certainly would have known about her. Theseus, you know we don't hire of counsel lawyers. But who knows. Give Lysias a call. He'll know what's going on."

The more Theseus reflected on Neaira, the hazier the image he had of her and what had transpired. Theseus wondered if it was all a hallucination.

12

Theseus always enjoyed the arrival of new associates. Every year, the firm would welcome a new crop of young law graduates to restock the associate ranks and add to the firm's ever increasing number of lawyers. The annual injection of fresh blood buoyed and energized the entire firm. There was a renewed sense of purpose and optimism.

When Theseus joined, he remembered walking into the firm full of vigor and self confidence. Theseus recalled the greetings from partners, senior associates and staff, which were on the whole enthusiastic and congenial. He was in awe of Aegeus and Melesius and many of the older partners. They were the titans of the law and larger than life figures. Theseus considered himself fortunate to have been selected to work at their firm and to have the chance to learn from lawyers of their caliber. The first days at the firm reminded Theseus of the homecoming given the young Olympians after the games. There was celebration and festivities in honor of the returning heroes and a deep sense of civic pride in their achievement. Theseus could not recall a time in his life that he felt more proud.

Alcaeus had set up a meeting with Theseus to discuss the upcoming new associate training program. The program was held each year to teach the new lawyers effective lawyering techniques and indoctrinate them into the firm's practice philosophy. It was typically organized and supervised by young partners or senior associates. Theseus had recommended that Alcaeus take on the program because Alcaeus was up for partnership. Theseus thought it would be looked on favorably by the executive committee.

"This has become a real headache, to be honest," Alcaeus told Theseus in his office. "I didn't realize running the program required this kind of effort. I haven't had all that much free time to devote to it, with Asterion and other transactions I'm on. I hope it comes off."

Theseus said the program would fall into place as it usually did, that he needn't worry so much. He asked Alcaeus who he had lined up.

"The usual suspects, I guess," Alcaeus answered. "Isocrates and Triton are handling a couple of sessions. Aegeon and Boethus, who do a lot of Pausanias' work, will take up the litigation side. I'll do corporate. Diocles will be helping me out with that. Melesius will give his traditional spiel. Oh, and Pausanias wants to address the new associates after Melesius."

A marked departure from custom, Theseus thought. Melesius always took the final speaker's slot.

"I don't really know what Pausanias has in mind," Alcaeus said. "Word is that some of the younger partners put him up to it. He's definitely motivated to speak."

Theseus said he didn't see the harm in it.

"I've got to get down to a meeting with the first years right now to tell them what to expect," Alcaeus said.

Theseus said he had about an hour before a client call and would tag along if Alcaeus didn't mind.

"Sure, that would be great," Alcaeus agreed.

All of the new attorneys came right out of the firm's summer program except for the few that joined after serving judicial clerkships. Because job offers were extended early in the last year of law school, most students glided through to graduation without much to worry about. Some competed for academic recognition at their schools and continued to be diligent in their studies, but most took it easy and finished without a lot of extra effort. Careers seemed secure and promising after landing a job with a prestigious firm.

Alcaeus and Theseus walked into the conference room where the associates were collecting. When the associates saw Theseus, they stopped talking. He laughed and told them not to be concerned. Their conversations would not go farther than the room.

A young woman named Ianthe said they were discussing the bar exam. After graduation, the new associates had about two months to prepare for the exam. Every lawyer needed to pass the two day test in order to practice law. There were no exceptions. The first day of the exam was multiple choice.

Lengthy fact patterns were presented followed by a series of nuanced questions that were designed to test one's legal analysis. The second day was all essay. The associates would sit for morning and afternoon sessions writing responses to hypothetical cases or legal issues.

"We all thought it was pretty easy," Ianthe offered.

"Not everyone," an associate said, who introduced himself as Sophos. "The multiple choice questions were difficult. I don't really know what they were supposed to be testing."

Theseus remembered that the nature of the bar exam had little if any relevance to what was taught or learned in law school. Law grads all took a standard bar review course in order to pass. The review course lasted about a month and ended a few days before the actual exam. Theseus recalled spending most of his time learning the tricks to answering the multiple choice questions. The questions were designed not to have clear or ready answers, so it was necessary to learn how to eliminate the wrong choices and back into the correct ones. The bar review was designed to teach the techniques for having a greater probability of selecting the right answers. The essay subjects were based on local law, which wasn't taught in the law schools. So the associates also had to study local law summaries prepared by the companies staging the review courses. Theseus thought that it was absurd that a review course was a prerequisite to passing the bar after three years of law school. But the review courses were money makers, and there was no apparent interest from the bar or the law schools to change the system.

"I hope I pass," Sophos blurted.

"Everybody passes," Ianthe said.

"Not everyone," Alcaeus volunteered. "There have been a few fails from our associate ranks over the years."

"What happens if you fail?" an associate who went by Thanatos asked.

"Well," Alcaeus said, "you can take the exam over. As many times as you like, in fact. You guys probably know the results are highly public. Anyone can call in to the courts and find out who passed. The list is even published in the newspaper. Because the results come out after you've already been here a couple of months, the humiliation of not passing is tough to overcome. There was one associate who called in and learned his name wasn't on the list. He was comatose. Didn't show up at the firm for days. Then the letter came that he passed. I guess they had his name misspelled on the pass list or they didn't hear his name right when he called. But word had gotten around that he failed. He could never shake the stigma. He left the firm within the year."

"Sounds dreadful," Ianthe said.

"I'll make sure to enunciate when I call," Sophos laughed.

"We're going to be jinxed it if we keep talking about it," Thanatos said. "Let's discuss something else. Where did people go this summer?"

After the bar exam, associates had about a month before starting work at the firm. The associates knew it would be their last block of free time for an extended period, perhaps for the remainder of their professional careers. Associates were encouraged to take advantage of the opportunity and most did. The associates were paid a generous cash stipend from the firm to help defray living costs over the summer. Many used the money for travel.

"I spent some time in Corsica," Sophos said. "A good place to get away from everything and just chill out."

"I went to Mount Tmolus on a hiking trip with a bunch of friends," Thanatos said. "We were hoping to find gold so we wouldn't have to work."

Theseus had himself taken a trip to Memphis, a place that always interested him. He remembered spending several days there and visiting the temple of Hephaestus and other archeological sites. Legend had it that Helen spent the entire Trojan War in Memphis under the protection of Proteus. Menelaos had to fight Proteus' son, Theoclymenus, before taking Helen back to Sparta. Theseus didn't think the account was plausible. From Memphis, Theseus traveled up the Nile beyond Elephantine hoping to find the city of dwarf wizards visited by the Nasamonians.

Aegeon and Boethus came into the conference room with a stack of materials for the litigation associates. Diocles arrived as well, looking disorganized and carrying drafts of an asset purchase agreement. These were for the corporate associates.

"All right," Alcaeus started, "let's get down to business. You guys have all had a couple of months to get acclimated to the firm. Now it's time to get to work. You have to sit through a week of lectures, workshops and seminars on different topics relating to our practice at the firm. Attendance is mandatory, so don't take on assignments from partners that need to get done during the week. You won't have time to complete them. You'll be split up by practice groups for a good part of the week."

The firm expected all new lawyers to declare their allegiance to either the corporate group or litigation when they joined the firm. In earlier times, young lawyers would be assigned work depending on what clients required regardless of the area of the law. But the age of the renaissance lawyer had long passed. Now all entering associates had to choose corporate or litigation. There was no time to test the waters. Taking the wrong path was often detrimental to one's career.

"For the litigators," Boethus jumped in, "we're going to teach you techniques for effective oral advocacy in court and how we expect you to draft persuasive pleadings. You'll be shown how to be assertive and uncompromising and to never allow opposing counsel to take the offensive. The firm has an aggressive litigation style, and you'll have instruction covering the firm's proven methods for winning cases."

"Corporate associates will learn how to draft contracts and write disclosure for securities offerings," Alcaeus said. "You'll be taught about the need for detail and precision in your drafting. When preparing an agreement, the firm favors staking out extreme positions so that any move to the middle most likely turns out favorably for our clients. We'll coach you on the art of negotiation and how to achieve client goals. It's all good stuff."

Theseus viewed the training session as the start of the

legal apprenticeship required for all entrants to the profession. Law schools were not in the business of teaching students how to practice. Young lawyers needed to learn from experienced practitioners how the law and legal system operated and how it could be used or manipulated to a client's advantage. Theseus believed an effective lawyer, whether a litigator or corporate lawyer, ultimately had to master language. Grammar and rhetoric were the lawyer's tools. An accomplished lawyer needed to communicate well and have a command of the spoken and written word. There was no doubt in Theseus' mind that these traits were at the core of every distinguished lawyer. Theseus regretted that the growth of the profession saw an erosion of these skills among the bar. But he credited the firm for its commitment to training. If nothing else, the effort was a reminder to both young practitioners and old of the attributes of the ideal lawyer.

"You'll also be tutored in the more mundane aspects of practicing law at the firm," Alcaeus continued. "For example, Triton will show you how to bill and record time. Lack of attention to recording time properly costs the firm money. We discovered long ago that if lawyers miss even an extra fifteen minutes a day, it costs the firm millions each year."

Ianthe raised her hand and asked if there were pointers on timekeeping.

"Let's put it his way," Diocles said. "You should bill every second of every day while working on client matters. Discussing a case or transaction in the halls or over lunch is time to be recorded. When I think about an issue for a client while on the bus or train or even in the shower, I bill it. While traveling, I bill one client for the travel time and another for work I do on the way."

Theseus was chagrined over Diocles' message to the new associates. He thought it shameful that young lawyers were so single minded about maximizing billable hours.

"And it's just as important how time is recorded," Aegeon said. "Clients didn't like reading that time was billed for lawyers merely talking to each other, even though that can be your most productive time. It's better to record the time as research, due diligence or file review."

"Make sure you submit your time to the accounting department daily or weekly," Boethus added. "Revenues are lost if you don't stay current. Associates have been let go for being recalcitrant in turning in time sheets."

"Now," Alcaeus said, "the highlight of the week will be the mock trials for the litigators and mock negotiations for the corporate lawyers. You are going to have some homework to do to prepare."

The exercises were designed to give the associates an early taste for the real thing, but in a controlled environment. The older attorneys at the firm signed up to judge. Associates would be split up into teams and given a hypothetical case or transaction. The teams would collaborate and divide up issues or assignments. The lawyers who judged critiqued the associates and offered constructive advice. These exercises were generally conducted good naturedly. On occasion they became competitive as the associates tried to impress the partners and earn an early name for themselves.

"Aegeon," Alcaeus said, "what's this year's case?"

Aegeon passed around the litigation materials.

"The case deals with false advertising," Aegeon explained. "The plaintiff is claiming that the defendant sold dietary supplements that promised weight loss and mental alertness, but actually caused severe depression. The plaintiff is arguing the defendant should be held liable for emotional distress and is seeking punitive damages. Each team will have a direct and cross of witnesses, and then final arguments. The judges will be senior litigators, and they will render final verdicts. You will not want to be on the losing end, believe me."

Alcaeus told Diocles to review the mock negotiations for the corporate associates.

"Right, uh, let's see," Diocles fumbled. "You guys will have an acquisition to negotiate. The company is a supplier of benzene that is used in industrial cleansers. Its plant was built on an old landfill that has environmental problems. The union workers at the plant are threatening a strike. The owner is motivated to sell, and the buyer is a private equity fund. Your teams will be assigned to represent either the buyer or seller. You'll have to negotiate some of the reps and covenants the buyer wants from the seller, as well as indemnification for unanticipated costs and a few other typical deal points. You'll also have to agree on the price for the business, which is the critical thing. You are required to come to agreement. No one leaves the negotiations until you get to a price. The lowest price for the buyer wins, or the highest price for the seller if you are on the sell side."

Theseus got up to leave for his call, feeling that Alcaeus had the training well in hand. He himself was not able to participate in any of the sessions, but he did want to catch Melesius' speech at the end of the week. His talk was an annual tradition at the firm. All of the firm's lawyers made every effort to attend.

On the final day of the training program, Theseus made his way to the room where the attorneys were assembling. The first year associates were sitting around a large oval conference table in the center, surrounded by lawyers sitting and standing in every corner of the room. Theseus was struck by the sight. He saw the symbolism with the young people in the middle and the firm's senior lawyers behind them.

Alcaeus was announcing the results of the mock sessions when Theseus arrived. Sophos' team won the litigation contest by getting the defendant off without penalty. His team argued that the incidence of depression among the pill takers was no different than the population at large, and in the absence of a direct causal relation between the supplements and depression the defendant was entitled to judgment as a matter of law. In the corporate negotiations, two teams actually had negotiated the same sale price. First prize was awarded to the team headed up by a new associate named Callicles, because they avoided an indemnity escrow for the seller. When the results were announced, the lawyers clapped and cheered for the winning teams. A sense of pride and camaraderie pervaded the room.

After the awards, Alcaeus commended the first year associates on their performance and thanked all the lawyers who participated in the training sessions. He then introduced Melesius, who rose slowly from his seat and walked to the head of the room. Melesius had white hair, drawn checks and cloudy eyes which gave away his advancing age. He always had his reading glasses on top of his head or on a chain around his neck. His clothes looked a little tattered and woefully out of date. He sported his customary suit vest and watch chain.

"Congratulations and welcome to those of you who are just now joining the firm," Melesius began. "We are very pleased you are here. We hope this is a time of great excitement and anticipation for you. For us, it is a moment of great promise. By joining us, you are taking your place among the ranks of the most prodigious legal minds in our profession. As a member of the firm, you will help shape the law as it will be years hence and contribute to the remarkable history of our country's jurisprudence. It is a privilege to practice law in our country and at the firm. But it brings with it responsibilities that must be taken to heart. You will be held to a high standard of conduct and expected to acquit yourself properly as an attorney at law.

"Now, I am curious how some of you came to decide on pursuing a law career. Perhaps there are a few volunteers that aren't shy about telling us their story."

A young man toward the front of the room raised his hand.

"Yes, you there," Melesius pointed. "Please tell us your name and why you want to be a lawyer."

"My name is Teucer," the young man said. "My father is a lawyer, and my grandfather was a lawyer. I never considered any other profession."

"All right, Teucer," Melesius said. "Not an uncommon answer. Many of us admit to a genealogy. Thank you."

"I studied the humanities in college," Callicles contributed. "I looked for a year for a job, but couldn't find one suitable. So I decided on a law degree."

Theseus

There was a smattering of chuckles.

"Ok," Melesius replied smiling. "No harm in that. How about you, young lady?"

Melesius motioned toward Ianthe at the other end of the table.

"I'm Ianthe," she said earnestly. "I have a degree in genetics, and want to pursue medical ethics law."

"A weighty but timely area of the law," Melesius responded. "Anyone else?"

Melesius looked around the room.

"Diocles," Melesius said. "I see you lurking way back there. Diocles here has been with us for a few years. Why don't you share with our new associates why you chose the law?"

"For the money, to be honest," Diocles said straight out. "It's the next best thing to investment banking, and hopefully a career that lasts longer."

The room let out a hearty laugh.

"All right, then," Melesius began again. "You have arrived at the firm for different reasons and from diverse paths. But you all share at least one thing in common. You've proved yourselves to be deserving of an offer from the firm. That is no small feat. Whether you realize it or not, you were hand selected by the firm out of the thousands who obtained law degrees last year. You are the ones who showed the most distinction and greatest potential. You now share an opportunity to become part of the grand traditions of the law at one of our country's finest law firms.

"So what does it mean to be a lawyer and a member of the legal profession? Let's try to answer that question. Maybe some of you have given it some thought. I hope so. Perhaps we should start with the qualifications necessary to practice law in our country. Do any of you know that you must meet certain admission criteria before you are allowed to practice?

"Callicles, are you aware that no one can be admitted to the bar unless he or she demonstrates general fitness for admission and good moral character? General fitness for admission to the profession means you possess the ability to learn the law, recall it, and through reason apply it. A lawyer must also communicate clearly and logically with clients, other attorneys and the courts. You all have, and will soon manifest, these traits in abundance, I am sure.

"Law school taught you the essential skills you need to practice. You learned how to find and analyze the law. That is no mean feat in our society, especially given our common law roots. The common law is the great memory of justice, and it is not readily discernible to the population at large. Unless you successfully completed law school, there is no easy way to find, read and understand the law. Only lawyers can adequately search and know the law.

"More importantly than this, you were taught in law school to think as a lawyer, a remarkable cognitive process that is lost on anyone who has not earned a law degree. Your law studies set you apart by distilling in you a mental capacity that is unique to lawyers. Only lawyers are able to analyze experience from general principles and grasp the consequences for human behavior that must follow. It is the genius of the case method. A lawyer's way of looking at the world, I tell you, is your most important asset. To think as a lawyer is a remarkable capability that you must learn to exercise prudently. The legal thought process taught in law school and applied in our courts has created a monopoly for lawyers in our judicial system.

"Because of the skills instilled in law school, lawyers yield great power in our society. Teucer is not surprised to hear it. He has undoubtedly seen it with his father and grandfather. You others will come to appreciate this more each day that you practice and as you move along in your professional careers.

"General fitness for admission also means you must conduct yourself diligently and reliably and have the ability to comply with deadlines and time constraints. Sounds rather pedestrian, doesn't it? But imagine, Ianthe, if you are not on time for a hearing or trial, or if Diocles fails to show for a closing. You will find that diligence and timeliness takes great effort and preparation, especially if you are juggling five or ten client matters at a time. You will get up before the sun rises and work well into the night to meet your commitments as a lawyer. You may not see daylight for days when engrossed in a case or transaction. While partners here are sure to place heavy demands on your time, remember it is not of their doing. The clients are to blame. They are the ones we work for.

"Now what about good moral character? To be admitted to the bar, one must have the ability to conduct oneself with a high degree of honesty, integrity and trustworthiness in your professional relationships. You must show respect for the law, avoid acts that exhibit disregard for the health, safety, and welfare of others, be truthful and use good judgment in financial dealings. A record manifesting a failure to meet these eligibility requirements constitutes a basis for denial of admission.

"There is more. Meeting the essential criteria for admission is just the start. Do any of you know what your first act as a lawyer will be? You will swear an oath. Ask most practicing attorneys today to recite the lawyer's oath and they will probably fail in the effort. Yet every lawyer must begin his or her law practice by taking an oath before our highest court. You will be reciting it in the coming weeks once the bar results are out. What is the oath? The lawyer's oath is to uphold the law. That sounds pretty straight forward, doesn't it? But the oath requires that a lawyer not pursue an unjust cause and only employ means that are consistent with truth and honor. In addition, a lawyer agrees to abstain from all offensive personality and advance no fact prejudicial to the reputation and honor of any party or witness unless required by the justice of the cause. A lawyer also promises not to reject or delay a cause for lucre or malice. These are things you will swear to as an attorney at law.

"What appears on the surface simple is now rather more complex. Teucer, what is an unjust cause? How are lawyers to act according to truth and honor? Why are lawyers prohibited from denigrating the reputation of an opponent or taking on a case for lucre or malice? Justice, truth and honor are high minded words, are they not? Did your course in legal ethics instruct you about lucre or malice? What did law school teach you about the meaning of these concepts? Very little is my guess.

"If you weren't instructed in law school as to these things, what are you to do? How are you expected to fulfill your oath and stay in good standing in the profession? Fair questions. Callicles, can you say that justice is a natural condition, a virtue or a social contract? Is justice something rooted in our human essence or part of our culture? Does it emanate from a divine source? Maybe at its base justice is merely social convention or nihilism. You needn't be too concerned. Whether you realize it or not, you all have inherent notions of justice distilled in you from your parents and earlier schooling. You are not without grounding.

"The nature of justice has drawn the attention of many celebrated thinkers throughout history. But I don't intend a pedantic discourse on justice. For present purposes, we can all agree that justice is about right and wrong, however you define it, and a system of justice attempts to set things right. A just society safeguards the person and defends property, protects right minded people who have respect for the law and punishes the wrongdoer. An unjust system, Ianthe, is arbitrary and partisan. It leaves malefactors to their own devices and encourages lawlessness. Civic virtue is replaced by greed, lack of trust and revenge. People are forced to live in fear and uncertainty in an unjust society. Injustice, if prevailing in a culture, causes great harm. The great tenet of our society is that all men have the right to life and liberty. Perhaps justice lies in protecting these fundamental rights.

"As lawyers, our oath prevents us from pursuing an unjust cause. We can't take on cases that have as their aim an unwarranted result. Imagine representing a thief and arguing that he is entitled to steal. Or defending someone who bludgeons another on the grounds that he did it for pleasure. Would you take the case of a company that sells harmful products to consumers based on the argument that it is profitable? Of course not.

"All right then. What about truth and honor? How do these virtues factor in? Teucer, if you need a lecture on truth and honor, I suggest you look for a different profession. Personal integrity is critical to any system of justice. Imagine a system where opposing sides can't trust each other or believe in each other's representations. Unless lawyers can be counted on to keep their word, the system breaks down and anarchy results. We must also act honorably, which I suggest means we treat each other with dignity and respect. Defamatory and false statements and attempts to humiliate, embarrass, harass or intimidate your opponents won't get you far. Picture going to court and having opposing counsel prejudice the judge by speaking poorly of you or your client. That you don't like paying taxes or don't support charities. That you grew up in an unpopular place or hold radical political views. That would seem ludicrous, would it not?

"Then there is lucre and malice. Lawyers can't take cases for money. That's certainly odd sounding. How can this be so? We are all money mad are we not, Diocles? But I tell you now that lawyers are prohibited from taking cases purely for the money. Lawyers also can't take a case because of some deep seated hatred for the opposition. Personal enmity clouds the mind and defeats reason. You will never win a case brought out of malice.

"Understand that the practice of law is a privilege that can be lost. You can be incapacitated from continuing to practice law by reason of mental infirmity or addiction to drugs or intoxicants. What if you commit a felony or are convicted of a crime involving fraud or moral turpitude? Conduct which tends to undermine the administration of justice or to bring the courts or the legal profession into disrepute are grounds for disbarment, suspension, censure or reprimand. Disbarment and suspension amount to banishment. Censure and reprimand are ostracism. You can lose your livelihood. Or your reputation. Reputation is everything to a lawyer.

"The most common reasons lawyers are disbarred or

suspended are alcohol or drug addiction, fraud and mishandling or stealing client funds. Avoid excess drinking. Stay off drugs. You cannot meet the daily demands of the work if addiction has you in its grip. Do not be tempted to deceive others in order to win a case. You will only be deceiving yourself if you do. If you take client money, always give it to the firm for safekeeping. Don't tempt fate by holding client funds yourself.

"Now, let me offer some simple advice. To keep your mind sharp, keep your body fit. You will have trouble maintaining the mental rigors of the work if your body is not kept in shape. Stay physically strong and you will find longevity and more productivity in your career. The body is the vessel for the mind. Make a habit of physical activity. Run, lift weights, play basketball or tennis. Commit to it on a regular basis. Squash is an excellent game you might try. Join a rowing club. Sign up for exercise with a colleague. You will be more apt to stick with it and enjoy it more. Even at my age, I don't neglect exercise. I walk the two miles from my home to the train and back every day, rain or shine.

"I also advise you to manage your personal finances well. Don't live extravagantly or beyond your means. Borrowing is like gambling, and is an addiction. Save your money and invest it conservatively. Pay your taxes. Do not put yourself in a financial position where you are desperate for a big win. Don't invest in a client's business. You will be compromised by it, and it will lead to ruin. Money woes have undermined many a promising career.

"Let's go on to talk about what the firm will mean to you. By joining the firm, you probably think you will be handling intriguing cases or major transactions for clients, that you will make momentous arguments before a judge or jury, or break down a difficult witness on cross examination. Or perhaps negotiate important mergers for large corporations. You doubtless expect to interact with powerful people and travel to many interesting places as you manage the affairs of firm clients. You may hope to earn large sums of money in the process. You are right to expect these things. Don't doubt that the firm will give you such opportunities.

"Be assured of the benefits the firm will give you. Yes, you will be paid handsomely. Do not worry about making money. That is the least of it. We are partners and a fiercely loyal lot. The firm is your family and your colleagues are your brothers and sisters. We acknowledge each other's contributions to the firm, varied though they may be. We demand excellence from each other, and we expect everyone to perform at their highest level. If you have problems professionally or personally, have confidence that the firm is behind you. You needn't suffer alone. We are a brotherhood, a clan. We look out for each other. We are each other's friends. We celebrate life events together, vacation together and socialize outside the office. We do it not out of necessity or to politic for our careers. We do it because we find ourselves interesting and interested people. We are sophisticated, each in our own way, yet fine people with a sense of humor. We take pride and delight in each other and like to have fun and enjoy ourselves. You will learn what I mean very soon, if you have not already. Take part in the firm, and become one of us.

"Today, we find the legal profession growing rapidly. Large numbers of lawyers are produced from many law schools across the nation. Women and minorities are graduating from law school in vast numbers. Law firms have become gargantuan in size, and lawyers are specializing as never before. Corporate lawyers don't try cases and litigators don't negotiate transactions. We have tax specialists, health care specialists, environmental specialists and housing specialists. The law profession evolves as our society does, and reflects the complexity of our nation and its people. The practice of law is competitive. Clients have a choice who they choose as their lawyers. Don't take clients for granted and never think you are the only lawyer that can represent them.

"You will spend the rest of your life learning how to practice law. I have been doing it for almost fifty years, and I am still learning. Put aside the notion that it will come quickly or without effort. The practice of law is an apprenticeship in the truest sense of the word. You need to learn how to be a good lawyer, and the firm will teach you. Our partners are the finest lawyers there are, and over time you will learn the trade from them. It won't always be pleasant, but nothing of value comes easy. There will come a time when you realize what it truly means to be a counselor at law, to advise your clients on how to protect their interests or achieve a just result on their behalf. That day will surely come, but for now it is a long way off. In the meantime, devote yourself to learning the practice of law and let us teach you how to do it properly. If you are diligent and patient, you will be ready when a new client comes to you for representation and you open your first client file at the firm. I tell you, that will be the moment you find yourself maturing as a lawyer. Treat your clients fairly, charge them a fair fee. Put your ego and personal interests aside in all matters. Don't let greed or malice cloud your view. Never lose sight of the fact that as lawyers we are bound by truth and honor and required to pursue justice. Do right by your practice. Bring honor to the profession and the firm and you will have a long, prosperous and rewarding career."

Melesius then finished. The young lawyers sat with inscrutable faces. Many didn't know what to make of what they had just heard. Several of the older partners began clapping, and soon the room broke out in applause.

A short break followed, then Alcaeus called everyone back to their seats. Pausanias walked to the head of the room and stood looking bemused. Pausanias was a commercial litigation partner who handled insurance defense cases. Theseus assumed Pausanias was in his mid-forties, but his boyish and athletic looks made him seem much younger. He had crisp blue eyes, a ruddy complexion and a bright white smile. His hair was reddish blonde and perfectly trimmed. Pausanias wore a winged collar shirt, yellow power tie and navy-gold striped grosgrain suspenders. He spoke fast and authoritatively. Theseus wasn't sure if Pausanias reminded him of Sarpedon or Pandaros, but no doubt a Trojan.

"My, that was masterful, Melesius," Pausanias said looking

Theseus

at the associates. "I never knew that I was so virtuous! Our country would be surprised to learn that lawyers are good and pure!

"Before we all get taken by Melesius' fine oration, let's hear what the law is really about. Justice? Do you want to start there? All right. Where is the justice when drillers for natural gas poison the drinking water of the locals? How about the executive who earns a huge bonus and then puts his company into bankruptcy because the company can't afford to pay its pensioners? Or the fast food company that doesn't pay for the bad health effects of the food its sells? What about the discount retailer that sells guns and ammunition to a manic student that lets loose in his sociology class? What about the media client that has become the propaganda tool of a political party? How about a bank that makes loans to unworthy borrowers and then asks the government for a bailout when the loans go bad? Where's the justice when an investment bank sells investment products it knows will lose money? These are your clients. How is it you can represent them if you can't pursue an unjust cause?

"Let's not pretend. Justice is not about right and wrong, it's about power. Whatever your ideas are of fairness or equality put them aside. Justice lies in the hands of the powerful. Look at history. Who has the greatest force, the most followers? Who has amassed the most money? That's where you will find justice. Kings, landowners or revolutionaries. The pattern is always the same. Those in control define justice and administer justice. Sometimes those in power are good, sometimes not. Sometimes justice seems right and correct, other times it feels totally wide of the mark. It all depends on your perspective and whether you hold power or are subjected to it.

"There must be something more to it, you say? What about legitimacy or fundamental fairness? Isn't there something inherent in people that makes them fight injustice and unfair treatment? Those of you who think that should work for Melesius, but not for me.

"In the early days, kings or persons of noble birth held the reins of power. They controlled property and labor. Social thinkers over time formulated theories that began to instill in the masses ideas that they didn't have their fair share, and they attacked the status quo. Everyone gets into the game at one time or another. Coups, insurrection, rebellion, riots and boycotts. Giving everyone the right to vote or to run for office. What's the difference in the end? It's all a play for power.

"I suggest that you take what I say to heart. You'll be a better lawyer. It's not always about force, weapons or the art of war, mind you. Ideas are part of the equation. Self righteousness, personal freedom and morality are call words for power grabs. Capture the collective consciousness of the people and you can defeat any regime. Liberate the public imagination and you can change the law or topple any government, no matter how strong or powerful. Give me your poor, your downtrodden and give me enough of them. Convince the underprivileged and the deprived of their self worth and power and do so in sufficient numbers and you have yourself an assault on the classical notions of what is just. Mix in a little education and free time and a social revolution is sure to follow.

"What drives people to seek power? Ego, selfishness, righteousness? There are isolated examples of this. But true power is the control of resources. All resources are limited. Those that possess resources try to prevent everyone else from getting them. Those that lack resources maneuver to seize them. Justice is the way we protect or distribute resources. Food, water, oil, minerals, money. A frenzied battle for resources. Power and justice, I tell you, is all about controlling and managing resources.

"What does any of this have to do with you or practicing law at this firm? Well, listen attentively to what I have to tell you. Our body of laws and legal institutions have as their purpose the orderly distribution of limited resources. There, that's it. Lawyers represent their clients to maintain or increase their share of resources. Lawyers do this according

Theseus

to set rules and procedures. It's a nonviolent process. People don't generally get killed by filing a law suit or going to court. But it is not necessarily peaceful. It's still a battle and it can be bloody. We are hired and paid by our clients to make sure they get more or keep what they have.

"As lawyers we have to fight as soldiers. We put on our suits and ties or blouses instead of war gear, pick up our briefs and legal pads instead of swords. The courtroom or the conference room is our battlefield. We win or lose based upon our training, hard work and sagacity. And at this firm we don't ever lose.

"Don't get too light headed listening to Melesius. We are not defenders of truth and honor. We represent corporations. Today it's the corporations that have the power. Understand what that means. Corporations are unique creatures under our laws, created to allow for investment and management of business enterprises. Corporations are the great leviathans of our age, and the law has developed to protect their interests. Corporations have rights like individuals. They can make contracts and commit torts and crimes. Their speech is protected. Advertising and campaign contributions are first amendment rights. Corporations are free to act as they wish subject to the futile attempts of the legislature to contain them. Little effect that has had over the years. Corporations have continued to grow in size and influence. Many corporations are larger and more powerful than whole governments.

"Corporations are supervised by boards and managed by the executive group for the benefit of stockholders. They exist for one purpose. Profit. You've been taught about the common law. Now hear this. The most important common law in our country is the corporate common law. The courts set the ground rules for how our corporations are to be managed and how they can be challenged. Understand the cases and the legal principles that apply to corporations. Boards are given great latitude in their decision making and the law makes it difficult to challenge their decisions. If a board decision is contested, it is always on the basis of a conflict of interest or a flawed decision making process. But even suits over management misconduct in the end turn on whether there is a fair deal for the profit seekers. Ultimately, you will find that corporations are held to one guiding principle. Maximizing returns for the stockholders. Our task as lawyers representing the great corporations is to help them achieve profit.

"Now, Melesius is a very learned man and a good lawyer. But don't be swayed by his rhetoric. You are not defenders of justice in the classical sense. If you want to do good, become a public defender. Your job here is to protect and expand the interests of corporations and the rich. We are all about advocating for wealth. There is no room for empathy for the common man. His avenue is the ballot box. Our domain is the court of law and principles of contract.

"One last word. Let me talk to you about the firm. Melesius makes the firm sound like some idyllic professional guild. Well, you're in for a rude awakening I'm afraid. The old ways are succumbing to the firms built for profit. We're in this for the money for the most part, so let's be clear about it. If you're not adding to the profits of the partners, you won't be here for very long. That's a simple fact. Now here's what you should be doing. Identify partners with large amounts of business and do what you can to work for them. Make yourself indispensable. That way you assure yourself of more work and another year employed at the firm. When it comes time for partnership, if you have made it that far, hope that the rainmakers are in your corner. You never know, but without that kind of support you will be looking for another job.

"Here's another thing. Don't waste too much time getting friendly with your fellow associates. You don't really have time for it and it will get you nowhere. Besides, truth be told, they are the competition. There's only room for a handful of partners here. Only a few make it. Keep that in mind. Your time is better spent getting to know the clients. And I'm not taking about trying to ingratiate yourself with the senior executives. That's the domain of the partners. If you try to show up a partner in front of a client, it's a sure ticket out of here. Besides, no intelligent executive would ever hire a young lawyer. They know associates don't have the experience, and an inexperienced attorney can spell doom for a businessman's career. Clients tend to hire lawyers that are older than themselves. They want to see gray hair. That's just the way it is. Instead, get to know your peers at these places and become their friends. If they are at all ambitious, they will move around to other companies trying to get ahead. Follow them. If they are successful, they will land a job soon enough where they can direct the legal work. You want to be part of that equation. These contacts will feed you down the road.

"Go home tonight and have dinner with your wife or friends. Go to a fine restaurant. Have something to drink. Catch a show. Go to a club. Enjoy yourselves. Get back here early tomorrow. After today expect to start working long hours. Your life is no longer your own. You are ours now. The games are over. This is not the summer program. Be prepared for what is coming at you. It's going to happen fast and you are going to be tested. Trust me. Many of you won't outlive the battles. There will be casualties. A few of you will survive, even thrive on the challenge and in time secure your place among the partners of this firm. We'll see. The future is calling. It's going to be a ride like you never expected."

13

Theseus thought a great deal about the speeches given by Melesius and Pausanias in the days following the associate training. The speeches were certainly antithetical, and they caused Theseus to reflect on the profession and what it had or was to become. Theseus wondered which speaker gave the truer or more prescient account. Melesius' speech reminded Theseus of the great funeral oration of Pericles, when Pericles extolled the virtues of the Athenian democracy and its free citizens. The speech was given in honor of the dead after the first year of the Peloponnesian War. Pericles did not mourn those who had lost their lives in the fighting as much as he celebrated the greatness of the city and its people. Pericles took account of the things that made classical Athens great. The citizenry had an abiding respect for the law, a free and open political life, a love of beauty and things of the mind, an adventurous spirit and incomparable bravery. Theseus speculated whether radical democracy wasn't the right model for the firm. A more egalitarian group one could not hope to find than lawyers in a law firm. Lawyers all received the same education and passed the same bar. They all took the same oath. No one held an advantage due to wealth or social status. There was mutual protection and security in the partnership. With so much commonality and identity of interest, wasn't it right to treat all lawyers alike and have them sharing equally in the management and benefits of the firm?

The speech given by Pausanias made Theseus think of Alcibiades' arguments before the Athenian assembly when he tried to gain popular support for the campaign against Syracuse. Much of Alcibiades' speech was about the inevitable need to expand in order for Athens to stay a dominant power in the Greek world. He was able to convince the people of the imminent danger of falling under the control of their adversaries unless their adversaries fell to Athenian supremacy first. The people were captured by Alcibiades' rhetoric and never gave a thought to the risks or

Theseus

possibility of failure. They embraced the aggression against the Syracusans wholeheartedly. But Alcibiades was not interested in sustaining the glory of Athens as much as securing power and wealth for himself. His goal was personal, and he sought to elevate himself politically. The course won by Alcibiades ultimately served to weaken the state and was followed by an oligarchic overthrow of the democracy.

The economic theory underlying Pausanias' view was that the firm needed to maximize its profits in order to pay for the best legal talent, and the best legal talent was needed to secure the best work from the highest paying clients. A circular form of logic, Theseus thought. Ironically, the rationale for this view was the preservation of the firm itself. Expand profit or die. Dominate or be dominated. One of the problems with this model was the natural selection in favor of the business generators. The highest drawing partners would be the ones tapped to lead and they would make certain they were paid the most. With only the wealthiest in control, there was no doubt how the firm would be run. Unproductive attorneys would have to be paid less or cut. Productivity requirements would increase, meaning greater billable hours for the rank and file. Anyone not contributing enough becomes dispensable in the name of the common good. Ultimately, Theseus thought, the firm becomes less secure and more unstable, and the risk of failure rises. A sad message to convey to young associates just now joining the firm.

Theseus soon turned his attention back to the purchase of Nemean for Minos. The agreement had finally been negotiated, and a date had set been set for the closing in Thebes. Diocles, Iollas and Calliope were enlisted to assist Theseus with the closing. Pedocles was to receive approximately eight percent of the stock of Asterion. The shares wouldn't be tradable for at least a year. Pedocles would be head of software development and appointed a director of Asterion. There would also be employment agreements for key members of Nemean management providing guaranteed bonuses and stock options over the first few years. If the public offering was successful, Pedocles and his top people stood to become very wealthy.

When Theseus arrived in the Theban lawyers' offices, he was surprised to find that little had been done in the way of preparation for the closing. Normally, a closing would be set up in a large conference room and all the closing papers would be neatly laid out and organized according to a closing index. None of this had been completed. Theseus walked the office to find Keos standing in a back hallway with a cup of espresso in this hand.

"Well, Theseus," Keos started, "back to wrap up Nemean are you? We didn't expect you until later in the day."

Theseus said he didn't see any documents out, and asked if Keos would be ready for the next day's closing.

"Of course," Keos replied, sensing Theseus' consternation.

As Keos and Theseus stood together, Keos' cell phone rang and he answered it straightaway.

"Yes, yes, he's here," Keos said to the caller. "I'm with him right now. I think you should come out. Yes, directly."

Theseus waited for an explanation.

"That was Rhesus," Keos said with a smile.

Rhesus was the Theban associate responsible for the closing. Theseus wondered what Rhesus was doing calling in on the cell phone. There was work to be done, Theseus thought, and he should be here. Before he could ask Rhesus' whereabouts, Rhesus appeared out of an office several paces from where Theseus and Keos stood.

Theseus walked with Rhesus back to the closing room, and they took seats with Diocles and Iollas. Theseus asked Rhesus where the closing papers were. The checklist Diocles had prepared for the closing showed over fifty different documents that would have to be produced for the closing, which included, along with the final purchase agreement, good standing certificates, copies of the companies' governing charters, lien searches, third party consents, employment agreements, trade name and patent filings, employee lists, copies of insurance and benefit plans, and so on.

"Oh, yes," Rhesus said a little surprised, "we can have those items for you shortly. Let me ask Keos."

Rhesus skirted quickly out of the room.

Diocles looked worried that he would be blamed.

"I went over the closing list with him before we left, Theseus," Diocles said. "Rhesus told me he would have it all together when we got here."

Theseus sat with Diocles, Iollas and Calliope in the conference room for nearly an hour. Neither Keos nor Rhesus was seen during that time. A lunch cart was brought in and the waiter stood to take sandwich orders. Theseus grew restive. He told Diocles to find Keos. Soon, Diocles returned with Keos in tow.

"Well," Keos observed, "I see Borus is here for your order. Tell him what you would like, he will make it up for you right here. I might recommend the ham and cheese brioche."

Theseus at that point had enough. He told Keos to put aside eating for the moment and start producing documents. Theseus commanded Keos to get control of the process and his people. He didn't want to have to say it again.

As Theseus was speaking, Pedocles appeared in the door. Pedocles wanted to know what the problem was, and looked at Keos.

"All will be as it should," Keos explained. "I see no reason for delay."

Rhesus came into the room with an unorganized stack of documents.

Theseus looked at the stack, and had it handed off to Iollas.

Theseus demanded that two computers be set up in the room with printers. He also asked for legal assistants and secretaries and a couple of fax machines. Theseus wanted operators and messengers on call. There should be at least one copier at the group's complete disposal. He told Calliope to get some folders and to lay out the table. He instructed

Keos to have his people available for the next twenty four hours straight.

Keos directed Rhesus to go out and arrange the computers and fax machines. He made a call on his cell phone and asked someone to find secretaries.

"I gather we are not ready?" Pedocles said blankly to Theseus.

Theseus said they were far from it.

"Keos, a word with you, please," Pedocles ordered.

Pedocles and Keos walked out into the hall.

Within thirty minutes, the conference room was abuzz with activity. Calliope had prepared folders for each document that would be required for the closing and laid them out neatly in order. Iollas was sorting through the documents produced earlier from Rhesus, and placed relevant papers in their proper place on the table. Diocles had the task of making sure the purchase documents and the disclosure schedules for Nemean were complete, and he spent time on the phone with the Nemean financial people to ensure the accuracy of the disclosures. Diocles discovered from the schedules that there were additional contracts that Nemean had not produced, which needed review. The fax machine was running nonstop as these contracts were sent from Nemean. Iollas reviewed each contract as it came over the fax. In the meantime, Theseus made heavy revisions to the legal opinion that would be required from Keos' firm for the closing.

Contributing to the racket were the legal assistants brought in by Keos. Their names were Aella and Clio. Theseus took note of their look. The women were equal in height or taller than most of the Theban men, and professionally dressed. One was blond and the other was a brunette, and both had their hair tied up in a bun atop their heads. Their manner of speech was direct. Focusing on each of their tasks, they gave off an aura of unflappability that seemed to settle the mounting tension in the room. In a strange way, Aella and Clio reminded Theseus of the Lydian working class girls who used their own devices to raise a

Theseus

dowry and chose their own husbands. Theseus wished these women were the attorneys in charge. He was certain they would put Keos and his men to shame.

By mid afternoon, much had been done. Theseus was relieved to find that the form of government registration papers for Nemean had been procured, and most of the third party consents to the transaction collected. Diocles had completed his review of the disclosure schedules and Iollas was revising the due diligence memorandum for the additional contracts that came in.

In the course of completing the due diligence, Diocles was informed of a piece of litigation that had been filed against Nemean about three months before. After paging through the case, Diocles brought it to Theseus' attention. Theseus wasn't pleased. The suit alleged that Nemean had hired away an employee named Eucles from Baricos Co., a Theban competitor, and Eucles had used proprietary code from Baricos to help develop Nemean's new software.

Pedocles was nearby when Diocles told Theseus of the case, and Pedocles said he knew of it but his lawyers told him the matter was not of much concern.

Keos was called back into the conference room to shed light on the claim.

"A typical case, but without any merit or consequence," Keos said. "These suits are filed whenever a programmer changes jobs."

Theseus asked pointedly why Keos did not think it important enough to bring it to his attention.

"I'm sure you have these kinds of things with your technology companies all the time," Keos replied. "You call them frivolous lawsuits, I think."

Theseus said the suit was certainly not frivolous as it claimed infringement of the very software that made Nemean valuable. He wanted to speak to the lawyer handling the case.

Keos produced a middle aged attorney by the name of Clinias. Pedocles, Keos and Theseus sat down with him. Clinias had spent some time with Eucles and learned that Eucles had indeed worked on code similar to the Nemean software while at Baricos. Pedocles had hired Eucles away from Baricos to help with the completion of the Nemean software. The case was up for a hearing in the next thirty days, but there had been no contact with Baricos' attorneys to date.

Theseus asked Clinias his assessment of the case.

"To be straight with you," Clinias said, "there are allegations that if proved to be true would be a real problem for Nemean, that is, a cause for concern."

Theseus inquired whether Clinias was aware that Nemean was being sold to Asterion, and did he think the case was material.

"Yes, certainly, I know of the sale," Clinias said, "and yes, if it were me buying Nemean, I would want to know about the case. But nobody has asked me so I assumed it was not deemed of much importance to anyone."

Pedocles started scolding Keos. It occurred to Theseus that Keos was like the wretched satyr Silenus, the indentured servant of the one eyed Polyphemus. Theseus stood up, grabbed his cell phone and left the room.

After about twenty minutes, Theseus returned. He said he just got off the phone with Minos, and the case raised questions about the propriety of moving ahead with the transaction. Minos would be willing to close nonetheless, under certain conditions.

Theseus then gave Minos' proposal. Pedocles would have to agree to a holdback of twenty percent of the Asterion stock he was to receive in the deal. When the case was disposed of, Pedocles would receive the shares less the cost of the case to Asterion whatever it happened to be, including any damages, settlement payments and attorneys fees. Asterion would take control of the case and try to settle it before the planned public offering.

"No," Pedocles responded adamantly. "It is illogical for me to give up such a large stake for a case we weren't even discussing yesterday."

Theseus said his option was to agree to the holdback or postpone the closing until the case was settled. There was

Theseus

too much risk for Asterion. If the case proved groundless, Pedocles would have lost nothing. If there is a delay, the opportunity to obtain a good price for his stock may pass him by.

"I will talk to Minos," Pedocles said.

Pedocles brusquely left the room.

Theseus, Keos, the associates and the legal assistants stayed back. All eyes turned to Theseus.

Theseus ordered everyone to continue working. He asked Diocles how things looked.

"I was just about to review the third party consents with Rhesus," Diocles said. "There is a small loan from Tityos Bank to Pedocles' company that requires change of control approval. Pedocles' office lease also requires the landlord's consent to the acquisition, and there are two or three approvals required from equipment finance companies that lease Nemean's hardware."

Rhesus had a blank stare. He appeared ignorant of the status of the approvals.

"The bank has said we should have its consent tomorrow, early," Aella said. "We spoke to the landlord and the finance companies and we should see their approvals this evening by fax."

Pedocles returned to the room, not looking too pleased.

"I have agreed with Minos to proceed as you propose, Theseus," Pedocles said matter of factly.

Keos looked relieved, even though it was a hard bargain for his client.

The associates along with Aella and Clio would continue working late into the night. Cautiously optimistic that things were falling into place, Theseus decided to return to his hotel for the evening. He left strict instructions with Diocles that he was to be woken up if any serious issues arose.

The next morning, the group reconvened at the Theban offices. Minos arrived midmorning with Pedocles. Minos conducted himself with his usual levity.

"There's only one thing better than this," Minos said eyeing Aella and Clio. "I hope everyone is in good spirits, because it's a fine thing we are doing, right Pedocles?"

Pedocles looked unsure about going ahead with the deal.

"You guys have been burning the midnight oil, I hear," Minos said to Diocles, Iollas and Calliope. "All for a good cause."

Minos then walked over to the legal assistants.

"And you, young ladies, I'm sure kept everyone on their toes," Minos said. "I can't say I know what part you played in this, but I'm sure everyone appreciated your contributions."

Minos let go a hearty laugh. Aella and Clio didn't react. His flirtations were not hitting their mark.

Theseus called the group together to review the documents to be delivered for the closing and to make sure everything was set for the signing of the purchase agreement. Theseus then noticed that Keos was not present. He asked of his whereabouts.

Clio said he hadn't been seen in the office. Pedocles was uncertain, not having talked to Keos that morning. Finally, Rhesus spoke up.

"Keos begins a holiday today," Rhesus said meekly, "so he is unlikely to be available for the closing."

Theseus was astonished. It went beyond the pale that Keos would leave for vacation before the closing. He demanded Rhesus get him on the phone and tell him to come into the office.

"That is doubtful," Rhesus responded. "Keos leaves his cell phone here when he goes on holiday."

Theseus asked Pedocles if he was prepared to proceed without his lead counsel.

"Yes, certainly," Pedocles said with a long face. "Let's proceed."

Theseus then told Diocles to lead the group through the closing documents to confirm everything was in order. Diocles spent the next half hour walking around the table noting the presence of the documents to be delivered and confirming signatures. The only matter that was required to be completed was the registration of the new ownership of

Theseus

the Nemean shares with the Theban corporate registrar's office. A notary was waiting outside to deliver the paperwork to the registrar.

Theseus then declared that they were ready to close and asked Minos and Pedocles to execute the agreement.

Minos was euphoric as he signed the document. Pedocles was expressionless. After Pedocles signed, there was dead silence.

Inking a deal was an anomaly to Theseus. For him, the simple act of signing the final agreement rendered incongruous the hundreds upon hundreds of attorney hours devoted to getting the parties to the closing table. But for the parties, they now had their bargain. Theseus knew that if the lawyers had done their job properly, the Eumenides would be contained. The parties traded fate for the laws of contract. Like in the trail of Orestes presided by Athena, the lawgiver was greater than even the Eumenides.

"Time to celebrate, my friends!" Minos finally exclaimed.

Minos stepped out of the room for a moment and came back with Borus pushing a handcart with several bottles of fine champagne. Borus dutifully popped the corks on two bottles, poured the champagne and passed out the glasses.

"Let me propose a toast," Minos said taking center stage.

"To Pedocles and the great company he has built," Minos saluted. "Welcome to Asterion, my friend. May we all become rich and retire before we are too old to spend it."

Pedocles finally managed a smile, and raised his glass.

"To all of you who have helped make this happen, my great appreciation," Pedocles said looking around the room. "And to you, Minos, who now must take the lead."

Theseus said there was one last detail. He told Rhesus to bring in the notary.

Rhesus did as asked, and the notary came into the room. He was handed the signed registration papers that needed to be filed.

Theseus told Diocles to accompany the gentleman to the registry office. The notary looked surprised.

"That won't be necessary," he replied. "I have done this

many, many times. I will return directly with confirmation of the filing."

Theseus said he insisted, and motioned both men out the door. Theseus, thinking of Keos, was not about to chance a possible diversion by the Theban functionary.

14

Theseus felt abnormally fatigued after finishing with Nemean, and he was not eager to go back to the office. If offered a taste of the plant of the Lotos eaters, Theseus thought, he would not refuse it. A few days respite away from his practice would do him good. He recalled Ariadne's invitation to meet her in Chalcis. Maybe now was a propitious time to reciprocate and make it up to her. Before he boarded his plane back to Athens, he gave Ariadne a ring.

"I could probably swing a day or two," Ariadne said pleasantly surprised by the call. "What do you have in mind?"

Theseus told Ariadne that he could be in Crete by the evening and that she should meet him at the port in Iraklion. He also told her to pack a weekend bag.

"Theseus, you have to give me more than that," was Ariadne's reply. "What I am supposed to bring?"

Not sure himself, Theseus just said to have comfortable clothes and maybe something for the beach. He then called Ophelia to alert her of the plan.

When Theseus landed in Athens, he walked through the terminal straight away to grab a taxi. When he reached the front of the taxi line, the cab driver put his bags in the trunk. The cabbie got into the driver's seat, rolled down his window and grabbed a green flag off the front passenger seat. Theseus had forgotten that the country was holding elections that day.

"The results should be very close," the driver said.

The cabbie turned up the radio which was set to a station carrying the returns. He hung the flag out his window and drove off. Traffic was heavy and car horns blared. Many vehicles on the road displayed red flags. People yelled at each other when stopped at intersections.

As the taxi spun around the city square, large intermittent groups of people waving banners were staging rallies. The election was hotly contested, and the national democrats and Pan-Hellenic socialists were both anticipating victory. The cab driver circled the square several times, all the while waving his flag and shouting at passersby. Theseus relished the spectacle and disorder of free elections.

When Theseus got to his flat, he quickly changed and found the overnight bag Ophelia had packed. Ophelia had left a large envelope for him and arranged for his driver. He was taken to the port of Piraeus, where a cruise charter was waiting. Theseus boarded and settled in for the long voyage to Iraklion. He had something to eat and napped. When he was about an hour away, he rang Ariadne.

"So where are we going?" Ariadne asked with some excitement.

Theseus realized he hadn't thought that far ahead, and said the destination would have to wait. He laid back in his recliner and pulled out Ophelia's envelope. He sorted through some letters, then saw a reservation slip for the Aegean Hotel in Agios.

The ship arrived in port on schedule, and Ariadne was waiting when Theseus walked off the pier. Ariadne wore a lace camisole under a denim jacket and tiered eyelet shorts, and her dark hair draped freely about her shoulders. She carried a duffle bag over her shoulder. Ariadne waved and greeted Theseus with an affectionate smile.

When Ariadne approached, Theseus awkwardly reached for her duffle. He did not embrace her. He was unsure of the etiquette he should follow, and did not want to be more demonstrative than was appropriate. Ariadne respected his standoffishness, but was confused by it. She apparently was expecting some greater show of affection from him.

"Theseus, what a wonderful idea for you to come," Ariadne said.

Theseus hailed a taxi and told the driver to take them to the Aegean.

"The Aegean Hotel, in Agios?" Ariadne shrieked. "Theseus, how did you know I've always wanted to go there. I hear it's very chic."

Theseus asked the driver how long the drive would be.

"Oh, about fifty kilometers to the east," the driver said

with a wide grin. "Yes, the very best. My favorite in Crete."

When they arrived, Theseus gave the driver a very generous tip, and did the same with the porter. The bags were taken to reception in the elegant lobby of the hotel. Ariadne excused herself to make a phone call while Theseus settled the room arrangements. The bellhop led them to two adjoining villas on the beach that shared a private pool. Theseus did not want to test Ariadne's virtue or appear presumptuous. Theseus recalled that Odysseus took pains to avoid having the good name of the maiden Nausicaa sullied after Nausicaa had found him threadbare and exposed on the shore of the island ruled by Alcinous, her father and king of the Phaeacians.

Ariadne was ebullient when they arrived at the villas. She had never seen such a lovely place. The villas had spectacular views of the Mediterranean.

"Theseus," Ariadne said looking overjoyed, "I don't know what to say. This is marvelous."

Theseus was pleased with the lodgings.

They had dinner next to the private pool, then strolled the hotel grounds as it was getting dark.

Theseus woke the next morning feeling refreshed. He knocked on Ariadne's door, and told her to wear something appropriate for touring. They went to the main hotel for brunch. After eating, Theseus had mopeds brought up and the two were soon on the coastal roads of Crete heading toward Cnossos. Ariadne rode ahead. Theseus could not remember feeling better. When they reached Cnossos, Theseus was eager to explore.

Theseus led Ariadne along the dusty path toward the archaeological excavations. They took up with a guide who walked them to the decayed walls that were once the foundation of the ancient palace. Theseus felt a sense of awe and wonder as he traversed the site. The guide spoke of the mysteries shrouding the ceremonies and rituals that took place there. Theseus knew that at one time, Cnossos was an early center of culture and trade in the Greek world. And it had a unique place in the development of the law.

Discoveries had shown that the first instances of written law could be traced to Cnossos.

Theseus gazed upon the famous fresco of bull jumpers, dolphins and partridges that had been restored at the palace. He imagined himself there when Cnossos was in its full glory.

"I don't know if it's the sun or air," Ariadne said looking weak, "but I feel faint and need something to drink. Why don't we find a place where I can rest, then maybe you can go on ahead."

Theseus located a bench shaded by a large olive tree, and fetched a bottle of sparkling water for Ariadne to sip. Theseus did not wander off, but stayed with her.

"Theseus," Ariadne said after regaining some strength, "how much have you been able to learn about Minos? I have serious reservations about Asterion."

Theseus laughed and told Ariadne that Minos was well in hand.

"I am afraid that you will find yourself in a situation that might be difficult to get out of," Ariadne pleaded. "Listen to me."

Theseus told her that he saw the pitfalls in representing Minos, but that there was no reason for concern. If Asterion goes sideways, he would see it coming. She needn't worry.

They returned to the villas and had a quiet evening. The next day was spent mostly near the water. Theseus enjoyed the sun and salty air. Ariadne again brought up Minos as the two where relaxing on the beach.

"Now that you've closed Nemean," Ariadne started, "Minos will move rapidly to do the stock offering."

Theseus knew that was in the plans, and said so.

"Well, you will have a problem with the deal team," said Ariadne. "Minos plans to hire an underwriting firm that is second tier, if that. He's been working with them already, and they are sleazy. He will want to use his current accountants, who have little experience with pubic companies. Minos will work you to keep them in because he knows he can control what they do. If you let that happen, you will expose yourself and your firm. You are going to need to get a top investment bank involved to sell his deal, Theseus, and a competent accounting firm to do the audit. You know there will be substantial international accounting issues."

Ariadne was right in her view that the deal would require reputable, competent professionals, Theseus admitted. Poor underwriters and unknown accountants were sure to create obstacles. Up until then, he hadn't given it much thought. He told her that he appreciated her observations, and he would address the issues with Minos when he first had the opportunity.

"He will fight you on this," Ariadne persisted, "like a lion cornered by hunters."

They spent the remaining daylight lounging on the sand. As Theseus looked about the landscape, it occurred to him that the splendid view paled in comparison to Ariadne's beauty. Theseus found Ariadne not only enchanting but a good companion. Theseus thought about the nature of this counterfeit creature. Was Ariadne like the blessed Alcetis or the cursed Clytemnestra, or a strange mixture of both? Theseus' mind raced until he decided his enquiry was a pointless distraction.

Theseus and Ariadne had dinner later in the restaurant and called it a night. Theseus was booked on a ship going from Iraklion back to Piraeus first thing in the morning.

15

Not long after Theseus returned from Crete, Minos invited Theseus and Tantalus to his summer residence on the island of Rhodes. Minos arranged to pick them up at the Athens airport. He was bringing a private plane, which would save five hours sailing time. Theseus soon learned that Minos was earning his pilot's license and would be flying the plane, but there would be an experienced copilot on board. Minos had Asterion buy into a time share that provided easy access to aircraft when needed. Although Asterion was technically the account for the time share, Theseus was all but certain no one other than Minos ever took advantage of the service.

The plane seated six passengers comfortably. Because Minos was flying the plane, Theseus and Tantalus stayed back alone in the passenger compartment with a flight attendant named Iole. Tantalus was noticeably excited having the young lady on board. Her blue black hair curled at her shoulders and she had a pleasing smile.

"Hey, Iole," Tantalus said to her, "what will you be doing tonight? Are you staying on Rhodes for the return flight? Why don't you hang out with us, you know, have a few drinks and dinner. We're staying at the Camirus Club. You can meet up with us later. Maybe you know some other girls on the island."

Iole was obviously accustomed to being propositioned by passengers, but didn't dismiss Tantalus' invitation out of hand. Theseus saw Iole pass a glance at him. She was trying to size up the situation, he thought. Theseus noticed her smart uniform, high heel pumps and scarf tied neatly about her neck.

"Well," Iole said, "I'm not scheduled to fly back until tomorrow, and I do have a friend I can call. But I don't know. Let's see how the flight goes."

Iole walked to the back of the plane. Tantalus leaned over to speak to Theseus.

"Come on, man," Tantalus whispered, "I bet that woman

is a handful. Mino's wife would love it if we can get her to dinner, so she won't be alone with a couple of stiff lawyers."

Iole came back to take drink orders.

"Will you be having dinner, too?" Iole asked Theseus.

Theseus answered that he supposed he would.

Iole smiled, and again went to the rear.

Minos came out of the cockpit of the plane in fine spirits. He was obviously aching to get off the ground.

"Buckle up, men," Minos crowed. "We are about to set sail. We'll be in Rhodes in about an hour. Iole taking good care of you guys?"

Minos gave Theseus a wink.

"I asked for her specifically for this flight," Minos quipped.

"She'll be with us for more than the flight," Tantalus said rubbing his hands together. "She wants to join us for dinner. Bringing a friend, too."

Minos looked at Tantalus bemused.

"Wasting no time, are we Tantalus?" Minos said.

"Damn right!" Tantalus replied beaming.

Theseus and Tantalus relaxed in their seats and Minos went back up to the cockpit. Within a few moments, the plane taxied to the runway.

"This is going to be better than I thought, Theseus," Tantalus proclaimed. "A good dinner and a couple of women. Fantastic."

The aircraft was positioned for liftoff. As the wheels came up off the ground, the plane lurched violently upward in a steep ascent. Theseus and Tantalus were jerked back into their seats.

"What the hell!" Tantalus screamed as he gripped the armrests of his seat. "Who is flying this thing? God almighty!"

The plane continued its upward motion and then started rocking to and fro. As the plane began to level off, it seemed to drop down repeatedly. Theseus and Tantalus felt their stomachs in their throats.

"Damn," Tantalus sputtered.

Tantalus looked as if he was going to be sick.

"Are you two all right?" Iole asked loudly from the rear. Her voice had a tinge of real concern.

The aircraft finally stabilized, but Tantalus was perspiring. Iole brought out ouzo to settle things down. Tantalus drank his quickly.

"That's what you call a textbook takeoff," Minos announced confidently over the intercom. "Now sit back and enjoy, men."

Tantalus didn't say a word for the rest of the flight.

The silence gave Theseus a few welcome moments with his own thoughts. Theseus started to wonder about Minos and his venture. Minos was gregarious and had that confident swagger common to many entrepreneurs. He didn't lack for charisma. Both men and women were drawn to him, it was clear. Theseus knew these qualities should not be underestimated, but they were far from guaranteeing success. Minos obviously was leading a fine life with all the accoutrements of wealth. Theseus questioned where the money was coming from. Asterion was still a fledgling company and wasn't generating any measurable revenues much less a profit. It could be some time before that occurred. Theseus thought it implausible the money all came from Talos Bank.

And why was he taken by Tantalus? Of all the lawyers he could hire, why Tantalus? Engaging the firm made sense. It gave Asterion credibility and ballast. But the relationship with Tantalus was a puzzle.

Theseus also asked himself why they were making this jaunt to Rhodes. They could just as easily have met in Crete or Athens and saved a day. Maybe Minos liked entertaining or just wanted to show off his seaside residence. Maybe Minos was one of those people that fit his work into the rest of what he was doing. Perhaps he was simply conducting business on the go.

Theseus then thought about Ariadne's warnings. He began to feel as if Asterion was a strange mixture of promise and danger, not only for himself but for the firm. There were

Theseus

many angles to the venture and wildly different potential outcomes. It wasn't at all evident to Theseus what the final conclusion would be. He felt he needed to get a better handle on the risks Asterion presented. Minos had to manage a significant acquisition quickly and efficiently, and he hadn't built out his staff or sales team or put a functional board of directors in place. Even if Minos was successful in all of that, he would have to maneuver a difficult process before the securities commission if he was to complete a public offering. The company had the potential to be a colossal failure for everyone involved.

While Theseus reflected on these things, the plane began to descend. The way down wasn't any better than the takeoff. The plane dropped precipitously which prompted another outcry from Tantalus. Minos took the plane in way too low, and Theseus could see the treetops almost touching the wings. The wheels hit the runway hard and the plane bounced up nearly out of control. Instead of taking the airplane up for another try, Minos brought the plane down again and braked hard. If they hadn't been belted, Tantalus and Theseus would both have been thrown into the cockpit. The plane veered to a stop just short of the runway's edge.

Iole appeared again from the back of the plane, looking a little tousled from the landing.

"So we'll see you later tonight, Iole?" Tantalus cajoled. "And you'll bring someone for my friend here?"

"I think that will work out," Iole said throwing a cursory look Theseus' way. "Hope you enjoyed the flight."

Minos had a limousine waiting. The group drove to Camirus, a secluded grounds covering a huge expanse along the east coast of Rhodes. In addition to slips for numerous yachts, the club had an equestrian center, pool, spa and fitness facility, tennis courts, lawn bowling and golf course.

Minos declared he wanted to get a round of golf in before dinner. Theseus had not known this was the plan and did not bring clubs or golf attire.

"Don't worry, Theseus," Minos said, "I'll have the pro shop get you what you need. What clubs do you play?"

Within minutes of arriving at the club, Theseus had a new pair of golf shoes, slacks, leather belt and shirt with a finely stitched logo. A set of clubs that matched his own was brought out to the range.

Minos was already practicing when Theseus came out to the course. Although Minos was athletic, it was evident he hadn't played golf when he was young. He had a stiff, jerky swing. Theseus found it painful to watch. At the top of the backswing, he stopped, rotated his hips and then swung down with his hands. This caused him to come over the top on the downswing, creating a massive slice. Tantalus showed, and teed up a few drives. He didn't manage to get a single ball in the air.

Minos and Tantalus carded big numbers over the eighteen holes. Theseus was content with a relatively good round on a difficult track.

After golf, Minos reserved a table in the club's dining room. His wife Daphne would be joining them. The men went to the bar and Minos sat down on a stool. Tantalus was looking around for Iole.

Theseus asked Minos what investment banks he had talked to about the planned stock offering.

"The banker is all set, guys I've worked with for a while," Minos said.

Theseus asked who they were.

"A group called Orthrus Financial Ltd.," said Minos.

Theseus told Minos he didn't know anyone there, and wasn't aware of their reputation in underwriting technology issues.

"They say they can do it," Minos said getting a little testy. "I've already signed an engagement letter with them."

"Where in the hell is Iole?" Tantalus asked.

Tantalus left to find her.

Theseus cautioned Minos that the firm would have problems working on the offering if Orthrus didn't check out.

"What's that supposed to mean, Theseus?" Minos snapped.

Theseus explained that a reputable and qualified underwriter was important because of the due diligence they would perform. They would do their own independent investigation of Asterion and help draft the appropriate disclosure in the prospectus. This was essential for development stage companies. A top firm would also provide the best market execution ensuring the widest possible distribution of the stock. That would be critical for the trading market. Theseus said flatly that unless Asterion used a qualified underwriter, one that had a deal list for bringing technology companies to market, the firm would likely step aside.

"Step aside then," Minos said fuming.

Just then Daphne came up carry two armfuls of shopping bags.

"Hey darling," Daphne said as Minos stood up and gave her a kiss. "You look bothered. Bad day on the course or something?"

"Oh, just having a little business chat with Theseus," Minos said cooling down.

"How are you, Theseus," Daphne said. "Nice that you could come."

Tantalus, excited, returned with Iole and her friend Polyxena in tow. Iole was wearing a short black dress with a low neckline. Polyxena was in a tight fitting cherry outfit. She had air blown bleached blonde hair, and wore bright lipstick and heavy blush. Theseus took note of Polyxena's wide eyed mien.

"Look what I found," Tantalus announced. "Ladies, we're in for a fun evening."

The party took its table in the main dining room. Iole worked to secure her seat next to Theseus and across from Tantalus. Daphne talked about her shopping and Minos ordered some light hors d'oeuvres.

The waiter, dressed elegantly in a black waistcoat and bow tie, asked if the table would be ordering wine for dinner. He handed Minos the wine list.

"Don't bother with that," Tantalus shouted grabbing the

wine list from Minos hands. "Waiter, bring me your other list."

The waiter responded that this was the restaurant's only wine list.

"No," Tantalus countered. "I want to know what you have in the back, you know, in reserve. Go check it out."

The waiter didn't care for Tantalus' attitude, but agreed to see if there was anything else they might have in stock.

"I'll bet he comes back with some good choices," Tantalus started in. "There is always something special for the high rollers."

Tantalus started to recount his good if not rare shots on the back side. But before he got too far the waiter had returned.

"Sir, as it happens, we have just received a case of rare Bacchus selections," the waiter said tersely. "Will that do?"

"Well, it depends on the years you have," Tantalus cracked, obviously pleased. "Tell us what you've got."

"I'll check the vintage, sir," the waiter said grimacing.

Minos seemed amused by Tantalus. Minos started talking about his round.

"I hit an unbelievable shot on that long par three," Minos said. "I only left myself about a ten footer for birdie."

"Yeah, but you three putted for a bogey!" Tantalus laughed. "You've got to give up those lessons. They don't make a damn bit of difference, Minos. I played as good as you and I've never had a lesson. It's not that hard a game."

"It's an easy game when you don't count strokes and pick up on half the holes," Minos said. "That was a pathetic move you made on thirteen."

Minos was referring to Tantalus's attempt to card a winning but inaccurate score on the hole. Tantalus had yanked his tee shot left into a crevice along the tree line and whiffed twice before he hit the ball. Tantalus tried to card a six on the hole, without counting his whiffs. Minos called him on the missed swings. Tantalus claimed they were practice swings. The argument got a little heated until Tantalus relented and admitted the whiffs.

Theseus

The waiter returned.

"It would appear we have several '95s, sir," the waiter said.

"Come on, my friend, what else?" Tantalus pressed.

The waiter cleared his throat.

"We also have '80, '82 and '83 bottles," he said.

"Now we are getting somewhere," Tantalus said hardly able to contain himself. "Let's start with the '82, then the '83. Hold the '80 for later."

"Very good, sir," the waiter said.

"Very good indeed!" Tantalus chortled. "We'll start with the best and work our way down."

Theseus caught Minos rolling his eyes. Tantalus was almost giddy. Iole and Polyxena were not sure what to make of Tantalus.

The waiter soon returned and uncorked the Bacchus '82. Theseus found the wine excellent.

Polyxena asked about what the men did, and Tantalus said he and Theseus were big time lawyers helping Minos build an empire.

"Oh, so you're in politics," Polyxena said evidently clueless. "That sounds interesting."

Minos and Daphne started talking about some of the furnishings Daphne had bought for their new home in the city, including a new grand piano. Theseus doubted either played a note. Iole nudged closer to Theseus and asked him why he became a lawyer.

Before he could muster an answer, dinner was served. Everyone ordered light, except Tantalus. He had a steak exceedingly rare and made a spectacle of himself as he ate it. The '83 and '80 bottles came and went, and Theseus thought the '80 was undoubtedly inferior to the other vintages. Tantalus' knowledge surprised him.

By the time dinner was over, everyone was feeling the effects of the wine. Tantalus was getting loud, and seeing Iole's interest in Theseus, started to fawn over Polyxena. When the bill came, Tantalus excused himself and left the table. Minos looked to Theseus to pick up the tab, which was exorbitant. The Bacchus proved to be a small fortune.

Tantalus came back to collect Polyxena and the entire table retreated to the bar.

Iole centered her attention on Theseus, and they talked for a time. Theseus found her to be quite charming.

"Do you think Polyxena will be safe with him?" Iole asked Theseus.

Theseus saw Tantalus groping Polyxena, and she was resisting.

"Why don't you and I go someplace, Theseus?" Iole said smiling. "Maybe somewhere a little more private. Those two look like they'll be busy for a while."

Theseus said that sounded like a fine idea, but he had matters that needed attention early the next morning. He told her perhaps another time.

"Oh, alright, maybe another time," Iole said thwarted. "It is getting late."

Iole got up to leave, and said goodnight to Minos and Daphne. Minos walked her out. Iole stopped on the way to check on Polyxena. Tantalus wasn't about to let her go, and Polyxena had stopped struggling. Theseus watched Minos escort Iole to the front door with his arm about her waist. As they stood talking to each other Theseus saw that Daphne was watching. She turned to Theseus looking mortified.

"Well," Daphne said, "I hope you boys keep an eye on Minos. He can get distracted."

When Minos returned, Theseus got up to leave.

"I'll talk to the bankers you recommend, Theseus," Minos said to him. "I want you guys on the deal. But you better be able to keep Tantalus under control. I don't want him screwing the thing up."

Minos took Theseus and Tantalus back to Attica midmorning the next day. Tantalus was tired and hung over. Iole hadn't shown for the return flight. Her place was taken by a young male attendant.

"That Polyxena turned out to be a handful," Tantalus said to Theseus as they took their seats. "How'd you do with Iole?"

Theseus said they had a nice time.

"Excellent," Tantalus responded tilting back his seat. "She was a real piece."

Tantalus quickly fell asleep and didn't wake until the plane landed in Attica.

16

Pirithous started urging Theseus to move on Aegeus' proposal to join the executive committee. He thought Theseus had waited long enough.

"Periphetes and Sinn were both great deals, Theseus," Pirithous told him. "You have people talking. I heard even Aietes was impressed."

Theseus was still not ready. Asterion was moving along but there was the public offering to do, and that was months off. Theseus was looking through his current work load to see if there was something notable that might develop. Just as he was doing this, Theseus received a call from Thero, a hedge fund operator that specialized in merger arbitrage. Theseus assisted Thero from time to time with legal questions on companies that might be on the block.

"There are reports out that the management of Damastes is starting to purchase shares," Thero told Theseus. "The company's stock has plunged. I wonder what management is up to? I've been accumulating the stock. Can you look into this for me?"

Theseus said he would, but advised Thero not to buy any more shares.

Damastes Drilling was a public company that had oil development interests in various parts of Attica and Laconia. Damastes' stock performance had lagged the market for years, and many investors had lost money in the company.

Theseus called Calliope into his office that evening and had her research Damastes' public filings. Theseus then contacted one of his energy partners. They talked about what the insiders at Damastes might be up to. Theseus' partner arranged a call for the next morning with an oil client called Chimaera Energy. Theseus thought they might know what was going on with Damastes. When Theseus got to the office the following morning, Calliope had completed her research.

"Damastes stated in its annual report that its last major oil field investment in Laconia was a disaster," Calliope told

Theseus. "They said tests had indicated that the Laconia field was dry."

On the call with Chimaera, Theseus asked what they knew about Damastes' dry well in Laconia. Chimaera said that the reports from the drilling were very preliminary. Chimaera also knew that some geological studies done on nearby areas showed potentially sizeable reserves.

Chimaera years ago had expressed an interest in possibly acquiring Damastes, and Theseus asked if that were still true. The company said they would look at it again. Theseus told Chimaera that it would have to act quickly if it wanted to preempt other bidders. There were indications Damastes might be in play. Chimaera said they would get their financial advisors on it. Theseus in turn had his people look for any antitakeover defenses Damastes might have in place.

About ten days passed, and then events began to move quickly. Chimaera's bankers performed a financial analysis of Damastes, and concluded that if the Laconia field was productive the stock of Damastes was significantly undervalued. The Chimaera board would be meeting in a few days to consider its options. Chimaera management told Theseus to start preparing a tender offer just in case the board decided on that course. Theseus called Alcaeus and asked him to oversee the drafting of the tender documents.

Theseus convinced Chimaera to hire a proxy services firm to analyze the Damastes shareholder base. A large number of institutional investors would prove ideal. Institutional investors were more oriented toward short term profits and likely to support a tender.

At the special meeting of the Chimaera board of directors, which Theseus attended, Chimaera's financial advisors presented their analysis. The Damastes stock was trading at a five year low. Even if the Laconia field was dry, at current prices the stock had little risk in it. The financial advisors agreed to deliver a fairness opinion to the board confirming their assessment of the stock's value. An engineering consultant told the board that the probability of substantial oil deposits in Laconia was high. The proxy firm reported back that institutional positions approached seventy percent of outstanding shares of Damastes. Theseus informed the board that the certificate of incorporation and bylaws of Damastes were clean of antitakeover defenses. No staggered board, no supermajority voting requirements, no shareholder rights plans. There were no legal hurdles for a tender. Chimaera management told the board that debt financing for a tender had been secured from a syndicate of commercial banks. The banks were willing to take the Damastes assets as collateral if the deal was successful.

Several members of the Chimaera board raised the possibility of engaging Damastes in direct talks and negotiating a friendly merger. Theseus strongly advised against this. Approaching Damastes to discuss a merger would introduce delay and give Damastes the opportunity to seek higher bids. Chimaera management also did not trust Damastes to negotiate a merger in good faith. The board voted to act aggressively and pursue the tender.

With everything in order, the board of Chimaera authorized a tender offer for a minimum of fifty one percent of the shares of Damastes at a substantial premium over the current market price of the stock. The offer would be launched the next day after the stock market close. Theseus had his team work through the night preparing the tender offer documents for filing with the securities commission. The wording of the fairness opinion to be delivered by the financial advisors to Chimaera's board was reviewed and finalized. The negotiations with the commercial banks for the loan were quickly concluded and the loan documents completed. Press releases were prepared.

The following afternoon, the tender offer was filed with the commission and a public announcement of the offer was released by Chimaera. The offer was required by law to remain open for twenty days, and Theseus knew that competing offers could emerge and Chimaera might have to increase its price. Theseus did not know how Damastes would react. There was the chance the Damastes board would reject the offer as inadequate and search for a white

Theseus

knight. A bidding war could erupt.

Theseus also knew the tender offer would bring lawsuits and administrative inquiries. Theseus had his litigators prepare defense motions to the myriad complaints likely to be filed.

Lawsuits were indeed filed against Chimaera attempting to enjoin the tender. The plaintiffs bar for shareholder suites was specialized, well organized and surly. Shareholders of record for companies likely in play were needed as plaintiffs, and the firms had them identified and compensated in advance for the use of their names. Off the shelf complaints were ready for filing within hours after a tender offer was announced. Securities fraud, board conflicts of interest and breach of fiduciary duties were the standard causes of action. The better plaintiffs' firms normally had statements of fact prepared for companies that were potential targets. Damastes must have been on the radars of several firms because the first few complaints filed were detailed and comprehensive. There was a race to the courthouse with this kind of litigation, because the earlier a firm's name was before the court the better the chance of being named lead shareholders counsel. That was where the big money was made.

Surprisingly, Damastes did not fight the Chimaera offer. Theseus learned the Damastes board had its own investment bankers review the offer and conduct a market check. No competing offers for Damastes surfaced. The Damastes board eventually came out in support of the offer. It came to light that the Damastes board was in fact unhappy with Damastes management and welcomed the offer as an honorable way to sell the company. Many of the Damastes directors stood to become exceedingly wealthy and had no reservation about a sale.

With the Damastes directors in line, Theseus worked quickly to dispose of the shareholder suits. He convened a settlement conference with the attorneys representing the shareholders. He was unsure going in to the discussions how rapidly and at what price he could achieve a settlement.

Theseus learned that Euippos, a savvy and experienced plaintiffs' lawyer, had been appointed lead counsel by the court. Theseus and Euippos were on opposing sides of a very contentious piece of litigation years before over some defaulted bonds, and came to like and respect each other. That was long ago, and nearly forgotten. At the settlement conference, Euippos greeted Theseus like Diomedes greeted Glaukos during a battle on the plain between the rivers of Xanthos and Sinoeis in Troy. Within a few hours, Theseus and Euippos worked out a settlement. Chimaera agreed to increase the tender price three percent and the suits would be dismissed.

By the end of the tender period, over ninety percent of Damastes' stock was tendered to Chimaera in the offer. The purchase of the stock was completed over the next thirty days.

Aegeus rang Theseus to say he received a call from the chairman of Chimaera's board.

"He said you were central to the whole maneuver," Aegeus told Theseus. "You had complete control of the process and every angle covered. He told me your intuition on what was to happen was uncanny and your tactics were simply superb. Theseus, we need to renew our discussion about you on the executive committee. I won't have you put this off any longer."

Within a few months new studies of the Laconia oil field proved out huge reserves, and the stock of Chimaera soared. Chimera was more than happy to pay the substantial fee the firm charged for its work.

17

With Damastes behind him, Theseus turned his attention back to Asterion. Minos agreed to talk to an investment bank called Typhon Securities at Theseus' recommendation. Theseus had worked with Typhon many times before. The bank had extensive experience in the burgeoning technology space and had a strong international distribution franchise. A Typhon banker named Axylus was called in to make the pitch to Minos. Theseus knew his reputation as a hard charging banker who took no prisoners.

Axylus invited Minos and Theseus to boxing night at the Acropolis Club in Athens. Theseus assumed Axylus wanted to size up Minos and secure the engagement. Tantalus somehow managed an invite through Minos, and Minos brought with him Asterion's outside accountant whose name was Nomion. A couple of Axylus' younger colleagues and a few traders from the underwriting desk at Typhon rounded out the group. Tuxedos were the required attire for the event.

"Hello, my good man," Axylus greeted Theseus at the reception before the bouts, "it's been a while. Where's this Minos fellow you told me about? I'd like to drum up some business here tonight. Thanks for bringing us in."

Axylus was of good height and wiry. His nose was long, thin and straight, he had a high forehead and his hair was ash blonde and greased back. Axylus' black tie underscored his well polished image.

"I've heard about some of your recent deals, Theseus," Axylus commented. "Wish we had been on them, to be blunt about it."

Tantalus arrived and was introduced by Theseus to Axylus.

"We've got to get this deal signed and delivered fast," Tantalus barked at Axylus as he surveyed the room. "It'll move like a bat out of hell, if you know what I mean."

"Well," Axylus said looking Tantalus up and down with a discerning eye, "let's see what we can do."

Theseus was presented by Axylus to Stolos, his younger senior manager. Stolos was slightly taller than Axylus with oiled hair in the Axylus style. His bearing and demeanor mimicked his boss. Stolos didn't have much to say, but seemed agreeable enough. Theseus assumed Stolos was like most of the younger investment bankers he knew, eager and hungry to make his mark. Well to do guys from good business schools who knew how to handle themselves. Axylus had Theseus also meet the traders. They were older and coarse in comparison to the bankers. Traders normally didn't mix well with the banker set. Many of them probably hadn't made it through college and had worked their way up from the mailroom. The traders would be in the background on the deal and Theseus would have little to do with them.

Theseus pointed out Minos to Axylus when he entered the reception area with Nomion. Axylus made his way over with Stolos. Theseus waited to see the practiced affectation of the bankers when they approached Minos. Investment bankers were at their disingenuous best with clients with promising deals. Axylus greeted Minos with a big smile and a slap on the back. Stolos flashed an exaggerated grin.

The reception eventually moved upstairs to the main dining room. It was a great ornate space with royal blue carpet and surrounding Ionic columns. Massive chandeliers dropped down from the ceilings. Large portraits of club presidents and captains of industry with gold frames hung on the walls. A raised boxing ring stood in the center of the room, and long dining tables hugged the ropes on all four sides. Serving stations for drinks were set up in each corner and the lines were forming.

Theseus sat down next to Minos. Minos was buoyant as ever. He was enjoying the banker's attention and was itching to see some high quality bouts.

"What could be better, Theseus," Minos said. "A couple of drinks, a few cigars, maybe a good fight or two. Beats the office."

Minos drew closer to Theseus.

"What do you think of this Axylus?" Minos murmured.

"He seems a bit high and mighty to me. Can he get my deal done? I don't know what kind of window we have with the market. I need someone who can produce."

Axylus came over and took a seat. He passed out cigars and had a waiter lay out four bottles of wine on the table.

Fight night had begun. There were to be eight bouts. The matches would feature two amateur boxing clubs, one from Scythia and the other from Chaonia.

Axylus stood up and handed out fight information and bout cards to everyone at the table. The information sheet showed each of the boxer's height, weight and won lost record. There was a bout card for each fight.

"Listen up," Axylus commanded. "Fill out your cards when the fighters come out. Take a good look at them before you pick. Once they enter the ring, betting closes. Fifty buck minimum per fight."

The table studied the boxer abstracts over dinner. The fare included black bean soup, arugula salad, porterhouse steaks and twice baked potatoes. Raspberry cheesecake was served at the finish.

"Hey, Axylus," Minos said "when do you think we can get the offering done? You think you guys can knock this thing out?"

"As soon as you have your financial statements consolidating Nemean," Axylus responded, "we can get started. How are those coming?"

Minos looked over at Nomion.

"We're working on them," Nomion said a bit nervously. "There are some issues to work out. Theban accounting principles are different than ours."

Axylus looked at Theseus and then at Minos. Nomion was not engendering confidence.

"I've been working with Nomion on the statements," Minos said. "They're coming along."

"We'll do a cross border offering for best execution," Axylus offered. "There will be great traction with institutions in Lydia. We'll need our lawyer friends to get going on the disclosure."

"Screw that, Ax ol' chap," Tantalus, sitting next to Theseus, jumped in. "Theseus will be all over the offering documents. You've got the best damn law firm on this. Minos knows it."

Minos just nodded.

"Where are the fights?" Tantalus continued, getting obstreperous. "Let's see some boxing!"

The referee appeared with the master of ceremonies and both entered the ring to whistles and cheers. The announcer greeted the crowd and introduced his female assistants, two buxom young ladies whose job it was to carry the placards for each round. They were in sequin cocktail dresses and spiked heels. The brunette wore red, the blond wore blue. The gentleman crowd did not hide their pleasure at the sight of the women.

"Tonight's fights are between two premier boxing clubs," the announcer told the audience. "All proceeds go to charity, so to give you an opportunity to donate we will auction off our beautiful assistants. Each winner will accompany one of our assistants in announcing the rounds. Let's start the bidding for the opening contest."

"I want some of that," brayed Tantalus raising his hand to make the opening bid.

The announcer worked the room in an effort to get the highest offer. Tantalus kept raising his bid, taking the first bout. He jumped from his seat and sprinted up the steps to the ring. Almost falling as he bent down through the ropes, he quickly had his arms around the two girls. The crowd laughed and jeered.

The first fight was a lightweight bout. The boxers came through the dining room entrance, and everyone had about twenty seconds to decide their bets.

"Go with the Scythian," Minos said to Theseus. "They are the better street fighters."

The boxers entered the ring and were presented to the crowd. Tantalus circled the canvass with the blond fight assistant carrying the sign for round one. Each fight would be three rounds with each round lasting three minutes. At the bell, the fighters came out swinging. Lightweights were usually quick and aggressive, and these boxers were no exception. The Chaonian entrant was taller with the longer reach. The Scythian tried to get inside quickly with a flurry of punches. Both were more inclined to hit than avoid getting hit, and a fair number of punches landed on both sides. The smaller Scythian took several right hooks that had him off balance, but he was able to land an upper cut that staggered the Chaonian boxer. The Scythian fighter landed more punches by the end of the first round, and his Chaonian opponent looked dazed. Blood started pouring out from over his left eye. The fight was mercifully called by the referee for the Scythian a minute into the second round.

The crowd was happy with the fight judging from the root and holler. Tantalus came back to the table beaming.

"God, the woman is something, let me tell you," Tantalus boasted. "I'm going after that later tonight."

The bouts went up the weight classes. Punches became less frequent but more powerful as the night wore on. Most fights were decided by the scoring of the judges, but like the first bout there were a couple of matches called. The young men were reasonably trained and exhibited solid boxing technique. Even with the heavy head gear worn by the amateurs, there were plenty of blood and red faces over the course of the evening. On balance, the Scythian boxers were winning most of the fights. Minos was overall the biggest winner, Tantalus the loser.

The last fight was a heavyweight bout between a young and round Chaonian and a very muscular, more mature Scythian. The table bet heavily on the Scythian. The Chaonian was on his heals from the start of the first round and took a lot of blows. Theseus didn't think he would make it the full three rounds. The second round was more of the same. The Chaonian was taking hits and his face was spilling blood. The crowd wanted a knockdown, but the Chaonian fighter stubbornly kept in the fight. At the start of the third round, the Scythian grew tired. His punches weren't landing. Theseus was reminded of the combat between Aias and

Hector that ended in a draw. The Chaonia fighter moved in and began connecting with strong punches to the head. The Scythian grew wobbly and the Chaonian boxer kept at him. The fight looked like it should have been called, but the referee let it go. With about a minute to go, the Chaonian landed a left to the face and the Scythian went down hard. The crowd roared. It took several minutes before they could get the Scythian to his feet.

The wager on the last fight was the largest of the night, with Tantalus throwing in the most. Theseus and Minos were the only ones betting on the Chaonian.

"I love taking other people's money," Minos said to Theseus as the bouts ended.

The traders got up and left. Axylus went to get a drink and asked Theseus to join him.

"We need to get a new accounting firm in quickly, Theseus," Axylus said. "I can't get this through our investment committee at Typhon with who Minos has right now. My guess is Nomion doesn't know the first thing about international accounting."

Theseus said he agreed, and told Axylus he should talk to Minos about it before the night was over.

Theseus noticed that Tantalus was gamboling with the female attendants near the ring. Nomion and Minos were at the table with Stolos.

Axylus walked back to the table and whispered something to Stolos. Stolos and Nomion got up and walked out of the room. Minos and Axylus began talking and Theseus could tell Minos was getting upset. Minos got up quickly and went right for Theseus.

"What did you say to Axylus?" Minos said to Theseus. "He won't do the deal with Nomion. What is it with you guys? You look out for each other, that's for damn sure."

Theseus told Minos he knew where Axylus was on the issue.

"How much delay will there be in getting a new firm involved?" Minos asked.

Theseus thought it would push the schedule back a couple

of months. It was that or not getting the offering done.

"Oh, what the hell, Theseus," Minos quipped. "All right, I'll talk to Nomion. You find me the right accountant. Don't let this thing get delayed more than six weeks. Make sure we stay on track."

18

Theseus received a call from Minos a few weeks after the boxing matches.

"I have a bunch of money lined up that I need to take in, Theseus," Minos said. "I want to sell promissory notes and warrants in a private deal. You have to get it papered and closed by the end of the week. Axylus has the details. It's really important that I do this quickly."

Theseus was surprised by the immediate need for cash and the choice to complete a bridge financing. He called Axylus to discuss the financing plan.

"What can I tell you, Minos wants some cash now," Axylus said. "He says he can't wait for the offering. Minos told me Orthrus has the money, that it's already lined up. The investors will get a note for six months and warrants to purchase stock at about a buck a share. This is a very rich deal, Theseus, and it puts a gun to our head to get the offering done, regardless of market conditions. I don't like it. What's Minos think he doing? It's not good."

Theseus understood. The investors buying the notes and warrants were looking for a quick profit. They would get repaid from the offering proceeds, and still have warrants that could substantially increase in value after Asterion does the public deal. The company would get the cash but at a hefty price.

Theseus asked Axylus why Minos said he needed the money.

"He says he wants it to pay off some expenses relating to Nemean," the banker said. "I really don't know. I think he already has taken in some of the cash."

Theseus called in Diocles to prepare the promissory notes and warrants. The warrants were to carry registration rights that would allow the investors to freely sell Asterion stock upon exercise of the warrants. Theseus told Diocles that the documents were needed quickly.

"Ok, but I've got a couple of other projects piling up," Diocles said. "Can it wait a few days?"

Theseus

Theseus replied no, that he wanted it on his desk by the time he got into the office the next morning. From Diocles' lack of a response, Theseus presumed that Diocles would be up all hours to complete the assignment. Theseus didn't think twice about it. That was part of the deal of working at the firm.

Diocles had the documents to Theseus on time, and Theseus took a couple of hours to review them. He made handwritten comments on the documents and turned them back to Diocles. Theseus told Diocles to get them out to Axylus and Stolos and see the matter through.

A few hours later, Theseus got a call about the notes and warrants from a potential investor. Such a call was highly unusual. Investors seldom spoke to company counsel. They typically interacted only with the company and the bankers. Theseus was guarded as the investor introduced himself as Phalius. He said he knew Tantalus. It was Tantalus who in fact put Phalius in touch with Minos.

"Minos told me to call you, Theseus," Phalius said. "He said you would be able to fill in a few details about the company."

Theseus told him it would be better if Phalius' lawyer gave him a call.

"I don't want to pull in my lawyers," Phalius said. "I'm thinking of putting up all the money and I want to move quickly. If I get the lawyers involved, it will take weeks and eat up my profit."

Phalius sounded a bit rushed. Theseus asked Phalius if the money was coming out of the fund he just raised.

"Yeah, what about it?" Phalius asked.

Theseus wondered if that was the fund Tantalus worked on.

"As a matter of fact, yes," Phalius bristled. "I had another law firm give me what I needed. You guys dropped the ball."

Theseus did not care for Phalius' bluster.

"I'm going to turn this call over to my associate," Phalius said rudely. "He's got some questions about Asterion."

Theseus was put on the speaker phone. He didn't like

how this was developing. Theseus asked if anyone else was on the call. It occurred to him that this could be some kind of set up, like the murder trap laid for Telemachos by Penelope's suitors.

"No, no," Phalius responded, "just us. Mydon, what do you have for Theseus? Make this quick."

Mydon asked about how Asterion booked revenues and how the integration of Nemean was proceeding. Theseus heard Phalius in the background. It sounded as if he was talking to someone else on another phone about some other investment. It occurred to Theseus that Phalius wasn't even paying attention. But Mydon continued with other questions, mostly about the planned stock offering and when it would get done.

Theseus was generally evasive with his answers. He deflected many by saying questions related to the business of Asterion were better addressed by the company itself. Theseus knew it was never a good thing for lawyers to be discussing the financial performance or prospects of a company, particularly with investors.

After about fifteen minutes, Phalius broke back in.

"All right," Phalius said, "I've got to run. But tell me first, how much does Tantalus have to do with this deal?"

Theseus objected to the question. Theseus said Tantalus was a tax lawyer and wasn't involved with the company on a day to day basis.

"I see," Phalius responded. "One last question. Is this company legit? I mean, am I going to get my money out of it?"

Theseus had had enough of the conversation. He told Phalius that was for him to decide.

19

Although Theseus had reservations about the short term financing arranged by Minos, he was impressed with how Minos went to work organizing the company after the acquisition of Nemean. He sent Ucalegon and a team of programmers over to Thebes to fine tune Nemean's software. He also began the construction of the call center in Stratus and acquired a site for the data center in Tegea. But for all these advances, he was still lacking a seasoned management team and board of directors. He required both in short order. Minos decided he would take the title executive chairman, Pedocles would be executive vice president for software development and Thrasycles was to be kept in charge of corporate strategy. He needed to add a new chief executive officer and chief financial officer to round out the management group.

Minos retained an executive recruiter named Satyros to help with the searches. Satyros' task was to find the right people to pull the different pieces of Asterion together and get revenues flowing. Theseus didn't have the highest regard for recruiters as a general rule. They made it their business to know people and keep the business gossip mills churning. They profited if people got fired and there were job openings to be filled. Conflicts among recruiters and their clients were rife. Stealing a candidate from a client company to fill a spot at another client was commonplace.

Theseus had come across Satyros on more than one occasion. Satyros was born of an ordinary family, and had the good fortune to marry a wealthy girl out of college. He lived in a mansion in one of the city's more affluent communities. Satyros drove an expensive car and traveled extensively around the world with his wife and children. Because of his spouse, he was able to fraternize with people in high places and get to know highly paid executives looking to make more money somewhere else.

When Satyros' firm got the assignment, Satyros set his people to work. To his credit, Satyros had no difficulty putting a credible group of candidates together for Minos.

Satyros' top pick for chief executive officer was Silenos. He was older than Minos, slightly undersized and had neatly cropped hair. Silenos had a metal piercing stare that matched his stiff posture. He graduated from college with degrees in accounting and finance and passed his boards on the first try. He served in the army as an officer for four years and was deployed as a comptroller for ammunition warehouses.

After his military service, Silenos worked for a number of years for a company that sold high resolution computer screens. When that company was sold, Silenos found himself out of a job. He hooked up with a venture capitalist named Tiro who invested in a variety of technology startups. Silenos operated as chief executive for hire for Tiro, working different companies at different times trying to get them positioned for sale or growth capital. Many of the companies didn't make it, but a few were hits. Silenos never cashed in with the successful companies, and was becoming frustrated. Other executives were making a killing running small tech companies and then selling out, but it was all passing Silenos by. When Satyros contacted Silenos about Asterion, Silenos looked at it as an opportunity to finally make some money. He liked that Asterion had immediate plans for a public offering. Silenos wanted an equity stake up front to come on board. Minos obliged, giving Silenos a healthy grant of stock options.

Satyros next brought in Cineas as the chief financial officer. Cineas was a young accountant without a strong finance background. Cineas was adolescent in appearance and had tightly curled light brown hair. He always wore sweaters, even with a jacket on. Theseus thought Cineas was bright but weak as a chief financial officer for a public company, but assumed Minos wanted someone who would do his bidding. Minos promised Cineas some options once the company did the public offering.

Thrasycles was not particularly happy with either Silenos or Cineas. He called Theseus to raise his concerns.

"We need a young, aggressive chief executive," Thrasycles

gripped to Theseus. "Silenos is too old. He doesn't get it. We need to move fast and be nimble. Silenos is a military man, which is not a good fit. Cineas is a bean counter, and doesn't know finance. I don't know what we are doing with these people. You should talk to Minos."

While Thrasycles carried on, Theseus understood the real message. Thrasycles wanted to be the chief executive. He was angling to have Theseus recommend him to Minos as the logical choice. There was no chance of that. Minos went ahead with both hires.

Silenos jumped in at Asterion with both feet. From an operating standpoint, his focus was on the revenue side of the equation. He didn't have a technical background, and would leave the product development to Minos and Pedocles. Silenos' experience was distribution and building out the marketing side of a business. Early on, Minos and Silenos debated the best approach. Minos wanted his call center in Stratus to generate leads. Silenos favored a national sales force, with professional sales people canvassing the market. In the end, they decided to do both. Minos would concentrate on setting up the call center, and Silenos would create a sales force, although somewhat scaled back from his original plan.

Both Minos and Silenos knew that generating organic revenue would take a while, and in the meantime they would rely on the tech service acquisitions Minos had closed to produce a revenue base for going to the public markets. Thrasycles identified a few more tech service firms that Minos wanted to move on. One was called Empusa Corp. and run by a young computer scientist. Empusa's revenues were mostly from hardware sales but it had a revolving credit facility that was available for draws. Silenos agreed to the Empusa purchase even though Empusa didn't fit well with Asterion's business. Minos believed that revenue was revenue and the market would treat increasing sales from whatever source as positive signs. Theseus guessed Minos wanted the company for its credit line.

Silenos was overawed at first by Theseus' credentials.

Silenos was not used to the attention of a top lawyer and grew to relish it. Silenos developed a close working relationship with Theseus, and began calling Theseus almost daily to discuss legal and business issues on hiring, employee benefits, trademarks and patents, company leases, equipment purchases and software licenses. Theseus normally would get other lawyers involved in the matters brought to him from Silenos, but he remained the primary liaison.

Following the Nemean acquisition, Silenos spent a fair amount of time mapping out the company's personnel chart and appointing people to head different departments. As Thrasycles suspected, Silenos believed organization and discipline were fundamental to success. Minos, on the other hand, didn't regard structure that highly and, being the founder, felt free to ask anyone at any time to do whatever was needed to be done. Because he bypassed Silenos more often than not, Silenos grew irritated with Minos and how he used people. Silenos felt this disrupted the work flow and scheduled timelines and created confusion within the company as to roles and responsibilities. Silenos expressed his frustrations frequently with Theseus but not with Minos himself.

With Silenos and Cineas on board, Minos called upon Theseus to help him put together a board of directors. The board would have to be in place before the company went public. Minos had several people in mind, including his father-in-law who helped him raise some friends and family money for one of Minos' ventures in the early days.

Theseus advised Minos against appointing his father-in-law. He told Minos to take a step back and think about board members that will aid in the success of the stock offering and can help grow the business.

"Yeah, yeah, I've heard it before, Theseus," Minos said. "Axylus has been singing that tune. Why can't I just set up an advisory board and put those kind of people on that. For window dressing. Then stock the full board with, you know, my people."

Theseus explained that advisory boards were perfunctory

and not seriously considered by any prudent investor. They had no voting power or authority, and were generally inactive. The market viewed them negatively. Besides, Theseus said, no legitimate director candidate would sit on an advisory board. The prestige sat with the corporate board. Theseus added that the exchanges were requiring independent directors on public boards. Institutional investors were skeptical of companies with boards controlled by management. If Minos wanted a successful offering he needed quality outside people.

"All right," Minos said, "I guess I can get my father-in-law a spot in the company, maybe for investor relations. I'll start looking around for the full board."

Minos mentioned Thrasycles, Pedocles and Silenos as possible management picks.

"Thrasycles has been angling," Minos said. "Silenos is expecting a spot, and we promised Pedocles when we bought Nemean. Should I put them on? What about Tantalus? He wants a board seat."

Theseus said Thrasycles was too young and inexperienced, and his competitiveness with Minos would not travel well in board meetings. Silenos was a reasonable pick, as most chief executives sat on their companies' boards. Pedocles made sense since his software was critical to the company's success. Theseus thought having Silenos and Pedocles as management selections was enough. As for Tantalus, Theseus responded absolutely not. He didn't have experience with public boards and wouldn't add much of anything of value. Theseus was actually appalled at the notion that Tantalus might serve as a director. Not only would he be unpredictable, but the potential liability he could cause the firm was huge. When a law firm does work for a company going public and has one of its own its attorneys on the board, there was an immediate conflict of interest that exposed the firm.

"Well," Minos said, "you tell Tantalus that yourself. I agree with you on Silenos and Pedocles. Let me give some thought to others. We'll talk."

Theseus would not hear from Minos again on the board

selections. Theseus learned after the fact that Minos decided on a seven member board. Minos, Silenos and Pedocles would be the inside directors. Minos went to Satyros for the others. After a lengthy search, Satyros produced four independent directors. The lead was Sargeus, who was resigning from his post as president of an insurance company. He was moving on to head an online asset management business offering alternate investments for high end deferred compensation plans. The second outside director, Bacenor, was retired from a big accounting firm after years of doing auditing work in the computer industry. The other two directors were Phormion, the elderly head of a regional bank, and Radamanthos, an economics professor at one of the city's graduate business schools.

Theseus was a bit perturbed that Minos had not consulted him on his selections, but he was satisfied Minos had a majority of independent directors on the board. Theseus thought Sargeus and Bacenor were solid choices, but questioned Phormion and Radamanthos. Sargeus had the necessary executive bent, and Bacenor's industry experience would be valuable. He was the logical pick for chair of the audit committee. But Phormion was an old school banker and Radamanthos was an academic that probably didn't have any experience with real world companies.

Tantalus wasn't pleased when he learned he wouldn't be on the board.

"Why the hell not, Theseus?" Tantalus protested. "Minos promised me. He told me if I brought Phalius in for the bridge, he would save me a seat on the board. We've got a whole lot of partners on corporate boards. Aegeus and Melesius serve on a ton. Hey, I'd be good with long range planning. Go back to Minos, would you? Tell him he's making a big mistake."

Theseus told Tantalus he understood the board seats had already been filled.

"That's really idiotic," Tantalus declared. "I thought Minos was sharper than that. This damn thing better work out."

20

Theseus' favorite daytime diversion at the firm when he had a couple of free hours was the lunch time basketball games organized by Aegeus. Aegeus was famous for his basketball. When Aegeus was younger, he would play every day at the downtown athletic club when he wasn't traveling. Now that he was older, Aegeus still tried to get out on the court twice a week. Chabrias, the club's locker room attendant, held one of the two courts open for Aegeus at half past noon every Monday and Thursday. No one else was allowed near the court.

Aegeus would be joined by combinations of business executives, bankers, accountants and firm partners. Some of the older men had been playing together since time immemorial. The games were full court and the play relatively good. Aegeus himself had played in college and was competitive on the court well into his fifties. After that, Aegeus slowed down quite a bit and had difficulty at times running the floor.

Theseus got into the games after he made partner and earned a standing invitation to play. Theseus played swing guard in high school, and had several scholarship offers from smaller colleges. His jumping ability was extraordinary and he had a good outside shot. Theseus tended to play down to the level of the competition, which Aegeus respected. Pirithous was also a regular.

These were Aegeus' games and he generally controlled the action. Aegeus would be as much referee as player, freely calling fouls and turnovers. No one argued with him, even though the calls invariably went his way. There was never any natural selection to the teams, such as the first five to make free throws. Aegeus would pick the players, taking the better ones for his team. He nearly always won. Whenever Theseus and Pirithous could play, they were on Aegeus' squad.

Aegeus would let Chabrias know if he wanted someone new in the games, but for the most part it was the usual group. On occasion, Aegeus would want to check out a new associate or lateral partner, and he would ask around to find out if the prospect was a player. If so, an invitation would be extended. If the lawyer was lousy, too good or didn't respect the older players, he was out. If Aegeus liked the lawyer's game and demeanor he might be asked back.

Tantalus decided he wanted to play, and cornered Theseus to see if he could arrange it.

"I want to show Aegeus a thing or two," Tantalus said. "I have a hell of a jump shot. Let me know when I can play."

Tantalus wasn't in the best of shape and didn't have much of a reputation as an athlete, so it was curious why he wanted to play.

It was a while before Aegeus warmed up to the idea. At first he was dead set against it. After mulling it over for a couple of weeks, Aegeus relented.

"All right, all right," Aegeus said to Theseus, "let him come out. We'll see what he's got."

Tantalus was ecstatic. He came to the gym early to change and warm up. Chabrias was unsure about Tantalus from the start. Tantalus walked out of the locker room donning a loose fitting jersey with the number one and "Mountaineers" across the front, gray sweats and new white leather high tops. Tantalus also wore goggles that looked like they were stolen from a chemistry lab.

Aegeus didn't know what to make of the goggles.

"What's with this guy?" Aegeus wondered aloud to Theseus.

It was quickly apparent that Tantalus hadn't played recently, if ever. He only dribbled right handed, and got about three inches off the floor when he went for a rebound.

"Let's go," Tantalus screamed at Aegeus. "How about you and me on the same team."

Aegeus would have none of that. Aegeus took Theseus and Pirithous, as was his custom, while Tantalus was put on the other team. Aegeus divided up the rest of the players.

The game was played to fifteen. Tantalus called for the ball early and put up a few air balls, as Aegeus' team took a quick lead. Tantalus tried to get up and down the floor, but quickly became winded. He took an ill advised drive to the basket and his shot was blocked by Aegeus. Tantalus fell to the ground clutching his knee. Aegeus quickly got him off the court and had Chabrias find a sub. Tantalus looked like he was in pain, but Theseus believed he had to feel relieved. Chabrias brought out an ice pack for Tantalus and he sat subdued on the sideline. Aegeus' team finished the game winning by a wide margin.

The lawyers went into the locker room to shower and get back to the office. Tantalus made his way from his locker to the shower stalls stark naked and carrying a basket of toiletries. After showering, a number of lawyers were at the sinks shaving. Tantalus came up and grabbed a hair dryer by each hand. Still naked, he put a foot up on the sink counter, fully exposed, and started blow drying his body up and down. It was a sight. He then laid a towel on the counter and set out his toiletries.

"I tell you, Aegeus," Tantalus griped, "that was a foul. If I had known you would come at me like that, I would have gone harder to the basket. Damn, I thought this was a gentleman's game."

"I caught the ball clean," Aegeus retorted. "You can't come out here if you are going to play like that. And put a goddamn towel on! I'm not interested in looking at what you've got."

Everyone laughed but Tantalus.

"God," said Tantalus, "last time I play with a bunch of prudish lawyers."

Tantalus was of course right. It would be his last time playing.

"Aegeus, I need to talk to you about Zosimus," Tantalus said as he shared the counter with Aegeus. "He's trying to take credit for some work I brought in. I've known these guys over at Ladon for years. I went to the same school as the head guy. So we now get hired for some big patent work. No way Zosimus should get credit for that."

Aegeus asked what the matter was about. Tantalus said

that Ladon Corporation had developed a new technology for solar panels. The technology was radical and had the potential to generate large amounts of power, ideal for manufacturing plants. It was the kind of innovation that was a game changer for the entire alternate energy industry. Ladon had been a small player with limited resources, but the new process had the potential to catapult the company to a leading position in its field.

Ladon planned to patent its technology prior to any field testing. The company wanted complete protection under the patent laws before word of the process got out into the market. Landon was afraid that the two dominant companies in the industry had the money and talent to develop competing panels once they learned of the technology.

Ladon hired Zosimus to handle the patent filings and advise the company on legal tactics. The goal was to stop or at least slow down Landon's competitors with patent infringement lawsuits. A defensible patent and properly executed litigation strategy could help Ladon with staking out its market position and raise cash for its operations. The payoff, if successful, would be huge.

Zosimus had an electrical engineering undergraduate degree and a master's in applied sciences. He had a strong client base in the computer industry, and had begun picking up clients in the clean energy sector. Zosimus had won a number of high profile patent cases early in his career and his reputation quickly grew. He was also an astute businessman. He realized that bet the company patent litigation could reap substantial windfalls for the successful litigator. Zosimus convinced Aegeus to let him take cases at deeply discounted rates so long as he could earn a large premium if he prevailed. Aegeus reluctantly agreed at first, but it turned out to be the right decision. Zosimus won his cases and earned gigantic fees. He became one of the better paid partners in the firm.

"I can tell you why that client is here," Tantalus said to Aegeus. "Me. I told Ladon what we could do for them. The engagement is a gold mine. Anyone can see it. Zosimus is a tool. I could handle the damn thing myself."

Complaints over billing credit was not considered good form within the firm and frowned upon. Most partners with issues would work it out among themselves, often splitting credits. In the event billing conflicts could not get resolved, Aegeus would step in. The chairman had the unfettered discretion to rule on any and all billing disputes. His decision was final.

"Let me ask one question, Tantalus," Aegeus pressed him. "Who got the call?"

"What do you mean, who got the call?" Tantalus asked back.

"Who did the client call, Tantalus?" Aegeus responded. "Who picked up the phone?"

"Well, that was Zosimus, I guess," Tantalus said meekly.

"Then its Zosimus' deal," Aegeus said firmly. "Matter settled."

"Not fair," Tantalus said to Theseus on the way back to the office. "I brought Ladon in. Served it up to Zosimus on a goddamn silver platter."

Theseus asked if Tantalus knew that Aegeus and Zosimus and their wives used to attend the opera together.

"Figures," was Tantalus' reply. "What's it take to get a break around here?"

"Hey, Theseus," Tantalus said moving on to another subject. "The increase in the billing rates that was announced is killing me."

Tantalus was referring to the modest billable hour rate hike the firm just instituted.

"The firm is going to put me out of business, Theseus," Tantalus said. "I can't keep raising my rates. My clients don't like it. They don't mind having the firm's name behind them, but there's a limit on what they will pay. We're pricing ourselves out of the market. Can't the firm see that?"

Theseus pointed out that the firm's billing rate increases were in line with other prominent law firms. He told Tantalus that holding rates constant for even one year hurt the firm in the long run. Clients could tolerate reasonable rate increases year to year, and even budgeted for it, but reacted adversely to large one year jumps.

"I think you've got it backwards," Tantalus argued. "If we lowered rates we would increase our business. We'd make more money. This way, we're asking clients to look around for a better deal and walk."

Lowering rates would force the firm to adjust associate salaries down, Theseus explained, which meant the firm could lose the best associates.

"Who cares about the associates," Tantalus shot back. "I'm telling you, we are just shooting ourselves in the foot."

Theseus finally told Tantalus that if he needed lower rates, he might find a better fit at another law firm.

"Not with Asterion in the door, no way," Tantalus said. "Minos is going to make my career."

21

The time for the public offering for Asterion was drawing near, and the bankers were determined to get to market before the new offering window closed. Within every market cycle, there is a period when investor appetite for purchasing securities in new companies is insatiable. The bankers' job was to feed the beast. They could earn substantial sums of money for themselves in the process.

Axylus organized an all hands meeting hosted by Theseus at the firm's offices. Minos came with Silenos, Thrasycles and Cineas. They were all wearing colored dress shirts, jackets and khakis. None of them had bothered with ties. Theseus took it as a sign of overconfidence. Axylus walked in with Stolos and an analyst named Cadmos. Axylus was wearing a heavy wool suit, a plaid dress shirt, wide purple tie and tasseled loafers. Stolos and Cadmos were similarly dressed. Two of the new auditors appeared. The lead audit partner was named Eetion. His hair was neat and graying on the sides. His junior colleague, Clonius, had a fatigued rank and file look about him. Both wore the standard issue navy suit, white shirt and red tie.

Underwriter's counsel also showed. The partner had the name Penthesileas. She was tall and fair, but showing her age. Derinoe was her senior associate. She had short dark hair and her scowl masked otherwise nice features. The third was a junior associate named Thermodusa, who had fiery eyes and copper hair. Penthesileas wore a knee length maroon dress with a scarf that lay across her chest like a war sash. She had big gold earrings and bracelets. Her compatriots were dressed to kill in tailored suits and heels. Penthesileas, Derinoe and Thermodusa reminded Theseus of the Amazons. Heracles, Theseus remembered, had his battles with them.

Theseus had not mixed with these lawyers before, and he knew almost the entire securities bar in Athens. Theseus didn't take it as a good omen. The importance of having experienced counsel for both the issuing company and the underwriter could not be overstated. The lawyers were the primary drivers behind the entire process. Besides, Theseus knew, the lawyers would work closely together and deals always went better with high caliber counterparts.

Alcaeus, Diocles and Calliope joined Theseus for the meeting.

Minos began by greeting everyone. He asked each attendee to introduce themselves and state their role. When Penthesileas' turn came, she took the opportunity to cite her deep experience in technology issues and securities offerings. Theseus thought her fatuous. She was obviously trying to impress.

"Thanks, everyone," Minos said after the introductions. "Great to have such a fine group for this project. As you all know, we've spent the last year getting Asterion ready for this day. We have a network of strategic service offices and, of course, our Nemean operation in Thebes. Asterion acquired Nemean to give us the integrated suite of software packages that will be attractive to the middle market. We have appointed a quality board of directors, and built a fine management team with Silenos and Cineas in the lead. We have added an inexpensive but capable call center in Arcanania to help generate revenue. Our hosting location in Tegea is in development. The pieces are all in place. We are ready to go."

Theseus saw that Thrasycles was upset that he wasn't mentioned by Minos.

Minos asked Axylus to give an overview of the equity markets.

"My pleasure," Axylus began. "We have a unique opportunity in the current market. Stock prices are high, the technology sector is hot and investors are bidding up to get new issues. If we catch this market right, we can have a very successful offering for Asterion. Cadmos, why don't you walk us through the market dynamics."

Cadmos distributed flip books and turned everyone's attention to the slides projected on the overhead screen he controlled with his computer. He spent the next twenty

Theseus

minutes showing the group economic data, industry statistics and market points with every kind of bar, pie and quad chart imaginable.

During the middle of Cadmos' presentation, Tantalus burst into the room. The nice flow Cadmos had going was totally disrupted.

"Minos!" Tantalus screamed. "Are we ready to go public? Hey, Axylus, what's taking so long? We should be rolling in dough right about now."

"Tantalus, sit down," Minos said, "let the young man finish his presentation."

"Good to have you, Tantalus," Axylus said. "We were just about to wrap up the market review."

"No one wants to hear this crap," Tantalus replied. "We all know where the market is. It's going through the roof. We're leaving money on the table!"

"Sit down," Minos ordered.

Tantalus took a seat. He started to ogle the Amazons.

Cadmos went back to where he left off and finished with the slides. He painted a picture of a healthy market for new technology issues. Pedocles was lost in the numbers, as was Silenos. Thrasycles asked a number of off point questions. Theseus guessed he was trying to put the bankers on notice that he was a mover at the company.

"We don't know how long the receptivity for new issues will last, so we need to get to market soon," Axylus observed.

Theseus was skeptical about the need to rush. Asterion had not yet fully integrated its operations or even successfully beta tested its software product. Minos was spending huge sums on his call and data centers, but it would be a couple of months before they were online. Theseus suspected that Axylus knew the risk in Asterion, and wanted to sell the stock before the company would disappoint with poor revenues and earnings.

"Let's hear about our stock price," Minos said. "What will we go out at?"

"We'll target a traditional price," Axylus responded. "Institutions like stock in a certain range. If you go too low you start attracting too many retail buyers or have penny stock issues. We'd want to avoid that."

"But what percent of the company are you selling?" Minos asked zeroing in on what kind of ownership dilution he would suffer.

"Probably thirty percent," Axylus said.

Minos thought for a moment. "Well, no more. I have to keep a control stake."

"That's all that I wanted to hear," Tantalus said as he got up and moved toward the door. "Minos, I'll catch up with you later. Get this mother done, will you guys?"

He left the room.

The group spent the next hour discussing the deal timeline and responsibilities. Penthesileas at this point tried to take over the meeting. She started chattering about getting a timetable together, drafting the registration statement and managing due diligence. Minos threw a glare at Axylus.

"Penthesileas," Axylus interrupted, "I believe Theseus has got a jump on a few of those things."

Penthesileas deflected the comment, and said underwriter's counsel should control the work flow.

"Well," Minos responded tersely, "let's see what Theseus has for us."

Penthesileas sat back in her seat.

Theseus had Diocles distribute a detailed timeline and the first draft of the company's registration statement. Theseus' team would have primary responsibility over the registration statement, which when ready would be filed with the securities commission. The registration statement included the prospectus which set forth the material information about the company investors needed to see. It was the task of both company and underwriter's counsel to ensure that the information provided about the company to the commission, and ultimately investors, met the standard of full and complete disclosure. The trick was not only saying what was true about the company and avoiding false statements, but not to omit information that would make what was disclosed misleading in any material way. What was not said could easily be, and often was, grounds for a lawsuit.

Theseus estimated it would take a good six to eight weeks to get the registration statement ready for filing. A number of all day drafting sessions were scheduled. While completing the registration statement, Theseus' firm would simultaneously handle the stock exchange application to get the stock listed for trading.

Theseus had the accountants discuss the company's financial statements, which would be included in the registration statement. Eetion said the company needed to have its historical statements restated for the Nemean purchase and pro forma statements for the other acquisitions Asterion had recently completed. Because Nemean was a foreign company, international accounting discrepancies needed to be reconciled. A large segment of the prospectus was devoted to the discussion of the company's financial condition and operating performance based on the financial statements prepared by Eetion's firm. Theseus knew that when offerings went poorly, financial disclosure was often the basis of shareholder lawsuits. The importance of the financial statements and commentary could not be underestimated. The accountants already had preliminary drafts of the numbers ready for the group to start reviewing.

When it came time to discuss due diligence, Theseus asked Penthesileas if she had her document request list ready.

"Not yet," Penthesileas came back curtly, "we've just been engaged. I'll have Derinoe draw one up over the next couple of days."

"We prepared a standard list," Alcaeus jumped in. "Take a look to see if you want to add anything. And we have collected all the documents keyed to the list. You can take a box with you."

The role underwriter's counsel played performing due diligence was critical to the underwriter. If the offering failed and the investment banker was sued, it could point to the intense investigation it conducted as a defense. Stacks of company documents, covering everything from its certificate of incorporation, bylaws and board minutes to its financing arrangements, leases, benefit plans, technology licenses and supply contracts would need to be reviewed by underwriter's counsel. Theseus anticipated the need, and had Calliope collecting the material Asterion documents for the past three weeks.

Axylus could see that Penthesileas was getting red in the face.

"Ok, then," Axylus said, "Penthesileas, you can pick it up from there. Let's move on."

Theseus felt confident that the group could meet Mino's target date for going public. Whether the company was actually ready was another matter. A great deal of work did lie ahead. The associate lawyers, junior bankers and accountants would be spending many late nights over the next several months.

Minos took Theseus aside after the meeting. Minos was concerned about Axylus and the Amazons.

"How could he have picked those women?" Minos said. "I'm afraid for my life with Penthesileas. What business does Axylus have bringing them in on this?"

Theseus told Minos he was reasonably satisfied with where they were, and that he thought he could control the Amazons. Theseus remarked he was more concerned about Mino's ability to get this company operating. Going public is just a step. If Asterion didn't hit its numbers over the first few quarters after the offering, the company was as good as dead. Investors will flee and not return, and there would certainly be lawsuits. Not a good scenario.

"Don't worry about that, Theseus," Minos said confidently. "We are ahead of the game. Say, what are you doing tonight? My wife and I are having dinner later with Pedocles. Care to come?"

Theseus said he appreciated the invite, but he had other commitments.

"Involving Ariadne, I presume?" Minos asked.

Another time, Theseus replied phlegmatically.

22

The firm's yearend holiday party was one of the two major social dates on the firm's annual event calendar and a long standing tradition. The holiday party was for everyone who worked at the firm, lawyers, secretaries and staff alike. The firm held it in the grand ballroom of a downtown hotel on the first Friday of December every year.

The holiday party was always a lavish affair. The offices were closed early on the night of the party. The dress code was suits and ties for the men and dresses for the women. Cocktails and abundant appetizers kicked off the evening. Drinking was usually heavy. To Theseus, the holiday event was akin to the ancient festivals held in honor of Dionysus. Wild, delirious behavior was the hallmark of the Bacchic worshippers, and he knew it was pointless to try to control the celebrants. Pentheus made the attempt and was torn limb from limb by the Maenads. There was no denying Dionysus was the son of Zeus.

An elegant dinner of holiday fare and desserts was served a couple hours into the party. Pirithous joined Theseus at his table. Cara and Rhea, two partners from the environmental practice, sat down with them, as did Lysias.

Pirithous and Theseus talked of sailing and the upcoming marathon. The firm was a big supporter of the major city event each spring. Both Pirithous and Theseus ran in the marathon and decided they would train together in the month leading up to the race. When training, Theseus always thought of Pheidippides' encounter with the god Pan on his run to enlist the aid of the Spartans against the Persians. It gave him more motivation when he put the marathon in that context.

Cara and Rhea turned the conversation to Aegeus' successor.

"Tell us, Lysias," Cara started, "how is Aegeus' search going? Has he picked someone?"

"Not to my knowledge," Lysias replied. "I think he has a few people in mind, but he is keeping tight lipped about it."

"I imagine Medea knows," Rhea said. "Word is Aegeus is keeping close company with her these days."

Rhea was searching for a reaction from Lysias.

"She does seem to have some influence with Aegeus," Lysias said with a frown.

"Medea's role in this is not good for the firm," Pirithous chimed in. "We all know that's true. She's cast a spell over Aegeus. Medea has her own agenda. She is likely angling to have herself or someone she dominates named chairman. Something needs to be done about it."

"Has anyone confronted Aegeus, you know, expressed to him the misgivings of the partners?" Cara asked.

"Believe me, a number of us have tried," Lysias responded.

"We all know how she works," said Pirithous. "I've see it firsthand. Medea not only tries to promote herself, but she attacks without quarter anyone she sees as competition."

"That's exactly what happened when Medea was elevated to the head of real estate," Cara added. "She sabotaged a number of other partners who were in line ahead of her. Two of them have since left the firm."

"The woman is ambitious and spiteful to boot," Pirithous continued. "She would kill her own children to get ahead."

"It's not becoming of partners to speak of each other this way," Lysias cautioned. "Have some faith in Aegeus."

"You need to make a move, Theseus," Pirithous said impatiently to Theseus beyond the hearing of the others. "Before it's too late."

Following dinner, Aegeus gave a brief speech extolling the virtues of the firm and thanked the staff for their support over the year. After that, the senior associates took the floor. A highly anticipated feature of the holiday party was the partner roast. Associates performed skits poking fun at the partners. Most of the time, the skits were done tastefully. But there were exceptions. More than a few associates handling the task didn't work at the firm a year later because offense was taken. Some partners had thin skins.

Diocles and Iollas took the podium for this year's

Theseus

performance. They had chosen to lampoon Tantalus.

Diocles and Iollas showed some ingenuity by creating a short film. They had the lights in the room lowered, and without fanfare, played the tape. There was a bit of laughter as the title "Death of a Lawyer" flashed on the screen. But there was an outburst when the credits read "Starring Tantalus." The first scene had Iollas, playing Tantalus, standing in a cemetery next to a freshly dug grave. There were headstones all around with the names of associates who had been with the firm but were either let go or had quit. Everyone knew that all of these young people either had worked with Tantalus or had unfortunate run-ins with him. Standing next to Tantalus was a dark hooded figure. Tantalus pulled off the hood, exposing Nikon. Tantalus grabbed Nikon by his nape and yanked him to the edge of the grave.

"You are a pathetic excuse for an associate, Nikon," Tantalus ranted. "You show no ability to work without sleep for days on end, or to read a partner's thoughts before he knows what he wants. You grow frustrated after redrafting a legal memorandum for the twenty fifth time. You pity yourself for missing the holidays with your family and having to cancel vacation plans. You lose your self esteem after endless brow beatings from partners. You are a fraud and unfit for the practice of law."

Before Tantalus was able to push the young associate into the grave, he was surrounded by the ghoulish, undead associates who had fallen victim before. They grabbed Tantalus by the arms and dragged him off into the darkness.

The gathering broke out in an uproar at the scene. But there was more to come.

The next shot showed Tantalus standing in front of a high bench with three black robed judges, all associates. Diocles, Nikon and Calliope sat in judgment. Diocles announced the verdict.

"For your heinous transgressions against the youth in the law profession," Diocles said sternly, "and your otherwise pitiful existence, you are herewith given the following punishment. First, you will be chained to a desk, with client files within your reach. Every time you complete work on a file, three more will instantly appear. When you finish the next, again three more will be found in its place. Second, you will be denied hot food and will eat only tuna salad sandwiches and tired raw vegetables. Each and every meal will be taken at your desk. Finally, your phone will ring without end and the red light will blink incessantly. You will know that your practice group head is on the line ready to tell you your services are no longer needed at the firm, but every time you touch the phone you will receive an electric shock resulting in excruciating pain. This is your punishment for all eternity."

The crowd howled out of control. There was applause and whistles and shouting.

The final scene showed Tantalus head down at a desk in an office with no windows. Clients files were stacked high all around him, and styrofoam food containers were strewn about. The blinking red light from the phone was the only illumination. The phone rang loud and continuous.

The partners reacted first with a standing ovation, and soon the whole room was up clapping and yelling. Everyone was in stitches. Except Tantalus.

Theseus looked for Tantalus and saw him at another table. The partners seated with him were hysterical. One slapped Tantalus on the back to get a rise. Tantalus was noticeably agitated, and got up and walked out of the room. If not for the fact that Tantalus was not well liked, Diocles and Iollas might be packing.

After the dinner, a band played for dancing. This was the aspect of the holiday party that Theseus thought made it somewhat dodgy. Spouses and dates were not invited to the party, a recipe for licentiousness. The unattached secretaries were on the prowl for single lawyers. The male attorneys hit on their female counterparts. Many rented hotel rooms for the night. The potential for debauchery was everywhere. The night never seemed to disappoint, and more than a few families were broken up as a result of the holiday party. Theseus recalled his vow to leave the party early. He did not

Theseus

want temptation to be his undoing, and he didn't care to witness others fall.

When the dancing started, there was general mingling. Theseus got up and ran into Tantalus.

"Where is Calliope, Theseus, have you seen her?" Tantalus slurred.

Tantalus was evidently inebriated and had a wild look in his eyes.

"I bet she's a dancer," Tantalus stammered. "Tell her I'm looking for her."

Tantalus made off in search of Calliope.

At the bar, Theseus saw Aegeus.

"You've had a good year, Theseus," Aegeus said. "Your string of deals in the last half has been impressive."

Theseus said he appreciated the comment, that it had been a decent run.

"Good for the firm," Aegeus said. "There's a buzz about the place that I haven't heard for a while. You've helped create that."

Aegeus grabbed the drink he ordered and mixed it with an olive stir.

"You've got strong leadership skills, Theseus," Aegeus commented. "We don't have an abundance of partners with your qualities."

Before Theseus could thank Aegeus for the compliment, Medea appeared. Theseus was caught off guard. She seemed to have been standing there the entire time.

"Enjoying the party, Theseus?" Medea said in a patronizing tone.

Medea made a motion to the dance floor and the intermingling of partners and female staff.

"Theseus doesn't seem to partake of the good cheer, Aegeus," Medea said. "He must think he's above the rest of us."

Theseus didn't bother with an answer.

"Why so hard on our young partner, Medea?" Aegeus replied smiling at Medea. "I respect Theseus' decorum and how he handles himself. There has to be a few adults in the room."

"I have misgivings about men unable to enjoy themselves," Medea said looking at Theseus. "Theseus needs to loosen up, that's all. Not interested in our fine young ladies, Theseus? It's strange for such a handsome unattached man not to take advantage of the adoration of so many women. Don't you think it peculiar, Aegeus?"

"Word is that our fine Theseus has some affection for a lovely woman, Medea," Aegeus said jovially. "A lady as beautiful as Aphrodite herself I have heard reported. And a lawyer no less."

Medea returned a look of jealous surprise. Aegeus' mention of Ariadne reminded Theseus that he had promised to ring her after he left the party.

Aietes and Tisias came up to join the conversation.

"Great speech, Aegeus," Aietes said. "You are without equal when lauding the virtues of the firm."

"There isn't anyone better," Tisias added.

"How goes the search, Aegeus?" Aietes asked.

"The search, the search!" Aegeus said aggravated. "Is that the only thing on people's mind? Please, leave an old man in peace for one evening, Aietes. There will be a time for that discussion. But not tonight."

"Yes, let's allow Aegeus an hour to enjoy the party," Medea scolded Aietes. "Aegeus has the appointment well in hand. I can assure you."

Medea took Aegeus arm and led him away from the conversation.

"She is his protectorate, I give her that," Aietes said to Theseus. "I trust the old man to make the right decision, don't you Theseus?"

Theseus' thoughts had drifted to Ariadne. He had no interest in remaining there with Aietes and Tisias. He bid them both a good evening and left to call Ariadne.

23

A night at the financial printer had attained an almost mythic status in the financial services industry. The financial printer was the central location where the deal participants convened to prepare the registration statement for a public offering for filing with the securities commission. Company management, the underwriters, the accountants and legal counsel all collected at the financial printer to fine tune and finalize the registration statement.

Theseus instructed Alcaeus, Diocles and Calliope to plan on arriving at the printer in Athens by early afternoon to get everything organized. He told them that they would likely be up all night getting the Asterion documents ready. Some deals required two or more overnights, but at least one was the norm.

Calliope was curious to know why so much time had to be spent at the printer.

"Staying at the printer for a couple of days and nights seems a bit overdone," she commented to Theseus and Alcaeus.

"It's just the way things have evolved for public offerings," Alcaeus said. "The printer will eventually typeset the text of the prospectus so it is ready for printing when the commission has finished its review. Things tend to move quickly after commission comments are cleared. The underwriters push to get the prospectus to investors. Downtime is avoided if the text is setup with the printer before filing."

"What does the commission do with the filing?" Calliope wondered. "What are they looking for?"

"The commission's task," said Alcaeus, "is to make sure Asterion's filing contains sufficient disclosure for investors to make an informed decision whether to invest in Asterion's securities. The commission doesn't have the authority to judge if the company's stock is a good investment or not. It is not allowed to substitute its own judgment for that of investors."

Theseus explained that the securities laws were based on the efficient market theory. The underlying premise was that the markets for stock and bonds worked properly only when the information about issuers was complete and accessible to all investors. Full public disclosure creates a level playing field. The commission's role is to ensure that companies selling securities to the public disclose everything material. The company must satisfy the disclosure requirements in order to pass muster with the commission. The securities lawyers take the lead role in preparing the disclosure and help shield the issuer and underwriter from liability for false statements or material omissions.

"That's why we will spend so much time at the printer," Alcaeus followed up. "We'll keep turning drafts of the registration statement until everyone is satisfied that the filing is complete and meets commission standards. It's an involved process. The lawyers, accountants and business people pour over the drafts hour upon hour. Markups are given back to the printer and clean drafts produced. Hopefully, by late in the evening or early the next morning, the markups will dwindle to a handful of changed pages and it'll be ready to go."

Theseus arrived at the printer a few hours after he had sent Alcaeus and Calliope over. Cineas, Eetion and Clonius were already well into the work needed on the financial statements. Theseus took a look at the financial discussion in the prospectus. He spent about an hour with Cineas and the auditors editing the sections dealing with the company's revenue growth over the past three quarters. Alcaeus and Diocles attended to the business description and Calliope was assigned the task of getting the stock ownership table completed.

The Amazons arrived before too long. Penthesileas, Derinoe and Thermodusa took over one end of the work room, spreading out their purses, briefcases and files. Theseus' early premonition about Penthesileas proved accurate. In the numerous working group sessions leading up to the final drafting at the printer, Penthesileas displayed a

Theseus

dearth of technical skills. Her writing lacked precision and her analysis was weak. As for Derinoe and Thermodusa, Theseus made sure Diocles reviewed everything they did. All in all, Theseus found the Amazons a sad excuse for securities lawyers. He and his team redoubled their efforts to make up for their shortcomings, and managed to keep up the pace of the work to meet the schedule despite their involvement.

"Let's get moving, Theseus," Penthesileas declared. "There's no time to waste. Have the accountants finished their audit?"

Theseus doubted Penthesileas had even read the financial statement drafts.

Toward evening, the investment bankers came in with Minos, Silenos and Thrasycles. Axylus and Stolos were content to let the lawyers and accountants do the work on the documents. They had the printer's customer service representative order up a serious dinner from one of the better steakhouses in town.

Theseus sat down with Minos and Axylus to talk about how the night would go.

"The last offering I did shot right out the box," Axylus boasted. "It was a technology company that was building a business to business exchange for machine tools. We made a ton of money on that offering. The one before that was also pretty successful. A software company that provided back office tracking of delivery orders. Investors ate it up."

"How do you keep up with all the different deals?" Minos asked.

"I book a lot of airline miles, that's for damn sure," Axylus laughed. "Say, Minos, how long have you had your place in Rhodes?"

"Oh, it's been a couple years now, I guess," Minos responded. "Theseus has been up there."

"I've had my beach house in Sicily for about six," said Axylus. "Bought it for cash with a bonus check. Love that place. The shore is untouched by human hands. I'll have you guys out sometime."

Penthesileas showed and started in with some blather

about her exotic vacations.

"I've been going to the south of the Black Sea for ages," she said. "No one really knows about it. Kind of a mysterious place. A lot of myths about the inhabitants, some of which are true."

Theseus saw that nobody was actually listening to her.

Dinner arrived and was set up in the printer's kitchen area. The printer laid out the delivery of mixed greens, filets, creamed spinach, hash browns and mousse cake. There was plenty for everyone, but the investment bankers ate first and let the rest of the team fend for themselves.

Minos, Silenos and Theseus joined the bankers for dinner. The meal was interrupted a few times by Cineas and Alcaeous wandering in and out with questions about how to rewrite this sentence or whether to add that phrase. Theseus would tell them what to do, and send them back to work.

Just as he was finishing dinner, Theseus was given a message from the printer's customer representative. There was a matter that needed his attention back at the office, so he excused himself for an hour or so. Before he left, he checked in with the work room. Cineas looked sufficiently disgusted by the lack of attention to the deal by the bankers and Minos. Theseus told Alcaeus that he wanted Diocles and Calliope to finish their proofing of all the changes to the registration statement submitted during the day.

When Theseus came back later in the evening, he walked into the work room. No one was there. He checked the kitchen, and that too was empty. He then heard boisterous laughs emanating from the game room down the hall. Financial printers were infamous for their game rooms. They had leather couches and chairs to lounge, magazines and papers of every variety, a fully stocked bar, refrigerator filled with drinks, beer and plenty of food. The pool tables, pinball machines and large screen televisions were the most important features.

Theseus walked down to the game room and he saw Minos, Thrasycles and the bankers huddled in front of the television screen. Diocles and Alcaeus were also in the room talking with Silenos, Cineas and the accountants over a foosball match. Calliope was standing with a pool stick in hand and looking over a shot. Theseus was surprised to see Ariadne sitting on the edge of a chair behind the men watching television. She was embarrassed when she saw him and got up.

"Thank god you've finally come, Theseus," she said in a low voice. "Get me out of here."

Theseus saw the men watching erotic scenes on the big screen, and cheering the different moves and contortions.

"I can't believe these guys," continued Ariadne. "I got into a billiards game with Calliope and before I knew it they were yelling like it was an athletic contest."

Theseus escorted Ariadne out of the game room.

"You're probably wondering what I'm doing here," Ariadne said. "Minos said you were about ready to file, so I thought I would stop by. I didn't realize things were moving so quickly. Are you really ready to go to the commission? There may be a few things you should know first."

Theseus looked for a place to talk privately. He took Ariadne into what he thought was an empty conference room. The Amazons were there on reclining chairs getting pedicures. Theseus was in disbelief.

"I figured it would be a long night," Penthesileas said cheerily, "so I thought we would take advantage of the downtime."

She noticed Ariadne.

"Are you with Theseus' firm?" Penthesileas said to her. "Why don't you sit down and join us? No charge."

Theseus walked out with Ariadne and found another room.

"There are two things really," Ariadne told Theseus. "The beta test on Nemean's new product came back mixed."

The report Theseus had received earlier was that the test was strongly positive.

"Minos has also been selling some stock," Ariadne added. "The broker who did the bridge has been parceling out shares from Mino's account."

Minos was warned by Theseus months before not to engage in any trading of his Asterion stock before the offering.

"Don't tell Minos you heard this from me," Ariadne pleaded. "Please."

Theseus told Ariadne that she should probably leave and ushered her out. He had the printer bring a car around.

"Let me know how things go," Ariadne said.

She gave Theseus an embrace and turned and got in the back seat.

Theseus returned to the work room and ordered Calliope to get everyone back without delay. He told her he didn't care what they were doing and not to take no for an answer. Minos, Axylus, the Amazons, the entire working group.

In a few minutes, everyone came in and took seats. Theseus asked for their undivided attention. A couple of matters needed to be sorted out before they could proceed.

"The beta?" Minos said after Theseus raised the issue. "That came out fine. The software is functional and integrates well with the platforms that are out there."

"I've read the test report myself," Silenos said, "and talked with the programmers. It's as Minos said. There's not a problem that I know of."

"Where have you heard different?" Thrasycles asked.

That's not important, Theseus said to Thrasycles. He asked if Diocles had a copy of the beta results.

"At the office," Diocles replied.

Theseus wanted to read it. Calliope was told to go get the report and bring it back to the printer straight away. Theseus then asked Minos about his stock trades.

"Stock trades?" Minos said angrily. "Where is this coming from?"

Minos looked at Axylus and then Thrasycles and Cineas.

"Ok, sure," Minos said, "I did a few trades a while back to pay some bills. But it was all cleared through Orthrus. They assured me it was all right to do. It didn't amount to many shares. Shouldn't be any big deal."

Axylus raised his eyebrows, and Eetion sat up straight in

Theseus

his chair. Penthesileas looked confused.

Theseus said the registration statement couldn't be filed until they were able to verify Mino's stock holdings and confirm there were no trading improprieties.

"What does that mean, Theseus?" Minos objected. "You're telling me we are not going to file? Bull. We're not holding this thing up."

"I agree with Theseus," Axylus said. "What you own is fairly important."

Minos turned to Thrasycles.

"You told me you cleared it," Minos said accusatorily. "Didn't you tell Theseus?"

"Orthrus said they were clean trades," Thrasycles responded defiantly. "I saw no reason to tell Theseus."

"So where does that leave us?" Minos asked. "I've got to raise Asterion some cash, damn it. It can't wait."

Theseus said he needed to see Minos' securities account statements from the broker. He could tell from the statements how big the problem would be.

"Thrasycles, give Orthrus a call," Minos ordered. "Now. Get the broker out of bed if you have to. Tell him to get to his office and get a copy of my statements. I want him to deliver them here personally. And within the hour."

Theseus asked if the registration statement was otherwise ready to be filed.

"I'm comfortable with management's discussion," Cineas said.

"The financial statements are good to go," Eetion confirmed.

"Silenos and I are signed off on the business," Alcaeus added looking over at a nodding Silenos. "Diocles finished with the executive compensation a while ago. The underwriting section was cleared by Derinoe. So I think we are generally all set."

"We need to talk about the risk factors," Thrasycles said returning to the room. "There's too many in there. Can't we cut back on them?"

"Thrasycles, I told you to raise that with Theseus and

Axylus last week," Minos said in a shrill voice. "What in god's name have you been doing?"

Theseus said he had been over the risk factors several times, and he thought the content was appropriate for a company in this stage of development. If anything, he might want to add something more about the risks associated with the Nemean software.

"It's what's in there about the management team," Minos jumped in. "All that stuff about lack of experience, not having a track record together, no history of success. It makes us sound like a bunch of bloody amateurs."

"I wouldn't worry about it, Minos," Axylus answered. "In this market, the more risk factors the better. Investors think the greater the risk the higher the returns. They don't even look at the prospectus, except for the front page and the pictures on the inside cover. Let it go."

24

"Fine morning, Mr. Theseus," Herodian said in greeting.

Herodian was dressed in his usual black trimmed gray security uniform complete with insignia arm patch and sterling buttons. Herodian was the head of the firm's security effort, overseeing staff guards and emergency systems. The way Herodian stared when speaking, it was often difficult to know if he was looking at you.

"Anything to declare, Mr. Theseus?" Herodian asked.

The firm's board room was not frequently used. It was reserved for only important client conferences and top firm business. Access was restricted. As if a customs officer, Herodian was asking the executive committee members to declare all electronic devices. These items had to be turned over and would be unavailable for use during the partner compensation review meetings.

Theseus walked down a long corridor and stepped into the large wood paneled conference room. This was Theseus' first meeting as a member of the executive committee since his appointment by Aegeus. To Theseus, the executive committee was like the great war council of the Greeks in Ilium, counting among its heroes Agamemnon, Idomeneus, Aiantes, Diomedes, Odysseus and Menelaos. The executive committee had assembled to settle on the annual incomes of the firm's partners. It was the most important meeting of the year.

"Theseus, we were expecting you," Aegeus said gesturing. "We've already started."

Demosthenes was in the middle of discussing the first candidate. Demosthenes was a banking lawyer that had been on the committee for some time. He was a husky man who was overly loud and expressive. He sported a nicely trimmed goatee, an unusual look for a lawyer but one he managed well. Demosthenes was a snappy dresser, known for his fedora and camel topcoat in winter and Panama hat and seersuckers in summer.

Demosthenes extended Theseus a polite greeting and

congratulated him on his appointment to the committee. The other committee members followed suit. Theseus appreciated the welcome.

"You are new to this process," Aegeus said. "But you will catch on quickly enough. There are a lot of names to cover and the spoils are ours to distribute. We had a pretty damn good year."

Aegeus formed the executive committee years prior to get input on important decisions from a few trusted advisors. Aegeus now used the committee so frequently that it had become the *de facto* authority at the firm.

In the old days, the oldest partners were paid the most and everything proceeded in lock step. All lawyers graduating the same year from law school earned the same amount, and each year their take home increased. That practice had gradually given way to a merit based pay scale. As the firm grew larger and the legal profession more competitive, there was mounting pressure to reward the most productive partners regardless of age. Theseus was a beneficiary of the change. His own meteoric rise in compensation matched his mammoth production when he made partner.

Demosthenes continued where he left off.

"Selegus needs to be brought down," Demosthenes said. "He's over paid. His practice has fallen off and the outlook for bankruptcy work is not good."

Demosthenes was gesticulating forcefully as was his habit.

"The whole bankruptcy team should be cut back," Demosthenes contended. "The practice is not growing. Selegus is a good example. He hasn't had a new client in three years. His hours were way down last year."

Theseus was a little surprised by Demosthenes' caustic tone. As the new member of the committee, Theseus held his tongue.

Isaios then jumped in. He was the firm's top executive compensation attorney. Isaios was a thin, gaunt looking man with short peppery hair. The heavy lines in his face fit his serious demeanor. Isaios was Selegus' presenting partner.

"Selegus had some personal problems last year," Isaios

said. "He was out for about six weeks with pneumonia and that cost him hours. He had his third kid last September. Selegus also lost the Cetus account because of a conflict. That wasn't his fault."

Cetus Containers was a large packaging company that filed for bankruptcy earlier in the year. Stheno Distribution Corp., a long time client of the firm, was one of Cetus' largest trade creditors. Selegus had been advising Cetus for the past eighteen months over ways to stave off bankruptcy and restructure its senior credit facilities. When the company decided to file for bankruptcy, Isocrates determined that the firm could no longer represent Cetus given the Stheno relationship. It was a blow to Selegus' book of business.

"Selegus himself lost that account," Demosthenes said forcefully. "He should have kept the company out of bankruptcy. It made the firm appear weak. He knew we represented Stheno. Look, bottom line is his billable hours and revenues have evaporated."

The executive committee was comprised of five partners. In addition to Aegeus, Demosthenes, Isaios and Theseus, the committee was rounded out with Hypereides, a class action litigator. Hypereides had a rotund shape and large gut. His face was scarlet colored, and he had puffy eyes. His hair was a dark shade of orange and looked dyed. He was always chopping on an unlit cigar.

The lawyers on the executive committee were among the higher paid at the firm. As with other key management positions in the firm, it was no accident that authority followed income.

Theseus spoke up. He said he was generally in favor of merit pay, but that bankruptcy was an integral part of the firm's commercial law services. The group as a whole had a fairly decent year. And when the economy slowed, the firm would be thankful it had a solid workout group. Bankruptcy was counter cyclical.

The committee members were surprised that Theseus, being young and newly appointed, so quickly asserted his opinion.

"I tend to agree with Theseus," Aegeus said. "He's got something there. Let's be cautious."

"All right then," Isaios started. "Let's go around the room."

The committee used a novel system to arrive at compensation levels. A presenting partner would review a lawyer's profile, history with the firm, billable hours, collections and writeoffs. Some cases merited little discussion. Others caused debates, like Selegus. In the end, the chairman would call on the presenter to throw out a number. The next member would give his number until all the members had their turn. The chairman kept tabs on the range. If the range was large, there would be more back and forth. The committee then would work toward consensus. Aegeus would have the final say, but he long ago set a precedent not to settle on an amount outside the initial range.

"We need Selegus and his team for the rainy days," weighed in Hypereides.

"I can live with the midpoint, but I could go higher," Isaios said. "We're only dropping him a little at that level. I think he can deal with it. He's young."

"Fine," Demosthenes said deflated. "We're still making money off him I suppose. Let's move on."

"Agreed then?" Aegeus asked.

Everyone concurred.

"Next is Diagorus," Aegeus indicated. "Hypereides, he is yours."

"Right," Hypereides started. "Diagorus. He tried several cases last years. Two went to the jury. Both victories in terms of dollars. In one case, he defended a media client in a libel suit. The company published an article about the drug habit of one of our top politicians. Yes, I think it was Eubulus. You all saw it in the papers. Turned out a couple of our client's sources had fabricated their stories to discredit Eubulus. They were actually paid to do it from the campaigns of Eubulus' political rivals. Anyway, the client was found guilty for libel, but the damage award was only a dollar. Diagorus made Eubulus look like such a rat on cross that the

Theseus

jury had no sympathy for him. Gave him nothing."

"Diagorus also did the Clytius Corporation trial," Aegeus added. "Huge age discrimination case against the company. They were letting go fifteen percent of their most unproductive salesmen. Problem was they were all older men. Diagorus got Clytius off. The company walked away scot free. They were thrilled."

"Diagorus clocked nearly twenty seven hundred hours," Hypereides said. "He logged about a hundred thousand travel miles. Didn't see his family the whole year. I hear his wife wants a divorce."

"Diagorus is the kind of lawyer that has built the firm and keeps it at the top of its game," Aegeus said. "He has what it takes. He's one heck of a lawyer and partner. If I were his wife, I would wait until he collects his bonus check before filing the divorce papers. You have a number in mind, Hypereides?"

Hypereides' number was very generous. The other members were not too far off.

"Sounds reasonable," Demosthenes interjected.

"Let's give him the top of the range," Aegeus said. "Any disagreement?"

Aegeus asked for a vote. Everyone was on board.

"All right, let's look at Charicles," Demosthenes said. "Isaios, you're the presenter."

"Charicles has developed a real specialty in mutual funds, and he's been instrumental in helping Archias build that business," Isaios began. "Charicles had been doing all the heavy lifting for Archias for quite a few years now. He is a real expert in designing funds, representing the independent boards and handling securities filings."

"Well, from the statistics here," Demosthenes asserted, "it hard to know what's been going on with him. He's not billing the hours he used to. His numbers kept going up until last year, and then fell off a cliff. Did we lose the clients he worked for?"

"That's not it," said Isaios. "The clients are still there."

"Then what's the problem?" Demosthenes asked. "Has

he decided to kick back?"

"Quite the contrary," Isaios replied. "It's Archias. He has the client relationships. Archias moved the work Charicles was doing to a couple of associates. Never really told Charicles about his plan. He just did it. The move has really left Charicles hanging."

"Was Charicles screwing up?" Demosthenes queried.

"Like I said," Isaios repeated, "Charicles is an expert in the stuff. That's not the reason."

"What then?" Demosthenes persisted.

"Archias felt that Charicles' billing rate was getting too high," Isaios said. "I guess the mutual fund business is becoming more commoditized and Archias felt he needed to start charging lower blended rates. The rates we bill for the work get disclosed in the securities filings and are easy to compare to fees billed by other firms. At least that is what Archias explained."

"You sound like you don't fully believe what Archias has said," Aegeus questioned. "Do you think there is something else?"

"To be frank," Isaios said, "I do. I think Archias pads the bills a lot, to keep his own hours up. The funds can't really sustain two partners charging high rates. Archias actually asked Charicles to cut his hourly fee, and Charicles refused. So Archias decided to move the work to the cheaper lawyers to protect his own hours. He figures he can use Charicles when he needs to, but otherwise the associates can do the day to day. I also think Archias is threatened by Charicles' growing reputation with his clients."

"This is not a good situation, Isaios," Aegeus replied. "What should we do?"

"Well, I say it's Charicles' problem," Demosthenes blurted out. "They are Archias' clients. He controls what goes on. He can choose who he wants to service his clients. That's our way. Charicles is going to have to find his own business. We'll have to cut his compensation until he develops his own book. That will send him the message."

"Do you have an opinion, Theseus?" Aegeus asked.

Theseus

Theseus said that he was concerned about several things. He was bothered that Archias tried to get Charicles to lower his fees and safeguard his own time. Charicles had supported Archias in the mutual fund business for years and now was being discarded by Archias for less qualified lawyers who had lower rates. That was not good citizenship. There was also the question of whether the firm should be continuing to support mutual fund services if the work was becoming cut rate. The firm charged premium rates for its lawyers because of the complexity of the matters it handled and because it had the best legal talent in the business. Theseus wondered if continuing to do work that lesser firms could do at lower rates made sense for the firm.

The other members of the executive committee didn't immediately react to Theseus' commentary. They were obviously pondering.

"The situation certainly doesn't seem fair to Charicles the way you put it, Theseus," Hypereides said.

"But it is Archias' business," was Demosthenes' reply.

"What do you suggest we do, Theseus?" Aegeus asked.

Nothing. That was Theseus' answer.

"You are going to have to expound on that," Aegeus said.

Theseus said that even though Archias was wrong not to use Charicles, forcing Charicles on Archias wasn't optimal since it would deepen the rift between the two. That would ultimately prove detrimental to the client relationships. If the work was easily done by other firms for cheaper rates, the work would eventually become uneconomic. The reason there was pressure on rates was because the mutual fund business was getting more competitive itself, and all the funds were looking for ways to increase their returns. That meant cutting professional fees. On the other hand, many mutual fund complexes were designing more intricate structures and strategies to differentiate themselves and attract new investors. That was the hidden opportunity. Whether he knew it or not, Archias needed Charicles' expertise more than ever. Eventually, Archias' business would erode to nothing if he didn't go after the new business, and Charicles was critical in securing it. Theseus said Charicles should be kept at his current level so not to penalize him for Archias' behavior. The firm should help Charicles get more exposure himself in the industry. Have him assume a leadership role on the bar association's mutual fund committee, and encourage him to speak at top industry seminars. In time things would work themselves out.

The executive committee sat without uttering a word. Demosthenes looked unconvinced.

"That sounds like a plan," Aegeus finally said. "Let's hear some numbers."

Hypereides, Isaios and Theseus proposed keeping Charicles where he was, while Demosthenes wanted a substantial reduction in pay.

"Ok," Aegeus decided, "he stays level. Isaios, sit down with Charicles and tell him what Theseus wants done. Hypereides, go talk some sense into Archias. He should realize it's in his own best interest to work with Charicles. Who's next?"

The executive committee reviewed another fifteen or so partners before Aegeus announced it was time for a break. Aegeus asked Theseus to step outside the room for a moment.

"I like how you've jumped right in, Theseus," Aegeus said. "I can see you've done your homework."

Aegeus was referring to the five large binders of partner self evaluations and statistics that were distributed before the meeting.

"By the way, how is Asterion going?" Aegeus asked.

Theseus told him Asterion filed the offering with the commission last week.

"Excellent," Aegeus said. "Any road bumps?"

Theseus mentioned his concerns with the software testing and Mino's stock trades. But he personally looked into both matters and felt comfortable that the offering should proceed.

"Always last minute issues, aren't there?" Aegeus said. "Say, I know that I have Damasias coming up, but I'd like for

Theseus

you to take him as presenter. I want to see if we can keep his income up there this year. It will sound better coming from you."

Theseus thought the request was odd, and wondered why Aegeus did not want to present Damasias himself. Damasias was a labor lawyer that had been with the firm for nearly half a century. In his day, he was renowned for his union busting tactics. One story had Damasias breaking up an organizing effort at a large chemical plant by having the company provide free lunches to all the scabs that crossed the picket line. The gimmick was so effective that the boycott against the company lasted only until noon on the first day of the strike.

The executive committee reconvened and worked their way through a fair number of partners. When it came time for Damasias, Theseus took the lead. He tried to portray Damasias in the best possible light, but in point of fact Damasias' numbers had dwindled to almost nothing in recent years. He had no remaining clients to speak of, and billed no more than a couple hours a day on average. Damasias developed the habit of coming in late morning and leaving mid afternoon.

"Damasias has seen his day," Demosthenes started. "I think it's time he bows out. If we cut him enough, maybe he'll resign gracefully."

"He does set a negative precedent," Hypereides chimed in. "No offense, Aegeus, but we can't keep the old guard around if they're not productive. The overhead is killing us. I mean, Damasias still keeps his corner office and has his own secretary."

Aegeus noted that Damasias was struggling with his wife's health problems. He didn't have any children, and the firm was everything to the man. Cutting him loose would be devastating.

"I wish we could do something for the guy," Isaios said. "But we can't really afford to carry dead weight. It's too competitive out there. Lawyers like Damasias suppress our profits per partner. We're not a charity."

Theseus noted that Damasias was still sharp, and the younger labor lawyers in his group often sought him out for his sage counsel.

"I just don't see how we can keep him around anymore," Demosthenes said.

Theseus thought for moment, then proposed a solution. He suggested that the firm move Damasias from his corner office to an associate office, and double up his secretary. That would cut his overhead in half. Theseus knew that Pirithous had just picked up as a client a large food processing company that operated production line facilities in multiple locations. The company's employees were heavily unionized, and a number of collective bargaining contracts were up for renegotiation. He would ask Pirithous if he could possibly use Damasias for some of that work. If Damasias' hours were increased just a bit, his numbers would likely work out.

As Demosthenes, Isaios and Hypereides reflected on the proposal, Theseus noticed that Aegeus broke a smile.

"Maybe we could go that way," Hypereides said, "and see how it goes. If there is something that can drop to the bottom line, it's worth a try."

The committee decided to keep his salary the same and see how this new arrangement would go.

"All right, then," Isaios said, "at this pace maybe we can get back to our clients."

"Or maybe I can get in some tennis at the club before the weekend for once," Demosthenes hoped.

Demosthenes was not going to get his wish. There were still plenty of partners to review. After that, the committee would take up the new candidates for partnership. Hypereides informed Theseus that the new partner process always ate up inordinate amounts of time. The committee would be fully engaged for the next several days.

25

Theseus knew that if any associate was asked his goal at the firm, the response would unequivocally be to make partner. The answer was never to become a good lawyer, or to have an intellectually challenging career, or even to make a good income. It was always to make partner. That was the prize for all the hard work in law school and the ungodly hours spent grinding away as an associate at the firm. Theseus knew that associates had no real concept of what it meant to be a partner, but that was not a deterrent. For the associates, being made partner was akin to laying hold of the Golden Fleece.

To Theseus, making partner was like attaining citizenship in classical Athens. The citizen estate was coveted above all things. When a young man had his name entered onto the register of the *demes*, he became a privileged member of the *polis*. The citizen was entitled to join in the assembly, hold office and take roles in the religious festivals. But perhaps more than anything else, citizenship conveyed the right to bring cases and defend oneself before the lawgivers. The benefits of being a partner at the firm were no less significant.

In the old days, most associates who survived until their seventh year were automatically elevated to partner. Similar to the children of citizen parents in Athens, associates up for partner did not encounter many hurdles. There was seldom debate about their entitlement. Making partner was the decoration earned for simply being a competent lawyer. But things were changing. The partnership process was giving way to the same pressures changing the way lawyers were paid. With the increasing focal point being money, partnership was now less of a birthright and more the reward for tangible contributions to the firm. Partner status was becoming a gift bestowed upon those that could be trusted to generate profits. Theseus thought it was like the action taken by the Athenian assembly toward the Plataeans after Plataea was besieged by the Spartans during the Peloponnesian War. The Plataeans refused to break their friendship with Athens that dated to the battle of Marathon, even in the face of certain destruction by the Spartans. To the end they remained loyal to Athens. For the Plataeans who had escaped the Spartan massacre, Athens favored them with full citizenship. The grant was in honor of their unbroken allegiance and support of the Athenian war effort.

The partner evaluation process followed by the firm had evolved into an obstacle course each associate had to maneuver. It started the day an associate walked in the door. Each new associate was assigned a mentor, typically a young lawyer who had recently made partner. The mentor was usually outside an associate's practice group to provide objectivity and a fresh perspective on an associate's development. The mentor was supposed to meet with the associate regularly throughout the year and coach the associate on the standards for partnership. The practice sounded good on paper, but the mentoring partners seldom followed through. Partners did not want to spend time on anything they couldn't bill, and associate mentoring was nonbillable and nonproductive. The associates themselves didn't embrace the practice either, probably because they had no genuine interest in constantly being lectured.

An associate evaluation committee comprised of younger partners existed to handle the annual performance reviews of all associates. Theseus served for three years on the committee.

The evaluation committee would collect written assessments on every associate from forms filled out by supervising attorneys. The forms required ratings on everything from lawyering skills to executive presence to determine whether the associate exceeds, meets or falls below expectations. Theseus understood these responses as code for on track, one more year or immediate termination.

Associates who were weak or deficient were weeded out usually by year five. At that point, an associate either hit the wall or broke through it. If one made it to the magic age, it meant he or she was an expert in a particular area of the law important to the firm, or good at servicing the firm's clients

Theseus

for other partners. And there was also always room for the rare senior associate who had a knack for bringing new clients to the firm. Poulydamas once chastised Hector that not all gifts are given to any man together. So it was with lawyers.

The associate evaluations were designed to identify any kind of questionable behavior that could be grounds for firing an associate. Misconduct could relate to lack of talent, poor professional judgment or simply egregious acts. Theseus remembered one case involving a promising young associate who did food and drug litigation. His name was Ates. He was the favorite associate of the partners in his group, but he had a temper and abused staff and junior lawyers. His verbal attacks on subordinates were vicious. Ates was unable to keep a secretary as many quit or asked for reassignment. The end came when he had found his secretary slow in making copies of a pleading he wanted. Ates decided he couldn't wait and walked out to the copier, grabbed the document from her hands and slammed it on the copier glass, smashing it to pieces. The secretary ran off in tears. Ates received a failing grade on "ability to work with others" and was dismissed.

Another associate named Diodotus happened upon some work for a client that leased plots of land for transmission towers. It eventually came to light that Diodotus was negotiating real estate documents for the client even though he didn't know the first thing about real estate law. On top of that, he signed and delivered legal opinions he cribbed off a firm form. Associates were prohibited from signing legal opinions. The client had no idea that what Diodotus was doing was off the map until a lawyer at another firm called a real estate partner he knew at the firm. Diodotus received poor marks on "exercises good judgment" and was let go.

The committee didn't rely solely on the evaluations. It would also sift through the reams of statistics produced on each associate. Law firms had become adept at collecting and monitoring the data that mattered. Billable hours, billing rates, revenue generation, collections and realizations could be captured and analyzed for every lawyer going back years.

There was no hiding. Theseus was aware that the heavy reliance on statistics encouraged associates to game the system and juice the data. Astute associates would angle for big ticket projects, the kind one could wake up and go to sleep with and bill every minute in between. It didn't matter that these were often the very worst types of matters to work on. Associates could get mired in hours of mundane document review that had no end. But they could get their hours.

At the end of the evaluation process, associates would be assigned overall rankings from one to five. "Five" was reserved for senior associates recommended for partner. "Four" was expected for midlevel associates. "Three" meant something needed to change for the associate to have any realistic chance of staying with the firm for the long term. A "one" or "two" meant the associate had three months to find another firm or profession.

For those few senior associates that came out of the process with a recommendation for partnership, the journey was far from over. The reports of the associate evaluation committee went to the executive committee. The executive committee considered the input from the associate evaluation committee, but also looked hard at the performance of each practice group and the effect of new partners on the overall profits of the firm. If litigation was having a down year or two, it might mean that no new partners would be anointed from that group. Or if the number of new partner candidates overall depressed the profits per partner below acceptable levels, the count would be pared back.

Many associates understandably had issues with the system. They couldn't comprehend that their intrinsic worth was not dependent on their legal skills or lawyering abilities. Profit trumped everything. Some associates were unable to grasp the situation and figure out the process. Those that did knew the formula. Put in the hours, support the partners, keep the blinders on and hope for the best.

Theseus was aware that many other large firms had created a lawyer class called income partner. Associates up for partnership at these firms were made income partner, but the real hitters were the equity partners. Income partners did not share in the firms' profits and had no voting rights with respect to partnership affairs. Pay was fixed, although the most profitable income partners could earn a bonus. This two tiered partnership structure gained traction in order to keep the number of equity partners low and profits high. Income partners could hold themselves out to the world as partners, which was important because clients preferred interacting with partners, but otherwise they were employees at will. If an income partner developed a large book of business, either by inheriting institutional clients within the firm or developing new clients, he or she would be elevated to equity partner. If not, the income partner remained a second class citizen and could stay with the firm as long as he or she was productive.

Theseus did not care for the income partner structure. To him, it bred competition among partners for revenue and business and ultimately was counterproductive. The two tiered partnership served merely to protect the take of the equity partners at the expense of all the other lawyers.

The firm never adopted the structure. The firm kept the time tested up and out policy. If partnership was not in the cards for whatever reason by the seventh year of practice, an associate was given his or her walking papers.

On the third day of meetings, the executive committee reviewed the recommendations for partnership from the associate evaluation committee. Alcaeus was the first senior associate up. He had joined the firm out of law school, and clocked strong hours year in and year out. Theseus came to rely on him to prepare documentation, monitor the work of other associates and see a transaction through without a lot of fuss. Alcaeus could be trusted to raise issues that needed partner attention and find ways to overcome obstacles. Seldom was Alcaeus found complaining about pay or the demands placed on him by the practice. Clients liked and respected him and he became the primary contact on many deals. He was even developing a few clients of his own. He had come out of the associate evaluations with a strong "five."

"The kid is very solid with his stats," Isaios said. "I don't see any deficiencies in his package."

"You work with him the most, Theseus," Aegeus interjected. "It's really your call."

Theseus said that Alcaeus was an excellent lawyer. He easily grasped issues, exercised sound judgment and always put client interests first. He was also someone that held the good of the firm at heart.

"All good stuff," Demosthenes said, "but we expect those traits from anyone who gets this far. What's his economic contribution going to be? Can we count on him to develop an independent book of business? I would have expected a few more clients in his column."

Theseus said he was confident that Alcaeus would be able to sustain himself and others in years to come. There was no reason to doubt it.

"He's in," Aegeus declared, cutting off Demosthenes.

Theseus wondered if that was repayment for Theseus' backing of Damasias.

"Who's next?" Aegeus asked.

Alcaeus was one of eight senior associates up for partner. Not all fared as well. An insurance defense associate was rejected because he worked for a partner who had recently lost a couple of major bench trials. An employee benefits associate who took off for maternity leave was also passed over. Without saying it, the committee didn't like the fact that she took the full three months of her permitted leave.

After the executive committee weighed in, a full partnership meeting to vote in the new partners was still necessary. Normally, this was routine as the executive committee's decision would carry the day. But every once in a while, a debate at the partners' meeting would ensue. This year happened to be one of those times.

Besides Alcaeus, four other associates were being recommended for partnership. When the partners met late morning the day after the executive committee had made its selections, Alcaeus and three others were quickly voted in. But an associate named Phylas wasn't so fortunate. Phylas' specialty was appellate cases. He had clerked for a judge sitting on the appeals court and joined the firm in his fifth year on some very good recommendations. Phylas had quickly developed a name for himself for his excellent briefs and oral arguments.

"I thought that we had a two year rule," Tisias started. "All associates need to be with the firm at least two years before they can be partners. Phylas is short of the two years by five days. He hasn't made the cutoff."

Tisias was sitting up front with Aietes and Bacis. Medea was right behind them.

"If that is correct," Aietes added, "then we can't make him partner, at least not now. I've been told we've always stuck to the rule."

"That's ridiculous," Lysias countered. "We promised the kid consideration after two years when he joined us. He's everything we hoped for and more. A week is certainly something we can and should overlook."

"But there's another problem," Medea said. "Isn't Phylas the son-in-law of Castor?"

Castor was sitting toward the back of the room. He was a corporate partner that represented big airlines. Castor was known to have designs on succeeding Aegeus.

"He is indeed," Castor responded. "What's that got to do with anything?"

"We have a rule against nepotism," Medea said. "How did Phylas get hired in the first place?"

The room burst into torrid discussion. After a time, Theseus stood to speak. He said that both the two year and nepotism rules were long standing principles followed by the firm and should be respected. Theseus reminded everyone that both rules were grounded in sound management theory and to deviate would likely lead to bad precedent.

"You see," Aietes followed, "even the great Theseus sees the merit in our view."

The partners started up again in heated debate.

Theseus asked everyone to hear him out. He continued by saying that if he recalled correctly, Phylas had asked the firm if he could start a month after he left the court. The firm readily agreed, Theseus said. The firm paid Phylas a small salary to cover the gap and added Phylas to the rolls for the firm's health plan the day he resigned his clerkship. Because of the stipend and insurance, Phylas had officially been employed by the firm for a period that exceeded the two year measure by several weeks.

"Very ingenious, Theseus," Aietes said. "But there's still the nepotism rule."

Theseus went on by saying that the nepotism rule only applied to blood relatives, sons, daughters, grandchildren. It had never been raised in the context of in-laws, although he couldn't recall a hire that fit that relationship. Indeed, Theseus added, there were a couple of the partners who had married other partners, and there was no action to ask one or the other to leave.

"That should settle it," Lysias said loudly.

Aegeus then stood.

"Enough quibbling," Aegeus said. "Theseus is right in this. Phylas should be admitted without further discussion. If we pass on him, he'll walk across the street and continue what he's doing, but for someone else. We've tried to jumpstart an appellate practice before without success. We are not to blow this opportunity. Let's decide."

Aegeus asked for a vote. The majority of partners loudly approved Phylas. Aietes and his crowd were the lone dissenters. Medea sat still.

"Excellent," Aegeus announced. "Lysias, invite our new partners in. And not a word of this debate to Phylas."

When the partnership did vote in new lawyers, custom required that they be called up to the meeting. As they walked nervously into the room, the partners cheered and applauded. The new partners lined up and shook every partner's hand as they left the meeting. After the congratulations, the new partners stood alone wondering what just happened.

Theseus

After welcoming the new partners, Theseus walked out with Pirithous.

"There is something crass in this whole process," Pirithous commented to Theseus. "We are losing our bearings, with all this emphasis on statistics, money and rules. I fear we are not promoting all the deserving candidates."

Theseus said he was also somewhat disillusioned. The money aspect was important, but he felt that the nobleness of the law profession suffered. He recalled the intellectual stimulation he felt as he studied the law, and how honored he was when the firm offered him a position. He had no thought of money or riches then. Nowadays, the exigency of the firm was profit. Theseus thought Theognis must have felt that same regret when he wrote his elegies. Money, although necessary to stave off the great breaker of men, poverty, was corrupting. The firm's drive for profit was almost shameful, and shame was the great enemy of *areté*.

"What's to be done with Diagorus, Theseus?" Pirithous asked.

Theseus didn't know what Pirithous was referring to.

"Diagorus went ballistic over his pay," Pirithous said.

The numbers for the partners hadn't been released yet, Theseus noted. Besides, Diagorus was treated generously by the executive committee.

"Well, someone leaked his take and he wasn't happy," Pirithous responded. "The guy's gone mad. He's bitter that he wasn't the highest paid in his group. Diagorus got wind of it while he was in the library. He knocked over a whole stack of federal reporters, nearly killing an associate. Herodian had to be called in."

For many partners, Theseus knew their annual compensation and how it stacked up with other partners was the only measure of their worth. Like Aias when denied the armor of Achilles, many could not accept the dishonor of not being given their due.

"Catch up with you later at the party," Pirithous said before leaving.

Pirithous was referring to the time honored soiree the

new partners had to host at a nearby pub following the partnership vote. The whole firm was invited, and the new partners had to pick up the tab. No discussion. The bill would easily be in the thousands, so if there were only a few partners that year, the pain for the new partners could be intense. By late afternoon, the mailroom employees would belly up to the bar and be ordering drinks and food. Secretaries and staff would filter in after business hours. Lawyers came in and out at all times. The night usually couldn't end soon enough for the new partners. Attorneys headed to other late night spots afterwards, and the next day handed over receipts to the new partners.

When Theseus arrived at the party, people were already crowding the bar. Theseus noticed Herodian off at a side table with a couple of men from the security team. A number of legal assistants and word processing staffers were laughing and talking. Theseus thought the cordiality and good spirits were good for everybody. It was also an occasion for the partners to talk about their work or the firm over a few drinks. The Persians used to discuss important decisions when drunk, and then reconsider the issues when sober. Similarly, decisions made while sober were revisited when drunk. Theseus saw merit in the practice.

Alcaeus was there with a drink, and Theseus congratulated him with a firm handshake.

"I just talked to Lysias," Alcaeus said looking distraught. "He told me about the capital contribution we now have to make. No one ever mentioned it. Is it true that I have to kick in that much money to the firm? Theseus, I can't afford that."

Theseus smiled and told Alcaeus that if couldn't write the check, the firm would arrange a loan with the firm's bank. The firm got the money up front, and the new partner had to pay back the loan out of his draws. Because of the size of the capital contribution and the bank loan repayment terms, the newly elevated associate often took a pay cut when he or she became a partner. Few new partners were ready for it. They were now tied in and had to earn their way out of the debt. A nice feature for the firm. Instead of walking into financial security, the new partners would be forced to work even harder.

By the time Theseus was ready to leave, the party was in full swing. All the employees had arrived, and many of the partners.

As he walked out, he ran into Aegeus and Medea.

"I liked how you handled Aietes and his crowd, Theseus," Aegeus said greeting him. "Well done. You were quick to put him down."

Aegeus' comment reminded Theseus of Heracles and Lityerses. Heracles slew Lityerses without thinking twice for the way Lityerses treated his house guests.

"Don't go thinking you are so clever, Theseus," Medea warned. "And I wouldn't be too dismissive of Aietes. You just may find yourself pitted against an opponent that is more than your match."

Aietes was not the one that concerned him.

26

Theseus was an ardent though irregular theatergoer and decided to invite Ariadne to a play at a local writer's workshop. Ariadne said she was planning a trip to Athens, and would stay over the weekend of the play. Theseus had Ophelia pick up tickets. Ophelia also reserved for Ariadne the guest quarters in Theseus' building.

The play was about the final days of Oedipus. It was one of Theseus' favorites. Theseus was fascinated not so much with the Oedipus story as he was with the interplay of the themes of fate, destiny and justice. As heinous as the crimes were that Oedipus committed, he was nonetheless shown favor by the gods when he died.

Theseus enjoyed the production, and he thought the actors had staged an excellent performance. Afterwards, he took Ariadne to an out of the way cafe not far from the theatre.

"The Asterion boys kicked off their road show this week," Ariadne said as they were sitting down at the cafe. "I was able to catch the presentation yesterday at Typhon's offices."

Theseus had forgotten that the investor presentations had started. The commission had reviewed the company's filing and came back with light comments. Theseus was somewhat surprised. The commission normally identified a long list of issues that often required extensive revisions to the registration statement. Accounting comments were often the most difficult and time consuming to address. Theseus thought the commission must have been overly inundated with filings given market conditions not to have given the filing a harder look.

After quickly clearing the commission comments, a preliminary prospectus, which was complete except for the final price of the shares to be sold in the offering, was printed and hundreds of copies delivered to Typhon and the underwriting syndicate. The bankers scrambled to reschedule the investor sessions, anticipating another couple of weeks back and forth with the commission. But they wanted to take advantage of the hot market. There was no time to lose building enthusiasm for the deal, so the investment bankers quickly got the prospectus out on the street. The next three weeks meant traveling from city to city hawking Asterion's stock. Athens, Argos, Delphi, Sardis, Miletus, Syracuse and Corcyra were all stops. They were cities where large numbers of institutional buyers resided.

Road show meetings typically took one of two forms. There were group meetings with small investment companies, family offices and high net worth individuals. A power point presentation was made by management and the bankers. Questions about the company and its prospects were raised and answered.

For the large mutual funds and pension investors, one on one meetings were scheduled. These meetings tended to be shorter. Institutional investors were prepared and did not wait for the canned pitch. They knew the industry and the competition. They dove quickly into management's business model and the risks and rewards facing the company.

In all of these meetings, Theseus knew decisions to invest more often than not hinged on the impression made by management. At this game, Theseus thought Minos was a master. He had an easy and natural way about him in front of a crowd. He smiled and laughed his way through difficult questions but was always confident. Minos made everyone feel that there was good money to be made if only they would back him.

Theseus asked Ariadne how she managed to attend one of the meetings. The bankers didn't like to see the lawyers during the roadshow.

"Oh, you know Minos," Ariadne smiled. "He always wants me around. Besides, it was the underwriter's due diligence meeting with their retail group. A dry run, really."

Theseus knew the bankers generally ran a meeting with syndicate members and brokers first. They could use it to freely discuss the company, get a sense of tough questions and hone management's delivery.

Once the show hit the road, the pace was frenetic. Multiple meetings and even cities could be scheduled on any given day. To counter the grueling calendar, the roadshow team traveled in style. A private jet was arranged by Typhon for transportation to save time. The hotels were five star and the restaurants the best in town. And there were always women. Sometimes from the investment firms, often pickups at the bars before or after dinner.

"I think you should probably look in on one of the meetings, Theseus," Ariadne suggested. "Thrasycles was talking off script, getting into some pretty aggressive earnings projections. He shouldn't be doing that. It's not even necessary in this market."

Theseus agreed he should attend a session, and decided to catch up with the group in Lydia early in the second week. When informed of Theseus' plan, Minos told Theseus that Axylus preferred if he didn't come, that there were no worries. Theseus was concerned about Thrasycles, so he insisted.

Theseus arrived in Sardis for the afternoon meeting. The meeting was held in a conference room in a plush hotel. There were about twenty attendees in addition to the Asterion people and investment bankers. He walked in as Axylus was completing his introduction. He saw Minos, Thrasycles and Cineas, but didn't see Silenos. Stolos was sitting with Cadmos and a couple of eager looking young women. Theseus assumed they were junior bankers brought to handle logistics and perhaps add some spice to the trip.

Minos took the microphone and talked as he walked around the room. He outlined the company's strategy and product rollout and the unique market opportunity. Thrasycles flipped through high tech color slides on the overhead as Minos spoke. The slides depicted futuristic infrastructure grids and assiduous programmers in front of terminals. Minos spent a fair amount of time on the call center operation in Stratus. Theseus thought the presentation was a bit superficial, but Minos had the attention of the audience. That was a good sign.

Cadmos followed Minos and addressed the economy, the tech industry and the size of the company's market.

Thrasycles went next. He talked about the history of Asterion and the acquisition of Nemean. Thrasycles was a little stiff and didn't budge from behind the podium, but managed well enough.

"Now let's talk financials," Thrasycles said. "Cineas, our chief financial officer, is here to answer any questions you have once I'm finished."

Theseus thought that Cineas should be discussing the numbers. Not having the chief financial officer give the financial presentation didn't convey the strongest impression. Thrasycles quickly walked through a slide showing Asterion's pro forma balance sheet after the offering. He didn't bother to show the company's historical income statements.

"What I really want to discuss," Thrasycles continued, "are our earnings projections."

Thrasycles put up a slide showing five year forecasts of revenues, profit margins and earnings per share. Theseus was aghast.

"As you can see," Thrasycles said, "we think we can achieve exponential revenue growth while keeping costs flat. The result is high margins and high profitability. If the market is as large as we think it is, or even a third of it, our earnings will skyrocket over the first five years."

Theseus didn't believe what he was hearing. The Stratus call center just went on line, and Silenos was only beginning to put together a sales force. He would have to hire an army of salesmen to come anywhere close to the revenue projections. The product testing was also only recently completed, and although apparently successful, the support costs were still uncertain.

Theseus made a line for Axylus and pulled him out of the meeting. He asked Axylus what he thought he was doing letting Thrasycles go on like that.

"Hey," Axylus said defensively, "I can't control what he does. Besides, the numbers paint a pretty vivid picture."

Theseus quickly explained that those numbers were not

likely to be achieved, or anything close, and both Asterion and Typhon could be sued over them. Axylus grew nervous and asked what they should do. Theseus responded that he should get Thrasycles off as soon as possible, and Axylus himself should announce that the flip book of slides handed out to prospective investors could not leave the room. Axylus was turning red. He took a deep breath and walked to the front of the room. Axylus grabbed the microphone away from Thrasycles and told the audience the meeting was running over and they had to wrap up.

"I'm not finished," Thrasycles protested.

"Unfortunately, we do have to move on to our next meeting," Axylus told the investors. "If you have questions that need answers, please contact my colleague Stolos here."

Axylus thanked everyone for their attendance and said he would be in touch to take their orders.

Thrasycles was hot. Minos sensed something was amiss, but went off to talk to investors as they left. Theseus made the two female bankers stand at the doors and collect the flip books.

When the room cleared, Thrasycles accosted Theseus.

"What's with telling Axylus to cut me off?" Thrasycles said demanding an explanation.

Theseus told him not now, that they could talk it over at dinner. Theseus caught up to Minos to make sure he also wasn't talking out of school.

Later that evening at the restaurant, Thrasycles was still stewing. Axylus had settled down after a couple of drinks. Minos was his charming self, seemingly unaffected. He sat right down between the female bankers, and quickly had their attention.

Theseus asked Thrasycles to go with him to the bar, wanting to avoid a row at the table. He said to Thrasycles that presenting aggressive forecasts and handing them out was dangerous if not reckless. Projections of the kind Thrasycles was touting could be the basis for stockholder suits if the company's stock price faltered after the offering.

"That's not what I was told," Thrasycles said skeptically.

Theseus asked him who at the firm told him differently.

"No one at your firm," Thrasycles said. "I know a guy at another firm who's a securities lawyer. I ask him, you know, for informal advice."

Theseus was beside himself. He told Thrasycles that he didn't know who he was talking to but didn't care. He would speak to Minos about this.

"Go ahead," Thrasycles shot back, "Minos has been talking to him too."

Theseus went to the table meaning to take it up with Minos. Using other lawyers behind the back of primary counsel was a harbinger of an oncoming storm.

Cadmos and Stolos had arrived, and Axylus looked like he had already forgotten the day's events. They were heavily into the drinking, and the two female bankers were sharing laughs with Minos.

"Why so glum, Theseus?" Minos asked. "I thought the day went extraordinarily well. Investors were pumped from the looks of things. Hey, Mnene, go cheer up Theseus."

Mnene took her cue and got up from her seat.

"I've heard so much about you, Theseus," Mnene started giddily, "and from the looks of you, it must be all true."

Theseus didn't like the direction Mnene was going, and motioned Minos away from the table. Theseus asked him what he was doing working with another securities lawyer.

"Is that what's upsetting you?" Minos said surprised. "Hell, don't worry about that. He's a guy that works with Orthrus, you know, who arranged the bridge. He's advised on a couple trades, that's all. You're our guy, Theseus. You're doing a hell of a job."

Minos' words made Theseus cringe. He had a bad feeling that this entire venture would blow up.

"What's the matter with Mnene, Theseus?" Minos asked slapping his back. "You want Strybele? Look, they are just kids doing their job. Axylus is putting them up to this. Take care of the client type crap. But they're good looking women. No harm in it, don't you think?"

Minos and Theseus sat back down and dinner was served.

The group enjoyed the best the restaurant had to offer. Afterwards, Theseus excused himself and found his way back to his room. He knew the rest were just getting started.

Theseus was awakened well before daylight by the telephone. Axylus was on the line.

"Theseus, thank god you're there," Axylus said panting. "You've got to get to the police station. They have Thrasycles."

Half asleep, it took a few moments for Theseus to collect himself.

"He and Stolos were stopped after leaving the bar," Axylus revealed. "Long story short, Thrasycles is in a holding cell. We need you down here."

Theseus got dressed. He felt like he was being called to retrieve the bodies of the Argos warriors who fell at Thebes after Cleon refused them proper burial. This was a duty he could not ignore. Axylus had his car waiting and Theseus headed right to the station. Theseus found Stolos sitting near the booking desk hung over. Theseus asked for the officer involved and took him aside to talk privately. In about twenty minutes, the officer told the guards to release Thrasycles. No charges would be filed.

Thrasycles came out looking horrible. His eyes were bloodshot and his left arm hung limp.

"Thanks, Theseus," Thrasycles said sheepishly. "Never get into a tiff with a cop."

Thrasycles said that he and Stolos had left the bar to go get something to eat at a late night diner. Just as they pulled out of the parking lot, they were stopped by the police. Thrasycles started arguing belligerently with the cop. When the cop decided he had enough and went to cuff him, Thrasycles resisted. The cop grabbed his left arm and jerked it violently behind his back. Before they knew it, he and Stolos were off to the station.

"Damn thing about it, Theseus," Thrasycles said, "it was Minos' fault. He said it was the best food in the city."

Axylus was waiting to take Thrasycles to the hospital to have his arm examined. He asked Theseus to help Stolos back to the hotel.

"I don't know what you said to get me out of there," Thrasycles remarked when they were leaving. "But I promise you I won't talk about projections anymore."

27

Medea stopped by Theseus' office a few days after Theseus had returned to Athens and announced that she had a good client prospect that she could use his help on.

"It's a company called Podarge Health Associates," Medea said. "They source and design outpatient medical facilities, and need to borrow some money. It's a good business from what I've learned. I have a meeting set up, and I was hoping you could go meet with them. I've already run a conflicts check. It was a clean search, so we are free to take them on."

Theseus asked Medea why she wanted him to handle the client.

"I know you think I'm some kind of a witch," Medea said with a slight laugh.

The image of the Gorgon slain by Perseus came to Theseus' mind.

"We have our differences, I suppose, maybe just going after the same things and getting in each other's way," Medea said candidly. "But we should try to get along. Aegeus has been encouraging me to work with you more. Besides, I think your personality matches the people at Podarge. The chief executive there is a sharp guy, named Melas. You two would hit it off. I would appreciate it if you could take this on. At least go meet with them. We can go together, if you don't mind putting up with me."

Theseus was skeptical, but Medea sounded sincere. Theseus felt that it would reflect badly on him if word got back to Aegeus that he refused to help. That would be contrary to the firm's code. So he agreed.

Medea said she arranged the meeting out at Podarge's offices in Eleusis. When the day of the meeting arrived, Theseus rang Medea so they could head out together. She didn't pick up.

"No, she not here," Medea's secretary said. "I haven't seen or heard from her today. I don't know where she might be. And there's nothing on her calendar about a meeting out at Podarge."

Theseus assumed Medea headed to the meeting on her own, so he would just catch up with her there.

When Theseus arrived at Podarge, he asked for Melas.

"He's traveling this week, Mr. Theseus," the young girl at the front desk told him. "Let me call Tydeus, he's our number two."

Theseus asked if Medea had arrived.

"No, no one by that name has been here today," the receptionist replied.

In a few moments, a man came out. He appeared overtired and his eyes darted to and fro when he spoke.

"My name is Tydeus," he said, "and you must be Theseus. I heard you might be coming in."

From the sound of it, Theseus had the clear impression Tydeus was not expecting him.

"Let's go back to my office," Tydeus said. "We can talk for a few minutes there."

Tydeus' office was overgrown with stacks of site plans and surveys for office layouts. He had to remove some papers from a chair for Theseus to have a place to sit.

"We're awfully busy around here," Tydeus said, "so pardon the mess. Melas said something about meeting some new lawyers. What is it we were supposed to meet about?"

Theseus explained to Tydeus what he was told by Medea.

"Oh, you're with Medea," Tydeus said. "Yes, yes, yes. She was here a couple of days ago. We just got a loan agreement from our bank. You should probably have it."

Tydeus walked out of his office. Theseus heard him give instructions to an assistant to run a copy of the bank document. He returned and spent a few minutes talking about Podarge and possible financing plans.

"Very preliminary, all of this," Tydeus said. "But maybe you could take a look at the agreement. You know, give us some quick thoughts."

Tydeus wrapped up the meeting fairly quickly and walked Theseus out. Theseus found the whole thing quite strange.

When Theseus got back to the office, he had a

commercial banking associate mark up the loan document and send it to Tydeus. Theseus called Tydeus several times over the next few days, but Tydeus never returned his calls. Theseus also tried to contact Medea but she also was unavailable. He decided to hold off on anything further until he heard back from Tydeus or Medea. He went on to other work.

The following week, Theseus received a call from Isocrates. Theseus took his calls, as many did, with some trepidation. No one liked getting a call from the firm's general counsel. Isocrates told Theseus that something had come up and asked if he had some time to meet with him and Lysias. Theseus had no idea what it could be about.

Theseus arrived at the conference room to find Isocrates, Lysias and Aegeus.

Theseus greeted them all, but was left cold by the lack of response. The three men stared hard at Theseus.

"Theseus, have you ever done any work for our client, Argus?" Lysias asked directly.

Theseus replied that he hadn't.

"Well, let me give you some background on the client," said Lysias. "If anything I say rings a bell, let us know. Argus Consulting Group has been a longtime client of Aegeus. Aegeus and the chairman of Argus, Neidias, met many years ago and Aegeus helped Neidias build his company from the ground up. Argus is now one of the leading health care consulting firms in the country. A couple of years ago, Neidias did an extensive search for a successor he could groom. He hired an outsider. He gave the man restricted stock of the company, but required him to stay on for five years before it was fully vested. For the first several years, Neidias was pleased with the executive's performance. The company continued to prosper. But before long, the man began to ask Neidias for more money and more stock. He took issue with Neidias' plans for the company and wanted to hire his own people. Neidias resisted. The man abruptly departed to set up his own operation and sued Argus over the value of the stock that he forfeited when he left. He also began soliciting Argus' clients. Aegeus recommended that Neidias counter sue for breach of the noncompete provisions in his employment agreement. The litigation has been going on for about eighteen months and is very contentious. The firm, of course, is representing Neidias and Argus. Any of this familiar?"

Theseus said this was the first he had heard of it. He asked who the executive was and the name of his new company.

"Do not play games, Theseus," Aegeus started in. "I've gotten to know you well enough to know that you are sly."

"Lawyers and law firms have a duty of loyalty to their clients, as you know, Theseus," Isocrates said. "It's serious when the trust between the firm and a client is broken."

Theseus demanded to know what all this was about.

"You really don't know?" Lysias asked.

"I should have listened to Medea about you," Aegeus said fuming.

"Aegeus, please," Lysias cautioned Aegeus. "Ever have any dealings with a company called Podarge or its chief executive, Melas?"

Theseus now understood. He asked if Melas and Podarge were the adverse parties in the Argus litigation.

"Don't take me for an imbecile, Theseus!" Aegeus growled.

"Please, Aegeus," Isocrates said. "When was the last time you saw Melas?"

Theseus said he had never met him, but had been out to Podarge's offices just last week to meet with the company's chief financial officer.

"I knew it was true!" Aegeus shouted standing up.

"Aegeus, sit down," Lysias pleaded. "Podarge filed a motion with the court this morning to disqualify us from representing Argus. They are claiming we have a conflict of interest. Your name is all over the motion."

Isocrates passed a copy of the motion to Theseus. Theseus read the details about his meeting with Tydeus and the work he had done on the loan document.

"You petty thief!" Aegeus vented. "Do you think you can damage my client associations in order to enrich yourself? I have signaled you out as a future leader of this firm, and in return you steal from me."

Theseus said there must be some kind of explanation. A conflict check was run and nothing came up on Argus.

"That can be easily verified," said Isocrates skeptically.

He dialed the firm's docket department which handles client conflict reports.

"No checks were run, no reports were made," Isocrates said getting off the phone.

Theseus told the group that there must be some mistake, that Medea told him herself that the conflict cleared.

"Medea?" Aegeus said angrily. "What does she have to do with this?"

Theseus said that it was Medea who asked him to take on Podarge.

"Don't try to lay this off on Medea," Aegeus shot back.

"Calm yourself, Aegeus," Lysias countered. "Let's call in Medea to explain. Isocrates, go and find Medea. Bring her in."

Isocrates called down to Medea's office and was told she was not there.

"Give me a few minutes," Isocrates said leaving the room.

Theseus, Lysias and Aegeus sat without talking during Isocrates absence. Aegeus was boiling.

Isocrates returned carrying a stack of documents that he dropped loudly on the table.

"Medea is gone," Isocrates said, "but you should look at these. They were sitting on her desk in her office."

Lysias picked the document on top and started slowly turning pages.

"Curious," Lysias said. "This appears to be a draft of Podarge's motion to disqualify. I wonder why Medea would have it?"

Lysias removed his glasses and looked intently at the other documents.

"These look like earlier versions," Lysias observed.

Theseus

"Aegeus, I assume are you familiar with Medea's handwriting."

"Of course I am," Aegeus said gruffly. "Give me those."

Aegeus grabbed hold of a heavily marked up draft. He stood up and went to the window while reading the document. There were several minutes of awkward silence.

"Get me Herodian!" Aegeus ordered as he turned around. "I want Medea's office locked and secured! Nothing is to be removed! Now!"

Isocrates left to carry out Aegeus' instructions.

"I owe you an apology, Theseus," said Aegeus. "It would appear as if Medea had set about to poison you. Her hand is all over these documents. She needs to go, and I will see to it."

Theseus asked if there was any way to salvage the relationship with Neidias.

"Oh, he will understand once I talk to him," Aegeus said ruefully. "A slip of our conflicts procedures is all he needs to know. But we will have to resign from representing Argus in the litigation. It wouldn't look good for the firm, and we don't want our internal affairs fodder for the media."

Aegeus became meditative.

"Was there ever a more devious, conniving woman in the world?" Aegeus wondered aloud. "A stupid old man falling for a younger woman's charms. How could I have been so blind to it? She almost had me convinced she would have made a fine chairman."

Easily understood, however regrettable, Theseus thought. For all his power, even Zeus succumbed to the charms of Hera of the white arms. While Zeus was rallying the Trojans, Hera came down from her golden throne and, hiding the zone given her by Aphrodite, distracted Zeus by her seduction. Her wiles gave Poseidon time to aid the Danaans.

28

Theseus had just sat down at his desk when the receptionist rang to let him know that Selene was on the phone and needed to speak with him. Selene was a corporate paralegal. The receptionist said Selene sounded very upset.

"Mr. Theseus," Selene said with a shaky voice, "I tried calling you last night. Bureau agents came to my apartment yesterday evening. I don't know, maybe it was about just after dinner. They were asking what I had to do with Stymphalae Flight Co. You know, that company of Mr. Minos."

Theseus said he had never heard of the company.

"Never heard of it?" Selene responded. "Mr. Tantalus had me form it a while ago. He said I should put my name down as the company's registered agent. I've only filed one annual report for the company. Nothing more, I swear. The bureau people came in to my place, and started questioning me about Minos. Two of them. A man and a woman. They kept asking what I had to do with him, what I knew about him. That sort of thing. Theseus, they were agents. They said they hoped I would cooperate. I didn't know what they were talking about or what it was they wanted."

Selene had been a fixture at the firm for many years. Theseus liked working with her because she was professional and efficient, and he could always count on her. She started with the firm as a secretary, but obtained a paralegal certification after taking a local bar association course. Paralegals worked exclusively for the lawyers and were trained to perform ministerial and administrative legal functions. Litigation paralegals prepared routine court motions, processed court filings, organized discovery materials and maintained case files. Corporate paralegals handled preparation of corporate charter documents, lien searches and closings of loans and acquisitions. Many paralegals, like Selene, approached the work as if it were a career. Others came out of college and took paralegal jobs without any training to help them decide whether to go to law school.

Theseus

One universal shortcoming of the job was the abuse paralegals suffered at the hands of lawyers. Paralegals were treated like metics. For whatever reason, many lawyers felt entitled to intimidate, berate and abuse paralegals. This was especially true of young lawyers, even those just out of law school. It was not uncommon for new attorneys, who had no knowledge of anything practical or useful, to order paralegals around like they owned them. There was a story that a first year male associate once made a female paralegal go out and buy him a new shirt, tie and underwear for a last second trip a senior lawyer needed him to make. The paralegal was ordered to return to the clothier three times to get a tie that was to the associate's liking.

Theseus could tell that the visit by the bureau had unnerved Selene. She seemed to be bordering on panic.

"They wanted me to tell them everything about Minos," Selene said frantically. "The last time I saw him, talked to him. Did I ever travel with him, like on his helicopter. Theseus, I never met the man, not once. I have never been on a helicopter, never! The bureau man did all the questions, and the woman just kind of smiled and looked around. I got scared. They told me Minos might be in some real trouble, and it looked like I could have something to do with it. They asked me about Stymphalae, and why my name showed up on the company's articles. I don't know what the man has done, but I was just doing my job. You know, following Mr. Tantalus' orders."

The receptionist called again and Theseus put Selene on hold.

"Theseus," the receptionist said, "there are two people here to see you. They say they are from the bureau."

Theseus told the receptionist to have them wait, and picked up the line with Selene.

"Oh, god," Selene said very rapidly. "I'm so sorry, Mr. Theseus, I gave them your name as one of Minos' attorneys. You and Mr. Tantalus. They told me not to tell anyone they came here last night. Please, Mr. Theseus, don't tell them we talked. The bureau, those agents, they said if I did they would

259

make it difficult for my brother. He's, well, had some run-ins with the law."

Theseus hung up on Selene and thought about calling Minos, but decided against it. He was better off the less he knew. Theseus told the receptionist to show the agents to his office.

Agents Erastus and Copreus were young and neatly dressed. Erastus had thick black hair and a penetrating stare. He wore a navy suit, white shirt and blue tie. Copreus had shoulder length brown hair and wore a dark suit with white blouse. Theseus wasn't certain if it was their demeanor or the circumstances, but both agents demanded one's attention.

Theseus asked for identification and the agents produced wallet badges. Theseus thought better than to request a close inspection. The agents sat down quickly without Theseus having offered. Both smiled. Erastus sat and crossed his legs. Copreus propped herself on the edge of her seat. Erastus went first.

"Nice office," Erastus said. "Quite a view. You must be very successful in your work."

Theseus acknowledged the comment with a look of impatience.

"We understand, Theseus, that you may be representing a man named Minos, is that right?" Erastus asked. "We have reason to believe that Minos is the registered owner of a helicopter. We are very interested in determining its present location. What can you tell us about that?"

Theseus said he had no idea what Erastus was talking about.

"The bureau has been investigating the increasing drug traffic with Megara," Copreus interjected, "and we're identifying the whereabouts of all aircraft registered here. Minos' helicopter doesn't appear to be located where it is registered and there is no flight log indicating he took it anywhere."

Theseus said that he had no direct knowledge of where the helicopter might be, much less that it even existed. Theseus asked the two agents if they had tried to contact

Theseus

Minos.

"We know where we can find him," Copreus quipped. "There's no point in trying to protect him."

Theseus stood to indicate the meeting was over. The agents got up out of their chairs.

"Look," Erastus said. "Minos is a client of yours. We thought you could help us locate the helicopter. Why don't you think this over and give us call."

Both Erastus and Copreus pulled out their business cards, which carried a gold embossed rendering of the famous bureau logo. Theseus showed them out to reception.

Theseus' main concern was the Asterion offering. Any kind of entanglement with the bureau involving drug trafficking, if made public, would deal a deathly blow to the planned stock sale. The mere suggestion of management involvement in federal felony crimes would turn investor interest in the offering stone cold. Theseus called Minos at his office.

"Oh, the helicopter," Minos said when Theseus recounted the bureau's visit. "I had it moved about a month ago. It used to be at a hanger at the Attica regional airport. I had it brought out to Piraeus."

Theseus asked why the flight logs didn't show the move.

"Well, look, Theseus, it was because of Talos Bank," Minos said. "I owe some money on the thing, and the bank was getting all nervous about the payments. I had some guys move it from Attica by truck. The helicopter is now padlocked out at a warehouse in Piraeus. Tell you what. I'll send over the bank loan on the helicopter, and you have your guys take a look at it. See what you can do, you know, to stall. I don't want the bank to get hold of it right now. The market's down for copters. After the offering, I'll pay the damn loan off. "

Theseus told Minos to send the document over and he would deal with the bureau. He called Hippias, the firm's white collar criminal lawyer. Hippias was the hardy sort, the type that never could keep his shirt tail tucked in. He always looked freshly shaved and wore only white shirts. He removed his suit coat whenever he was in a meeting. Hippias took a job as an assistant state's attorney out of law school and in time was elected for two terms as the city's top prosecutor. Hippias gave it up for a lucrative career at the firm.

"Yeah, I know Erastus," Hippias told Theseus. "He's relatively new over there. A bit of a stuffed shirt. Has a political agenda."

Theseus explained the situation with the helicopter. He also informed Hippias of the Asterion offering, which was to price the following week. Time was of the essence.

"I'll talk with Erastus," Hippias said. "Get me clearance to the warehouse from your client, and I'll take Erastus out there so he can see it for himself. I'm sure we can sort this out."

29

The Asterion offering was scheduled for pricing midweek. The bankers preferred to price on a day when investors could be found in their offices and there would be active trading on the floor of the exchanges the next day. The beginning and end of the week were usually the worst days to launch a deal.

The market had continued hot for technology stocks. Theseus knew that market demand was almost at a frenzy. Companies that could not have raised a dime two years ago were now deals waiting to get done. Investors were riding the technology boom. Stocks of enterprises with no revenues or profits were oversubscribed five or six times at the opening of trading.

Axylus was primed to go with Asterion. The road show was well received and Axylus' trading desk had built a strong book of buyers for Asterion shares. Price talk was at the top of the range indicated in the commission filings. Theseus got a call from Stolos. He had Penthesileas on the line.

"Theseus," Stolos started, "the stock is going to be a blowout. We want to upsize the deal. Demand is just incredible. Minos has signed off."

"The registration statement will need to be amended," Penthesileas alerted Theseus as if he wasn't aware. "We do this kind of thing all the time. We'll help you through it."

Stolos said Axylus was proposing a twenty percent upsizing for the offering. That would mean a huge increase in new capital for Asterion. As promising as it sounded, Theseus was concerned that Minos didn't have a strategy to deploy that amount of cash. Theseus rang Minos up at his office.

"It's fantastic," Minos declared. "With that kind of cash, we'll be set. The company will have a war chest that could last years. What are you worried about, Theseus?"

This was not a venture investment, Theseus said to Minos. A private company could sit on a pile of cash to develop its business over a prolonged period. A public company was different. Public firms could not carry cash too long. The return on investment was too low. Asterion would have to report strong earnings in its early quarters after going public to be successful. That meant using cash for building out the company's infrastructure, sales force and, ultimately, generating revenues and profits. Minos didn't have a plan that matched the amount of money Axylus wanted him to take.

Typhon, Theseus guessed, was pushing the upsizing hard. The bankers stood to make more fees if they could place the additional stock. The bankers were not necessarily in it to help the company. They were motivated by the money. Theseus remembered a deal years back where the banker promised a company a minimum share price. After five months of work and crushing fees and expenses, the banker announced to the company that the market would only take the stock at half the originally estimated price. The company was incensed with the banker, but was told it would be prevented from accessing the capital markets later if they didn't go ahead with the sale. It was now or nothing. So the company went ahead with the stock offering at the depressed price. On a group conference call before the deal closed, the bankers could be heard laughing at the stupidity of the company's chief financial officer for falling for one of the oldest tricks in the book. Promise a highly inflated price to hook the company and secure the business. After all the sunk costs and management time devoted to the deal and potential market fallout from a busted offering, the company would be forced to take a more realistic but much lower price. One of the bankers obviously forgot to mute the phone.

"Yeah," Minos said to Theseus, "I hear what you're saying. But we have to take the money and run. Hell, I don't know if we'll have a second bite at the apple. That is one boat load of cash."

Minos gave the bankers their marching orders. Theseus got Alcaeus and Calliope over to the printer to start revising the prospectus to reflect the increase in the offering size. The Amazons and Cineas would likely be with them through the night readying the revised commission documents and filing an amendment to the registration statement the next morning. There would be no fun and games at the printer this evening.

At the office the next morning, Theseus focused on finalizing the underwriting agreement between the bankers and Asterion. Penthesileas was being difficult in the negotiations. She held out for unreasonable positions on many of the company's representations and warranties.

"That's not market," Penthesileas would whine. "We just won't take that wording."

After a great deal of back and forth, the last issue came down to the definition of indemnifiable damages. Penthesileas demanded that the company protect the bankers from any claims of whatever kind or nature that could arise from their role in the offering.

Theseus was willing to allow for proximate damages caused by the company, but nothing else. Penthesileas couldn't grasp the concept of proximate cause. Theseus proposed reasonably foreseeable direct damages, but Penthesileas wouldn't budge.

"We just won't do the deal unless I get what I want," Penthesileas threatened. "I'll tell the underwriters they will have to walk."

Theseus asked himself if it was possible that Penthesileas was more stubborn than Antigone or more spiteful than Electra. He was growing weary of Penthesileas' Amazon bravado and knew he could get no farther with her. Time was running short. He was also confident Axylus would not pass on the offering. He told Penthesileas there would be no deal and hung up.

As Theseus expected, Penthesileas called back with Axylus on the line.

"What's going on, Theseus?" Axylus cried. "What do you mean we're not doing the deal?"

Theseus described the issue.

"My god, Penthesileas," Axylus screamed. "Are you out of your mind? Give him the language he wants. I don't have a problem with it. We're ready to go."

"But you're exposing the bank," Penthesileas started to argue.

"Stop," Axylus demanded, "no more of this. Theseus, we are good on the wording you propose. I'm signed off. Where are the signature pages, Penthesileas?"

Penthesileas said she would send them over.

"It's those goddamn Amazons causing trouble again!" Theseus heard Axylus remark to someone as he was slamming down the phone. "Last time they're on one of my deals."

The pressure mounted as pricing was drawing near. The last open item Theseus had to deal with was the bureau. Theseus still hadn't heard from Hippias. He had his secretary track him down.

"I think we're good, Theseus," Hippias said when the secretary got him on the line. "I'm out at the airport in Attica with Copreus. Good looking lady, by the way, though a little chilly for my taste. I had the helicopter brought back this morning. The bureau will be fine."

When the market closed that afternoon, signatures pages on the final underwriting agreement were exchanged. The underwriting syndicate was now committed to buying the entire upsized offering of Asterion stock at the offering price less the underwriting discount. The syndicate was at risk if it couldn't place the stock with investors at the offering price. Theseus knew that there was very little chance Typhon or the others would lose money. Underwriters were loath to take the risk of a failed offering and took every precaution against it. Axylus had a strong book for the offering and was expecting huge demand.

Once the underwriting agreement was signed, a press release went out to the market announcing the stock offering and the price. The stock exchange was alerted. Asterion stock would begin trading the next morning. Some off market trading would probably occur that evening.

Minos called Theseus and wanted him in Crete early the next day when the Asterion stock started trading.

Theseus

Theseus arrived at Asterion's offices just before the market opening. Asterion's people were collected together in a conference room. Minos, Silenos, Pedocles, Thrasycles and Cineas were all there. The entire crew. The room was decorated with balloons, streamers and posters with Asterion's ticker symbol. There were three large screens in the room. One showed the exchange's trading page for Asterion, another was tuned into one of the financial channels, and the last was a live feed into the stock exchange trading floor. Cineas had also set up an open conference line to Typhon's trading desk.

The conference room was tense with anticipation before the opening. There was little talking. Even Minos had nothing to say. Theseus sensed a mixed feeling of hope and dread.

When the opening bell sounded and general trading commenced, there were no immediate reports of trades in Asterion stock. There was unintelligible shouting from Typhon's trading desk, causing no one in the conference room to stir. The lack of reported trading meant there was a dramatic imbalance in orders. The overall market started to surge. Time was suspended as everyone waited for the first trade.

"It's unbelievable," a voice came through on the speaker.

It was Axylus.

"Minos, your stock is about to skyrocket," Axylus broadcast. "It's going to open really high. Get ready."

A loud cheer went up in the conference room. The expectations were now uncontrollable. About twenty minutes after the market opened, Asterion's first trade was reported. The stock opened at double the offering price. There was pandemonium in the room.

Minos had made sure all the employees had stock options, and Theseus could see everyone's mind working calculations of their new found wealth. Minos started uncorking the champagne, and by late morning the office was in hysterics. Employees were grabbing and hugging each other. Thrasycles and others were dancing on chairs and desks. By noon, the stock price was up three fold. Employees were announcing the purchases and trips they planned. Theseus was reminded of Odysseus' crew on the island of Aiaia, where they found the great hall of Circe. The men, hungry and worn from their endless voyage, were lured by the food Circe offered them. But they fell victim to Circe's dark magic and were transformed to swine. There they remained captive until Odysseus came to their rescue.

Theseus walked out of the conference room to check in with Diocles to make sure the post offering work was being handled. Phones were ringing off the hook throughout Asterion's offices but went unanswered. Computer screens were idle. Desks were empty.

When he returned he didn't see Minos or Silenos. He found them sitting in Minos' office. Both had lit up cigars. Minos handed one to Theseus.

"Well, my friend," Minos said, "we did it. Thanks for everything you've done. You were magnificent throughout. A real pro."

Theseus took the compliment in stride.

"Silenos here is already getting into how we spend the money," Minos chuckled.

"I've got three top sales people ready to sign up," Silenos said pleased. "They wanted to see how the offering went first. I think we've probably hooked them."

Both Silenos and Minos laughed.

The three discussed what was happening at the call center in Stratus. Minos said it was built, staffed and operational. Theseus asked when he planned on having a board meeting.

"Yeah, we should set something up," Minos said. "Let's talk about that later. I need to get home right now. Construction is almost done on our house, and Daphne has some art pieces she wants me to see. Now she has some real money to spend."

By early afternoon the office was vacant. Everyone had checked out to continue celebrating elsewhere or start spending money. Theseus felt an eerie still in the office. The phones had stopped ringing.

30

At the start of summer, the second year law students selected from the fall campus interviews joined the firm as legal interns. The firm invited between thirty and forty in for the summer. From this group the firm hired most of its fulltime associates after they completed their third year in law school and passed the bar exam.

When the summer associates arrived, they doubled up in offices or worked out of cubicles in the law library. The firm normally did not give them individual offices. The summer people selected projects out of an assignment book maintained by the firm's recruiting coordinator. Legal research of some kind was the typical assignment, often in support of litigation, a client memorandum or a legal treatise written by a partner. The coordinator tried to keep the book filled with interesting things to work on, but it was largely hit or miss. By the end of the summer the projects became fairly sparse.

The firm paid the summer interns handsomely for less than three months' work. Billable hour requirements were nonexistent and the firm required just one or two writing samples from a summer associate. Otherwise, the summer program was designed for the interns to get acclimated and to show them a good time. Practice groups competed in hosting summer activities such as tours, boat rides, sporting events, wine tasting, bowling, golf and more. One year the environmental group offered guitar and piano lessons to the summer class. The firm actually brought in a collection of baby grand pianos and acoustic guitars.

Just getting a position in the summer program usually meant a permanent offer. The need for young lawyers at the firm was so great as the workload of the firm grew, a summer intern needed to pull some boneheaded stunt not to get an offer. There was one female intern who started up an affair with an unmarried partner and began to talk incessantly with the other associates about her midday liaisons with the partner. The summer associates became tired of the talk, and a couple of enterprising interns followed her and the partner to a nearby hotel. They took photographs that ended up in a few choice locations in the firm's office. No one ever found out who posted the pictures, but the female intern was not invited back. It was not so much that she was having the affair as the way she lorded it over the other summer interns. Unacceptably bad form.

Another summer associate was refused an offer after he was discovered getting high in a stairwell with a couple of the mailroom employees. They were found out by a partner who used to walk the stairs for exercise in the early afternoon. At first the sentiment was to give the intern a pass until it was learned that he was actually supplying drugs to staff workers. There was some indication that a few of the partners were also buying from him.

A variety of collateral benefits to the firm came from the summer program. All the planned outings and social events included associate attorneys and partners. The socializing from these events was good for firm morale and cohesiveness. They also presented an opportunity for partners to recruit promising associates to their practice groups.

Lysias had asked Theseus to attend one of the professional sporting events scheduled as part of the summer activities. It was hosted by the corporate group, so Theseus felt some obligation to attend. The firm made available its corporate suite at the stadium, which had a sweeping view of the field. There were seats for about twenty outside and room for plenty more inside. The bar was stocked and the catered food was enough for an army. A desert cart came by every half hour.

When Theseus arrived, the suite was already fairly crowded. A large number of summer people and partners from a variety of practice groups were there. Theseus noticed Adrasteia and Timais, who he had interviewed in the fall. He had heard that the three he recommended were all extended summer offers and had accepted.

"Mr. Theseus," Adrasteia said approaching, "I came by

your office a couple of times to see if I could get involved in any of your projects. You seem to be out a lot. I heard about the stock offering you did. It's been the talk of the summer. I guess that's been keeping you occupied. Sounds really interesting. If there is anything that I could do, let me know. I did get to work on some insider stock ownership filings for the commission for Melesius, which was kind of fun. Other than that, it's been more like employment law research. Not exactly what I want to do."

Theseus replied that he would certainly keep her in mind, but corporate projects were hard to come by over the summer. There usually was little research or other discrete assignments available on corporate matters. More drafting of documents and due diligence, which took up large amounts of time. Not the kind of thing the firm had in mind for summer associates.

Lysias and Tantalus came into the suite after a while. It sounded as if they were in the middle of an argument.

"Lysias and I are having a little disagreement," Tantalus said. "Maybe you can help me out."

Theseus said he would be happy to weigh in.

"Well," Tantalus explained, "I've been telling Lysias that I should be the new chair of the firm's tax group. We need someone who's good at getting business, you know, like myself. He seems to think otherwise."

"The tax group has never been a revenue generator," Lysias said looking at Tantalus. "Our tax people are service providers to our other practice groups, particularly corporate. We want the best tax lawyers, not salesmen. We need our tax specialists to analyze complex transactions and advise on tax efficient structures, bring in creative ideas. They shouldn't be spending time on developing their own independent block of business."

"See what I mean, Theseus?" Tantalus groused. "He's missing it. With guys like me who can bring in business, we could double the practice. Look at Asterion. I brought that baby in, and look at the fees we earned. Think of what else I could do given the chance. As I see it, the tax lawyers are paid for their hours, whereas everyone else around here gets credit for revenues. Take Theseus here, for example. He works other deals like mine, but he has his own independent business. He generates tons of work for other groups, and I know he is well paid for it. That should be me, too. If I was head of the tax practice, I would change the thinking of the group. Get them to hustle for new business."

"That's not what the firm needs, Tantalus," Lysias reiterated. "We've tried that approach with tax a couple of times in the past. It simply doesn't work. We need our tax lawyers to have their noses in the code. It's one of the most difficult areas of the law. They need to be current and innovative, not distracted. Business development takes a lot of time and effort. It's just not a quality we want in our tax people. You included."

Lysias had had enough and walked away.

"Damn it, Theseus," Tantalus said with disappointment, "you should have jumped in there. I know you agree with me. I mean, I hit a home run with Asterion. The way that stock has surged, we've made a name for ourselves. The city's premier securities firm. Hey, I know you've just joined the executive committee, so you're probably wanting to take it slow. I don't blame you. I've made up some marketing materials. You should see them. There'll be a flood of new business when I'm through."

Theseus asked if the marketing department has looked at what he was doing.

"Not yet," Tantalus replied, "but they'll be floored."

Before Tantalus could get another word off, Timais came up to talk to Theseus.

"Hey, Theseus," Timais interrupted, "been out sailing this summer? A good season for it, don't you think."

Tantalus glared at Timais.

"And who the hell are you, friend?" Tantalus shouted. "Can't you see we're having a discussion here? Where do you get off interrupting partners, you two bit twerp. Get lost, or I'll make sure you don't get an offer."

Timais was stunned by Tantalus' tirade.

Theseus

"Give me your name," demanded Tantalus. "You're done, goddamn it."

Theseus pulled Timais aside and said not to listen to Tantalus. He would catch up with Timais later.

"Can you believe these young jerks," Tantalus said to Theseus. "They think they own the place. They have it too easy during the summer. All these parties and events. If it were me, I'd make 'em work the summer, hard. If you don't clock the hours, you're out. Teach 'em what the law is really like. Parties? Maybe a lunch before we kick them off back to school. That's it. This whole summer fiasco is upside down. How much does the firm spend on this crap anyway? Theseus, you ought to look into that."

Tantalus walked over to the refrigerator, grabbed a beverage and sat down in the seats at the far end of the suite, away from the summer associates.

Theseus received a call from Silenos and he went outside the suite to take it. Silenos wanted to go over how the company was spending the offering proceeds. He said Minos and Thrasycles were traveling, so it would be a good time for Theseus to come by the new offices. Theseus agreed.

Before leaving, Theseus took the opportunity to talk with a few of the interns and partners he hadn't seen in a while. Like Adrasteia, the interns were earnest and trying hard to make an impression. Theseus thought it was refreshing. If only the partners had the respect and high regard toward each other that the interns showed, the firm would be the better for it. Theseus made a point of talking to Timais.

"I didn't mean to interrupt, Theseus, really," Timais started looking nervous. "I do want to get an offer here. Maybe I should go talk to Tantalus to clear things up."

Theseus advised against it and assured Timais that Tantalus wouldn't even remember the incident if asked. Timais looked relieved.

On the way out, Tantalus started in again about being head of the tax group.

"But what I really want," Tantalus said, "is to get on the executive committee. You and me on the committee,

Theseus, we'd shake things up. Turn this place around, you know, get rid of the dead weight. We got too many older partners sitting around collecting paychecks. We should clean 'em out. Think about it. I know it probably wouldn't happen right away, but in a couple of years. Heading up the tax group would be a start. Maybe you can work on Lysias and Aegeus. I think Aegeus would support it."

Theseus said he would see what he could do.

"By the way," Tantalus went on, "I picked up some brochures on this sports car they are selling in Mycenae. I'm thinking of putting an order in, having it brought over. Use a little of the extra cash coming my way from Asterion. I think you should pick one up too. Come by my office tomorrow, and I'll show you the brochures."

Theseus wasn't sure what Tantalus was talking about. He knew about the Mycenaen cars and their price tags. Theseus was aware of what Tantalus made, and the car was out of his reach. Tantalus would likely get a little bump from the Asterion fees but not enough to make a difference.

"Hey, who is that summer intern over there?" Tantalus asked motioning to Adrasteia. "You know her? I think I'll go over and introduce myself."

Theseus saw Tantalus head after Adrasteia, who was talking with Timais and a couple other interns. As Tantalus approached, Theseus saw Timais make a quick move to get clear of another lashing.

31

Theseus often thought of the story of Glaucus and the Milesian gold when he completed a successful offering for a client. Glaucus, known widely for his honesty, was approached by a man from Miletus who heard of Glaucus' reputation. Fearing unforeseen misfortune, the Milesian asked Glaucus if he would hold half his money. Glaucus was told to keep the money safe until someone came and produced the other half. Many years later, the Milesian's son came to claim the money. Glaucus feigned forgetfulness and told the son to come back at a later time. Meanwhile, Glaucus asked the Delphic priestess if he should lie and keep the money. The priestess said that asking the gods to consent to a crime is the same as committing it.

Minos did not take long to start spending the proceeds from the stock offering. His first move was to secure new, elegant office space at a prestigious business address. Minos retained a young, noted interior designer named Chersiphron from Crete to design and furbish the offices. The reception area was grand with the Asterion name and logo prominently displayed. The look was very high tech and futuristic. The ceilings rose about twelve feet throughout and had aluminum sheathings that were contoured to resemble ocean like waves. The waves washed over green metallic desks and pallid yellow dividers and walls. The space was communal, except for the conference room complex off the reception area and the executive offices tucked far in the back. Asterion occupied an entire floor in the building.

"Not my favorite colors," Silenos laughed as he gave Theseus a tour, "but no one asked me. The young people seem to like it, so I guess that's good. I'm amazed at how quickly this was put together. I think Minos had been planning it for some time."

The executive suites were reserved for Minos, Silenos, Thrasycles and Cineas. The largest office was, as one might expect, reserved for Minos. He had more than enough room for a large desk, couches and chairs for a sitting area and a conference table. Silenos office was more reasonable. The quarters for Thrasycles and Cineas were surprisingly small.

"I know what you're thinking," Silenos said. "He's keeping corporate strategy and finance in their place. Thrasycles was actually pretty upset with the layout. He tried to get Minos to give him my office. Nothing doing."

Theseus sat down with Silenos in his office. He had his whiteboard set up with an array of drawn boxes and arrows.

"What I wanted to talk to you about, Theseus," Silenos started with some seriousness, "is our burn rate. We have already spent a fair amount of the proceeds from the offering. We still have plenty of cash, mind you, but if we keep spending as we are we will use it up before our revenues start kicking in. Not the perfect scenario."

Silenos said that Minos paid back the bridge and made a large outlay for the Tegea data center. He also paid himself for what he claimed were advances he made to keep the company going before the offering.

Theseus said he thought that was the purpose of the bridge.

"Minos came up with a truck load of bills and receipts that predated the bridge," Silenos explained. "Cineas came in to see me about some of it. He sounded concerned that the records weren't in order. Cineas said it was difficult to tell what was business related and what was personal."

Theseus pointed out that the prospectus laid out the use of proceeds from the cash raised in the offering. Material deviations from what was disclosed could be a problem.

"Well," Silenos responded, "you should look into that with Cineas. There's something else. Minos is looking at a couple of new acquisitions. Thrasycles is pushing hard on one of them. Minos also wants to build another data center in Magnesia."

Theseus was surprised to hear of this. He had not been told that Minos was going in that direction this quickly.

"I don't think we can afford it right now," Silenos felt. "We need to concentrate on what we've got. A new data center is a big concern because the cost would be huge and it won't generate revenues for some time. It's a sunk cost at a time when we need to show something on the bottom line. The one we have in Tegea isn't hosting much traffic. It's basically sitting idle."

Silenos sat collecting his thoughts.

"Minos and Thrasycles," Silenos spoke carefully, "are only interested in buying things. They are obsessed with acquisitions. They take calls from the bankers all day long with this proposal and that. I can't get Minos to concentrate on the basics. We only have a short window to start generating our own cash flow. I've been looking at some of Cineas' projections, and I don't see it happening soon enough."

Theseus asked him if this was something he should take up with the board.

"Probably," Silenos responded, "but Minos would ring my neck if I tried to. We've only had one board meeting since the offering, and that was more for show. I don't think the board has any idea what's going on. How can they? We do have insurance coverage for our officers and directors, don't we?"

The directors and officers policy was firmly in place, Theseus said.

"Check with your people to see if the coverage limit is high enough," Silenos directed. "Maybe you can find time with Minos to discuss where he thinks he is going with this. Try to get him to focus some on blocking and tackling."

32

"I just bought a table at the Hebe benefit," Minos said to Theseus on the phone. "Had to shell out a ton of money for it. Good thing you got the offering done, old man. Couldn't have afforded it otherwise."

The Hebe Foundation was one of the higher profile charities in Crete and its annual fund raiser was on the social agenda for most of the business barons and socialites in town. The benefit raised big dollars for Hebe, almost its entire operating budget for the year.

"I need you to be there," Minos said. "I've got someone coming I want you to meet. Tantalus and Leda are coming. I already invited Ariadne, so you can bring her."

Inviting Ariadne would have been enough for Theseus, he knew. But he thought it would be a chance to go over Silenos' concerns. Besides, the charity circuit was an ideal source of new business. It was good to be seen at these events.

Theseus caught a midday flight to Crete, rented a car and went by Ariadne's apartment. He parked the car in front of the building, and the doorman took the keys. Theseus went up and knocked on Ariadne's apartment door. She looked ravishing in her white one shoulder evening gown.

"Theseus, hi," Ariadne said sensing Theseus' pleasure in her appearance.

She smiled and gave him a kiss on the cheek, and turned to collect a wrap and small purse.

They drove to the Hebe benefit, which was held in a large canopied tent set up in a vacant lot next to Hebe's main building. Hebe was housed in a two story warehouse that had been donated by a wealthy commercial real estate developer. The charity was founded to give disadvantaged teenagers exposure to the arts. Inner city schools in Crete were devoid of the fine arts for lack of money and other resources. Hebe gave those with some talent access to canvas, paint, cameras and film. Hebe's founders believed artistic expression could lift the soul from a life gripped by poverty and crime.

Event goers were greeted with a red carpet reception. The waiting valet took Theseus' car, and Theseus escorted Ariadne up the walkway. The entrance was crowded with arriving guests, and the local newspapers were there to catch the glitterati. All activity seemed to halt, however, when Ariadne and Theseus passed. Everyone stopped to look. They were a handsome couple, elegant and imposing. Cameras began flashing as they stood in line waiting to get in.

"Do we have to stand here with all these people staring at us, Theseus?" Ariadne whispered in Theseus' ear. "It's making me a little antsy to get inside."

Theseus took her hand and led Ariadne up to the front of the line and people let them pass without objection.

Inside, Theseus was given their table number and a paddle for the live auction that was to follow dinner. He then saw Thrasycles with his wife standing off by one of the drink tables.

"Hello, Theseus, Ariadne," Thrasycles said. "Nice to see you both. This is my wife Clymene."

Clymene stood transfixed as she was introduced to Theseus and Ariadne. She was diminutive standing next to the two of them.

"Clymene, could you walk over with Ariadne to get a drink?" Thrasycles said, breaking the spell. "I'd like to talk to Theseus quickly, if I might."

"Why, uh, yes, of course, dear," Clymene said. "Ariadne, let's go over here. It's less crowded. I do love your earrings. Where did you get them?"

Ariadne looked at Theseus as if she needed saving. Theseus knew Ariadne didn't care for being one of the wives. It wasn't her world.

"Theseus," Thrasycles said when they were left alone, "I have issues with Minos. He's been taking a lot of money out of Asterion. For himself. He's come up with huge bills he said were owed him from the time we started the company. Credit cards, lines of credit, you name it. He's even wants reimbursements for payments for a helicopter, if you can believe it."

Theseus said he had heard about the helicopter and that he was sure Cineas would handle it. Theseus didn't want to be caught up in a fight with Minos just right then.

"Cineas won't really tell me what is going on," Thrasycles complained. "Look, I've been talking to a couple of the new directors. I think we need to move Minos out of the day to day. He's going to mess up the company."

Theseus was surprised by the comment. He told Thrasycles that Minos was still the controlling shareholder and he shouldn't entertain notions of removing him from management. Theseus said if he tried to sway the other directors on this point, it would likely turn out badly for him.

Theseus went looking for Ariadne. He found her with Minos and Delilah. Tantalus and Leda were with them. Delilah had the look of money in a sleek black dress. Theseus thought Leda looked a bit racy for the occasion in a tight purple number and six inch heels.

The setup in the tent was quite elaborate, with grass green carpet and abundant floras throughout. It was hard to believe that it was a temporary structure. The organizers created an aura of Dorian culture. There were busts of gods and goddesses surrounding the seating area.

"We have a couple of people at our table which I haven't seen yet," Minos said. "I want to be sure you sit next to one of them. A guy named Phylos. I'm looking to buy his company. Make an impression."

Tantalus overheard the remark, and butted in.

"He'll do the deal, Minos," Tantalus interjected. "The stock is soaring. The company is the hottest thing going right now."

After a couple of drinks and hors d'oeuvres, Theseus escorted Ariadne to the table.

"What did Thrasycles want with you?" Ariadne asked curiously.

Theseus said Thrasycles was a little miffed at Minos' success and wasn't getting the attention he craves. Theseus thought Thrasycles would eventually calm down.

Theseus

Two other couples were already seated. Phylos introduced himself and his wife. The other couple was from Rhodes and had come over for the event.

The evening got started when the master of ceremonies took the podium. She was one of the anchors on the local nightly news and a recognized celebrity. She opened with an impassioned plea for money, while cataloguing the good works of Hebe. She went down a list of the colleges that Hebe graduates were attending. It was not an unimpressive list. Theseus wondered why charities always had news people as their emcees. It was clear from her opening she was reading off a script and didn't know much about the organization.

The dinner of figs and red mullet was served promptly. The finest assyrtiko was poured. After dinner, a few awards were given out followed by the keynote. The main speaker was a popular national artist named Faenus who gained some notoriety with his unusual sculptures. His topic was the uplifting effect of art. While he spoke, Theseus thought that Hebe was an easy sell. The audience embraced the upbeat message and reacted positively to sound bites celebrating art as the way out. Despair was the more important issue. Theseus felt that the realities of domestic violence, unemployment, drug abuse, teen pregnancies and dropout rates facing the young urban teenage population were better served by homeless shelters and mental health agencies. But many of those agencies struggled in attracting donors and private funds. Hebe was different. It was feel good stuff. People opened their wallets freely to contribute to art training for a select few.

The night moved on to the live auction. Hebe was auctioning off a variety of vacation packages, summer homes, golf junkets and other assorted items. The highlight was a new sculpture by Faenus, created just for the evening. Guests could bid up to any amount for any item. The higher the better.

An auctioneer had been hired to manage the bidding. He was good at his job. He would read off an item, then start the bidding at a preset minimum. Paddles were lifted to submit a bid, and the auctioneer raised the stakes until another bid surfaced. The auctioneer worked the crowd like a pro, playing off one bidder against another, or three or more at the same time. He had a knack for identifying the men with egos, and worked them hard to get them to increase their bids. He was able to make most of the items competitive. This was how many of the bidders established their manliness, Theseus thought, spending money and out bidding the next guy. It wasn't prowess in battle or winning races at the Olympic Games. It was only the money. Theseus was somewhat put off by the spectacle.

The final auction item was brought to the podium and unveiled. It was a Faenus sculpture, a five foot bronze piece that resembled two intertwined stick figures. A grasp rose from the audience, and then applause. Theseus thought the sculpture bordered on grotesque. The auctioneer set the minimum bid. The bidding started slow, but the auctioneer played the crowd to get more action. Minos raised his paddle. Spending more of the offering money, Theseus thought.

"I'm not going to let you take it that cheap," Tantalus challenged.

He lifted his paddle high and outbid Minos. Minos smiled and countered with a topping bid.

Tantalus followed suit. Another two bidders surfaced raising the price even higher. Minos topped all comers.

"You're not going to win this, damn it," Tantalus said raising his paddle.

There was excitement in the crowd over the item and the bidding. Soon it was down to Minos and Tantalus.

Leda grabbed Tantalus by the arm.

"What are you doing, Tanti?" she cried. "You can't afford that."

Tantalus wrestled free.

Minos and Tantalus went back and forth several times in quick succession. Suddenly, Minos stopped bidding. Tantalus, having been caught up in the competition, now had a look of terror. The bidding had exceeded his means, Theseus knew.

"Let him have it," Leda pleaded.

Tantalus realized he was in over his head.

"Ok, Minos, I give up," Tantalus said. "You can take it."

"You have the final bid, my friend," Minos replied. "It's yours."

Tantalus looked ashen for a moment. Then he laughed at Minos.

"What the hell, I'll take it," Tantalus jeered. "Probably can flip it for a nice profit at Phidias'."

The auctioneer announced Tantalus' final winning bid and the sculpture was his. The gathering responded with appreciative applause. Minos raised his glass to Tantalus and chuckled.

Following the auction, the band started up in fine form and many of the patrons stepped onto the dance floor. Ariadne looked pleadingly at Theseus to dance with her. At weddings it was appropriate, he thought, but not at benefits with important people in attendance. Tantalus must have seen his opportunity, as he abandoned Leda and grabbed Ariadne's arm. In an instant, Tantalus was making a spectacle of himself on the dance floor.

Minos and Thrasycles had also gotten up from the table, and the wives went off with Leda in their own separate direction. Theseus had an opportunity alone with Phylos.

Theseus asked Phylos what he had been discussing with Minos.

"I don't know what he's told you," Phylos said. "Minos has wanted me to come up here for a while. My wife loves Crete and it's been some time, so I thought why not. We spent a day touring. Lovely here. I also had some time with Silenos and Pedocles the past couple of days."

Phylos looked around.

"He wants to combine my company with Asterion," Phylos said. "Our businesses are similar. We have a collection of information technology consultant offices in important markets not covered by Asterion which are doing relatively well. And we are looking at data centers. But to tell you the truth, I am not really interested in being part of Asterion. The whole public thing scares me, to be honest. It may take quite a bit of time before the backbone is robust enough to do the things Minos wants to do. I don't think we are quite there yet. And I question whether Pedocles' software is really workable for the lower middle market. It needs a lot of customization and it's not as cheap as Pedocles claims. I have some private money backing my company, which gives me a lot of time to see how things develop. It keeps me nimble and flexible. Minos doesn't have that advantage. Time is not on his side. The public markets today don't give you time."

Theseus asked Phylos what Minos could offer him that would change his mind.

"Cash," was Phylos reply. "Buy me out and I'll find something else to do."

Ariadne returned and sat down next to Theseus. She had left Tantalus dancing with another woman who looked like she had too much to drink.

Phylos turned to Ariadne.

"The two of you are married?" Phylos asked.

"No," Ariadne said smiling at Theseus. "Just a couple of attorneys trying to find a few fun moments together, I guess."

"So you too are a lawyer," Phylos said. "I wouldn't have thought so beautiful a woman would take to such a grueling profession."

"Not so bad, really," Ariadne said accepting the flattery gracefully. "It has its moments. But challenging it certainly is."

Theseus thought Ariadne's remark an understatement for women in the profession. There was no question that the law was often unfair to women. The big firms were still more or less old boys' clubs, and women hadn't been admitted as partners in the numbers they should. In the early days of the firm, the only women around were secretaries, and many partners ended up marrying them. That was their frame of reference. The older partners were not quite able to treat female lawyers with the same regard that they had for their male counterparts. Theseus also knew the escalating hour requirements for lawyers worked against the women at the firm. The competing demands of family and career were difficult to juggle and almost irreconcilable with the requirements for making partner. When a woman was elevated to partner, it was more often the exception than the rule. Men could endure the almost endless demands on their time. Women as a group less so. Marriage and child rearing for women did not fit well within the firm's practice model.

Theseus was aware that demographics were at work against the old ways. Women had increasingly secured a greater number of seats in the law schools. With so many law graduates now women, the firms had no choice but to hire a substantial number of them. The firm started adopting and touting female friendly policies, such as generous maternity leave and alternative work arrangements, but the billable hour requirements remained fixed. When it came time for partnership, women just weren't making the cut. Many departed the firm for more accommodating in-house counsel positions.

For those women who did make it, they either were unmarried, like Ariadne, or, if they had a family, had either a full time nanny taking care of the household and kids or the husband stayed at home. The latter scenario was not an available option for many female lawyers so they became casualties of the system.

With the growing number of female lawyers, Theseus thought, perhaps it was just a matter of time before things changed and women would come to dominate the legal profession. If that happened, Theseus wondered how the big law firms would cope. With women assuming power, it was conceivable that women would discriminate against the men just as men had discriminated against the women. Theseus wondered if it would be the Amazon takeover that men dreaded. With women like Penthesileas in control, there was reason to be afraid. Theseus did not want to be around to witness the slaughter.

Theseus didn't see any point in continuing the conversation with Phylos, since it was clear he would be taking a pass on Minos' offer. Phylos eventually excused himself to go find his wife.

Theseus suggested to Ariadne that they call it an evening. Ariadne agreed and they discreetly made their exit. Theseus retrieved his car and brought Ariadne back to her apartment. Ariadne kicked off her shoes and the two sat out on the balcony couch looking out over the city lights. Ariadne laid her head on Theseus' shoulder.

"You know," Ariadne said, "I worry whether Minos has got this thing together. Thrasycles causing problems, Silenos asking questions. Are you at all concerned?"

Theseus was surprised Ariadne mentioned Silenos. He asked her what Minos was telling her about Silenos.

"Oh, nothing really," Ariadne responded. "Only that Silenos has been poking his head around too much."

Theseus said that Silenos was the president and would be the first to go if things don't work out.

"I suppose so," Ariadne said, getting more comfortable.

Theseus and Ariadne sat together for a long time. Theseus reflected on his conversation with Phylos. He started wondering if Asterion would indeed cut it.

33

Towards the end of each summer, the firm threw an extravagant party at Aegeus' country club for all of the firm's lawyers and summer interns. Staff was not invited. Next to the holiday gala, the event was the highlight of the firm's social calendar. Golf, tennis, swimming, poker and late night drinking were all part of the itinerary. To Theseus, the games reminded him of the Phaeacians' pentathlon held in honor of Odysseus. Everyone competed for prizes, and the competition was sportsmanlike. Once in a while a brash associate with the personality of a Seareach would upset the decorum with a display of unwelcome flamboyance or insolent behavior, like laying down a challenge to an older partner in a sporting contest. But that was the exception.

The golf course was usually opened early for anyone who wanted to go out, but the official scramble would not start until after lunch. Theseus and Pirithous often arrived at dawn to get in a morning round. They had to play quickly to get in eighteen holes, but the two usually didn't have any difficulty finishing. If they caught up to another group, they generally just played through. Theseus and Pirithous had a standing bet of five dollars every time they played together. The bet was more than enough to make the matches competitive. Theseus knew that Xerxes thought the Greeks weak because their athletes competed for nothing more than laurel. Xerxes obviously failed to grasp the concept of honor. Perhaps that was his great failing.

Theseus and Pirithous both broke free for morning golf this year. When finished, the two headed into the clubhouse for lunch. The patio and inside dining area were already packed. The grill was lit and the buffet was plentiful. Theseus and Pirithous sat down with Aegeus and Aietes.

"Out for an early round, I take it?" Aegeus greeted them. "I like that you do that. It's good that our lawyers come out and take advantage of the club. There aren't enough opportunities for us to socialize outside the office as a group. I think it's healthy."

"I have to admit I look forward to this event and try hard not to miss it," Pirithous responded. "It's one of the best traditions at the firm."

"People do seem to enjoy it, which makes it worthwhile," Aegeus said in agreement.

"I wonder how many billable hours we are losing?" Aietes said. "There's millions we are leaving on the table just from this one day."

"Aietes," Aegeus countered, "leave it alone. The collateral benefits can't be measured. Just look at the smiling faces."

"There are a few smiles missing," Aietes said. "Unfortunate turn of events with Medea, wouldn't you say, Theseus?"

Theseus did not want to get drawn into that subject and thought it bad form for Aietes to bring it up before Aegeus.

"I think most of us are glad she is gone," Pirithous said firmly. "She had a polarizing effect on people."

"Disloyalty is something we cannot permit, Aietes," Aegeus said eyeing him closely. "From anyone."

Aegeus was obviously not over the sting of Medea's behavior. Theseus knew Aegeus was embarrassed he had Medea as his confidante for so long.

"Loyalty is an important virtue," Pirithous said. "Actually, I would have it as one of the most important. Even the law recognizes that partners have a duty of loyalty to each other, it's that important. Violations should never be tolerated or condoned."

"You cannot hold everyone to that standard," Aietes responded. "There are those who are driven by motives greater than loyalty."

"Such as?" Pirithous asked.

"Such as power," Aietes said. "Those who seek to attain power cannot be shackled by loyalty. If loyalty reigned supreme, no one would ever challenge authority. There wouldn't be change. No evolution. No advancement. History tells us as much. I'm not just talking law firms. It's true in politics same as the arts and sciences. Loyalty in and of itself is simply a survival tool. People learn to be loyal in order to be secure. And misplaced loyalty can be dangerous."

"I cannot agree," said Pirithous. "Theseus, you must have an opinion."

Theseus stated that he agreed with Aietes that loyalty is learned, but not as some coping mechanism. It was taught as an ideal. Strength, courage, soundness of mind, moderation and loyalty. Without loyalty, there is no trust and without trust there is anarchy. No organization or society for that matter can be void of it. Theseus speculated that in its right context loyalty is an essential component of culture.

"Culture?" Aietes said laughing. "I think not."

Who was the greater hero, Theseus asked Aietes, Achilles or Agamemnon?

"Achilles, of course," Aietes replied. "He was stronger, more courageous and feared. Without him, the Greeks would never have taken Troy."

Theseus explained that if that were true, the Greeks would have followed him instead of Agamemnon. But they didn't because the Greeks were loyal to the king. As much as they might have admired Achilles, it was Agamemnon that led the army.

"Very clever," Aietes said. "You have an annoying way of twisting everything. I think I'll go sit by the pool."

Aietes got up and left.

"He is one to be watched," Pirithous commented.

"If I have learned anything of late," Aegeus said, "it's to be a better judge of character. Don't you two have more golf to play?"

Theseus and Pirithous finished lunch and went back to the course for the scramble. They were in the same foursome as always. Rhea and Timais were part of the group. Theseus had asked specifically that Timais be paired with him and Pirithous. Theseus wanted to make sure Timais was fully recovered from the verbal beating he received from Tantalus earlier in the summer.

"We will be having a fifth on our team," Rhea said to Theseus as they collected at the carts. "They have so many people signed up, they had to increase the size of some of the groups."

"Hey, Theseus," Cassiopeia said walking up.

Cassiopeia was a municipal bond lawyer that Theseus knew but seldom worked with. Theseus said he didn't know she played golf.

"I don't really," Cassiopeia giggled. "My boyfriend and I went to a golf clinic a few weeks back, you know, to learn the game. Putting is my favorite part. I haven't been out on a course yet, though."

Theseus knew that Rhea was respectable and observed the etiquette of the game. He assumed Timais knew how to play. With Cassiopeia on the team it could be a long afternoon.

"Everyone says that golf is a good client activity," Cassiopeia said, "so I'm trying to pick it up."

There was a misconception that a good golf game could attract clients, Theseus thought. Although he had a low handicap and played a fair amount with accountants and other referral sources, Theseus could count on one hand how many good opportunities actually came from the golf course. Clients hired lawyers based on reputation and service, not how long and straight they could drive a golf ball.

The group headed out to their assigned tee box to await the shotgun start. When the gun sounded, each golfer took turns hitting their tee shots. As Theseus expected, Cassiopeia couldn't make solid contact with the ball. Pirithous gave Cassiopeia some simple advice on proper form at address. He showed her how to bring the club back over the shoulder until the club was parallel to the ground. Cassiopeia looked flustered.

"Maybe I'll just stick to putting," she quipped.

The group managed the round well enough. Timais proved to be a good player and Rhea kept the ball in play. Cassiopeia picked up whenever she needed to. The team actually carded some low scores and Theseus thought they might even have a shot at a trophy.

On the back nine, while the team was on the twelfth tee waiting to hit, Theseus saw Tantalus cutting across the fairway in a cart. He was waving his arm at a group over on the fifth green. Theseus noticed Diocles and Iollas with a couple of the summer interns lining up to putt.

"Hey, goddamn it!" Tantalus screamed. "Diocles! What the hell do you think you're doing out here! You should be in Stratus!"

Tantalus drove the golf cart right up onto the green and jumped out of the cart while it was still moving.

"I told you that you needed to be out in Stratus this week!" Tantalus yelled getting into Diocles' face. "Get your behind off the course!"

Diocles stood motionless. He tried to make a reply.

"Don't give me any of your crap!" Tantalus shouted at him. "When I tell you to do something, you do it. Am I clear? Now get your butt into the cart. You're on the next flight out. What clubs are yours?"

Tantalus grabbed Diocles' golf bag off another cart.

"Get in!" he ordered Diocles.

Tantalus sped off leaving tire tracks on the green, then cut back across the fairway.

"Can never trust associates to do their work!" Tantalus hollered at Theseus while waiving himself through.

Diocles looked straight head.

"Like it's a walk in the park or some goddamn game!" Tantalus scowled.

Theseus noticed Timais had moved out of sight behind some bushes. The rest of Theseus' group just stared dumbfounded.

"He's mad," Pirithous said after watching the entire affair. "Someone needs to get control of him. What's going on in Stratus that's so important?"

Theseus said he didn't know, but would find out later.

The group finished the round and turned in their score. After showering and dressing, Theseus went to the cocktail reception. Tantalus and Diocles were nowhere to be found. Theseus saw Calliope and asked her if she knew what was happening in Stratus.

"I heard about the ruckus on the course," Calliope said.

"Wish I could have seen that. I have no idea what's going on."

Theseus was walking about the reception waiting for dinner when he overhead a spat between Demosthenes and Alcaeus. Aegeus was there listening. Demosthenes and Alcaeus had played each other in the final round of the singles tennis tournament, a match Alcaeus apparently won. Demosthenes had been a highly ranked amateur in his day, and Theseus knew he took the game seriously.

"You were foot faulting the entire game, Alcaeus," Demosthenes exclaimed, "so I think you should forfeit. Aegeus, you were there, you saw it. You can't have a fair match when your opponent does that. Alcaeus didn't even try to stop it."

"Demosthenes," Alcaeus said, "you could have called it during the match. You must have thought you would win as it was, because you didn't say anything. I'd say I won the match fair and square."

Demosthenes grew furious.

"Let's have those here be the judge," Demosthenes demanded, "or else swear to me now that you weren't over the service line. I won't have you take first prize after that display."

The scene reminded Theseus of the chariot race during the contests held by Achilles in honor of Patroklos' death. Antilochos had been accused by Menelaos of trickery in the race. Menelaos refused to accept that he had been beaten and demanded that Antilochos take an oath that he hadn't used questionable tactics to win.

Theseus could see that Alcaeus was growing nervous over Demosthenes' reaction.

"You are a better player than I, no doubt," Alcaeus said to Demosthenes. "I'm sure it was just dumb luck that I won. And you are probably right that I went over the line a few times, maybe even on a few critical points. You should take first."

"Come with me to the awards table," Demosthenes said in a huff to Alcaeus.

Theseus

Aegeus turned to Theseus.

"Very gracious of Alcaeus," Aegeus said. "And politic too. I can see why you like him, Theseus. I was a little worried he would take up Demosthenes' challenge. That would not have been wise. Not only would it have incited Demosthenes all the more, I at least did catch a few foot faults."

After an hour at the reception, Theseus and Pirithous sat down together for dinner and were joined by Lysias, Alcaeus and a couple of other lawyers.

"What possessed Tantalus out there?" Lysias asked Theseus. "Everyone has heard about it. Aegeus is pretty upset with the damage to the fifth green."

Theseus said he didn't know the reason for Tantalus' outburst.

"Well, I hope that it's not bad news for Asterion," Lysias said. "If the company stumbles, it would be a bad thing for the firm."

Theseus didn't disagree. The discussion moved on to other topics while dinner was served.

Afterward, Aegeus presented the awards for the golf and tennis tournaments. Theseus' group came in second in the golf based on their adjusted score. The team went up to pick from an array of golf equipment and attire that were set out as the prizes. Cassiopeia was beside herself. Theseus noticed she selected an athletic bag filled with a designer cap, head covers, gloves, sox, golf balls, tees and ball markers. The bag and each item were in various shades of pink.

"Look at all this stuff," Cassiopeia said beaming. "I'll have to get some golf shoes and a golf bag to match."

Theseus sat back down at his table.

"You and Pirithous shouldn't be allowed on the same team," Lysias said. "You guys win something every year. Say, will you be playing cards later?"

Theseus said he most likely would.

When the tennis awards were given out, Demosthenes rose to claim a handsome engraved glass vase as the champion's prize. Theseus noticed Alcaeus looking a little down in the mouth.

After the awards were given out and before dinner broke, Demosthenes came up to Theseus' table.

"Alcaeus, here, take this" Demosthenes said handing him the trophy. "I want you to have it. You played a great match. I didn't know you were that good. I've won too many times, so it's only fair. What do you say we have a rematch some weekend if you can break away from Theseus' deals? I'll have you out to my club."

Demosthenes walked away pleased with himself and in good humor.

Theseus thought the matter well played by Alcaeus. No less so than Antilochos when he was challenged by Menelaos.

For many, the card games were the highlight of the event. Associates were each given chips for the evening, but partners had to play their own money. The firm hired blackjack dealers for the novices, but the partners tended to converge on the poker tables.

Melesius reigned supreme at the card games. He fashioned himself a player and generally fared well. He would light up a cigar, set the stakes and tell stories about the firm from the old days. When things got going, lawyers would gravitate to Melesius' table to watch the play and hear the stories. Many were repeated year to year, but they always drew hearty laughter.

Melesius customarily reserved a seat for Theseus at his table. Theseus joined with Demosthenes, Lysias, Isocrates and Castor for a game. After a few hands, Melesius started with one of Theseus' favorite tales.

"Now Cecrops, one of the firm's founding partners," Melesius began, "was a diminutive man but had a well earned reputation as a brawler. He was working late on a big railroad merger and had gone with a couple of other lawyers to a downtown bar for a late supper. Cecrops was telling the others how the opposing attorney was being difficult and refused to be sensible in the negotiations. Cecrops' client was getting impatient with the situation and began worrying that the merger target was getting the upper hand due to the stonewalling by its lawyer. The more Cecrops talked about the deal, the more furious he grew. As it so happened, the opposing lawyer walked into the bar with a couple of other fellows, probably his clients. The lawyer was twice Cecrops' size. Upon seeing the lawyer, Cecrops started to seethe. Before the other firm lawyers could stop him, Cecrops got up out of his seat. The lawyer told Cecrops if his client didn't increase the merger price, the target would walk away from the negotiations. Cecrops couldn't restrain himself and gave the lawyer a fist in the gut. When the lawyer bent over from the blow, Cecrops wacked him upside the head. The lawyer toppled over, out cold. The next day, our client's offer was accepted without much more delay."

Melesius dealt a few more hands before some asked him to tell the car story.

"Well, gentlemen," Melesius said, "if I must. When I had just joined the firm out of law school, I was asked by Erechtheus, who ran the firm at the time, to tackle a special project. Erechtheus asked me to accompany him to the docks in Pireaus to receive a shipment from Phoenicia. Erechtheus kept the nature of the shipment secret. I imagined that it must involve something highly sensitive for a firm client such as diamonds, bearer bonds or a cache of smuggled weapons. Erechtheus picked me up in a taxi and we headed to the harbor. We met a customs agent near a large container ship, and Erechtheus signed some papers. We waited. About thirty minutes later, a large crane went into gear. From the dock, I saw a large automobile dangling from the crane. The car was lowered to the dock not far from where we were standing. Luxurious, russet and glistening."

" 'Melesius, my boy,' Erechtheus said to me, 'this is my new car. Now, I want to have the car at my summer home this evening for some weekend events my wife and I will be attending. I need you to drive me and the car up there. You can catch a train back to the city.'

"I was naturally disappointed about the whole thing, but what was I to do? Erechtheus had me along to drive the three hours to his country estate. So I got behind the wheel and Erechtheus took the passenger seat. As we departed the docks, I got to thinking.

" 'Mr. Erechtheus,' I said, 'I grew up in a village on the way to your home. Do you think we could stop by and say hello to my mother? I haven't seen her in some months and she would be pleased to meet you. I'm sure she would love to have us for lunch. She's a great cook.'

" 'Well, I don't see why not,' Erechtheus said. 'We'll need to stop for something to eat on the way. It's fine with me. Why don't you stop and call your mother and tell her we'll swing by.'

"So I made the call, and we were on our way. Erechtheus started reading a couple of documents, but soon tilted the passenger seat way back and feel asleep while I drove. When we got to my mother's, Erechtheus was still sleeping. He had the seat so far back he couldn't be seen from the outside. As I drove down my mother's street, the neighbors were all out on their front porches as if waiting to see what had become of the young man who left to become a big time lawyer. You can imagine the surprise and shock on the neighbors' faces as I drove by in a magnificent luxury automobile."

The lawyers gathered round laughed and applauded.

Theseus always felt a bit nostalgic when he heard Melesius' stories. He wondered what it would have been like practicing at the firm in the early days. He admired the older partners' sense of dignity and camaraderie. They never cited money or prestige as the reasons they became attorneys. They were intelligent, ambitious men, but they embraced the traditions of the law and were proud of the profession.

Calling it an evening, Theseus went out to the valet to retrieve his car. He saw Tantalus standing alone ahead of him. Tantalus looked like he had too much to drink.

"How much did you win at cards, Theseus?" Tantalus asked.

Theseus said he had collected on several good pots.

"If I played with those old farts, I'd clean them out," Tantalus slurred. "That's why they won't let me in their games."

Theseus

Theseus just stood waiting for his car.

"Hey, Theseus, I've been thinking," Tantalus said. "I've got this great idea about hosting a business development dinner, or maybe a lunch or a seminar. We'll invite top clients to hear about the success of Asterion. We can get all of your underwriters to come. We can drum up a huge amount of business from it. It'll be a bonanza."

Theseus was dubious about the idea. Theseus couldn't recall ever staging a client development program to promote the firm's success in a particular transaction. Besides, Theseus believed that clients did not want to hear about what the firm did for other clients. Human nature being what it was, clients had egos and wanted to feel that they had the full attention and commitment of the firm. They didn't care to know about anyone else. Parading selected clients in front of others was ill conceived.

"I'll have marketing get on it," Tantalus suggested. "About time the marketing department did something. We have all these people in marketing, who aren't even lawyers. They don't have the foggiest idea what lawyers do, yet they're always telling us how we need to polish our message and get in front of people. Who knows what they do most of the day. I'm tired of footing the bill for those people."

Out of curiosity, Theseus asked Tantalus who he proposed to be the main speaker.

"That would be me," Tantalus said. "Don't worry, I'll get a role for you if that's what you're concerned about. You can talk about the commission work or some such. I'll have Minos up to the podium too. He's good for lightening things up."

Theseus told Tantalus to let him know when he firmed up his plans. In the meantime, Theseus thought to himself, he would get Lysias to make sure the idea didn't go any further.

34

The first cracks in Asterion surfaced later in the summer. Theseus received a call from Cineas, who wanted to meet as soon as possible. Theseus was on the road with a client negotiating a large collateralized debt offering, but he was returning to the office that evening. Cineas, sounding nervous, asked that they meet in Athens away from Asterion's offices. Minos wasn't to know. Theseus told Cineas to come by his athletic club early the next morning.

On the flight back to the city, Theseus thought about the potential issues Cineas could possibly raise. Silenos had already mentioned his concerns about the Minos reimbursements and costs of the new data center planned for Magnesia. Perhaps another acquisition was in the works. Maybe Cineas was just on edge about the company hitting the street's earnings estimates or managing its burn rate. The heat always fell on the chief financial officer. Cineas was relatively new to the game, so he probably needed some hand holding. Theseus hoped it was nothing more, but one could never tell. Shortsightedness and bad luck often undermined good businesses. Theseus had a theory that the demise of the Athenian democracy could be traced to two causes. The first was the revolution in Corcyra, which before its bloody conclusion eroded the noble Greek character, and the second was the plague that ravaged the spirit of Athens when the city was besieged by the Spartans early in the war. One was caused by man, the other by the gods. Man's weaker instincts and simple misfortune are equally destructive to many promising enterprises.

Theseus was able to get in some weights and jogging before meeting with Cineas. The club was relatively quiet given the time of year as most of the members were with their families at the shore enjoying the end of summer. Theseus preferred the club when it was slow. He could get in and out quickly.

When Theseus was dressing, the steward came by his locker to let him know that someone had arrived for him in the dining room. He collected Theseus' gym clothes so they could be washed and ready for Theseus' next workout visit.

"Hello, Theseus, good morning," Cineas said when Theseus arrived for breakfast. "Thanks for meeting. This really is a great club. Beautiful place. Must cost a pretty penny for dues."

Theseus said he thought that probably was right. He explained that the firm picked up the tab for partners to join the key clubs around town. Theseus told Cineas that the firm actually paid for one downtown club and one country club for each partner. The partners had to cover the downstroke, but the firm would pick up the monthly dues and assessments. Not a bad deal really. The only drawback was the firm's three member rule. The firm wouldn't foot the bill for more than three partners at any one club. They wanted people to spread out. Not all partners could get in to their first choice.

That didn't seem to be a big drawback to Cineas.

Theseus asked Cineas what was going on out at Asterion.

"Well, Minos does know how to spend the cash, no doubt about that," Cineas answered. "I wish our expenditures were for more productive assets and not as much window dressing. Minos is drawn to the look more than I like."

Theseus wondered how Silenos was doing.

"Silenos, well, he's married to his chalk board and flow charts," Cineas said. "He's trying to build a sales force and figure out how to price the software. He's butting heads a little with Minos. Silenos wants to market to big companies. Minos likes the smaller firms. I tend to agree with Minos on this one, given that the larger companies have their own servers and programmers. That's a big part of what we are selling, you know, our hosting services."

Theseus suggested that it sounded like normal growing pains. He asked Cineas what he wanted to talk about. Was Asterion hitting the earnings estimates?

Cineas didn't respond straight off. He took a moment to select the right words.

"It's not the numbers as much as what's behind the

numbers," Cineas said looking around the room. "Our Stratus call center is booking some healthy revenue. I was really surprised to see how much. Way above our projections. I didn't think we had the place staffed adequately to generate those kinds of sales. So I started checking on some of the customers we were selling to. I tried to get some hard data on them, but couldn't find anything. Nothing. I had one of our people work with a credit reporting firm to locate what they could on these companies. Again, nothing."

Theseus said there were a lot of new companies out there, so they probably weren't included yet in the business data bases.

"New companies don't put in these kinds of orders," claimed Cineas. "Not in my experience."

Theseus said maybe he wasn't looking in the right places. He told Cineas to send him a list of the companies he was concerned about. Theseus would have an associate or paralegal search for their organizational filings in the public records. Some useful information was likely to surface.

Cineas seemed comfortable with Theseus' suggestion. Breakfast was served and the two men went on to other subjects. Cineas talked about his kids for a while, and his wife who worked for an advertising firm. Theseus learned that Cineas was a big sports fan, and Theseus offered to see if the firm's box was available for any weekend games left in the season. Cineas could take his family if he wished.

Cineas and Theseus finished and they got up to leave. At the front door of the club, Theseus extended his hand to Cineas.

Theseus said he was sure there's a good explanation for what Cineas was worried about. He told Cineas to send the names over right away, and Theseus would get someone on it. Theseus asked if Cineas would be attending the closing dinner.

"Oh, yes, I'm going," Cineas said. "I've never been to Aetolia, or fired a bow gun for that matter."

Theseus said he would see him there.

Theseus

When Theseus got to the firm, he went to Nikon's office. He thought Nikon would be a good one to do the corporate records searches. His light was off, which was unusual. In fact, his office was cleared out. Maybe he got a better office, Theseus thought. He caught an associate rushing by and asked where Nikon had moved.

"Nikon left the firm a couple of days ago," the associate said. "He got hit with a few bad reviews, as I heard it. He saw the writing on the wall and quit. I think he is going to work for the family furniture business or something."

Theseus then went to see Iollas. He was there, but packing boxes.

"Can't help you, Theseus, I've been let go," Iollas said forcing a smile. "The evaluation committee didn't buy into my business plan to start an entertainment practice. They said it wasn't part of the firm's long term strategy. They don't want associates doing anything but the work doled out by the partners. I'm history."

Theseus wondered why he wasn't told, especially since he worked with Iollas regularly. Theseus didn't really want to talk to Iollas about leaving, but felt the young man needed a few minutes of his time. He told Iollas that he appreciated his hard work and thought he was a good lawyer. He said that the firm wasn't for everyone, and Iollas would find his spot.

Iollas looked depressed and down, like he had lost his shield. Theseus wondered what that felt like. Life in the big firms was brutal for the young lawyers, and becoming ever more so. Theseus asked himself why the firm found it necessary to do this to people. It would be one thing to let Iollas go because he didn't have the requisite lawyering skills. But in his case, he was fired for wanting to develop his own practice.

Theseus said to Iollas that he shouldn't let this setback beat him, that he should stand up to it and be prepared to fight another day.

Iollas didn't appear to be listening. Theseus told him to call a lawyer he knew at a small firm that did some representation of authors and entertainers. He wished Iollas the best and left.

When Theseus got back to the office, he called Diocles. His secretary answered.

"No, Diocles is not here," the secretary relayed to Theseus. "Tantalus sent him off in a hurry to see about some client matter. He left yesterday. I think he was going back to Stratus if you want to know."

Frustrated, Theseus called Calliope and passed the Asterion assignment on to her.

Theseus told Calliope he would be back next week. He wanted her to get the company names form Cineas and have the searches completed by the time he returned.

35

The closing dinner was a tradition that followed every successful public offering. The investment bankers would typically organize and pay for an epicurean feast at an exclusive club or in a private room at a high priced restaurant. Only the top deal participants were worthy of an invitation. The Asterion transaction called for something special.

Typhon booked reservations for two days of game hunting at a country estate in Aetolia. Arrangements were made for the group to stay overnight in the manor house, which was built many years ago as a summer retreat by a shipping magnate from Salamis. The owner's heirs had abandoned the estate and the acreage became overgrown by brush and wild plants. A local developer discovered the property and bought it to raise horses. When he toured the estate, he was amazed by the amount of wildlife there. He decided to reopen the manor for hunting and began stocking the estate with game. The estate soon earned a reputation as one of the finest hunting grounds throughout Aetolia.

The entire Asterion contingent attended the outing. Theseus and Tantalus represented the firm. Eetion from the accounting firm was invited. The Amazons were not. A fleet of utility vehicles hired courtesy of Typhon drove the group to Aetolia from Athens. Axylus, Stolos and Cadmos met the convoy at the estate. There would be eleven hunters in all, but with the supporting cast the hunting party was twice that number. The plan was for a modest supper and an early rise the next morning.

Tantalus had other ideas. He talked Timarchus, the estate manager of twenty years, into a quick visit to a nearby pub, and the group headed out with Timarchus and a few of the crew to a nearby village. For the middle of the week, the village pub was busy. Timarchus and his men mixed with the locals, who at first kept their distance from the out of towners. Stolos grabbed a table and ordered several rounds while Minos, Tantalus and Theseus took positions at the bar. Tantalus downed a couple of pints and started getting loud.

The place began filling up and the group found themselves at close quarters with the regular patrons.

Tantalus intruded into the conversation of a couple of the residents standing next to the bar. Theseus thought by their looks they weren't interested in engaging with Tantalus in conversation.

"So what the hell do you people do way out here, anyway?" blurted Tantalus.

"What do you mean out here, mate?" one of the men responded in a heavy voice.

"Out here," Tantalus countered with a portentous laugh. "We're in the middle of nowhere. It looks like nothing much goes on around here. I suppose you people spend all your time in Attica anyway."

"Only been to Attica once, friend," said the man. "That was enough."

A few more of the locals grew closer.

"You've got to be kidding me," Tantalus spouted off. "What's there to do in this forsaken place? Only been to Attica once! What the hell!"

Tantalus' loud machinations were not traveling well in this company.

"Why don't you go back to where you came from," another local said pushing up to Tantalus.

Timarchus appeared as things were heating up.

"Now, now, Gryllus, my man, no need for any of that," Timarchus intervened. "Mr. Tantalus, how about another pint?"

"A bit defensive are we?" Tantalus said not letting up. "I bet you people can't even drink. Come on, let's put some pints on the bar. Who'll step up?"

"Mr. Tantalus, let it go," Timarchus said. "We have a schedule in the morning."

"Screw that," Tantalus pushed back.

Tantalus grabbed a pint and directed Gryllus to do the same. The crowd gathered close around.

"All right, then," Timarchus said, "as you want it. Mr. Tantalus. Gryllus. On my signal."

Tantalus and Gryllus started downing the pints. Gryllus finished first without losing a drop. Half of Tantalus' beer went down the front of his shirt. The pub was in hysterics.

"Again, goddamn it!" Tantalus shouted.

Tantalus ordered the next round. As before, Gryllus slammed his pint on the bar well before Tantalus. The challenge dissipated the earlier tensions. Axylus ordered rounds for the bar. The hunting party and the locals began mixing and shared laughs over the contest. Everyone was feeling good.

That continued until Urania came into the pub. Urania was a handsome local woman in her late twenties by the looks of her. Urania and Gryllus were obviously an item. The night ended abruptly when Tantalus tried to move in on Urania. Before anyone knew what was happening, Gryllus had landed a punch to Tantalus' face. Tantalus reeled and hit the floor. A couple of the regulars grabbed Gryllus and held him back, while Timarchus pulled Tantalus up off the floor and out the door. The group was quickly in the vehicles heading back to the estate. Tantalus' nose was bleeding profusely, and he held his head back with a scarf over this face.

"That mother," Tantalus groaned. "He blindsided me. Goddamn cheap shot. Didn't see it coming."

Back at the manor house, Timarchus managed to get Tantalus to his quarters. Theseus and the rest retired to their rooms for the remainder of the evening. Morning came much sooner than desired. Theseus woke before sunrise and found a full breakfast already prepared downstairs. After breakfast, the group was escorted to a room where everyone was fitted with proper hunting attire.

Once dressed, the hunters gathered outside for instructions from Timarchus. Everyone would be given a bow gun with a quiver of steel headed arrows. Timarchus illustrated how to load and shoot the bow and pointed out the safety features. He described firing techniques and the ideal shooting distance. The party was taken to a range for practice and to ensure the weapons were functioning.

The hunting party afterwards loaded into vehicles and was off. The estate was carved into large swaths of land by long winding narrow country roads. The high dense hedges along the roads made visibility on the curves difficult. There was barely room for a car going one direction. Theseus thought the vistas of the fields and groves were spectacular.

Theseus could only imagine the cost of the weekend affair, but he knew it was of no consequence. The bankers took the expense in stride as if they were picking up a lunch tab in the financial district. All part and parcel of doing business in high finance.

Timarchus led the entourage to parts of the estate where the game would be plentiful. The group was shooting for wild boar. The caravan first pulled up alongside an old stone stable. Opposite the barn was a white farmhouse. The sun had slipped back behind gathering gray clouds and the wind was cold. The ground was wet and soggy. The hunters disembarked from the vehicles and made their way onto the fields. The staff followed up from behind with a pack of hunting dogs.

Timarchus instructed everyone to spread out but remain in a horizontal line. Bows were to be carried facing downward as they marched. Timarchus warned that when they came across the boars, they would have to react and fire quickly. There was also the possibility that the boars could attack, which was why the dogs were there.

Minos was exhilarated and delighted with the scene. The bankers acted nonchalant as if hunting boar was old hat. Silenos marched like he was on military patrol and Thrasycles stayed close to his flank. Pedocles and Cineas were noticeably on edge. Then there was Tantalus. Although he wore a swollen nose and otherwise looked drawn from the prior night's beating, he was vocal about his abilities with the bow. Timarchus took care to place Tantalus at one end of the firing line and kept a close eye on him. Timarchus never had a casualty in all his years of leading hunting parties and Tantalus was not going to be the cause of the first.

"Damn," Minos said to Theseus, "I love this. What a

rush. This is what it's all about, don't you think? Makes the whole offering worthwhile."

When the party came across the first pack of boars, there was great excitement. Arrows flew high and low. The boars ran every direction, but the dogs kept them from running at the men. Minos was the first to strike, hitting a large boar above its hind leg. The animal fell yelping. The rest of the pack scattered unscathed. When the shooting stopped, Timarchus drew a gun to settle the writhing animal.

With bows down, the men moved close to inspect the carnage. Theseus could feel the group's excitement. Everyone was breathing heavy. Pedocles and Cineas looked nauseous.

"Well done, Mr. Minos," Timarchus said checking the feather color of the arrow. "Very rare to fell a boar on your first try. Very rare indeed."

Minos was beside himself.

The staff roped the boar on a pole and carried it back to one of the trucks.

The group covered more ground before moving to a fallow a ways further onto the estate. By late morning, they had stopped at four or five locations. Besides Minos, Theseus was the only other one to strike a boar. But Timarchus was pleased. The two boars would make a fine meal that evening and no one had gotten hurt.

The party gathered in the parlor in the early evening. Axylus' boss, Erasicles, had arrived for dinner. Erasicles ran Typhon, and Axylus thought it a nice touch to have him drop in. After meeting Erasicles, Theseus understood where Axylus and his minions got their look. The assembled group was taken through the manor kitchen to the outdoor pit where the boars were being cooked. Everyone was subdued from the events of the morning. Soon the group was led into the grand dining room. A long oak table was set with fine country flatware and goblets. After courses of soup and greens, meat from the boars was served.

Minos sat next to Erasicles, who was at the head of the table, relishing every moment. Axylus, looking very smug, tapped his glass. As if scripted, Erasicles rose to give a toast.

"They say the world is embarking on a new age of technological development," Erasicles began. "The global economy has seen in a very short time new products and systems based on telecommunication and computer advances that could not have been imagined only a short time ago. For the first time in human history, people have access to almost limitless information and communication devices that can reach millions in an instant. Some go so far as to claim it is the dawn of a new intellectual era. Not only do we now have the means for tapping information like never before, it is available at very little cost. The technology is accessible to anyone with a keyboard. There are no barriers to entry. The corporate giant and the man on the street are equal in this new age. The implications are profound. A sole proprietor has an equal chance as the company that has a thousand employees.

"Of course, having these new technologies available to us does not mean success for everyone. That is perhaps the most interesting part. The path to riches will not be paved by the old ways that defined the prior industrial age. Success will be defined by intellectual capital, not hording of material resources. Those with the brightest minds that can foresee the relevance of advancing technology will be the victors. Foresight is the key concept here. The ones that show the most ingenuity will prevail. The masters of the new order are the architects and designers of evolving applications. The old corporate behemoths that don't adapt and change will be left crumbling and become distant memories years from now.

"We, as investment bankers of the new order, are committed to raising the financial capital to match the ambitions of the most creative minds. Our bank is devoted to underwriting those promising businesses destined to lead the economy into the next century. We are uniquely positioned to draw capital from the most astute investors of our day. Whether it's the retail or institutional market, we know where the smart money is. And we can leverage our knowhow and contacts to fund the brightest ventures."

As Theseus was listening to Erasicles, he wondered if the street fashioned itself as a modern day Ploutus. Like Ploutus, the street was worshipped for its ability to confer great wealth on the base no less than the righteous.

"The future belongs to those who embrace its promise and challenges," Erasicles carried on. "Asterion is one of those companies that captures the spirit of the new economy and its potential. With the success of the Asterion offering, Minos takes his place as one of the champions of the new age. He has acted brilliantly and with resolve in building a strong foundation when he acquired Nemean and laid out his data center plans. There is no one else to our knowledge who has done what he has done. All he needs to do is wait and his dream will be realized. But you and I know Minos will not wait, but continue to add companies and people to create an even greater and more prosperous Asterion. Minos, our bank wishes you and your company everything you deserve. We are honored to have played a part.

"Let me add that the Asterion stock offering was one of the most successful of the year in the global equity markets. The stock rose threefold from its opening price on the first day of trading. Asterion has made a few people in this room very wealthy, very wealthy indeed. But we are hardly finished. My guess is we will be back in the market with an even larger follow-on. My congratulations to you, Minos, on the success of Asterion. To the future!"

"Here! Here!" the table chanted.

Minos was beaming. He had arrived.

36

Theseus was about to get on a flight in the late afternoon when he heard the news. Silenos called him on his cell and told him Asterion's stock had plunged in the day's trading. Silenos said that accounting irregularities had surfaced involving the Stratus call center operation and Cineas was calling in the auditors to look at the books. Silenos also said there had been a huge cash drain and the company's liquidity position was deteriorating. That was the extent of the conversation before Theseus had to board.

Theseus was alarmed by what he just heard from Silenos. Theseus knew that any time a stock dropped ahead of financial problems, a crisis was certain to follow. He reflected on the possible complications that could arise over the following days. The commission might look into recent stock trades to determine whether there was any insider trading ahead of the collapse of the stock price. The stock exchange would also likely inquire into unusual trading patterns. The filing of civil fraud claims on behalf of shareholders, however, was a bigger concern, especially if there were accounting issues. If shareholder suits came, the entire Asterion board of directors and management team would be named as defendants.

Upon landing, Theseus rang his secretary. Minos, Tantalus, Cineas and Axylus had all called and wanted to speak. Theseus called Minos first. Minos was out on location at the new data center site in Magnesia.

"The stock's taking a pounding," Minos said. "Something has spooked the markets. Axylus said rumors are circulating that our numbers aren't good. He's worried there will be more pressure on the stock tomorrow. I don't know what is going on, but we've got to stop the bleeding. How about a press release, Theseus, to settle things down? Let's say we're going to beat the street's earnings estimates this quarter."

Theseus advised against any public announcement, at least not until the board met and could get a grip on the situation. Theseus told Minos to convene an emergency board meeting for the next day. Minos agreed and said he would get Silenos on it and be back in the office by tomorrow morning.

Organizing the agenda for the board meeting was the first order of business. The board would have to be fully briefed on the accounting issues and stock trading and the potential consequences, including possible commission investigations and civil lawsuits. The company's insurance coverage for the directors and officers and their indemnification rights under state law needed to be reviewed with the board. Axylus would have to address the market crisis. There needed to be a presentation on all segments of the company's business, particularly Stratus. A little later in the evening Theseus called Silenos to walk through the agenda.

"Board meeting? Tomorrow?" Silenos said unawares. "Didn't know about it."

Theseus asked if he had spoken with Minos.

"I haven't heard from him in a couple of days," Silenos replied.

Theseus told Silenos he had the authority to call a meeting and to do so without delay. He recommended that Silenos personally call every director to make sure they could attend. He also told him to make certain all the directors came to the meeting in person.

"I'll try to get it set up for early afternoon tomorrow," Silenos replied.

Theseus gave Isocrates a call to let him know what was happening. If things got out of hand, there could be exposure for the firm. Isocrates said he would put the firm's loss carrier on notice.

Theseus spent the next several hours putting a cadre of lawyers together that would be needed for damage control. He called Dardanus, who specialized in advising audit firms, at his home. He then dialed Eleon, a securities litigator, who was still in the office. Theseus had Alcaeous and Calliope pour over Asterion's prospectus and other commission filings to spot potential disclosure problems. He left the office early the next morning, hoping to get a couple hours sleep.

When he arrived at his flat, he found Ariadne asleep on

the couch. He was more than a bit surprised to see her.

"Oh, my god, Theseus," Ariadne said when Theseus woke her. "What time is it?"

Theseus said it was pretty late.

"Ophelia was here when I came by," Ariadne said with heavy eyelids. "She let me in. I thought better of calling you at the office. I don't intend to stay, but I did have to talk to you. It couldn't wait."

Ariadne said she knew about the problems with Asterion's stock, and where the market rumors started.

"I can't talk about it, at least not right now," Ariadne said. "But the problem is in Stratus. I think you need to get out there as soon as possible."

Theseus told her about the board meeting later that day.

"Of course you need to be here for that," Ariadne said. "But go to Stratus right after."

She collected her things and moved toward the door.

"Trust me on this," she said. "I will be leaving for a while. I have matters to attend to on Naxos. You can find me there when this all clears up."

Ariadne left Theseus feeling deeply concerned about the prospects for the company. Stratus was obviously the issue. What was lurking there he had to find out. He wondered how Ariadne knew and where she got the information. It occurred to him that she was the source of the market rumors. That would be a dire breach of professional ethics if that were the case.

Theseus undressed and laid down hoping for a couple hours of sleep. His mind drifted until he saw himself standing next to Apollo, who was arguing Orestes' case against the Eumenides. Apollo was asking Theseus to help him make the right arguments. Theseus was torn, believing the Eumenides were right to haunt Orestes. Theseus woke abruptly when his phone rang. Cineas was on the other end.

"Theseus, the numbers aren't adding up," Cineas said. "Last night when I left the office I didn't think we had a problem. But I had the auditors stay late and check our internal accounting records to try to verify this quarter's revenues. They picked up sales entries from Stratus for the last couple of months, which were peculiar. All involving those companies I gave you. There was a whole bunch of repeating transactions. Every few days the same amounts from the same customers were recorded. And some of them were unusually large numbers. They couldn't just be from our software sales. They were just too big. The accountants were here when I arrived this morning and they are still here. My best guess is that Stratus has been bundling computer equipment into our services, and booking as revenue the cost of the equipment as well as the service contracts. We don't buy equipment for our customers, Theseus. They arrange their own financing for their computer hardware. We can't afford to carry it. Our revenues and profits are overstated at least fivefold for the quarter. I can't reach anyone in Stratus. I'm hoping there is a logical explanation, but I can't find Minos either."

Theseus got off with Cineas and called Minos at his office. He wasn't there. He then called his house and Daphne answered.

"I don't know where he is," Daphne said. "I heard him come in late last night, and he was gone when I got up. Theseus, what's going on?"

Theseus' attempt to reach Minos on his cell phone failed. He didn't answer. Theseus called Calliope and left a message. He wanted to know what she found out about the list of companies Cineas provided. He then quickly got dressed and headed to the office. When he arrived, there was a lineup of lawyers waiting for him. His secretary said Silenos called and that the board meeting was set. Everyone could make it, except there was no word from Minos. Silenos also asked what should be done about the earnings call with the analysts scheduled for later that afternoon. Theseus was not aware that the call was on the calendar.

Theseus had Dardanus step in. He asked him if he would get in touch with Cineas to discuss the accounting issues and be prepared to address the ramifications with the board.

Eleon was next. He was a pro at time intensive, complex

securities litigation. He came into the office with three associates. Theseus and Eleon began to plan for the shareholder suits that were surely coming. Theseus talked quickly about the accounting issues and the need to coordinate efforts with Dardanus. Theseus asked Eleon his thoughts about engaging a public relations firm to strategize appropriate responses for the press and analyst community.

In the midst of the discussions with Eleon and his team, Tantalus burst into the office.

"Get the hell out!" Tantalus screamed, looking at the associates. "All of you move your butts out of here. Not tomorrow, now!"

The three associates collected their legal pads and left in a hurry.

"Sorry, Eleon, but I need to talk to Theseus," Tantalus said. "It can't wait."

Eleon was angry at the abrupt rudeness, and walked out without a word.

"I bought into the offering," Tantalus confessed. "Axylus gave me an allocation. God, Theseus, I took out a second mortgage to buy that damn stock. I already talked to Axylus, and he said the stock would bounce back. But holy crap, Theseus, this looks awful."

Tantalus had no idea, Theseus thought to himself. His investment not only raised the risk of liability to the firm, but opened himself up to insider trading charges. Theseus wondered what Tantalus and Axylus were thinking.

"Look, I can read your mind," Tantalus said. "The stock was purchased in an offshore account, so I don't think anyone will catch on. Axylus may have sold some of it before the crash."

Theseus told Tantalus he needed to find himself a good lawyer.

"Screw that," Tantalus said. "This will all pass. And don't say anything to Isocrates about it. He'll blow the whistle on the whole thing."

At that point, Theseus' secretary walked in and said Silenos was on the line. Tantalus slumped down in a chair.

Theseus didn't bother to put the call on the speaker.

Silenos reported that the stock exchange had halted trading in Asterion stock citing a massive influx of sell orders. Not a promising sign, Theseus thought. Silenos also said the exchange wanted the company to make an announcement.

Theseus said that would have to wait until after the board meeting. Theseus also instructed Silenos to postpone the analysts call.

Theseus heard Cineas' voice over the phone.

"Looks like what we expected," Cineas said. "The Stratus people were aggressively booking revenues through hardware sales over the last quarter. But there were no offsetting charges on the cost side. It all dropped to the bottom line. Stratus was generating what appeared to be huge cash and profit numbers. It's all a facade."

Tantalus could tell something was off by Theseus' line of questioning and tone of voice. He jumped from his chair and flew out of the office.

Theseus asked Cineas to trace how far back this went. The company might have to restate its prior financial statements. When that hit the street, the stock would plummet. Theseus ran down the hall to catch Alcaeus, who was looking at the company's commission filings. He told him to stop his review and call the accountants. They needed to prepare a press release addressing the accounting issues. Theseus told him to contact Dardanus and write something about the board instituting an investigation. He wanted a public announcement following the board meeting.

When he arrived at Asterion's offices with Dardanus and Eleon for the board meeting, Theseus found a horde of reporters and camera crews. Theseus wondered what Ariadne had done. Things were spinning out of control.

Theseus managed to make his way through the throng that had gathered at the elevator bank. When he reached Asterion's floor, there was no one at reception. Phones were ringing. Theseus went straight to Silenos' office. Employees were scattered and huddled in groups. Very few were apparently working. As Theseus walked past, conversations stopped and he was given many grave looks.

Cineas and Thrasycles were together in Silenos' office. They looked like they had been arguing.

"I am preparing to inform the board of our findings," Cineas said. "I'm not sure how they will react. What are you going to say to them, Theseus?"

"We're going to tell them that Minos has screwed the company, that's what," Thrasycles said. "Am I right, Theseus?"

There was no time for an answer. Asterion's receptionist came in and said all the board members had arrived, except Minos. He was not in the office and had not been heard from. No one was sure where he was.

The meeting was convened in Asterion's main conference room. In the center of the room was a huge round table rather than the commonplace rectangle or oval. Hovering over the table was a ring of sleek monitors. Theseus noticed the Asterion logo projected on the screens next to a smiling Minos.

Theseus wanted the session closed, meaning everyone but the directors would have to leave the room. Except for Cineas, who needed to make his report to the board. Thrasycles demanded that he be allowed to stay. Given there was no time to debate it, Theseus agreed. Everyone sat down at the conference table. Theseus asked Silenos to work the monitors and put up the agenda. The first item was to review the trading in Asterion's stock and its implications. Theseus had arranged to have Axylus available for a tie-in over a conference line to address the board. Bacenor, the vice chair, asked if a board meeting could be officially convened without Minos present. Theseus knew that proper notice of the meeting had not been given in accordance with the company's bylaws, but he felt it essential to carry on with the meeting. Theseus said that a quorum was present and the vice chair could call the meeting to order. Bacenor obliged.

None of the directors, including Bacenor, showed any initiative in stepping up to take control of the meeting. Theseus quickly reviewed the agenda and had Silenos dial

Axylus. He promptly picked up his phone.

"The picture isn't pretty," Axylus said. "The stock has plunged from its high and sell orders continue to be heavy. The stock still hasn't opened, so it's likely to be down. How much it's hard to say. We don't see any buyers out there. We would suggest a firm statement from the company about the situation to calm the markets."

Phormion asked if Typhon could provide some support for the stock.

"Negative," Axylus responded. "Our compliance department won't allow it. We still have some of the stock in inventory. We would actually like to get out of our position if the opportunity is presented."

Theseus asked Cineas for a report on the financial statements and the auditor's findings. Cineas described what he thought was happening in Stratus, but said nothing was yet confirmed.

"If it is true," Cineas said, "there won't be any earnings to report."

The directors sat blankly staring at each other.

Theseus had Silenos drop off Axylus and call in Dardanus and Eleon. Dardanus started to assess the implications of the accounting issues. He said that best case was the problem was not as severe as it looked. The company should issue a statement that the board was investigating sales recognition practices at its call center but at the present time there was no evidence of any wrongdoing. That, Dardanus said, might give the company some time and hopefully loosen up trading.

"The downside is," Dardanus warned, "if it comes out later on there was fraud, the board and the officers will be sued. Delaying the inevitable will make it that much worse."

The company's insurance for directors and officers was then reviewed by Eleon. He told the directors that if claims came in for fraud, the company may have to litigate the insurance coverage.

"What are we supposed to do if the insurance doesn't hold up?" implored Radamanthos. "How do I afford defending myself? I don't have the kind of money some of you may have."

"I need to be able to sell my stock," Pedocles stated flatly. "How am I to do that?"

Theseus instructed Pedocles and the rest of the directors that a trading blackout would be imposed until further notice.

Pedocles looked pale.

"We can deal with those issues later," Bacenor intoned. "We need to get a statement out. What should we say, Theseus?"

Theseus recommended that the company issue a press release as Dardanus suggested right after the market closed. A draft had already been prepared. Theseus asked Silenos if he could print some copies and distribute them.

"All right," Phormion chimed in, "what's next?"

"We need to remove Minos," Thrasycles said loudly. "He's destroying the company and something needs to be done. You don't need any more evidence. Stratus was his idea, and he was running it. No one knows what's going on there, except that it's imploding. I'll offer to step in as chairman. Silenos can remain as president and Cineas as finance chief."

The directors were flabbergasted when they heard Thrasycles' proposal.

"But Minos owns most of the stock," Sargeus shot back. "How could we possibly remove him? He would simply replace us."

"There's no other way," responded Thrasycles. "Minos has mismanaged the company if not worse. I am fully capable of running the company, and I know what needs to be done. The time is now to make the move. The market needs to know that we have this under control."

It occurred to Theseus at this moment that Thrasycles reminded him of Pisander, an oligarch who conspired to overthrow the Athenian democracy during the Peloponnesian War.

Theseus said that Thrasycles should leave the meeting.

"I don't see why that's necessary, Theseus," Thrasycles said. "I think the board sees the merit in what I'm saying.

There is no other viable option."

Theseus now insisted that Thrasycles go. Despite the crisis, Thrasycles was blind to everything but his own aggrandizement. Theseus said the board needed to be able to discuss the matter in private.

"I'll be right outside," Thrasycles said on his way out. "I'm not going anywhere."

When he was out the door, Silenos spoke up.

"If he's appointed chairman, I'm gone," said Silenos.

"Of course he can't be chairman," Bacenor affirmed. "He is just a kid and has no relevant experience. And I don't see us kicking Minos out."

"Nor do I," Sargeus added. "But I do agree with one thing he said. We need to do something that will make a statement. "

"Right," Bacenor said. "I think Cineas should go. He's the head of finance for god's sake and there is a big accounting mess. Cineas has to be held accountable."

"Wait a minute," Silenos replied. "This wasn't Cineas' doing. At least I don't think so. He's the one that flagged the problem."

"Well, that may be," Sargeus said, "but it's on his watch. He should have had tighter controls over what was being reported. I agree he has to go."

"Thrasycles also," added Phormion. "I don't trust him. Let's throw him out as well."

The board debated the moves at greater length but ultimately agreed with that course. They asked Silenos if he would inform the two.

"I'll do it," Silenos said, "but I want Theseus there. I don't want any trouble."

The press release was reviewed and approved by the board. The terminations would be included in the public statement. The board members all agreed to make themselves available for further meetings or calls as events unfolded.

"I may have to resign, Theseus," Radamanthos said as he left the meeting. "I don't like what I'm seeing and I can't afford to get mixed up in this."

Theseus said he might find it difficult to extricate himself at this point.

After the board members left the office, Silenos and Theseus met with Cineas. His eyes welled up with tears when he was told.

"What am I supposed to do?" Cineas said crestfallen. "I've got kids, bills to pay. I'm the one who caught the problem. I was doing the right thing. Why am I catching the blame?"

Silenos said the board needed to let the market know they were taking strong action.

"Can you keep it quiet, at least for a while?" Cineas pleaded. "No way will I get another job if this comes out."

Silenos told him it would be in the press release.

"Oh no," was Cineas' reply.

Cineas got up and walked out. Thrasycles was waiting to come in.

"What's with Cineas?" Thrasycles asked. "He didn't get canned, did he?"

Thrasycles learned the answer from the look on Silenos' face.

"Wow," Thrasycles said. "I guess that makes sense. We'll have to find someone to step in pretty quickly to cover finance. I know some people who could do it."

Silenos and Theseus just stared and listened.

"Who's going to tell Minos?" Thrasycles asked. "That should probably be you, Silenos. You're the president."

"I'll call him," Silenos replied, "but not with the news you think. The board decided to terminate you immediately."

Thrasycles was in shock.

"They what?" Thrasycles said disbelieving. "That's impossible. It's Minos who tanked the company. I'm the one who built this place, and he's the one that destroyed it."

Theseus told Thrasycles it would be best if he collected his personal things and left promptly. He would have to leave his computer in the office.

Thrasycles sat with his face in his hands.

Theseus

"I can't believe this," Thrasycles said resisting. "I'm going to get a lawyer. You'll be hearing from me."

He stood up and walked out. Theseus followed him to his office to make sure he didn't take any company property.

"I mean what I say," Thrasycles repeated as he left the office.

The press release was issued shortly thereafter.

Later that evening, Theseus finally got a call from Minos. It was unclear where he had been during the crisis.

"Thanks for covering the board meeting, Theseus," Minos said. "I got held up in Tegea over some problems on the size of the pipes. I was in the air when the meeting started and couldn't call in."

Theseus reviewed what transpired at the meeting.

"The board did what?" Minos said in astonishment. "They booted Cineas? Without me? Damn. I suppose Thrasycles had a hand in that."

Thrasycles was let go too, Theseus told him.

"You're joking," Minos sputtered. "His father will be after me. What else went on in that room?"

Theseus told him about the press release.

Minos couldn't believe what he was hearing.

"The stock will be crushed!" he screamed.

Minos said he knew about the Stratus numbers and insisted the accounting was proper.

"It's just a matter of timing," Minos said. "We felt that it would be a good idea to get into the reseller business with the hardware and started that up in the last quarter. The equipment orders turned out to be bigger than expected. We had to book the revenues but couldn't book the expense of the equipment because we didn't have time to put the purchase orders in with the manufacturers. All just timing. Things will start to smooth out next quarter. Thrasycles knew all about this. I thought he was working with Cineas on it. Didn't he say anything?"

Theseus said Thrasycles didn't mention it.

"Letting Cineas go like that, it's just nuts," Minos said. "Hey, Theseus, got to go. The wife is calling."

When Theseus got back to the office, he stayed at his desk late to make sure he was covering everything he could. He recalled what Minos said about Tegea. He went to see Argeius, an intellectual property lawyer at the firm who had done some work on the data center. He wanted to know what Argeius knew about what was going on with Tegea. Theseus remembered Phylos' comment about the pipes and it had started to bother him.

Argeius was pouring over a pile of documents when Theseus walked in on him.

"Asterion?" Argeius said peering out over his glasses. "Tegea? It's been a while since I looked at things there, Theseus. But if it's the pipes, that might not be good. Quite a few hosting centers have begun to experience problems because the cable capacity is too small to accommodate large software interchanges and data flow. The internet infrastructure isn't big enough in many places. Even if the data centers can handle the traffic, the connections with the customers may not be adequate. The pipes back and forth are just too small."

Theseus asked Argeius if he could get down to Tegea tomorrow to determine if there was a problem.

"No can do, Theseus," Argeius responded. "I have to finish drafting a master license agreement for an outsourcing client. Then I have to fly out to a conference late tomorrow. I'm on a panel so I can't cancel."

When Theseus got back to his office, he got a call from Cineas. He was very upset.

"What the hell happened?" Cineas wanted to know.

The board needed a scapegoat, Theseus told him. The chief financial officer was always the easy choice if there were accounting problems. Cineas was also the final member of the management team. Last in and first out. He was an easy mark for the board.

Theseus told Cineas it wasn't appropriate for them to be speaking. Theseus represented the company, and Cineas was on his own. His interests were now adverse to the company's and he would have to retain his own counsel. The firm would not be available to help him dig out. Theseus gave him the names of two lawyers from small firms that did employment cases. He said goodbye and hung up.

Before he could even think, Aegeus was at his door.

"How bad is it, Theseus?" Aegeus asked. "Asterion, I mean. I've been watching the stock. Looks like a nightmare. Does the firm have any exposure?"

Theseus told him what he knew. He also said that Tantalus had bought Asterion shares.

"My god," Aegeus gasped. "Have you told Isocrates? The firm is going to be pummeled for this. Tantalus by himself is enough to bring us down. I can't believe I lived to see the day."

Aegeus stood pensive for a moment.

"I never did tell you what stands between Minos and me," Aegeus said. "You should probably know. Years ago, I had a referral from a client to look out for a young man who was involved in some business transaction with a group from Phaselis. He had just moved here, and struck me as someone who was determined to make his mark in business at an early age. He didn't have a lot of experience it seemed to me. Anyway, it turned out the business was shady and the Phaselites not the sort you want to get involved with. They were dealing in some sort of contraband. I think it was stolen credit cards, or something like that. The young man got into a tight spot when he found himself in the middle of a bureau investigation. The bureau had been watching the Phaselites for some time. I tried to help him extricate himself from the situation, and told him to cooperate with the bureau."

Aegeus sighed heavily.

"The young man was Minos' son, Androgeos," Aegeus divulged. "Minos apparently fathered the boy when Minos was quite young. From what I learned later, Androgeos had come to Attica to prove his mettle to his father. Strike it rich and return home a self made man. I guess he needed to show his father what he was made of and this was his way of doing it."

Theseus thought of Icarus, who took flight over the sea

on wings designed by his brilliant father, Daedalus. Ignoring his father's warning, Icarus flew too close to the sun and perished when he plunged into the water after the wax holding the feathers together melted away. Theseus always wondered if the cause of Icharus' demise was his own desire to prove his manhood to his father or Daedalus' inattention to Icarus as a boy.

"Well, things didn't turn out so well," Aegeus said. "Androgeos got in over his head. The bureau set him up as a mole and used him to corner the Phaselites. But the game turned deadly. Androgeos boarded a ship for Phaselis and didn't return. Minos never saw him again. I think Minos has always held me accountable. It's probably the reason I let Tantalus bring him in as a client, to make amends."

Theseus said that the ambition of young men to please their fathers led to many ruined lives.

"I sometimes have terrible dreams at night about that boy," Aegeus admitted. "I see Minos plotting the death of my own son. I worry that will come to pass in some strange way. Maybe Minos has finally gotten his revenge."

Theseus was about to respond, but before he could speak Aegeus was gone.

Stratus, the apparent source of many of the problems, was the next item of business. Theseus booked a flight to Stratus with a stop in Crete. He wanted to see Silenos before going to Stratus. Silenos was now in charge with Minos absent. When Theseus arrived in Crete, he found the office in a chaotic state. People were scrambling to and fro, rushing in and out of offices, talking on their phones. Theseus thought this must have been what it was like when the battered Athenian army marched away from Syracuse with Gylippus in pursuit.

Silenos was sitting in his chair talking to a couple of his customer service reps.

"Guys, don't go anywhere," Silenos instructed. "Give me a few minutes with Theseus, then we'll get back to it."

Silenos looked besieged, but he was surprisingly calm and composed.

"I'm just beginning to see what we're dealing with," Silenos said. "The board has no idea."

Theseus envisioned the slaughter of the Athenian troops under Nicias when fleeing Syracuse.

Silenos started explaining. Nemean's software was not functioning as promised. The product was not able to integrate effectively with the new operating systems that were being introduced in the market. The standard legacy platforms housing the software were being upgraded and replaced much quicker than expected and Pedocles' people were months away from introducing new versions of the product. Sales were drying up. The costs of Asterion's marketing effort had also skyrocketed with the hiring of the sales team. But without a demonstrably viable product, the sales people were out there sitting on their hands.

Silenos also confirmed that the data center in Tegea was under pressure. The size of the pipes made installations slow and unreliable. Customers were complaining and canceling contracts. The new data center in Magnesia would have the same problems.

"Then there is our cash position," Silenos said. "We have spent a lot of money on all these new people and offices. Stratus is a sink hole. Pedocles has hired a ton of programmers to fix his software. It's been like a sieve. And Minos has treated our reserve as if it was a personal bank account."

Silenos handed Theseus a spreadsheet showing payments over the last sixty days from Asterion to companies Theseus had never heard of.

"These are Minos controlled finance companies from what I understand," Silenos said. "Minos told me Tantalus formed all of them, some offshore. Minos and his father-in-law used these companies to help finance Asterion before the offering, or so they say. Look at this one."

Silenos pointed to an entry for Brontes, Ltd.

"Brontes is a company Minos owns," said Silenos. "He had Asterion reimburse Brontes for loans he claimed were made to the company. There is no record for these loans.

No documents. Never were shown on Asterion's books. I'm not saying the loans weren't made, but we have nothing to prove it. The same holds for all these other companies. Look down the list."

The total amount of payments to Brontes and the other companies was alarming.

Theseus asked Silenos how he found out about the payments.

"You don't want to know," Silenos said. "By the way, you better get someone out to Stratus."

Theseus said it was his next stop.

37

Theseus placed several calls to Diocles, but had not heard back from him. Diocles' secretary had given Theseus the address of the Stratus hotel where Diocles was staying. Theseus was able to catch a very early flight and arrived at the hotel late morning. The hotel was one of Arcanania's oldest and, as it turned out, most expensive. Theseus thought the choice of accommodations for an associate sent out to handle a few corporate matters was certainly open to question.

Theseus left his bags with the concierge and went directly to Diocles' room. His secretary had provided the number. Theseus knocked several times before he heard any movement in the room. Eventually, the door was unlocked and opened very slowly.

"Oh, god almighty," Diocles muttered.

He was half naked and his hair was disheveled. Theseus obviously woke him up.

"I've been meaning to call, Theseus, but now is not a good time," Diocles pleaded.

Theseus pushed his way into the room. Diocles had a full suite. The room smelled of stale food and liquor. Food trays from the night before remained, clothes were strewn about, and stacks of files and papers were piled high on the floor. It looked as if Diocles had not been out of the room for days. On the sofa table, there were opened liquor bottles and a mound of white powder next to a half empty vial. Theseus noticed several wads of large denominated bills.

"Hey, baby, you all right?" a young woman's voice called from the bedroom. "What's going on?"

Theseus could see her through the door to the bedroom propped up under the sheets. She was not yet awake.

"Mother of heaven," Diocles mouthed.

Diocles went into the bedroom and told the girl she had to go. She wasn't too pleased to be rushed. She got out of the bed and got dressed. Her hips swayed seductively in her red skirt as she came barefoot into the sitting room. Her blouse was unbuttoned. She barely gave Theseus a notice as she looked for her shoes and purse.

"It was nice, darling," she said.

The girl gave Diocles a kiss on the cheek.

"Call me anytime you're in town. You too," she remarked at Theseus.

On the way out, she removed several bills from the table and put them in her purse.

" 'Till next time," she said with a wave of the hand.

Diocles sat hunched down on the sofa.

"Listen," Diocles started, quivering. "Tantalus wanted me to come out here. He set me up at this place, gave me some cash. He told me to sit tight for a week or so and not to call you."

Looking around the room, Theseus spotted a laptop computer on the desk which was hooked up to a printer. Theseus picked up a stack of documents and started paging through. They were purchase contracts.

"Tantalus had me search state databases and come up with lists of random companies," Diocles acknowledged. "I had to do it, Theseus. Tantalus threatened to get me thrown out of the firm. I have student loans, an apartment. I just bought a car. I had to do what he said."

Diocles told Theseus he had been out to the call center a month before and had met Tantalus there.

"They had this guy, Medeius, running the place," Diocles said. "There were a couple of offices and a slew of call stations. About fifty employees making calls. It looked legit to me. What did I know? They had me sit down with Medeius. He was a finance type, you know, a numbers cruncher. I should have known something wasn't right. He gave me sheets with equipment specifications and prices, and computer printouts of sales. The names of the companies I found were on the sales printouts. Medeius told me the callers contacted the companies and closed sales with them. I was told to draft up the contracts for each one of these accounts. A huge number of sales. Medeius was on me the whole time I was there. He was in a big hurry."

Theseus told Diocles to clean up and get dressed.

Theseus

Theseus wanted to get out to the call center.

Diocles happened to have an expensive sports car at his disposal, and within the half hour they were on the road. Theseus looked out over the beautiful Arcanania mountains as Diocles drove north out of the city. Theseus thought it was hard to imagine that this could be the site of a colossal fraud.

They pulled off onto a gravel road, which wound up and down along a mountain ridge for several miles and ended at an open gated chain link fence. Driving ahead, they arrived at a collection of trailers and a warehouse facility with metal siding. The warehouse had a white roof and lime green corrugated walls. There were sun lights built into the roof, but no windows. The front double doors were boxed by large lanterns that were lit.

The place was deserted. Diocles was given a key to the front door from when he was doing the contract work. Upon entering the building, Theseus walked through a narrow corridor with an office on the left and right. The walls to the offices were clapboard and there were boxes piled high and opened file cabinets. At the end of the corridor was the large call center space. There were rows of desks and chairs. Everything else had been cleaned out.

Theseus and Diocles returned to the hotel in the early evening. Theseus had a message from Isocrates that the firm had received word that the commission was looking into the trading in Asterion stock. Aegeus wanted Theseus back in the office.

Theseus scheduled an early flight the next morning. He ordered Diocles to hire a security company and go back out to the call center and have the entire premise locked down. No one should be let in. Diocles was then to have all of his work papers and computer equipment boxed up and sent directly to the firm's offices. He was to return as soon as all that could be accomplished.

38

Theseus' secretary sounded unnerved when she told him Lysias had been down to his office several times.

"Mr. Lysias needs to see you right away, Mr. Theseus," she said. "Something about some calls he received. He didn't look happy. I think you should go up to see him right away."

"Theseus, the commission contacted Aegeus yesterday," Lysias said when Theseus swung by his office.

Theseus said he knew.

"Well, they want to come in to talk about the company and the trading in the stock," Lysias said. "They're from the enforcement division. Attorneys from justice are coming along. They mentioned Tantalus. They'll be here in about an hour. Aegeus told me that Tantalus is in over his head. Aegeus is worried about the firm in all of this. He's catatonic. I've never seen him this way."

Theseus updated Lysias on what was happening with Asterion. He repeated what Tantalus had told him and related what he learned while in Stratus.

"Let's go ahead and meet with the commission and justice when they come," Lysias said. "I don't want any information volunteered, obviously. But let's find out what it is they are concerned about. I'll get Hippias and have him sit in with us. We need a criminal lawyer there. Let's try to keep a lid on this. If we get implicated in any wrongdoing and it comes out, Aegeus is fearful our public clients will drop us like hot iron."

Theseus went to see Tantalus.

"Theseus, how the hell are you," Tantalus said greeting him. "Hey, I got some box seats for a concert tonight. Why don't you come along? Should be a kickass show."

Theseus asked Tantalus about Stratus.

Tantalus raised his eyebrows.

"What about Stratus?" Tantalus asked. "Hell of a spot. Really gorgeous country."

Theseus told him he had paid a visit to Diocles there.

"Diocles?" Tantalus shot back. "That kid's a total waste of humanity. I never trusted him. The firm should have let him go a while ago. What did he say?"

Theseus told Tantalus what he saw there.

"Look," Tantalus said, "Minos needed some contract work done and I sent Diocles. Minos said they were clicking on all cylinders and wanted some help keeping up. That's all I know."

Theseus told Tantalus the commission was coming by with justice. He said they asked for him. Theseus asked what they might have learned.

"How the hell should I know," Tantalus said looking away, not sounding too concerned. "I don't know what they know. Maybe they have some dirt on Minos."

Theseus was not inclined to play any games with Tantalus. He turned to leave.

"Hold on, Theseus," Tantalus said peering down at his desk. "I had a message from someone at justice too."

Tantalus stood up and walked over to the window.

"I did a little more trading than I let on," Tantalus said. "Minos gave me a bunch of stock when he did the bridge with Phalius."

Theseus asked how much.

"Oh, probably a couple hundred thousand shares or so," Tantalus said. "I sold a bit of it through Orthrus before the road show. I needed the money. Hell, if I had known what the stock was going to do, I would've waited. I left a lot on the table."

Tantalus swung around.

"Don't look so surprised, Theseus," Tantalus said. "You know everybody's doing it. The bankers, executives, the lawyers, the accountants. Everybody is in on this technology thing. People are getting rich. Why shouldn't I? You probably bought some Asterion shares yourself."

Theseus had heard enough. He told Tantalus not to talk to anybody about this and to stay away from the commission and especially justice. He directed Tantalus to take some time and get out of the office. Theseus didn't want him at the firm when the commission and justice arrived.

Uncharacteristically, Tantalus said nothing more.

Theseus called Silenos. Silenos told Theseus that he had just received by fax a letter from the commission that they were looking into the company and its stock trading. Theseus directed Silenos to call a meeting of his managers to let them know of the letter and to tell everyone not to talk to regulators or reporters. He also cautioned Silenos that no one destroy any documents.

"Too late for that," Silenos said. "Someone was here early. There are a couple of bags of shredded paper. Can't really say who was doing it. Does Thrasycles still have keys to the office?"

Theseus told Silenos to put the bags in a secure space and get rid of any shredders.

Theseus then had his secretary try to reach Minos on his cell.

"There's no answer," she said, "and his service isn't taking messages. His box is full. Theseus, I've got a couple of messages from a woman named Ariadne. She said it's urgent."

Theseus thought the calls from Ariadne more than odd given the timing. He was too busy to get back to her, but grew incensed thinking she was the government's informant.

"It looks like some people are here you are supposed to see," Theseus' secretary said putting down her phone. "They are waiting in reception."

Theseus knew it was typical for the commission to make some informal inquiries of parties that they suspected of violating securities laws. That was usually followed up with a notice of investigation and request for documents. If the matter was serious enough, a formal notice would be issued that a civil claim was to be brought. The recipient of the notice had the opportunity to submit its reasons why a case was unfounded before the commission would proceed. Theseus needed to ascertain who the target of the commission's investigation was and what the charges might be. He had no doubt whatever the focus of the commission was, it was serious. Justice would not be there otherwise.

Theseus caught up with Lysias and they both went in to the meeting together. Hippias was already there. The commission had sent two attorneys from its enforcement division, one man and one woman. The male attorney was named Stichius and the woman went by Acantha. Stichius wore a ruffled grey suit, steel framed glasses and a forced smile. Acantha was young, red haired and wore the basic business blouse and skirt. There was one attorney from justice named Toxeus. Toxeus was the white shirt, button down type. From his demeanor, it was evident he would not be one to lighten up the proceedings.

"We appreciate you meeting on such short notice," Stichius started. "We are looking into some unusual trading activity in Asterion stock. Simply exploratory at this point. The company should have received something from us already today."

Theseus asked if the commission had opened a formal investigation.

"Well, let's put it this way," replied Stichius. "We have serious concerns about what we have learned. Where we go from here, we'll just have to see. We are hoping you will cooperate with our inquiry."

Theseus, Lysias and Hippias traded glances.

"What can you tell us about Laelaps?" Acantha jumped in aggressively.

Theseus said he had never heard of Laelaps.

"Laelaps Investment LP is an offshore fund that invested in the Asterion offering," Stichius explained. "The fund seemed to have sold out its position before the stock tanked. The timing concerns us."

Theseus said they couldn't be of much help to them.

"You have an attorney named Tantalus with your firm, don't you?" Acantha asked. "What role did he play in the offering?"

"Tantalus is a tax lawyer with the firm," Lysias said hiding his alarm at the mention of his name. "He may have done some tax planning for the company and its chairman, but nothing else that I'm aware. Why do you ask about Tantalus?"

"He appears to have been an investor in Laelaps," said Stichius. "And from what we can tell, Tantalus worked with some foreign lawyers to set it up. He himself was a director."

"We'd like to speak with him, if he's here," Toxeus jumped in.

Theseus said Tantalus was out of the office and couldn't be reached.

"Let's set some ground rules, here," Hippias said in response to Toxeus' request. "If you want to talk to Tantalus, you'll have to manage that separately. He should have his own attorney present. We also want to know your intentions with respect to the firm."

"The firm should have nothing to be concerned about, that is, if it did nothing wrong," Toxeus said dryly.

Toxeus gave the impression he would find nothing finer than to bring a large firm down by scandal.

"What can you tell us about a Mr. Pedocles," Acantha came right back. "He works for Asterion, doesn't he?"

Theseus replied that he became the director of software development when Asterion acquired his company.

"Well, it looks like Mr. Pedocles may have a large stake in Laelaps," Stichius came back. "You see our concern."

Theseus was becoming more uneasy. The obvious implication was an insider trading ring involving Tantalus, Pedocles and who knows who else. Hippias motioned to Theseus that this meeting should be over.

"There's one more thing, although it probably doesn't concern you," Stichius said. "We've learned that a block of shares in the offering were sold to a number of executives in other companies. They may have flipped the shares by the end of the first day of trading. Two of those executives are with companies that have filed registration statements to go public. They share the same underwriter as Asterion. Did you know about any of this?"

Hippias stood up.

"We had best cut this meeting short right now," Hippias

said.

"If there's nothing to hide," Toxeus replied, "there are a few more things we'd like to ask."

"I don't think so," Hippias said as he walked over to open the door for the visitors.

"We appreciate that we raised a few things that might be of concern to you as company counsel," Stichius said as he, Acantha and Toxeus got up to leave. "We'll likely be talking about some of these things further. But tell me, where can we locate Minos? He seems to have disappeared."

"Have a good day," Hippias said with finality.

39

Theseus spent the next several weeks managing the Asterion crisis. He pushed all of his other matters onto other lawyers at the firm. The company was in a free fall. The stock price was now trading well below the public offering price and investors were losing their shirts. Customers were walking away from contracts and new business was nonexistent. The operation in Thebes was hemorrhaging and employees were looking for other jobs. The data center in Tegea sat idle with no traffic. Asterion was unable to get its arms around its accounting issues and notified the commission it would be late in filing its quarterly reports. The stock exchange was threatening to delist the stock. Justice had opened a grand jury investigation into Asterion and the commission was looking at civil fraud claims.

On top of all of this, three shareholder suits had been filed within the first week of the collapse of Asterion's stock price. Phalius had also sent in a letter threatening the firm with litigation for misleading him into making an investment in Asterion. Theseus was outraged when he heard. Phalius had gotten his bridge loan paid back, and now wanted something for the warrants. He was out of pocket nothing, but still was looking for additional profit. Theseus was worried that Phalius would cite his call at the time of the bridge as the source of the fraud. That could be extremely damaging to Theseus' reputation and cost the firm dearly. Blood was in the water.

Theseus toiled around the clock trying to keep things together. The markets were relentless when a public company stumbled. The firm demanded that Asterion pay a large retainer for the firm to continue to represent it. Silenos was happy to oblige. He really had no choice.

For good or ill, Minos resurfaced and was in the office a fair amount. Minos did not seem the least bit phased by the legal problems facing the company. He kept working on deals of some kind or other, perhaps trying to find a buyer for Asterion. Theseus thought that was a long shot. What new plans he was concocting, no one could know. He acted as if he had already moved on to other opportunities.

In many respects, Theseus could not blame Minos. Theseus knew that the prospects for the company surviving were dim. Even if some semblance of an operating business could be salvaged, the weight of the government investigations and shareholders suits would consume what meager resources remained. As with many companies facing certain doom, it was all about managing the lawsuits. That would be the case with Asterion, Theseus supposed. Silenos would have little time to devote to tasks other than reviewing legal strategies, responding to discovery requests or answering extensive interrogatories. Even if the company was successful in beating back the barrage of legal challenges, the settlement costs and burgeoning legal fees would weigh so heavily on the company that it would eventually be crushed.

Aegeus came by to see Theseus one evening while he was sorting through the Asterion issues. Aegeus looked distraught.

"I never thought I would see the firm embroiled in such a tangled mess as Asterion, Theseus," Aegeus said. "Never in my life. People are saying the firm was complicit in the whole thing. Other firms are licking their chops to come after our clients. I feel totally responsible for this happening. I should never have agreed to do this for Minos. It was against my better instincts. Never take an engagement because you feel you owe somebody something for events that happened long ago. Sometimes it's better to let things be."

Aegeus said to Theseus that he appreciated his efforts to try to contain Asterion and he knew things would be worse but for Theseus' involvement.

"You know Melesius has decided to retire," Aegeus said as he was leaving. "The retirement dinner is in a few days. I know you are up to your neck in Asterion, but you should make every effort to attend."

Theseus was surprised by Aegeus' tone of voice. His request came across more like an order. He didn't normally impose on his partners that way.

"He specifically requested that you and Pirithous come," Aegeus said. "Don't ask me why. He didn't mention any other lawyers. Melesius always looked upon you two differently than the other lawyers your age. He doesn't really care much about the rest, except, of course, for us old lions. We'll all be there."

For the older lawyers like Aegeus and Melesius, the firm was still a brotherhood, Theseus thought. The retirement of one of their ranks was the chance to bear witness to what the firm meant to them during their lives. For so many of the other partners, the firm existed merely to produce an income and support a lifestyle. They owed little to the firm other than billable hours. They were apathetic about most everything else, like the retirement of a colleague. Theseus didn't want to think of himself as one of those lawyers. Theseus promised Aegeus he would attend.

By the time Melesius' retirement dinner rolled around, Theseus was ready for a break. He had been totally consumed by the mounting problems at Asterion. Theseus joined other mostly senior partners before dinner started and reminisced over his experiences working for Melesius back in the day. None of the other associates wanted to work for him. Melesius was demanding, and associates did all they could to avoid taking on his projects. Theseus stood up to the challenge, and Melesius always respected him for it. They got to know each other well early on.

As dinner started, Melesius, true to form, told stories about the firm when he was a young partner. Other old timers added color and details. There was a great deal of laughter and pride in the room. Theseus sat back and enjoyed the display of camaraderie from an earlier time. After dinner, Aegeus rose to say a few words.

"Now," Aegeus began, "our good friend and colleague Melesius has been with the firm for over fifty years and decided it is time to step away. He's been an uncompromising lawyer that always put his clients first. Melesius was a true firm leader and a devoted family man. He and his wife Calonice of forty five years raised two boys."

Theseus

Aegeus conspicuously said nothing more about the wife or the two sons. There was a reason for this, Theseus knew. Calonice was an alcoholic and had been suffering from dementia. No one had actually seen her for years. The oldest son was in and out of rehab from substance abuse and couldn't hold down a job since graduating from college. He was living at home. The second son dropped out of school after his junior year. It may be unfair to say that Melesius was embarrassed by them, but he never did talk much about his family.

"Melesius graduated at the top of his class in law school and was a member of our maritime fleet," Aegeus continued. "He was very proud of his service to his country. He joined the firm when there were only a handful of lawyers. Melesius quickly distinguished himself with his sharp mind and professorial style. His most important client was Termerus Corporation, which the firm has represented for a very long time."

Aegeus told the story of Melesius and Termerus. Melesius was riding the train home to the suburbs late one evening when he took up in conversation with a young graduate engineer named Trakas. Trakas thought he had developed a promising new high density storage device. The engineer had some family money and asked Melesius about what was necessary to set up a corporation. Melesius incorporated the young engineer's company which was called Termerus. By the time Melesius was forty, he had taken Termerus public and represented the company in countless acquisition transactions. He had invested himself in the company, and by the time he was fifty was a millionaire many times over. Melesius served on Termerus' board of directors for decades. Early on in his relationship with Termerus, he introduced a young banker to Trakas. The banker, who was Melesius' friend from high school, ended up underwriting the public sale of Termerus. That forged an everlasting bond between Melesius and the banker. The two were constant mutual referral sources for their entire careers.

Theseus remembered that Melesius told him several times

his career was built on luck, and that he should never underestimate the importance of good fortune. If not for that fateful meeting with Trakas on the train that evening, his career would certainly have been much different. The Termerus business, of course, produced other business, which led to even more business, and so on and so on. Pretty soon he had all these younger lawyers doing the work for him. And if he hadn't invested in Termerus, he would never have made the money he did. Not as a lawyer. It was a pretty good deal. Melesius would tell Theseus not to get too overconfident about his own good luck, because it could easily turn out the other way. Be thankful for what it is you have, Melesius would say to him, and never look for more than what you need. Theseus knew the gods punished those who asked too much.

After Aegeus finished, Melesius stood to say a few words. Melesius was gracious in his remarks to Aegeus and the other senior partners, and a few choice stories from the old days evoked some warm hearted laughter. Theseus noted the conviviality and nostalgia that pervaded the room.

"My time has come to step aside and let the younger generation have its due," Melesius carried on. "I am glad for it. I came to the realization that I have outgrown my usefulness and no longer have a place in this profession, if you can call it that any longer.

"My contemporaries and I were proud to be practicing lawyers. We felt we were part of a grand history. We believed the law was the foundation of a great society and we were privileged to help shape it. We worked with and for the best. That was the way it was in the beginning. It was something special to make partner. It meant you were a damn good lawyer. It wasn't about revenues or profit.

"Midway through my career, business got pretty good and we started hiring a lot of associates. All that hiring was the profession's undoing I'm afraid. Having all those young lawyers we found made us money. We began to enjoy the power and prestige that came with it. We bought bigger homes, drove nicer cars. We hired ever more associates. We got drunk on the nectar and reshaped the practice of law in the process. We commercialized the practice and by doing so have led the profession astray. Today, a young lawyer needs to make business sense before he can become a partner in a law firm. He needs to be part of a profitable group or have his own clientele. He may not be the best lawyer, but that no longer matters. He needs to convince us that he can be counted on to generate revenue.

"Law has become an industry unto itself. It's big business. There are innumerable law firms earning outsized revenues. Partners at these firms earn tremendous salaries. Businesses now exist just to service the law profession. Accounting firms have groups that specialize in law firm audits. Banks have separate departments that lend only to law firms. Executive search firms move practice groups from firm to firm. Consultants come in and help right size firms and sell a marketing strategy. All these companies feed the beast and profit from it. Can anyone tell me how the legal profession is different today from the auto industry or the insurance industry? Please enlighten me if you can tell the difference.

"How often today do we lawyers talk of doing justice? That's left to pro bono efforts for which we don't get paid. Justice today is merely a result. If you win for your client, you've achieved justice. Justice means you've gotten them off, won a false judgment or tricked the opposition into a bad deal.

"We've taught our young partners to value money and wealth above all else. We've dispensed with integrity and honor as necessary qualities. Those traits do not add to the bottom line so they have been discarded as an unnecessary expense. I don't blame the young partners for this, it was our doing. We weren't aware of what we were in the midst of creating. The younger lawyers simply followed our lead. They have now embraced profit with a vengeance. The young partners are the ones who push the steady increase in billable hour requirements. Do they think there are an infinite number of hours that lawyers can work? Or the rates lawyers can charge? There is a mad rush to quantify and measure lawyer productivity. This is nothing more than a rallying cry for cutting staff and expenses, and forcing lawyers to do more with less. We used to each have a secretary. Today we want four or five lawyers per secretary. The goal of course is no secretaries. Efficiency is an excuse for marginalizing human labor. We have even given our clients the reasons not to use us. There are outsourcing alternatives that our clients now adopt because we refuse to accept lower fees.

"We have a new management class of lawyers that never existed before. We used to conduct our affairs as a partnership. Partner votes were taken and meant something. Today, we pay other lawyers to manage the firm. The management class is populated by the lawyers that have the most revenues in the firm and make the most money. Are the highest paid lawyers the ones most capable of managing the firm? Can anyone tell me what training these lawyers received to earn their station? None that I know of. These lawyers were not really elected to lead. They seized control and the rest of us stood by and watched. The rise of the lawyer management class is a coup really. We have abdicated the reigns to the profit seekers out of fear. Fear that the firm would collapse if we lost these people. Now they actually work less and no longer spend time on client development and practicing law. They obsess with cutting expenses and getting everyone else to work smarter.

"The reality is law firms have weak management teams. That's why they pay outside business consultants who are not lawyers to teach them how to increase revenues per lawyer and profits per partner. They receive from non-lawyers complicated sounding models and growth strategies. They judge their firm by where it's plotted on the quadrant. The two axes are revenue and profitability. We have assumed that any law firm with low profits per partner is a poor quality firm destined to fail. The consulting firms have a stock set of recommendations to move all firms to the upper left quadrant. That is now the measure of success.

"We haven't even begun with the personal cost that has come with our supposed prosperity. I probably drove my wife mad with neglect. I don't know my children very well. Many of us have pathetic personal lives and superficial relationships. Perhaps there is the justice in all of this.

"So I say to you my time has come to step down. As I look at the future of law, I cannot say where it will go. I don't see much good in continuing on the present path, but I am at a loss for alternatives.

"The future belongs to a new generation. We have not taught the young people very well in my estimation, and that is our great failing. Perhaps they will shake off this fog that clouds the profession and reestablish the glory we had. That is up to our younger partners and those that follow them. Farewell, and best of luck, is all I can say. May the god of justice lead the law to more noble and better times."

Melesius sat down. There was an awkward rustling in the room, but very little else. Melesius was there in his chair, staring straight out at no one, looking as if the life had left him.

Aegeus finally rose from his seat.

"Few of us will match Melesius' accomplishments," Aegeus said with some discomfort. "He was a giant in the firm and a giant in the law. He will be missed."

The partners applauded politely as if nothing Melesius said registered. Afterward, the lawyers quickly scattered. Some raced to their cars. Others pulled out cell phones and began dialing. Many caught taxis back to the office or went to catch planes. The business of the firm would continue on more or less as usual and without anyone taking heed of Melesius' exhortations.

Theseus was reminded of Solon, the great lawgiver of Athens, and his view of happiness. Solon was visiting the great Lydian king, Croesus, at Sardis. Croesus gave Solon a tour of his immense royal treasure, and then asked Solon who was the happiest man he had ever seen. Solon replied that it was an Athenian named Tellus, who had sufficient means, had fine sons and grandchildren, and died in battle defending his city. Tellus was given the honor of a public funeral. Solon said that the turns of fortune made it impossible to declare any man, wealthy or poor, happy until his death. Such were the vicissitudes of man. Croesus, upset that Solon didn't regard him as the happiest man alive, dismissed him as a fool.

Theseus understood why Melesius wanted him and Pirithous there to hear his farewell soliloquy. Melesius had taken the occasion of his retirement to convey to them a simple truth. A man's virtue and honor, once attained, can be easily lost if reason forgets or the will slackens. Purpose of mind can never waiver nor can vigilance be abandoned.

40

The official notice from the commission arrived a few months after Asterion's stock collapsed. The commission was alerting Asterion that an investigation of the company was ongoing and it was probable that a civil action would be filed against Asterion and its board. The commission's case would be premised on fraudulent misrepresentation of the company's financial condition.

The immediate goal, Theseus knew, was to have the commission drop its case. News of a commission complaint would be the last nail in the coffin for Asterion. A claim of securities fraud was the death penalty for fledgling public companies. Customers would walk, banks would stop lending and the markets would repel any attempts at raising new capital. The taint from a looming fraud charge was enough to cause operations to shut down even if the case lacked merit. For businesses that required growth in revenues, nothing could be worse. Theseus likened it to the fate of the Mytilenians after revolting from Athens during the war with Sparta.

Theseus huddled with Hippias to devise a way to head off the commission's case. Stichius was likely to be handling the matter from the commission, and Theseus agreed with Hippias that Stichius had career aspirations and would not be inclined to settle.

"We should go higher up, Theseus," Hippias said. "Let's get an audience with the head of enforcement to try to derail this thing. It's our best shot."

Theseus concurred and let Hippias arrange a meeting. Stichius tried to prevent that from happening. But a second call from Lysias to Cabrius, the head of enforcement at the commission, was enough to overcome Stichius' obdurate posturing.

Hippias was inclined to take an aggressive stance with the commission when they met, and argue that the firm would fight long and hard against any suit brought against Asterion. His view was that it would be difficult to prove the fraud allegations, and the firm could tie the case up in courts for years. Theseus wanted to pursue a different tack and try for a quick resolution. After not insignificant debate, Hippias acquiesced and agreed to Theseus' approach. Theseus developed the argument and coached Hippias on how he wanted it presented to the commission. Theseus thought it would be best for Hippias to make the presentation.

Hippias and Theseus arrived at the commission's office promptly at the appointed time for the meeting. Theseus traded a few pleasantries with Cabrius, but Stichius wanted to get down to business. Hippias took off his suit coat and Cabrius gave Stichius the nod to start. Stichius identified what he believed was a strong case against Asterion. Stichius thought he could get the case through discovery and to trial in short order.

Theseus and Hippias listened to Stichius courteously and without interruption. When Stichius finished, Hippias took his turn.

"What you just outlined, Stichius," Hippias stated, "would certainly be insurmountable if it all proved to be true. There's no doubting that. And we definitely don't want a long protracted battle with the commission. The company doesn't really have the money for an all out war. Besides, with your experience in these types of cases and the resources at the commission's disposal, we would have a hard time convincing Asterion to fight.

"Asterion is a small, developing company that has a good business plan. Where things went wrong we don't really know yet. We are pretty confident that the disclosure at the time of the offering was correct, although it is easy to feel that wasn't the case given the cascading events that followed the public offering. Hindsight doesn't always lead perfectly to the truth.

"There have been quite a few offerings from companies in this market that probably shouldn't have been floated. Asterion may be one of them. But we are here to ask the commission to reconsider its plans to bring an action against the company. Faced with a commission complaint, the company would probably fold. We're not sure that's the result the commission really wants. We are in a market cycle that is witnessing the funding of countless new technologies. Investors are snapping up new issues every day. The demand is enormous. Not all companies will be winners. That is the way with the market. There will be losers, and investors understand this. Bringing a case against Asterion would undoubtedly have a chilling effect on new issues. The commission's charge is to protect investors, not to substitute its judgment for them. The commission shouldn't be deciding which companies go public and which ones don't. That's the market's function. Suing Asterion in this climate is something the commission needs to think hard about. It could be politically damaging to the commission.

"Let's talk about the effect a commission action would have on the company itself. Asterion has grown from a few employees to a hundred in a very short time. Its employees are generally young, technology types. These young people are amazing to watch. They are entrepreneurial and excited about the future and want to help mold it. That's why they sign up with a company like Asterion. If you walk into the company's offices, you can feel the energy and excitement. People are happy and motivated, from the secretaries to the executives. There is a buzz that comes from being on the front lines of change. The employees embrace it and live it. Most have a share in the company through stock options, and that is part of the attraction. It's like owning a piece of the future for them. Our government policies should be supportive of these young people. Asterion's employees had nothing to do with the financing or the problems the company faced. Although there are obstacles, the company still has a chance to succeed. A commission complaint would be making these young people accountable for something that was not their fault. As we said, an action for fraud against Asterion, once announced, would likely mean the end for the company. The company isn't sitting on a pile of cash. The proceeds from the offering have largely been spent. The company needs revenues to survive. Sales will dry up if the commission lodges a formal complaint. You would in effect be throwing the employees out on the street and dashing their hopes and their dreams in the process. We urge you strongly not to take that course.

"You may decide that you will drop the case against the company to save the employees, and instead focus your attack on the board. We can understand why you might consider this. The board is ultimately responsible for setting policy and has oversight responsibilities for the company's management. It is a logical target. You might even prevail in this. But have you thought about who you will attacking? The board has four independent members, all of whom joined the board right at the time of the offering. Count among them a retired accountant and an academic. This is not the type of high profile group upon which to set a mark. Find a board that truly was gaming the system. Asterion's board was not.

"If you feel the boards of companies like Asterion need a wakeup call, let the securities bar handle that. There are already several securities cases filed on behalf of the stockholders. That's enough of a reminder to boards. These cases will run out years, as they usually do.

"There is still an opportunity here for the commission if you feel that you need to make an example out of this tragedy. Go after the investment bankers. They are the ones between the issuers and the investing public. The law imposes obligations on the underwriters to make sure there is complete and adequate disclosure about companies selling securities to the public. But their role is much larger than that, as you know. They are the gatekeepers to the market. It is their job to make sure only viable companies sell their securities publicly. The investment bankers are experts in sizing up companies and measuring their worth and chances for success. The underwriters are the ones that should be held accountable. Imagine if they took their job seriously and only underwrote companies they believed in. You would see far less failures and fewer busted offerings.

"The investment banking community has taken on this

aura of invincibility because no one takes them to task. They will sell anything to the market to earn their spreads. Instead of playing their designated role in raising capital, they engage in all sorts of questionable practices to make more money. They purposely under price issues in order to flip stock on the first day of trading. They place issues with favored clients and executives from companies whose business they are after, only to trade them out of their positions at hefty profits after the stock has risen. They know when large orders are coming in and buy and sell ahead of the orders to make a quick return. You know these practices are going on. We don't have to tell you this. The bankers believe that they are immune from commission suits on the basis that all they do is make markets and put buyers and sellers together. Since when did the underwriters become simple securities brokers? They have a greater role in the new issue market, and the law recognizes that. Investment bankers are supposed to be the guardians of the market. It's worth repeating. Their job is to make sure only legitimate companies with good prospects raise money from the public. They have totally abrogated their historic role. Go after the bankers. Make them your target. They can afford it. They are making money hand over fist in this market. Free-riding, spinning or front-running. Call these practices what you will, but be assured that they are rampant out there. You will have better publicity and actually help change the chicanery that is currently going on if you pursue the street. That's our view. We hope you will consider it."

Cabrius and Stichius were not expecting what they heard. Theseus could see Cabrius' mind turning. Stichius was circumspect. Theseus was surprised that Cabrius and Stichius did not outright reject Hippias's proposal. Instead, Cabrius simply told Theseus and Hippias that the commission would consider what was said and get back to them.

Hippias couldn't contain himself on the way back to the office.

"You know I didn't believe in this strategy, Theseus," Hippias admitted. "I thought it was a real long shot. The commission plays hard ball and usually doesn't back down. I'm not saying they will bite, but they certainly didn't dismiss our position out of hand. It will be interesting to see what they come back with."

Theseus thanked Hippias for his work on the matter, and told Hippias that his presentation was excellent. Theseus said that Cabrius was under pressure to come up with a major enforcement case. He had practiced on the street for years, and decided to give government service a try. Cabrius was going into his fifth year at the commission without a splash. There was talk that the street had Cabrius in their back pocket and controlled the enforcement agenda at the commission. Asterion was inconsequential on the whole. Theseus felt that hearing from the firm on the market abuses would give Cabrius some confidence in pursing that route.

"Could be I even learn from this," Hippias chuckled. "Maybe the soft approach isn't so bad. Let's see where it goes."

41

Lysias called Theseus with some unwelcome news.

"The commission and justice are here," Lysias said. "They are going after Tantalus. You better get down there."

Theseus quickly went to Tantalus's office. There was a crowd at Tantalus' door. Office personnel were standing at their desks wearing frightened looks. Theseus edged his way into Tantalus' office and saw he was being handcuffed by Toxeus. Theseus heard Toxeus reading Tantalus his rights. Stichius motioned Theseus to step out of the office.

"Mr. Tantalus is being charged with securities fraud and insider trading over the Asterion stock," said Stichius. "Looks like your firm has a serious problem on its hands. A shame to see a stalwart of the legal profession bloodied like this."

Stichius was enjoying the moment. Theseus wondered if Stichius resented the fact that he went to a second tier law firm and couldn't get an interview at any big firm.

"The investigation is continuing," Stichius said. "We may be back."

Theseus went to see Tantalus.

"You're going to be behind me on this," Tantalus exhaled concern. "I mean, the firm will see me through this mess, right?"

Theseus didn't answer.

"I've had to fight my entire career," Tantalus said rationalizing. "No one ever gave me anything. I didn't have a mentor that made it easy. I was always knocking heads with senior partners, other lawyers, clients. But I made it. I built a solid practice. Asterion was going to get me to the next level. You know, get me enough so I didn't have to worry about the hellish hours, the money. It would have gotten me into the management ranks. I would have been a hell of a firm leader."

Theseus noticed the sculpture Tantalus won at the Hebe auction. It was even more grotesque than he remembered. Tantalus saw Theseus looking at the sculpture.

"It all started going wrong when I bought that goddamn thing," Tantalus deadpanned.

Tantalus stared straight at Theseus.

"Is the firm going to cut me loose?" Tantalus asked.

Theseus told Tantalus he would find him a good criminal attorney. He offered to call Leda for him.

"Leda's gone," Tantalus said with disgust. "Split. Can you believe the bitch! She packed up and left a few weeks ago. I think she's shacked up with a banker."

Theseus began to feel sorry for Tantalus.

"Hey," Tantalus then said inexplicably, "they are building a race club and test track out by me. A couple of dealers started it. They let you keep your cars out there. I was about to put in to be a founding member. I'll have to get you out there. They just laid the track and broke ground on a clubhouse and everything. Can you see it? I always wanted to be a race car driver."

The agents took Tantalus by each arm and started to escort him out of the office.

"Theseus," Tantalus shouted from the elevator. "Tell Minos he owes me a round of golf in Rhodes when I get back. He never gave me a chance to win my money back. The cheap bastard."

Tantalus was gone.

When Theseus returned to his office, his secretary told him that Silenos was on the phone.

"They nabbed Tantalus?" Silenos asked cautiously. "Anyone else?"

Theseus said no one else at the firm.

"Well, we got a delisting notice today," Silenos told Theseus. "No quotes on the stock. We'll have to start checking the pink sheets."

Silenos paused before continuing.

"I'm resigning at the end of the week, Theseus," Silenos said. "It's not my way to walk away from unfinished business, but I've got another opportunity with Tiro. He must think I learned something here. Anyway, I may be unemployable if I stick around Asterion much longer. I gave

Theseus

Minos my resignation letter. He was on the phone and didn't have much of a reaction. It's been a pleasure, Theseus. Let's hope fate has something better in store for us, huh?"

Silenos hung up. It would be the last time Theseus would ever speak to him.

42

Herodian was behind his desk waiting for everyone to arrive. The sight of Herodian was somehow comforting to Theseus. He was present as always, without a notion of the weighty matters to be decided in the room behind him. Like so many others in the firm, Herodian performed his tasks without ever letting on what he was thinking or feeling. Did he enjoy his job? Did he resent the lawyers with their big take home pay? How was his health, his family? Did he love his wife? Had he saved enough for retirement? Herodian made Theseus think of the importance of daily labor. Without people like Herodian, society would abruptly stop functioning. He and those like him were essential to maintaining everyday life. Theseus felt there was great dignity in Herodian's work even though it went unrecognized and unnoticed. Herodian did not have the opportunity to be driven by ambition, money or fame. Theseus assumed he accepted his role at the firm and station in life. He was self possessed, comfortable in his own skin, Theseus thought. Herodian had been at the firm for more than thirty years, and had never missed a day. He worked his way up to become head of the security team. Herodian never graduated from high school, but raised five kids all of whom made it through college. A very respectable legacy.

"Good morning, Mr. Theseus," Herodian said with a sideways glance. "Your cell phone, please?"

The executive committee was gathering to assess the fallout from the Asterion debacle. The publicity had sullied the firm's reputation and there was the prospect of losing clients. Tantalus had been arrested. Shareholder suits had been filed. Phalius was likely to pursue his own separate claim directly against the firm. Aegeus was certain the firm's competitors were on the offensive, calling the public companies for the work the firm had been doing for decades. The new issue market was still robust, and it remained to be seen if the leading underwriters on the street would move away from the firm and encourage its corporate clients to do

Theseus

the same.

The conference room was silent when Theseus entered. Aegeus, Demosthenes, Isaios and Hypereides had grim expressions. Pausanias was at the head of the table. Everyone was looking right at him. Pausanias was smiling. Theseus wondered what he was doing there.

"This Asterion mess has changed things," Pausanias said. "It's been a good run, but I can't take the risk of the firm stumbling. I'll be joining another firm. I'm taking two other partners and five associates. My whole team."

Theseus knew Pausanias' new firm. It had strived for years to achieve the size and profitability of the firm. They were on a lateral hiring binge and offering large guaranteed payouts to partners from other prestigious law practices.

"I can take a couple of weeks to transition, or I can leave in a few days," Pausanias continued. "Whatever you want. But I'm gone."

Pausanias had come into the firm as a first year, and developed his practice with long standing clients of the firm. Theseus wondered if he ever brought in work from the outside. Theseus doubted that Pausanias was at all concerned about the firm losing its clients. He thought it was Pausanias' bid to grab all the billing credit he could. It was the game of musical chairs played out in the modern law firms. Lawyers like Pausanias wanted a bigger piece of the action and would move from firm to firm to get it. The Asterion fallout was Pausanias' excuse to make the break.

Aegeus told Pausanias a reasonable transition would be proposed and said that he was sorry to see him go. Once Pausanias left the room, Aegeus said he wanted Pausanias thrown out posthaste. Like the Samos soldiers who took the oath to save the Athenian democracy, Demosthenes and Isaios went into action. Demosthenes called Herodian and told him to round up security. Pausanias was to be promptly removed from the premises. His office was to be locked, his phone confiscated, his files secured and his computer access denied. Pausanias was not to be allowed to remove a single piece of paper. Isaios called accounting to get a list of all the clients Pausanias had worked on for the last five years. He was also to make sure the firm would tie up his capital indefinitely.

"What about the others?" Isaios asked.

"I want Theseus to talk to the partners who are going with him," Aegeus said. "Theseus, can you manage that by day's end? Tell them that Pausanias will not be successful in drawing clients away from the firm. His new place is an upstart and they are risking their careers. Promise them Pausanias' lead clients. I'll get Lysias to talk to the associates. Let's give them a bump in salary and tell them partnership is looking good for them. If they decide to leave, we will treat them the same as Pausanias."

The executive committee also put into motion the firm's client retention policy. Each of Pausanias' clients would be contacted by a senior partner. Other partners would be assigned primary service responsibility. The firm would dispatch lawyers to meet face to face with clients as necessary. No client files would be transferred out of the firm without a signed authorization by the client and not until all outstanding invoices for legal services were paid in full. That usually took some time.

The executive committee spent the next hour reviewing what needed to be done to stave off further fallout from Tantalus's arrest. The firm's public relations consultant was fully engaged to handle the media. Tantalus was to be portrayed as a rogue attorney acting on his own without any knowledge of anyone else at the firm. Only Aegeus was allowed to speak to the press. Internal memos were to be prepared and distributed to all personnel with instructions not to respond to reporters' calls.

Aegeus then discussed handling the ongoing commission inquiry of Asterion. Theseus said that Lysias just told him he had gotten a call from Cabrius at the commission, and it was pulling back its investigation of Asterion. Word was the commission would be announcing a major sweep of the bulge bracket investment banks and the street's trading practices.

"That's an amazing outcome, Theseus," Aegeus said

Theseus

surprised and obviously pleased. "Absolutely fantastic!"

"What do you know about this guy Thrasycles, Theseus?" Demosthenes asked. "From what we've already learned, he was the one that tipped off the bureau about what was going on at the company. Apparently, he had been feeding them information for quite some time. Why the bureau didn't bring in the commission earlier and stop the offering is beyond me."

Theseus was taken aback by the revelation that Thrasycles was the informer. He thought it was Ariadne. Theseus felt regret at his lack of trust in Ariadne.

"He's got a deal with the government, so he got away clean," said Demosthenes. "Who knows who he'll point the finger at."

"This Asterion debacle may continue to be a dark cloud over the firm for some time," Aegeus said to Theseus as the meeting was breaking up. "I never thought I'd see anything like this."

Theseus told Aegeus that he did not look well and asked about his health.

"Oh, I'll be fine," Aegeus replied. "There is a lot of talk among the partners about what happened. Much of it is directed at you, I'm afraid. You may as well know, Theseus, that I was looking at you to succeed me as chairman of the firm. Among all the partners you are the one for the job. I don't know if that can happen now. It is weighing on me more than Asterion itself. The partners are upset. Castor is angling. Aietes is up to his tricks and gathering support. He wants a seat on the executive committee, and I don't know if I can stop that. I put you up to this, Theseus, and it may prove to be my, your, undoing."

Theseus expressed his appreciation for Aegeus' confidence and assured him that things would likely turn out fine. Theseus was not convinced that would be the case, and from Aegeus' downtrodden look, neither did he.

Theseus went down to talk to Aegeon and Boethus, the two partners who Pausanias identified as leaving with him. He decided to talk to them together. Both were young, and both depended to a large extent on Pausanias' clients for work.

"What am I supposed to do, Theseus?" Aegeon asked. "The last couple years, most of my time has been with these clients. Without that work, I'd have nothing to do. I'm screwed."

"Yeah, and Pausanias has arranged a huge increase in pay for us," Boethus said confidently. "We are going in with a big raise from what we make here, guaranteed for two years. Besides, the market is changing. The money is flowing to the younger guys out there. We can't sit around hoping for a big payday down the road. It may never come. I'm busting my butt, and getting little for it. Not what I think I deserve, certainly. If you can tell me this firm will pay me what I'm worth, maybe I'd listen. But I probably wouldn't believe it anyway."

Theseus told the two they shouldn't underestimate what it means to be partner at the firm.

"Don't think we haven't given that some thought," Aegeon said. "We'd be walking away from one of the most respected firms in the country. Clients will wonder why we left the firm. They might think we were let go. But this Asterion problem has me spooked. This could really cost the firm a lot. Pausanias thinks so. And I've heard Aietes talking."

Theseus told them Asterion would blow over. He said their new firm was all about making quick money. Aegeon and Boethus would find no collegiality or loyalty there. Partners would be fighting amongst themselves for clients. Theseus told them that when their guarantee was over, they'd be shown the door if they hadn't produced. The two would be out on the street looking with Pausanias.

Aegeon and Boethus began to look a little unsure. Theseus stopped talking in order to give the partners a chance to respond. Neither did.

Theseus told the two they had until this evening to figure out what they wanted to do. He got up to leave. Theseus warned them they wouldn't be welcomed at the firm in the morning if they were still intent on leaving. Pausanias was already gone, by way of a security detail. Theseus said that for what it was worth, he hoped they would stay. Theseus told them to call him if they wanted to talk further.

Theseus walked out. He headed back to his office to work on a few client matters that he had been neglecting. When he got to his office, his secretary told him Axylus was on the line. Theseus picked up.

"Theseus, it's been a while," Axylus said in greeting. "How the hell have you been? Listen, I've got Penthesileas on the line."

"Hello, Theseus," Penthesileas said gravely.

"Hey, you've seen the commission's announcement, haven't you?" Axylus asked. "You know, about the sweep."

Theseus said he already knew.

"Word is you put Stichius up to it," asserted Penthesileas.

Theseus said he didn't know what Penthesileas was referring to.

"Don't pretend with me," Penthesileas threatened. "You traded Asterion for the street."

Theseus said that whatever actions the firm took on behalf of Asterion was confidential and not a subject for discussion.

"Holy Toledo, Theseus," Axylus interjected, "we are all a little nervous over here about the sweep. Erasicles is very concerned."

"Looks like you won't be working for Typhon or any other investment bank any time soon," Penthesileas said. "They'll cut your firm off once they know what you've pulled. And I'll make sure everyone knows."

Theseus said that it was not appropriate for him to discuss the matter and ended the call. He thought about Penthesileas' threat, and knew that it was a risk in the strategy. But his duty was to Asterion, and it was the best play he had. He was compelled to pursue it.

The phone rang again and it was Axylus.

"I had to get Penthesileas off the line," Axylus said. "I didn't know she would come on like that. Listen, Erasicles wanted me to ask you if your firm would handle the commission's case for us if we get pulled in. I don't know what happened with Asterion, but I can't believe you got them off. That's the kind of legal work that we want over here. We've had enough of Penthesileas and her crew."

Theseus said he would ask the firm's general counsel if the firm could represent Typhon. He didn't see why not.

"Great," Axylus said. "Look into it and get back to me. Erasicles will be pleased to know you can represent us."

43

Asterion sputtered along for a time but the inevitable collapse of the company finally came. Theseus wondered if the rise and fall of Asterion was a record of some sort. He couldn't recall another company filing for bankruptcy so quickly after a public offering. Perhaps he would have Calliope research it.

Theseus had stopped talking altogether with Minos or anyone else at the company for that matter. By the time the company finally went down, the firm was owed a considerable amount of money in fees, and the executive committee had voted to stop representing the company to avoid further losses. The firm was out of pocket for its own outside counsel to extract it from the mess caused by Asterion, and that was enough.

As it turned out, the firm avoided being named in the shareholder suits filed against the company and the board of directors. Phalius, however, sued the firm claiming that it misled him into investing in the company. The complaint alleged that he never got the chance to sell his warrants and they were now worthless. Phalius valued the warrants at five times the offering price, which would have earned him a small fortune if he had sold at the peak. He pointed to a conversation with an unnamed firm lawyer who told him that Asterion was a rock solid company that would have an exponential rise in revenues over the next three to five years. The lawyer told Phalius that the warrants were as good as gold. Theseus knew that he never spoke to Phalius about the warrants. Theseus learned later that the unnamed lawyer was actually Tantalus. He allegedly had hounded Phalius into making the bridge and taking the warrants.

As with any long time client whose fortunes were battered, there was always hope for a rise from the ashes. Theseus wondered if that might be the case when he was asked by Lysias to appear at a bankruptcy hearing for Asterion. Lysias wanted Theseus to go to see if there was any hope the firm could recoup some of its fees. Theseus thought that there might be a role for the firm in the bankruptcy. He knew that in bankruptcy the lawyers were paid first before any other creditors. Maybe he could yet turn a decent fee from Asterion's collapse.

When Theseus walked into the bankruptcy court, there was only one other person there. He was an attorney named Nicostratos. His firm had been appointed the lead counsel for the shareholders.

"So you are the great Theseus," Nicostratos said in greeting. "Pleasure to meet you. I didn't expect anyone from your firm to show up here. This should be an uneventful hearing. I am told the judge won't even show, just the magistrate. He is supposed to approve counsel for the creditors committee and discuss the prospects for a bankruptcy plan. Word is that there is a company interested in buying some of the assets. Not sure what there is to buy. We are only interested in the insurance coverage. If you are here looking to collect past due fees, good luck. There won't be anything left from what I can see."

Just then a man in a light blue jacket popped his head out from behind the door leading to the judge's chamber. He took a quick look around and then went back in and closed the door.

Several other people came into the courtroom. There was an attorney named Phaeax who wanted to be appointed counsel to the creditors committee. He had with him a gentleman from a server supplier that sold equipment to Asterion for the Tegea data center. Asterion had put in a large order just before the company failed. Unfortunately for the supplier, the equipment was delivered to the data center just in time for the bankruptcy filing. The supplier obviously hadn't investigated the creditworthiness of Asterion.

Another attorney showed who claimed he represented a group who wanted to buy the company. His name was Lamachus.

"Sure I know you," Lamachus said to Theseus. "You're with the firm that did the offering. Crazy turn of events, huh? Maybe not as crazy as Minos buying the company back though."

Just as Lamachus spoke, in walked Minos.

"Theseus," Minos said. "How are you?"

Minos looked as sharp as always. He hadn't lost that swagger.

The man in the light blue jacket came back in through the door and took a seat at one of the attorney tables. He seemed to be in a hurry.

"Ok," he said. "My name is Gallus. I'm the appointed magistrate. The judge won't be coming. Let's get started."

Gallus had everyone in the room introduce themselves. Theseus found it more than a bit awkward not having a client to represent.

"Alright, then," Gallus continued. "I call this meeting to order. Public notice of this meeting was sent to all known creditors and stockholders of the company. If there isn't any objection, I will go ahead and appoint Phaeax the attorney for the creditor's committee. I believe that, Mr. Lamachus, your client here has a proposal for the company. Let's hear it."

Lamachus cleared this throat, then began outlining the plan. An investor group led by Minos would purchase debentures issued by Asterion based on the value of the remaining assets of the company. Lamachus produced an independent third party appraisal showing the fair value of the assets. The proceeds would be used to pay off some of the outstanding accounts payable of Asterion, although at a fraction of what was owed. The debentures would be convertible into shares of Asterion at the time the company exited from bankruptcy. The amount of the equity issued upon conversion would dilute the existing shareholders to a small percentage of the company.

"Well," Gallus said, "get the plan on paper and into the court as soon as you possibly can. The judge is inclined to liquidate the company based on what he sees. We can have a vote of the creditors on this and get the company out of bankruptcy within ninety days. If there is nothing else, let's call it a day."

Gallus then got up and returned to the judge's chambers.

Minos also got up. He flashed his characteristic smile.

"I should have you over to Rhodes for some more golf," Minos said to Theseus. "I'd like to see that swing of yours again. Pure."

Minos picked up his briefcase.

"Too bad how it turned out for Tantalus," said Minos. "He got in over his head, I guess, couldn't resist the temptation. What some guys will do for the money."

Theseus thought the remark ironic coming from Minos. Theseus asked Minos what he wanted to do with the company.

"It'll get me back in the game," Minos replied. "I'll probably get the stock listed on the Smyrna exchange to make it look like there's something there. I've got a few brokers lined up to promote the stock. There are a couple technology firms I'll probably acquire once I have some stock again. It's an amazing thing, Theseus. You find people who have built a nice little business, generating some revenues. They come into some cash, find it's good to have. Lets you buy some fine things. People start treating you a little different, pay attention to you. Then a guy like me comes around. He offers them some stock in a public company. Now what they have isn't nearly enough. They want more. Public stock can get it for them. It can surge in value overnight. You can't get that with cash. They don't really understand the stock market or the fundamentals. If they do, they turn a blind eye to what they know. These people, they grab the stock quickly, and ignore everything they've built. The lure is too great for them. It's incredible. But what is it they get really? Wealth on a piece of paper, which goes up and goes down on a daily basis. It works out for some. But when prices plunge, devastation. Their life is destroyed. What is it about owning stock in a public company, Theseus? Call me when you have an answer to that. For me, I get my hands on the cash flow from the business. They've given that up taking my stock. I get a majority stake, so I'm in control. If I can get enough of the cash out, well, it doesn't really matter to me what happens to the stock."

Theseus

Theseus asked Minos how he intended to avoid getting pulled down by the bureau and the commission.

"I should get out unscathed," Minos said. "There is really nothing there to lay on me. I know you think I did this for the money. But you misunderstand me, Theseus. Greed is not my thing. I make my money from everyone else's. I can't do a damn thing unless my employees show up for work, a bank lends me money or someone takes my stock. I just provide the opportunity. If it wasn't me, it would be someone else."

For the first time, Theseus understood Mino's blueprint. It didn't matter what the business was to Minos, whether computers, machine tools or bicycles. Minos was into the human nature game and discovered a way to profit from it. Avarice was his trade. He learned that greed made people abandon foresight and reason. Minos did business with people cursed with wanting more than was meant for them. His victims were incapable of dodging Apollo's arrows.

Theseus said goodbye to Minos and walked out of the courtroom. He recalled the words of Zeus who said, with Aigithos in mind, that greed and folly doubled the suffering of men.

τρίτο μέρος

DYKE

By nature, they say, to commit injustice is a good and to suffer it is an evil, but that the excess of evil in being wronged is greater than the excess of good in doing wrong, so that when men do wrong and are wronged by one another and taste of both, those who lack the power to avoid the one and take the other determine that it is for their profit to make a compact with one another neither to commit not to suffer injustice, and that this is the beginning of legislation and of covenants between men, and that they name the commandment of the law the lawful and the just, and that this is the genesis and essential nature of justice—a compromise between the best, which is to do wrong with impunity, and the worst, which is to be wronged and be impotent to get one's revenge.

Plato, *Republic.*

α

Theseus was returning to Attica by sea. His mind wandered as he sailed, as if every wave that buffeted the ship jogged a new memory. Theseus reflected back on Asterion and wondered if the whole tragedy could have been avoided. What was evident at the beginning, he thought, that he should have seen? What did he miss? Surely there were signs. He remembered Ariadne's repeated warnings. At that moment it occurred to him that he had all but forgotten her.

Theseus realized that he failed to appreciate Ariadne's efforts on his behalf. She had made every effort to guide him through the labyrinth. He decided he must go find her. Naxos was the last place Theseus knew her to be, so he ordered the crew to chart a course to Naxos.

Theseus had his men sail in haste. When he reached the island, Theseus had the ship maneuvered into shallow waters. He looked out over the pristine beaches and rocky shoreline.

"How could I have been so vain?" Theseus said to himself. "I left the woman alone and lost in this place."

He ordered the crew to drop the anchor and moor the ship. Theseus leapt from the boat and made his way alone onto the island. Each village he entered he inquired of Ariadne's whereabouts. The residents of Naxos looked askance when he asked, and were evasive with answers to his questions.

"We don't know who you speak of," they would say, or "why is it you are searching for this woman?"

Theseus sensed that the people were not honest with him and he grew angry and frustrated.

Theseus persisted in his search and made his way onto the inner part of the island. The population was sparse the further he went inland, but he was certain he would find Ariadne. He reached one of the highest points and came upon an old vagabond. He had a full length beard, wore a patchwork of tattered clothing and walked with a large stick to steady himself.

"Old man," Theseus said, "I don't know why you are here

so far from the people of this island. You must be a seer or priest of some sort. My guess is you are wise and knowing of what happens here. Tell me, have you heard of a woman called Ariadne? She is dark haired and beautiful as if a child of the gods. She was lost here some time ago. She is looking for me and I her."

For a long while, the old man just sat there.

"What madness drives you on this quest, Theseus?" the man finally said.

Theseus was stunned the man knew him, but his heart beat with renewed hope that he would now find Ariadne.

"I shouldn't speak to you of Ariadne," the man went on. "The people of Naxos have been instructed not to mention her name lest they bring a curse on this land. You should abandon your search and go back to your home and not think of her again."

Enraged, Theseus drew his sword and threatened the old man.

"I will end your profligate days here if you do not tell me where you have hidden her," Theseus shouted. "I mean what I say so you are wise to speak the truth to me."

"I can see that you are wild in your affection for this woman," the man said quite unruffled, "but striking me won't draw her near. The gods have great sympathy for me, so perhaps I can tell you of Ariadne without their wrath coming down on the island. But before I do, put away your sword."

Theseus pulled back and did as he was told. The old man sat upright on a rock and spoke of the fate of Ariadne. During her stay on Naxos, she acted very sad as if left behind by someone dear to her. Ariadne received the hospitality of the inhabitants and lived on the island for a time. Soon, Dionysus appeared and took Ariadne away. No one knew where Dionysus was to take Ariadne, but Dionysus warned the people not to speak her name or great misfortune would befall the island. Many say Ariadne left Naxos with great reluctance, but was resigned to a marriage to Dionysus.

"It was not your destiny to be with Ariadne, nor for her to be with you," the old man said. "The path you chose for yourself and your present duties take you in different directions."

"Tell me, sir," Theseus pleaded, "what will become of her?"

"If you must know," the old man related, "Ariadne comes to an unhappy end. The story will be told that Dionysus himself called on Artemis to fell Ariadne with her bow on the isle of Dia. No more can I say."

Theseus' body fell limp when he heard this. He wailed out loud but did not curse Dionysus for fear of the god's reprisals.

Theseus' crew had grown concerned over his whereabouts and began their own search for Theseus. They arrived to find Theseus prostrate on the ground. The men gathered him up and brought him back to the ship. The waters were now roughed by strong winds from the south, and the crew had difficulty getting the ship away from the shore.

Seeing the trouble, Theseus himself grabbed an oar and with great strength brought the ship into open waters. Like a mad bull, he rowed ferociously through the massive swells in the sea. The crew was astonished at this great exhibition of power and strength. Theseus scanned the horizon and looked at the placement of the sun, and drew a course for Attica. He sculled without food or rest until the cliffs were in sight.

β

Upon his arrival in Attica, Theseus prepared sacrifices to the gods at water's edge, fulfilling a promise he made if he was favored with a safe return. While performing the necessary rituals, a messenger from the city approached him. Aegeus, the messenger announced, was dead. The news brought Theseus to his knees. He was overcome by great sadness and self loathing, certain he had some measure of blame for Aegeus' demise. Theseus made his way back to the city filled with remorse. Reeling from the loss of Ariadne and now Aegeus, Theseus thought about leaving Attica permanently and returning to Troezen. He had made up his mind to do this when he received a visit from Lysias.

Lysias implored Theseus to reconsider.

"The city is now without a leader," Lysias argued. "The council has just recently adjourned a conference to decide what actions to take. Demosthenes has stepped in as archon for the time being. I think you should lay claim to be Aegeus' successor. Will you do it? The situation is precarious."

Theseus was wary.

"Why do you place this burden on me?" Theseus asked Lysias. "Surely there are others better suited to the position. Haven't you considered Isaios or Hypereides? What of Demosthenes? These men have experience and are prudent and sensible. All are logical choices. You yourself, Lysias, are more capable than I."

"You should hold yourself with the same esteem others have for you, Theseus," Lysias responded. "Besides, Isaios and Hypereides are too long in years. Demosthenes is mercurial. As for me, I am just an old simpleton. We need someone with vitality, someone who will be decisive and far-sighted. You have the respect of the elders and great influence with the people. These are traits no one else holds. Aegeus wanted you as his successor. He made it known to me before he died. If you decline, we will be left with the likes of Aietes."

Theseus was unsure of the proposal. He questioned his

own ambitions and whether he would be dedicated to the task. Part of him wanted to retreat to the shores of his birth to live a quiet and contemplative life.

"Let me attend to the interment of Aegeus," Theseus replied, "and then I will give you my answer."

"The council has selected you to give the funeral oration before the burial," Lysias added.

Theseus was reticent, knowing that the honor to speak at the funeral of a great man was normally reserved for a statesmen believed to have the highest intellect. But out of his great respect for Aegeus and in deference to the Areopagus, Theseus agreed.

The occasion of Aegeus' death was an opportunity to display his great stature in Athens and tout his many contributions to the city. According to the funeral rites, Aegeus was to be buried within three days. The women of Aegeus' household prepared his body by anointing it with oil and wrapping it in fine white cloth from shoulder to toe. He was laid out on a glistening bier at the palace for the family to comfortably accommodate mourners. Aegeus' women sat on couches near the bier and sang songs as the men venerated Aegeus with open palms. A great many people, some traveling long distances, came to pay their respects. Aegeus' household provided for everyone's needs, with food, wine and resting places ample and accessible.

At the time of Theseus' speech, a large crowd had gathered at the palace. All of Aegeus' friends and acquaintances that were present collected near where Theseus stood. The women and children assumed their station dutifully behind. The sun had moved past the midday sky and the shadows from the trees were growing long. Theseus was versed in the traditions of funeral orations and intended not to deviate from the norm.

"My dear friends and colleagues, family members and citizens of Attica, do not expect much of me as I speak," Theseus said. "A man stricken with grief cannot be counted on for lofty words. In that state one cannot think clearly. I am ill equipped to talk of the great Aegeus who we grieve this day. But concede me my shortcomings and I will do my best.

"Here lies a great man, a high-hearted citizen and statesman that earned the respect and admiration of so many. A man such as this comes once over many generations, and we are left with a void we cannot hope to fill. Aegeus had many civic and professional achievements and was recognized for his dedication and commitment to many worthy causes. Aegeus had wisdom we find rare in our times and was known for his stewardship. Despite his great wealth, he remained always a humble man and honored the gods in the appropriate way. If all men with riches acted as Aegeus, what a city we would have.

"Aegeus' sense of honor was something that never failed him, even when challenged. He was a staunch defender of our way of life and fought off those who would undermine our constitution. Aegeus believed in the values of citizenship and civic duty. His leadership was founded on devotion to public service and maintaining the integrity of the *polis*.

"Upon the demise of a great man like Aegeus, the tendency is to think that his life was without strife. Like all mortal men, life brought its share of grief and pain to Aegeus. He lived without an heir. Imagine how this was a weight upon him. An old man without a son is a sad creature. But he faced this trial with resolve. In his final years, Aegeus' goal was finding a successor. Others thought to test his authority, and some devised devious schemes to undermine him. He fought off many unworthy suitors. But his obsession to identify a worthy heir wore on Aegeus. He became despondent and withdrawn. A sense of hopelessness gripped him in his final days until it managed to take his last breath. It is sad to think this was his condition in the closing hours.

"Although despairing of his failure to continue his line, Aegeus can nonetheless be counted among our great men. Happiness, some say, comes to those who have wisdom and honor the gods in all things. If this is the test Aegeus, was a happy man. Creon of Thebes he was not. He never acted rashly or out of ignorance. The good of the state was foremost and required informed leadership. He looked ahead

Theseus

and thought of the consequences of his acts. Aegeus sought out the advice of his counselors and used the assembly to measure the wishes of the people. Oracles were members of his household, and never did Aegeus move on important decisions without seeking direction from the gods. For this we can claim he was happy in his life and a good man.

"As a people, we learn from the lives of our heroes and try to emulate them. We teach our young to edify those who act with virtue. What more worthy hero can there be but one that sets the city above all else? Aegeus put the *polis* first, and for this we praise and honor him most of all. As Hermes now comes to take him across the dark river to where the shades gather, we bid him farewell. We can honor him with a promise to uphold the *polis* he held so close to his heart."

After the eulogy, dirges were sung and many expressed their grief.

The funeral procession began before dawn the next day. Aegeus was to be laid out in a special burial ground outside the walls of the city. Aegeus' bier was placed on a cart adorned with flowers and reeds. The cart was drawn by a magnificent gold chariot which was driven by Theseus himself. Aegeus' colleagues, dressed formally in grays and whites, followed behind the cart. The women and children came after the men. Everyone walked in silence as required by law. Athens had strict rules that a funeral procession be conducted peacefully so as not to disturb the public. Women were expected to contain their woe and avoid any public display of emotion.

When Aegeus was laid in the tomb and the door was sealed, the presiding priest beckoned the gods to take Aegeus to a blissful place in the underworld where he could enjoy peace and tranquility in perpetuity. Prayers were said and sacrifices appropriate for the occasion followed.

The crowd then dispersed to return to their daily routine. The women left first, as was the custom, and the men departed after.

Theseus was downcast and his mood gloomy.

"He was a father to me," Theseus lamented to Pirithous.

"I am responsible for this tragedy."

"This womanly grieving does not become you," Pirithous said to Theseus. "Are you the first man ever to lose his father? Do not be so conceited. Every son must part with his father and throw off the ties of youth. That time has come for you even if sooner than you wish. His death was not of your doing. His own despair brought him to his end. Now stop with the self pity. The city borders on insurrection. Aegeus' death and Tantalus' upcoming trial are causing fissures that threaten the peace. Theseus, you must stand up and take the reins. I don't know of anyone else better fit for the purpose."

Pirithous saw that his words were not registering with Theseus.

"Do not fret over this anymore, Theseus," Pirithous said. "Come to my house later today so I can keep an eye on you. Men in your state shouldn't be left alone."

Theseus met with Pirithous over food and wine that evening. Pirithous invited several young women of uncertain birth, hoping they would lighten the mood and help Theseus relax. The men reclined on couches as the women served them. Pirithous told tales of Theseus' many great deeds and the women giggled and laughed. Theseus was embarrassed by the adulation heaped upon him by Pirithous, but enjoyed the attention nonetheless. Pirithous motioned the women away when it came time for Pirithous and Theseus to talk.

"You are a true friend, Pirithous," Theseus said, "and you have managed to pleasantly distract me with your hospitality and these lovely girls. But now you must help me decide what it is I should do. I am ambivalent and lack resolve."

Though the hour was getting late, Theseus and Pirithous sat and spoke for a long time. There were no noises within the halls of Pirithous' residence save their own voices.

"I have sensed for some time now that changes in our constitution are necessary, perhaps inevitable," Theseus said. "We are living in a time of new ideas and great opportunity. Despite our internal problems, we manage to march ahead. Our citizens are loyal, but they demand equality and respect from our leaders. They are the ones who control our prospects, not the higher class."

Pirithous looked hard at Theseus.

"Theseus, my friend," Pirithous said, "the future of our city and our place in history is at stake. This is your time and you must embrace it. Pittheus would have expected no less of you."

γ

There remained the question of Tantalus. A young man named Sthenelus had submitted a *dike* against Tantalus for theft, and the Areopagus had set a date for the case. Tantalus' story had captured the imagination of the people. To many, he was symbolic of the contemptuous behavior of the rich and prosperous toward the freemen. The aristocracy feared that Tantalus' case was causing unwanted foment among the people. They wanted the matter dispensed with quietly and without fanfare.

Demosthenes assumed the position of lead archon on the council pending the final resolution of Aegeus' succession. It was widely viewed that Demosthenes, counted among the privileged, would cause the Areopagus to levy only the slightest penalty on Tantalus, if any at all, and let him go free.

Lysias approached Theseus to discuss his concerns about the Tantalus case.

"Tell me of this Sthenelus who brings the charge against Tantalus?" Theseus said to Lysias.

"I don't know much about him," Lysias responded. "I understand he had a substantial inheritance and lost it all in Asterion. He's left with a mother and three sisters without the means of support. A tragic circumstance to lose all one's wealth like that. A pitiful situation."

Theseus felt empathy for Sthenelus.

"Has Sthenelus had any instruction in the courts and proper methods of argument?" Theseus asked.

"Not that I know of, Theseus," Lysias said. "From what I hear, he is a young man that only recently attained his citizenship. I am sure he has never appeared before the Areopagus."

"That is unfortunate," Theseus remarked.

Theseus thought back on his training with Antiphon and the learning that was needed to be effective before the lawgivers.

"It is," was Lysias' reply, "especially now that Demosthenes sits at the head of the council. I am not confident Demosthenes can be trusted to administer the case fairly. I think his bias will be in full display."

Lysias paused for a moment ruminating.

"We can't ignore the importance of the case," Lysias told Theseus. "The situation is more unstable than anyone would care to admit, and the case has the potential for causing unwanted turmoil. The economy is not strong. Our farmers' yields are down and trade has declined. Public faith in the governing class is dwindling and frustration mounting. Inflation is eroding the people's wages, working conditions are oppressive and the educational system is closed to their children. There are rampant rumors of corruption and fraud within the law courts, which we know to exist. The ruling class has accumulated great wealth and even greater power, and the people are growing bitter. The Tantalus case may prove a catalyst for abrupt and disruptive upheaval. I am not alone in my views. The outcome of the Tantalus case could be the tipping point if not handled correctly."

"I agree with what you are saying, Lysias," Theseus said. "I have seen the tensions among the classes building. There is no doubt the Tantalus trial has the potential for upsetting the status quo."

"You should give some thought, Theseus," Lysias said, "to taking a public position on the case. Perhaps have a role in it before the council."

"If what you are suggesting is that I stand up for Tantalus," Theseus responded, "that I will not do. The man is abhorrent. Besides, Tantalus must answer the charges himself. That is the way of our law courts."

"You misunderstand me, Theseus," Lysias replied. "I'm not suggesting you appear in defense of Tantalus. Rather just the opposite. You should take up the case against him."

Theseus was intrigued. The idea had not occurred to him.

"The nobility will take solace in the fact that you are handling the case," said Lysias. "Whatever the result, there will be a better chance that both sides will agree that justice will have been done. Think on this."

"I see the merit in your proposal," Theseus said.

"I also believe that if you take part," Lysias said, "it may have a bearing on the outcome of who Aegeus' successor might be."

"You are too old to be called clever, Lysias," Theseus said understanding the point. "Let's call it wisdom in your case, given your age. But I need you first to do two things for me. Bring around this Sthenelus so I can meet him. And on the day the Areopagus gathers, I will need a large crowd of our citizens present, to emphasize the importance of the issue if you will."

"I'll contact Sthenelus myself, and put Alcaeous and Diocles to the other task," Lysias said.

The Areopagus convened for the Tantalus trial at its usual place on the hill of Ares. As planned, a great throng of citizens gathered outside early in the morning. The council members were apprehensive at their presence.

Demosthenes opened the session promptly after Sthenelus and Tantalus took their seats. Tantalus looked haggard and distracted. The restless mood of the citizens was palpable, and Demosthenes wanted to move the matter along.

"We have before the Areopagus today a claim for theft against Tantalus brought by Sthenelus," Demosthenes began. "Before we proceed, there is a request from the hand of Theseus to have the Areopagus hear his preliminary thoughts about the case. Although an unusual request, both Tantalus and Sthenelus have agreed to let Theseus speak before the allegations of Sthenelus are heard by the council. Good Theseus, you have the council's full attention."

Theseus stood to address the members of the Areopagus.

"Esteemed lords," Theseus began, "our fair city, honored by Athena herself, has suffered a heinous wrong. A great fraud has been perpetrated on us. Minos of Crete has stolen from us in a plot both shrewd and despicable. With promises of riches and wealth, he asked our people to support a venture that proved our undoing. This we did, without suspecting foul play. The loss has been great and ours to bear. Minos has fled back to his homeland, beyond the reach of our laws and our courts.

"We now know that we were misled, and it has cost us dearly. The wealth of many of our people has been depleted and lost forever. If the ignoble Minos had acted alone in this, we could perhaps admit that we ourselves are to blame, that we should have been more suspicious and less trusting of a foreigner. But perhaps the greater crime in this affair is that some among us, citizens of our own great city, assisted Minos in planning and carrying out the fraudulent scheme. There is one man among us whose part was greater than all the others. He is here before you, the one named Tantalus.

"Not only did Tantalus aid and abet Minos in the fraud, he profited handsomely from it. He walked away from this debacle a richer man, leaving poverty behind for others. This was his goal and mission from the start. But unrelenting Fate tore the veil that hid this crime from view.

"Tantalus now stands accused of stealing, but he believes himself entitled to his spoils and above reproach. His attitude is the principal reason I am compelled to come before you today."

For the first time, Tantalus appeared to have an interest in the proceeding. He seemed baffled, as if not expecting the gist of Theseus' remarks. He started to shift in his seat as he listened to Theseus' speech. He turned repeatedly to the Areopagus to read the council's reaction.

"The Areopagus has Tantalus' case before it," Theseus said. "The claim brought by Sthenelus is for theft. But it is my contention that this charge should be withdrawn."

A gasp rose from the turnout as Theseus spoke these words. Tantalus looked bewildered. Demosthenes raised the scepter to calm the Areopagus and the surrounding crowd.

"This is most peculiar, Theseus," Demosthenes said sounding confused. "Young Sthenelus, have you been adequately advised in this? Are you aware that dropping your case has serious consequences? Bringing false charges before the Areopagus carries severe penalties."

Sthenelus stood and nodded that he understood.

"Let me finish," Theseus said addressing Demosthenes

and the council. "The penalty for theft is paltry in comparison to the harm done by this man. Sthenelus and I now join to submit a summons for a public claim. We stand ready to levy a new indictment. We do so not for ourselves, not just for those that have lost their fortunes, but for the good of the city and our state."

The council sat puzzled. Tantalus cried out in objection. Demosthenes stood and instructed Theseus to make his intentions clear.

"My lords, let me explain," Theseus continued. "The losses occasioned by Tantalus' acts are not in question. But as I look at the evidence, it is obvious to me that Tantalus did not merely steal or act from ambitious greed to augment his wealth. No, what I find paints a picture of a man whose brazen, shameless conduct is nothing less than an affront to our civil notions of decency and decorum. Sthenelus and I have prepared a *graphe* to charge Tantalus with *hubris*."

The Areopagus sat stunned. A roar rose from the crowd. Tantalus moved to strike Theseus and had to be restrained. Men in the crowd left their seats and rushed both Theseus and Tantalus. Demosthenes tried to restore order but could not be heard over the din. After many minutes, Demosthenes ordered everyone to their seats and Theseus and Tantalus resumed their places. Demosthenes addressed the Areopagus.

"Theseus brings a new but more serious gravamen before us," Demosthenes began. "As I hear it, Theseus now moves to accuse Tantalus with hubris, a rare and grievous charge. Hubris is a crime of outrage against the state and the people, and requires proof of behavior so craven that unchecked it threatens civil society. There is precedent for the indictment, but, to my knowledge, a successful case has never been brought before the lawgivers."

Theseus acknowledged that was indeed his intention. A debate ensued among the members of the Areopagus as to how to proceed. Several elders wanted the matter dropped as improperly brought. Others, especially those who knew Tantalus, considered the charge to have some merit. There were many side conversations, some heated, among the court members. Theseus counted on the Areopagus' fear of open revolt if they were to deny his proposal. The clamor of the citizens before the council could not be ignored. After further argument and debate among the council members, Theseus stood again to address the Areopagus.

"Members of the council," Theseus said firmly, "there is more to what I seek. Because the crime of hubris is a crime against the people, I ask that the matter be heard by the Ecclesia. Let the assembly of the people determine if what this man Tantalus has done is punishable. It is the people who suffer from the likes of him, so let the assembly decide the issue. I also ask the indulgence of the council to allow me to make the case before the Ecclesia."

Near bedlam erupted at Theseus' words. Shouts from the gallery grew louder and more strident as the council looked on with disapprobation. Tantalus sat with a blank face, as if oblivious to the turn of events. A commotion persisted for a time, but Demosthenes finally reclaimed order.

"A novel and unprecedented request is made by our learned Theseus," Demosthenes stated. "Never before has the Ecclesia sat as a court or lawgiver. We can only guess what harm can come of it. Let the question be posed to the council, and it will be decided."

Demosthenes asked for a vote from the council. There were a collection of votes heard in support, and silence followed the call for the dissenters. Demosthenes had no choice but to announce that the Areopagus would refer the case to the Ecclesia.

Anticipation in the city grew to hysteria in the days preceding the hearing before the Ecclesia. Tantalus became nothing less than a public enemy in the mind of the people. Theseus knew that the upper class viewed the developments with anxiety, but with the business now set in motion, there was little that could be done to change direction.

The Ecclesia gathered to hear the case against Tantalus on the day prescribed by Demosthenes. The Ecclesia that assembled numbered five hundred strong. The arguments began early in the morning to ensure that the case could be heard and decided by sunset. Theseus thought the atmosphere was remarkably calm. The Ecclesia took their seats slowly under the murmur of hushed exchanges. Observers sensed that the Ecclesia was keenly aware of the magnitude of the proceeding and its implications. The congregation grew respectfully silent as Demosthenes started the hearing with a statement of the case. Theseus was then directed to begin his argument.

Theseus stood upright and paced the center stage with dramatic effect.

"Great citizens," Theseus began, "you all are aware of the original charges read against Tantalus. Perhaps some of you share in the loss of your savings because of this man. You know that in our system of laws, the complainant must convince the lawgiver of the charges he brings. He must prevail in his argument. So I have not undertaken my task lightly. But what I know of the crime and of Tantalus has convinced me that Tantalus must be held to account.

"The wicked Minos and Tantalus conspired to perpetuate a fraud against us. With Tantalus' help and knowledge, an elaborate scheme was invented to fool us and to loosen our hold on our precious savings. Minos acquired ventures that would prove to be failures but told us of the riches that would be ours if we turned our money over to him. Tantalus himself had arranged for some of that money to be hidden. It was never used, never intended to be used, for a legitimate purpose. Only Minos and Tantalus knew where the money would settle, and conspired to divvy it up among themselves and their co-conspirators. A great harm was to befall our city.

"Throughout the course of these catastrophic events, Tantalus acted with characteristic contempt for notions of decency and fair play. Tantalus laughed at the number of freemen who gave up to Minos their hard earned obols. Steadfast, he evaded those officials who were on to him. Feeling above reproach because of his birth and position in society, he now flaunts his ruinous scheme.

"We all have accounts of Tantalus' reputation and some of you may know the man himself. He was born into a family of means and given the customary education reserved for the rich. Tantalus had the benefit of the best instruction in the arts and sciences and provided gymnastic exercise to develop his strength and agility. He was taught about the immortal gods. If only each of us had these advantages! How easy it would be to step into society with such patronage. But what did Tantalus do with these gifts of rank? He grew selfish and conceited. He embraced entitlement. Tantalus learned to take whatever he wanted and from whom he pleased without regard to ownership or character. Tantalus freely abandoned respect for the gods. He came to disdain slaves and lower classes alike as weak and pathetic. He embraced wine and women as his idolatry. He rejected social conventions and standards of morality. Unchecked, Tantalus grew increasingly reckless in his behavior and began to act with impunity toward others in his affairs. Tantalus' nihilism has culminated in great damage to our people and our city.

"Tantalus leveraged his upbringing to secure a prominent position in the law class in our city. How did he acquit himself in this role? He ingratiated himself with rich people and did the bidding of those who could make him money. Tantalus is known for his resourceful ways to avoid paying dues for religious festivals and military campaigns, and he shared his tactics with the highest bidders. He found ways to hide assets and make investments that could not be understood or deciphered. This is not what we would declare a career of distinction.

"Let us also weigh Tantalus' treatment of our young, perhaps his most insidious attribute. He delighted in abusing the young people who worked for him, and had them engage in licentious and deplorable behavior. He handled the young people within his sphere with contempt and scorn. They were nothing but tools in his schemes. Tantalus toyed with their innocence and bought their loyalty with his street women and wine. He led his charges into veniality and disgrace. He ignored his duty to set examples of proper behavior. Are not the elite responsible for teaching our young men conduct worthy of good citizens and setting the standards of moral virtue? I tell you that the man that preys upon the young for his own gratification is godless and the lowest form of humankind. A civil society cannot tolerate this sort of depravity.

"Virtue and honor have eluded this man. Tantalus not only committed the acts necessary to carry out his theft, but he did so in such an openly outrageous and deplorable fashion that he mocks our standards of moral decency. Tantalus stole from us, yes, yet laughed in our faces as he did so. Why? His motive could not have been to attain money, which he already possessed in adequate supply, or to gain fame and influence. No, good citizens, this arrogant man acts with total disregard for anyone or the state. He is narcissistic and contemptuous of everyone. His extreme preoccupation with his own self left him no room for boundaries, and caused the losses we have suffered.

"You may be thinking to yourself, excessive pride is a state of being difficult to prove, so why not be satisfied with a verdict for theft and let the matter be? Do not be too easily swayed in this manner of reasoning. We have abundant witnesses to prove the outrage that afflicts us all. Look upon the front seats to see the lineup of witnesses assembled. Pirithous and Lysias are prepared by oath to attest to Tantalus' sins. Hippias is here to testify, as is Stichius. Diocles and Timais were victims. Eleon and Herodian have seen the rude behavior. Their presence and good reputation are enough to condemn Tantalus.

"You may say that hubris is a crime against man properly left to Zeus himself for punishment, and not something to be decided by mere mortals. We have abundant examples of prideful men being brought low by thunderous Zeus. But are we to wait and wonder when and how this will come to pass? We are only men, and cannot fathom the minds of the gods. Would it not be better that we dispense justice ourselves, when it is clear that the gods would support us?

"Our laws teach that wounding, destruction of property, slander and loutish behavior are grounds for redress under the proper circumstance. Any one of us can be held accountable for these acts if directed at others. But what if the harm caused is not limited to one individual but undermines the whole? Do we not recognize the *polis* as worthy of protection in her own right? Is she not more central to our well being and safety? Why should our city suffer from the likes of Tantalus? We need not concern ourselves with decadence in one's own private surroundings. What harm is there to others in this? In the public sphere it is another matter. It is dangerous for a man to engage in imperious behavior that brings harm and dishonor to the *polis*. This is particularly true if the perpetrator has a position of power and authority. Outrage is detrimental to the public and threatens the peace and stability of our city and challenges our standards of decorum and civility. Would the grey-eyed Athena look favorably on us if we did not safeguard the *polis*? Do not think that our patroness would condone it. I implore you not to tempt the goddess' wrath.

"You may say to this, why should we condemn a man who has the benefit of a noble upbringing and education? Let him be required to associate with good men, and his nefarious behavior will pass. Why does he need to be destroyed?' I say to this, good citizens, that his rearing is the very reason that he should suffer the utmost consequence. Consider similar acts of outrageous behavior from a metic or a slave, those who have not benefited from the right instruction or example. These men we can safely say have hope for rehabilitation. They can be taught what is good and right, not having learned it before. But to think that is true for an aristocrat is sheer folly. Have they not already been taught of virtue and good citizenship? What more is there for them to learn? They know what is right and good, and choose to ignore it. Neither the gods nor their fellow citizens are enough to dissuade them. No, I say, the aristocrat that ignores and turns his back on his noble education is not one for reform. He is a menace to our state and way of life."

Theseus stopped to check the level of the water clock and saw it dropping.

"So I finally come to the conclusion of my argument," Theseus said in closing. "You have clear indications of Tantalus' outrageous behavior that cannot be corrected. So I ask you now, are we ready to seek redress for his excessive pride and shameful acts against us? That, my friends, is the decision before us. Are we to allow ourselves to be subject to the arrogance of the wealthy? For if we let this monster Tantalus go unpunished, we are assuredly agreeing that the duplicitous gentry can act free of repercussions, that they have the right to cause us harm with impunity. We discarded the government of oppression long ago. Let us not revisit that sorry history and succumb to the impulses of the rich and powerful. Do not doubt that they will act the way Tantalus has acted if undeterred. If we allow this course, we will be deserving of the lasting pain and oppression we will suffer.

"Tantalus is but one man, albeit a wrongdoer that has left a trail of destruction. But let him be an example to persons of his persuasion. Will we allow Tantalus and his kind to make a mockery of our laws, our government and the rights of all freemen whether poor or rich? Are we to live and toil under their loathsome stare, and cower under their scorn and contempt? Tantalus, like other men of his breed, is consumed by his own insufferable pride and self indulgence. We will be stricken by our own insanity if we let him go free."

Theseus took his seat.

The Ecclesia rose up with a loud, unbroken cry. The citizens at once shouted support for Theseus and condemnation of Tantalus. Demosthenes raised the aegis to silence the crowd and maintain the order. After a while passed, the assembly settled down.

"We have yet to hear from Tantalus," Demosthenes rebuked the crowd. "Lest we judge too soon, we are compelled to hear him out. Our system of laws requires that both parties are given their due. So take your seats and withhold your reprisals for a few moments more."

Theseus

Tantalus sat with his head in his hands and no one could see his face. All eyes were fixed intently on him. When he raised his head, he let out a grating laugh and glared at the elders before panning the assembly. He had the look of delirium about him.

"What a speech we have heard today!" Tantalus bellowed sardonically. "My adversary should be awarded a prize! Best drama it should be! His theatrics are worthy of our applause. Amazing! Let us render the verdict while his oration still rings in our ears! Away with Tantalus!

"Is this the way it is to be? Unassuming and so sincere, this man Theseus attempts to persuade you of some great societal mischief. Something that threatens the very foundations of our city! Words of doom spoken so eloquently and with such force from such a man! What a rarity for us to have someone unaccustomed to bird watching give us his predictions. Perhaps we have discovered a new oracle who can glimpse our future. I say this man should be elevated to the heights of Delphi if he is so proficient a fortune teller.

"But what do we know of this soothsayer, this Theseus? A man with a talent for speeches! From all appearances, he himself is a man of money, which he condemns me for. He is not one of the commoners he now cajoles.

"I can tell you he loiters about the law courts. And what has he learned from it? A command of our laws? Perhaps an inclination for sophistry and clever argument? Perhaps something more sinister?

"Our good Theseus is on the attack now, that is clear, but did you know he used to be my friend? It is true. I entertained him at my house and he drank my wine. We traveled together. We worked in concert, he and I, on many things. I told him of my ambitions and confided in him. I thought he supported me in my endeavors. How wrong I was! Now I stand tricked by him. Imagine how you would feel if your best friend betrayed you for his own advantage. What worse crime could there be? I think you would agree with me that any man who turns on his friends should not be trusted.

"Theseus maintains I was at fault for my part in Asterion. You should be aware that he had his own role to play. He advised Minos and guided Asterion throughout the whole affair. He was paid handsomely for it. He now blames me for all the trouble, acting as though his hands were clean. We should question him on how it is that he was blind to what transpired and what he could have done to prevent this misfortune."

Tantalus walked over toward where Theseus was sitting, and then continued with his rant.

"My brothers, are you aware of the reward for the volunteer who prosecutes a public case? This man Theseus will be given a third of the penalty levied for the pleasure of bringing the dispute before you! A third I tell you! A handsome sum. High speech and soaring discourse cannot hide the true motives of this man. Consider the irony! Theseus claims to seek recovery for the financial losses of our citizens, yet he stands to earn a fair amount himself. What kind of trust do we place in the words of such a man? How can we believe what he says? Will you let him incite and sway you for his own profit? Will you be played the fool?"

Tantalus paced frantically back and forth across the floor of the arena. He stroked his hair as he gazed skyward.

"Now let us view this calumny brought against me in its true light," Tantalus beckoned to the Ecclesia. "I stand accused of manufacturing some plot to take your money from you like a robber under cover of darkness. My accuser says I duped many innocent people. But let the gods be my witness. I tell you first that this regrettable mess was not of my doing. Not at all! The cad Minos is truly to blame for this debacle. Minos devised the plan and orchestrated the fraud. He is the one that fled with your money and laughs at you from afar! If you want redress, I say raise an army and march on Crete to reclaim what he stole. Take his possessions, scorch his land. Teach him that men of his character are not welcome in this city. Minos is your culprit.

"I was but an ignorant instrument to his devious designs.

No, you say? Theseus claims my greed put me in the middle of this catastrophe. Ha! Whose greed did he say? I say it is your own! Minos promised you wealth and benefits in exchange for your support of his doomed venture. You raced to give him your money. You threw it at him. 'Take it, please!' you pleaded. You fantasized about having returned to you three or four times what you gave him. You took Minos at face value without difficulty and without question. Now with the money gone, you complain of your losses and want someone to pay for your own shortsightedness and greed. But don't lay these concerns at my feet! Don't come now and look to Tantalus for reimbursement. I tell you there is no merit or virtue in it.

"On top of this, I am being condemned for my personal habits. Tell me when this has ever occurred in our history, that a man was convicted of eating too much good food, speaking too loudly or enjoying too often the company of women? Ridiculous, I say.

"And of corrupting our youth? Enlighten me as to what duty I have to the young people who chose to work for me. Let them pursue other interests if they care to. What is it to me? I am not responsible for them or their choices.

"Listen further to what I have to say. In our great city, we have laws that condemn killing and homicide. What does that have to do with us? I tell you that you are in danger of committing genocide! If you find against me this day, you all might as well take to the streets and slaughter all men of rank. Insane, you say? No, I tell you. Our city was built on the shoulders of great men, heroes who protected our inhabitants and bestowed countless benefits on them. They were our leaders, and we loved and respected them. These were men of high means, mind you, people of distinction, of the upper class. How could it be otherwise? They had the resources and wisdom needed to govern. The lower classes certainly did not. Picture ordinary citizens leading our state! Impossible! Only those from noble families and of the highest social order have such capacity. Without our aristocracy our city would be hopeless. Your attack on me is an attack on nobility. Do not be mistaken or tricked into thinking some other way. Persist in this course and tempt rebellion, chaos and bloodshed for our great city. The gods themselves have ordained this. Do not doubt my words. A verdict against me would be blasphemous and an affront to the social order. What madness that would be!

"What profit is there in having the great men of our city scorned and brought low? Yes, count me among the great men we cannot live without! Don't laugh. Tell me the merit of punishing the privileged for triviality. Do you wish men like me to withdraw to our homes and retreat from all commercial and social association? Who would pay for our army, equip our ships for trade and provide our public feasts? What a city we would have then! Imagine no one with a proper upbringing and instruction attending to the affairs of our state, our commerce and our sacred rituals. A sorry state we would have indeed. Men like me create prosperity and opportunity. We use our wealth and knowledge to advance the interests of our city. We increase industry and give workers labor to perform. We captain our triremes. We build our temples and public places. We commission the arts. Don't question our motives. You have no right. We are entitled to act in our own manner. We bring honor and fame to Attica!

"I am tired of this charade. You have no business judging me. Do not tempt Fate with what you decide here today! You will bring nothing but shame upon yourselves. The gods will curse you, I tell you! Our city will pay the price. Condemn me and you condemn everything proper and true! Walk away from this mishap before it is too late. I will forget this whole affair, as you will. Otherwise be prepared for what comes! I dare you to denounce me before the gods! Bring on your own demise, what do I care! You people are pathetic I tell you! You will look back on this day and see the beginnings of Attica's great decline!"

Tantalus finished.

The assembly erupted. Freemen hurried to attack Tantalus and had to be restrained. There was wild thrashing about and scuffles ensued. Tantalus looked demented and menacing. He stood and shouted profanities at Theseus and made obscene gestures at him. Tantalus succeeded in inciting the assembly all the more and the scene bordered on open riot.

Demosthenes once again stood to reclaim order. When calm had been restored, Demosthenes directed the assembly to render its judgment. When the vote was called, the Ecclesia vociferously returned a verdict against Tantalus. Tantalus was staggered.

With the verdict given, all that remained was the sentence. Demosthenes rose to address the Ecclesia.

"Let the punishment be as the law requires," Demosthenes stated. "No one but Sthenelus has claimed damages, so let Tantalus pay for the loss of Sthenelus' inheritance. We can all agree that justice will be done if we require this of Tantalus."

A crescendo of disapproval came from the assembly. Demosthenes was alarmed by the reaction.

Theseus rose once more.

"Good archon," Theseus' voice resonated above the clatter. "May I once again address the assembly?"

The assembly shouted its support of Theseus.

"If you must," Demosthenes said nervous and frustrated.

"Tantalus is found to have committed outrageous and wanton acts against the people of Athens," Theseus contended. "In retribution, I say the man should be punished as follows. First, let Tantalus' possessions be confiscated by the state and given to all those who can establish their losses. For my part, I will waive any claim I have to compensation. Whatever largess remains is to be turned over to the city treasury. Second, Tantalus should be stripped of his citizenship and banished from ever appearing within our city's walls. Let him wander the countryside like a beggar and be compelled to live off the goodwill and charity of those that pity him, if there be any. And if it is found that he be buried here, let his bones be dug up and tossed far beyond our boundaries."

The assembly enthusiastically voiced their endorsement of the proposed punishment. Tantalus cried aloud cursing the cruelty of the sentence.

Demosthenes was frozen. The crowd noise was growing louder and more raucous.

"There is no precedent for what Theseus' proposes," Demosthenes finally said.

A chorus of boos rained on Demosthenes' statement.

"Yet, the crime of hubris, having been committed, perhaps demands a more onerous punishment," Demosthenes said.

Cries of approval came from the crowd.

"So be it," Demosthenes said relenting. "Let the assembly have its vote. Those who favor the punishment proposed by Theseus stand and give us your voice."

The crowd stood and the resounding "aye" was to be heard miles away.

"Those against, speak now," Demosthenes followed.

An eerie stillness followed.

"The assembly has voted," Demosthenes announced. "Tantalus must give up all that he owns. Those who can establish their losses will be paid. Anything remaining is claimed by the state. Forthwith, Tantalus is banished from the city, and if it is found that he is buried here, let his remains be dug up and tossed out of our land."

Demosthenes ordered that Tantalus be taken from the assembly and led to the outskirts of the city.

δ

"The king is dead," Theseus declared to Lysias and Pirithous. "Gone and never to return."

"A strange thing to say, Theseus," Pirithous responded. "You are king now, the heir to Aegeus. You stand as archon of the Areopagus."

Theseus, Lysias and Pirithous were on their way to the Ares and a meeting with the council. This was the first gathering of the Areopagus since Theseus became head of the council.

"Theseus is speaking rhetorically, I think, good Pirithous," Lysias said. "Demosthenes and his supporters are panicked over the Tantalus trial and fearful of its aftermath. They intend to consolidate the power of the aristocracy in the Areopagus and arrest any further aggrandizement by the Ecclesia. The king on his own is helpless to stop Demosthenes and his sympathizers, I'm afraid."

"A turn of events unlikely to be reversed," Theseus concurred.

"But as archon, you still have the greatest influence, Theseus," Pirithous argued. "The other members of the council will follow your lead if you are of a mind to deter Demosthenes."

"They might for a time," said Theseus. "But eventually they will move even against me. That is the way with men. They ultimately will act in their own interest."

"Well, why trouble yourself with it?" Pirithous queried. "Why not let the Areopagus be the sovereign?"

"Because I fear the ultimate resolution, Pirithous," Theseus countered. "How this will play out is of concern to me. The Areopagus is in the exclusive grip of the upper class. There will be inevitable conflict with the people."

"I think I see what you are saying," replied Pirithous. "It would be as if the likes of Tantalus held free reign."

"Tantalus is suggestive of an aristocracy that acts without self restraint," Theseus said. "The people are fully aware of it."

"Which is why you brought the Tantalus case before the Ecclesia," Lysias followed. "It was a dramatic way to illustrate the danger."

"What are we then to do?" Pirithous asked. "Who is to rule? Who will administer justice?"

"Excellent questions, Pirithous," Theseus said. "Let us ponder what I think you are really asking. What makes a system just? Shall we start there?"

"A reasonable suggestion," Pirithous said. "Let me be so bold to say that a just system is one that recognizes first the laws of the gods, and then the authority of the ruler."

"You are truly a traditionalist, Pirithous," Theseus smiled, "and may the gods keep you for that."

"The ways of the immortals are not always clear and sometimes contradictory," Lysias responded, "so I don't know if their law is the starting point. Don't take what I say as blasphemous, but men themselves must agree on what laws should govern our secular affairs."

"Do you concur, Pirithous?" Theseus asked.

"Yes, it sounds reasonable, even though our temple priests might take offense," responded Pirithous.

"Even if we agree on manmade law," Lysias added, "I dare say a just system must yet be fair so that everyone is inclined to abide by the same rules. Otherwise, people won't go along."

"Please, Lysias," Theseus directed. "Make clearer what you mean."

"The system must not appear to be arbitrary or favoring one kind of person or group in particular," Lysias said. "There must be equal treatment and evenhandedness."

"Aptly put," Theseus replied. "But who should we have in control of this system?"

"Since the king is gone, as you say," Pirithous said, "control will be in the hands of noblemen."

"Our current predicament," added Lysias.

"Are the wealthy naturally inclined to a just system?" Theseus asked.

"They are the best educated and contribute most to

society, do they not?" Pirithous quipped. "Tantalus made that argument, and there is more than an element of truth in it."

"Let us think on that for a moment," Theseus reflected. "Do you know the story of Capaneus? He was one of the Argive generals when Argos attacked the seven gates of Thebes in support of Polynices."

"Capaneus was killed in the battle," Lysias stated. "He was struck by a lightning bolt while on a ladder attempting to scale the Theban walls. Witnesses say it was Zeus himself that brought him down. He was given the highest burial honors among those killed the day of the fighting."

"Do you know why Capaneus was given this high honor?" Theseus pressed.

"Capaneus was a very prosperous man," Lysias said, "yet his riches did not make him vainglorious. He placed duty above his wealth. A rarity many would say. Men of means don't often hold the common good above their possessions or their very lives."

"If loyalty to the state is uncharacteristic of the wealthy," said Pirithous, "we can't leave the laws to them alone."

"Why is it that wealth can be the enemy of justice?" Theseus asked. "Do either of you have an opinion?"

Neither Lysias nor Pirithous had a view.

"The wealthiest among us live with fear and greed," Theseus surmised. "They fear losing their property and are forever wishing more. The rich are motivated mostly along these lines."

"Are you suggesting that those that are poor are more inclined to justice?" Pirithous asked. "That doesn't seem to follow, certainly."

"I agree with Pirithous," Lysias said. "That way of thinking isn't intuitive."

"Destitute men are equally unsuited for the task," said Theseus. "They are driven by want and the necessities of their own poverty. And they envy the rich. Not what we would call stellar traits for a lawgiver."

"If we are to discount the roles of rich and poor," Lysias

said, "we are left with those in the middle, the freemen."

"That is how I see it, Lysias," Theseus said. "Our common citizens must have an important role to play in the justice system."

"Am I hearing that the commoners are to be given the authority over justice?" Pirithous interjected. "I see obstacles there."

"Go on, please," Theseus said.

"The upper class won't allow that," Pirithous explained. "They have too much at stake."

"Your point is well taken, Pirithous," said Theseus. "Perhaps justice requires some measure of equal sharing among the classes. That may be our way clear."

"What do you mean by equal sharing, Theseus?" Pirithous asked. "We already said that the rich are motivated mostly to protect and increase their wealth. You can't be suggesting the ordinary people must be given a share of the rich man's property. That would result in armed conflict."

"I hope that is not the direction you are taking us, Theseus," Lysias followed. "We are not Sparta. The wealthy in our city would not follow a system that takes their property from them. They would view that as *unjust*."

"I cannot argue your point," said Theseus. "And do not think that is what I advocate. But hear me out. The equality I speak of is not tied to wealth."

"That is good to hear," Pirithous said. "But what then can all the people have together?"

"They will share power," Theseus said, "over the laws and the courts."

"Sounds simple enough," remarked Lysias. "How is this power to be divided, exactly?"

"The aristocracy is now in control of the Areopagus," Theseus said, "so let us start there."

"Perhaps we should admit burghers to the council," Lysias stated. "That would be novel. But a way to ensure the voice of the people is heard."

"How would these men be chosen for the Areopagus?" Pirithous asked. "There could be unwanted competition for

Theseus

the seats."

"Let them be selected by lot," Theseus said.

"I see problems with that," countered Pirithous.

"How so?" Theseus asked.

"Some may be picked who are not qualified to serve," Pirithous said. "Governing is a serious affair."

"Well stated," Theseus responded. "How can we overcome Pirithous' objection?"

"Educate all those who wish to sit on the council," Lysias recommended. "Have them take an examination of the law and the courts. Throw in a study of ethics so all are knowledgeable as to how to behave. Those who pass the test can be included in the lottery."

"Excellent suggestion, Lysias," Theseus said.

"Add to the list of subjects the major issues of the day," Lysias urged. "Economics, war, trade and whatever else is of pressing importance to the state."

"An interesting idea," Theseus said. "And why not require the test be imposed on all members of the Areopagus, the noblemen included."

"That would result in qualified candidates," Lysias said.

"But I still see problems," Pirithous persisted.

"Let us hear them," Theseus followed.

"Well, many freemen may not have the means to serve on the council," Pirithous said. "The role would be demanding of one's time. We wouldn't want those serving forced to make money by taking bribes or selling their votes. And then there is the potential for the rise of a political class, those who wish to make their seats on the Areopagus permanent."

"Why don't we propose a stipend for those who serve, according to need of course," Theseus said. "And we will impose limits on how long anyone can sit on the council."

"That should satisfy your concerns, Pirithous," noted Lysias.

"Forgive me," Pirithous said, "but I am still bothered by these proposals, Theseus. Why should our aristocrats agree?"

"Because it will be shown to be in their best interest," Theseus explained.

"How so?" Pirithous asked.

"I envision great things for our city," Theseus stated. "We have the potential to be unique in all of Greece in war, trade and culture."

"Have you a prophesy from Apollo about our future?" Pirithous wondered. "If so, tell us what the god has ordained."

"Apollo has not given me such insight," Theseus said. "But you make a valid point, Pirithous. Perhaps we should send a delegation to Delphi to ask about our plan when it is time."

"A favorable reply from the Pythian oracle would certainly encourage support from all corners," said Lysias. "We should be careful how we pose the question to be asked."

"Yes, of course," Theseus replied. "How the question is framed can determine the answer we receive."

"I am not in favor of trying to trick the gods," Pirithous objected. "Let's stop that line of discussion. But tell us why our city is great."

"The answer lies with the fabric of our people," Theseus posited. "We have a unique mix of Ionian individualism and Dorian nationalism. We value our freedom but recognize the importance of the state. No place else in the Hellenic world can boast of these qualities."

"You are reminding me of something, Theseus," Lysias interrupted. "Do you recall the battle between Poseidon and Athena for sponsorship of our city?"

"I do indeed," Theseus said.

"We know that there was a mighty row between the gods to secure that patronage," Lysias stated. "Athena won out."

"Yes, that is right," Theseus responded. "Why would she battle Poseidon if she didn't recognize the glory we would achieve?"

"Exactly so," Lysias added.

"Now, as I see it," Theseus continued, "the city has a whole must change. Our population is growing, and Demeter has not blessed Attica with the farmland to support our increasing numbers. For us to prosper, the city must look to mercantile trade as the primary source of our strength and power. This means shifting the economy of the city to artisanship and seafaring ventures."

"Those things would certainly add to our prestige if that were successful," Lysias confirmed.

"For us to achieve this, it will require the refocus of all of our people, nobles and freemen alike," Theseus said. "We must encourage our citizens to leave the countryside and take up work in the city and at sea. We must ask the rich to fund artisans and a first rate mercantile fleet. And a navy to protect our expanding interests abroad."

"Why would anyone agree to this, Theseus?" Pirithous queried. "People may want to live as they do now."

"The rich will be enticed by ever greater profits and more wealth from an expanding economy," Theseus said. "They will see the opportunity in it."

"And the commoners?" Pirithous asked.

"They will need to be shown the potential benefits to them and their families," said Theseus. "They will have a greater part to play in governing the city. They will find in it the means for their own security and protection."

"I think you will have difficulty getting people to leave their agrarian ways and pack up to live in the city," Pirithous came back.

"We will encourage the transition," Theseus said. "Let the city award citizens who agree to this with five hundred drachmas and those that teach their children a trade another two hundred."

"That may work," Pirithous stated, "but will it be enough?"

"We will expand the law courts and all freemen will be allowed to serve as magistrates and judges," said Theseus. "We will provide a wage for service to make the positions available to those who could not otherwise afford to take up the role. The Ecclesia will also be given more authority to voice the will of the people, and veto laws decided by the Areopagus. The people, I believe, will see this as a just system."

"When true justice is done," Lysias said, "one is said to give *dyke* and the other to receive it. At its base, fair and equal justice is an exchange. Your proposals, Theseus, are embedded with this notion of *dyke*, only applied more broadly to our constitution."

"Well said, Lysias," Theseus said. "An apt analogy it will serve us well to remember."

"There is one last reservation that I have," Pirithous said. "I fear the danger from the more politically inclined members of our new system. Those among the aristocracy may resist the will of the people. What if they stay recalcitrant in the face of popular opinion? What safeguard will we have to protect against the rich that don't have the best interests of the city at heart?"

"The same could be said of citizens who are swayed by demagogues," said Lysias. "Glib orators can have a deleterious effect on the people. The prevalence of these types could prove an intractable obstacle to the ultimate success of our plans. We could see renewed strife among the classes."

"You both raise legitimate issues," Theseus agreed, "ones we haven't yet addressed. Let us propose that every third year both the common people and the rich can ban one person from serving or appearing before the council or the assembly or taking an appointment as a magistrate."

"Are you suggesting that our leaders can be ostracized?" Pirithous said with some surprise.

"Precisely so," Theseus responded. "In fact, let those who are ostracized live outside the city for ten years. They will remain citizens and keep their property, but they cannot appear within our walls unless recalled."

"An onerous remedy, Theseus," Lysias commented.

"But an effective one, surely," Theseus replied.

"But won't it discourage even well intending people from participating in public life?" Pirithous asked.

"The lure of having a role in the framing of our laws and administering justice is a strong one," Theseus said. "And

Theseus

few would ever admit that such a fate could befall them. That is not the way with men. I doubt it would be a serious deterrent."

"That would most certainly serve as an effective check on our public officials," Lysias stated. "A very intriguing proposal if I do say. From the sound of it, Theseus, there will be much to present to the council today."

"There is one other matter that we must discuss before we plot this new course," Theseus said.

"Tell us," pressed Pirithous, "we are almost upon the Ares."

"Let us slow our pace, then," Theseus said. "This last subject may be the most critical of all."

"You have my attention, Theseus," Lysias said.

"Mine as well," Pirithous added.

"Thank you, gentlemen," Theseus replied. "Our reforms must in the end create a stronger, more unified city. One that endures and flourishes. For this, all citizens must be willing to declare an oath to our city and undertake a commitment to civic life. Our people must come to her defense in war and remain loyal in times of internal strife. This will be expected from all citizens."

"I agree that this must underlie all that you propose," said Lysias. "Yet this may be the most difficult to achieve. How are we to do this?"

"We must educate our citizens in civic virtue," Theseus responded. "We will require that all of our people learn the responsibilities of citizenship. Children from the youngest age will be given civic instruction and taught citizenship and how to participate in the affairs of the state. The city itself will provide the means for anyone unable to do this for their children. Unless the young are educated properly, I fear our reforms would not have longevity."

"Right minded citizens will certainly help to sustain our new commonwealth," Pirithous said. "But how will lectures on civic virtue alone teach our people? Not everyone likes sitting in the classroom. Perhaps there are other things we can do also."

"Do you have thoughts on this, Pirithous?" Theseus asked.

"Let us declare citywide games to celebrate the young men who complete their education and are added to the voting registries," Pirithous said with some excitement. "This will create pride among our citizens. And let us hold these games annually in honor of Athena, our city's patroness."

"Excellent," replied Theseus. "But let us not stop there. Let us also look to the arts and stage performances to help teach our people the value to us all of our joint duties to the state."

"Athena herself will be pleased with this plan," Lysias said. "The grey-eyed goddess will approve of a system that is based on well reasoned principles. Let us ask for her guidance and protection in this."

"We have arrived at our destination, gentlemen," Theseus announced. "Today we will propose the foundations for a new constitution."

"One last thing, Theseus," Pirithous added.

"Yes, Pirithous," Theseus said. "Be quick with it. We are being called before the council."

"What would Heracles think of these proposals?" asked Pirithous.

"A most excellent supposition!" Theseus laughed. "Let me follow that with another. If our great Heracles had time to save only one man from the chains of Hades, and he had the choice between a man who possessed *areté* and one that held *dyke* dear, who would he select?"

"May Zeus have pity on us if it were between the two of you that Heracles had to choose," said Lysias smiling. "Let's leave that debate for another day. Come, the council waits."

GREECE

Illyria

Macedonia

THAOS

Chaonia

+ Mount Olympus

THESSALY

CORCYRA

MAGNESIA

EUBOEA

IONIAN SEA

ARCANANIA
AETOLIA
Stratus*
Delphi* Leuctra* Thebes
LOCRIS Thespia* Plataea
Mt. Cithaeron

BOEOTIA
+Mt. Parnassus *Chalcis
Eretria

ATTICA
Eleusis *Athens
Megara *Marathon

CEPHALLENIA

Corinth*
Elis Mycenae *Argos SALAMIS
Mantinea* ARGOLIS Epidaurus
Peloponnese *Troezen
*Tegea
Messene*
MESSENIA *Sparta
Pylos* LACONIA

CYTHERA

MEDITERRANEAN SEA

CRETE

Theseus

BLACK SEA
*Colchis
*Bzantium

*Troy

Lydia
AEOLIS
ANATOLIA

AGEAN
SEA
*Sipylus
*Smyrna
+Mount Tmolus
*Sardis

IONIA
SAMOS
*Miletus

DELOS
NAXOS

Phaselis*

RHODES

DIA
*Iraklion Agios
*Cnossos

GLOSSARY

Acantha, securities commission attorney.
Achilles, Greek hero.
Adrasteia, law student and summer associate.
Aegeon, young litigation partner.
Aegeus, king of Athens and firm chairman.
Aella, legal assistant representing Nemean.
Aeolis, northwest coastal region of Anatolia.
Aethra, mother of Theseus.
Aetolia, mountainous central region of Greece.
Agamemnon, leader of the Greeks during the Trojan War.
Agios, coastal town in Crete.
Agora, central marketplace in Athens.
Aiaia, island home of Circe.
Aiantes, Greek warrior in the Trojan War.
Aias, Greek warrior in the Trojan War.
Aietes, government lawyer and lobbist.
Aigaion Corporation, telecommunications company named for the creature that battled the Titans.
Aigithos, plotted the murder of Agamemnon and took his wife Clythemnestra.
Alcaeus, senior corporate associate.
Alcetis, devoted wife of Admetus who offered herself to death to prolong his life.
Alcibiades, Athenian general and statesman during the Peloponnesian War.
Alcinous, ruler of the Phaeacians and father of Nausicaa.
Aloadae, boarding school named for the great giants that stormed Mount Olympus.
Amazons, female warrior tribe that lived without men.
Anatolia, otherwise known as Asia Minor.
Anaxis, chairman of Aigaion Corporation.
Androgeos, Minos's son.
Antigone, daughter of Oedipus.
Antilochos, young Greek warrior in the Trojan War.
Antiphon, Theseus' law teacher.
Aphrodite, goddess of love and beauty.
Apollo, god of the sun, reason and prophecy.

Appolomedes, Athenian citizen.
Arcanania, region in west Greece.
Archelaos, a king of Smyrna in Aeolis.
Archias, mutual fund laywer.
Areopagus, Athenian council of elders.
Ares, god of war.
Arete, wife of Alcinous and gracious host to Odysseus.
Argeius, intellectual property lawyer.
Argolis, region of east Peloponnese.
Argonauts, Greek heroes led by Jason to find the Golden Fleece.
Argos, city in Argolis.
Argus Consulting Group LLC, health care company named for the hundred eyed monster that could close only one eye at at time.
Ariadne, Cretan princess and Mino's attorney.
Artemis, god of hunting, wild animals, birth and virginity.
Aspasia, Pericles' companion and courtesan.
Asterion, Inc., Mino's software company.
Ates, junior associate attorney.
Athena, goddess of war and justice.
Athens, major city in Attica.
Attica, region of east Greece.
Axylus, Typhon investment banker.
Bacenor, director of Asterion.
Bacis, regulatory partner and lobbyist.
Baricos Co., software company named for a manticore.
Boeotia, region of east central Greece.
Boethus, young litigation partner.
Borus, office server.
Brontes, Ltd., company owned by Minos named for a cyclops.
Byzantium, city on the Bosporus in northwest Anatolia.
Cabrius, head of enforcement at the securities commission.
Cadmos, financial analyst with Typhon.
Cadmus, founder of Thebes.
Callias, Megaran ambassador to Athens.
Callicles, first year associate.
Calliope, junior associate.
Calliphon, son of Polymedes.

Calonice, wife of Melesius.
Camirus, luxury club in Rhodes.
Capaneus, Argive general in the battle against Thebes.
Caras, environmental lawyer.
Cassiopeia, municipal bond partner.
Castor, corporate partner.
Catalus, pro bono partner.
Cecrops, first king of Athens.
Cephallenia, large island in west Greece.
Cetus Containers, Inc., packaging company named for the sea monster slain by Perseus.
Chabrias, locker room attendant.
Chalcis, town in Euboea.
Chaonia, region of northwest Greece.
Chaos, primordial chasm from which Gaia, Eros and Tartarus sprang.
Charicles, mutual fund partner.
Chersiphron, architect of Cnossos in Crete.
Chimaera Energy, Inc., oil company named for a fire breathing creature part lion, goat and snake.
Cineas, chief financial officer of Asterion.
Circe, socceress that drugged Odysseus' men.
Clinias, employment attorney representing Nemean.
Clio, legal assistant representing Nemean.
Clonius, accountant for Asterion.
Clymene, Thrasycles' wife.
Clytemnestra, killed her husband Agamemnon upon his return from the Trojan War, and mother of Orestes and Electra.
Clytius Corporation, company named for a giant slain by Hecate in the battle for Mount Olympus.
Cnossos, ancient palace in Crete.
Colchis, region on the eastern coast of the Black Sea and destination of the Argonauts.
Connidas, Theseus' tutor.
Copreus, bureau agent.
Corcyra, large island of west Greece.
Corinth, city in the northeast Peloponnese.
Corsica, large island west of Italy.
Cosmas, law student.

Cottus Company, telecommuication equipment manufacturer named for the creature that battled the Titans.
Creon, king of Thebes.
Crete, largest Greek island southeast of the Peloponnese.
Croesus, king of Lydia defeated by Cyrus and the Persians.
Cronos, Titan son of Gaia.
Cymone, Athenian widower.
Cythera, Greek island south of the Peloponnese.
Daedalus, famed Greek artisan and father of Icarus.
Damasias, senior labor partner.
Damastes Drilling Corp., oil development company named for a robber on the road between Athens and Troezen.
Danaans, decedants of Argos.
Dardanus, litigation partner.
Darius, a king of Persia.
Deioces, king of Media chosen to rule for his wisdom.
Delilah, wife of Minos.
Delos, Greek island in the south Aegean Sea.
Delphi, city in cental Greece and site of the Temple of Apollo.
Demaratos, Athenian general.
Demeter, goddess of agriculture.
Demosthenes, banking partner and member of the executive committee and the Areopagus.
Derinoe, junior lawyer and one of the Amazons.
Dicaeus, Athenian citizen and relative of Cymone.
Diocles, corporate associate.
Diomedes, Greek warrior in the Trojan War.
Dionysus, god of wine.
Dorians, a Greek people sharing common heritage and ancestry.
Ecclesia, Athenian assembly of the people.
Eetion, Asterion's independent public accountant.
Electra, sister of Orestes.
Eleon, securities litigation partner.
Elephantine, island in the Nile river.
Eleusis, town in west Attica.
Elpides, boyhood friend of Theseus.
Elpidius, government trade lawyer.
Empusa Corp., technology company named for a demigod that

devoured men in their sleep.
Endios, Pedocles' chauffeur.
Enticles, Athenian citizen.
Epaminondas, famed Theban general.
Epidaurus, region of the northeast Peloponnese.
Erasicles, chief executive of Typhon.
Erastus, bureau agent.
Erechtheus, former firm chairman.
Eteocles, son of Oedipus who fought Polynices for the throne of Thebes.
Euboea, island region in northeast Greece.
Eubulus, Athenian politician.
Eucles, employee of Baricos.
Euippos, litigation attorney.
Eumenides, goddesses of vengence.
Eurystheus, king of Argos who imposed the twelve labors on Heracles.
Eurytus, owner of Hind Scientific Company.
Faenus, popular artist.
Gallus, court magistrate.
Gelon, father of Nicodromos.
Geryon Corp., technology company named for a monster with three heads.
Glaucus, citizen of Sparta.
Glaukos, warrior of Troy.
Golden Fleece, fleece of the golden ram sought by Jason and the Argonauts.
Gorgon, female monsters with snakes for hair who turn to stone those who meet their gaze.
Gryllus, native of Aetolia.
Gylippus, Spartan general who defeated the Athenians at Syracuse.
Hades, brother of Zeus and ruler of the underworld.
Haemon, son of Creon and wooer of Antigone.
Hagnon, Aegeus' house servant.
Hebe Foundation, charity named for the goddess of youth.
Hecate, goddess of sorcery and prosperity.
Hector, Trojan hero.
Helen, wife of Menelaos taken by Paris to Troy.

Hephaestus, god of crafts.
Hera, wife of Zeus and goddess of marriage.
Heracles, Greek hero.
Hermes, messenger of the gods.
Herodian, firm security guard.
Hind Scientific Company, laser technology company named for the Ceryneian Hind sacred to Artemis.
Hippias, white collar crime partner.
Hyblesios, shipping merchant.
Hypereides, class action litigation partner and member of firm executive committee and the Areopagus.
Ianthe, first year associate.
Icarus, son of Daedulus.
Idomeneus, Greek warrior in the Trojan War.
Ilium, also known as Troy.
Illyria, region of west Greece.
Iole, flight attendant.
Iollas, corporate associate.
Ionia, Greek region in west Anatolia.
Iraklion, port city of Crete.
Iris, goddess of sea and sky.
Isagoras, Athenian magistrate.
Isaios, executive compensation partner and member of the firm executive committee and the Aeropagus.
Isocrates, firm general counsel.
Janos, commercial finance partner.
Jason, Greek hero that led the Argonauts to Colchis to retrieve the Golden Fleece.
Keos, coporate lawyer for Nemean.
Laconia, region in the southeast Peloponnese.
Ladon Corporation, solar panel manufacturer named for the dragon serpent slain by Heracles.
Laelaps Investment LP, investment fund namd for the mythical dog that always caught its prey.
Lamachus, corporate lawyer.
Larissa Minerals Ltd., company named for a nymph local to Thessaly.
Leda, Tantalus' girlfriend.
Leodamas, traveling sophist.

Theseus

Leuctra, town in Boeotia near Thebes and site of Nemean's operations.
Linus, Heracles' music teacher.
Lityerses, man who killed his guests after challenging them to a contest.
Locris, region of Greece along the Corinthian Gulf.
Lotos, an addictive plant that makes men forget.
Lydia, region of west Anatolia.
Lysias, counselor to Aegeus and firm lawyer.
Macedonia, kingdom in the northeastern pennisula of Greece.
Maenads, female worshippers of Dionysus.
Magnesia, southeastern region of Thessaly in eastern Greece.
Mantinea, city in the central Peloponnese.
Marathon, town in east Attica.
Markarios, warrior from Epidaurus.
Medea, consort of Aegeus and real estate partner.
Medeius, manager of Asterion's operations in Stratus.
Media, a kingdom of Persia.
Medusa, the Gorgon slain by Perseus.
Megara, coastal region near west Attica.
Megistas, Athenian citizen.
Melas, chief exectuive of Podarge.
Melesius, senior corporate partner.
Memphis, city in Egypt in the Nile delta.
Menelaos, warrior in the Trojan War and husband of Helen.
Messene, city in the southwest Peloponnese.
Miletus, city in Ionia.
Minos, ruler of Crete and chief executive of Asterion.
Mnene, junior investment banker at Typhon.
Mount Cithaeron, mountain in central Greece.
Mount Olympus, highest peak in Greece located in Thessaly.
Mount Parnassus, mountain above Delphi in central Greece.
Mount Tmolus, mountain in Lydia.
Muses, goddesses of literature and art.
Mycenae, city in the northeast Peloponnese.
Mydon, assistant to Phalius.
Nasamonians, a people of north Africa.
Naupactus, costal town in Locris.
Nausicaa, daughter of Alcinous and Arete who provided aid to

Odysseus.
Naxos, large island in the Aegean Sea.
Neaira, trust and estate lawyer.
Neidias, chairman of Argus.
Neleos, son of Odius.
Nemean Software Systems Ltd., Pedocles' software company named for a fierce lion.
Neoptolemus, son of Achilles.
Nereus, Titan of the sea.
Nessus Technologies, Inc., computer manufacturer named for a centaur.
Nestor, elder Greek statesman.
Nicias, Athenian general during the Peleponnesean War.
Nicodromos, Epidaurian noble and father of Markarios.
Nicostratos, shareholders counsel.
Nike, goddess of victory.
Nikon, junior associate.
Nisos, Athenian commander and father of Appolomedes.
Nomion, Asterion accountant.
Odius, Athenian citizen and father of Neleos.
Odysseus, Greek hero.
Oedipus, king of Thebes who unwittingly murdered his father and married his mother.
Ophelia, Theseus' housekeeper.
Orestes, Agamemnon's son who avenged his father's death by killing his mother Clytemnestra and her consort Aigithos.
Orpheus, unparalleled musician and bard.
Orthrus Financial Ltd., investment bank named for a two headed dog.
Paeon, healer of the gods.
Pandaros, Trojan warrior.
Paseas, court judge.
Patroklos, companion to Achilles.
Pausanias, litgation partner.
Pedocles, founder of Nemean.
Pegasus, winged god-like horse.
Peisistratos, loyal companion to Telemachos.
Pelias, Greek king who sent Jason to retrieve the Golden Fleece.

Peloponnese, southern pennisula of Greece.
Peloponnesian War, extended war between Sparta, Athens and their allies.
Penelope, Odysseus' wife.
Penthesileas, Typhon's counsel and one of the Amazons.
Pentheus, Theban king that denied the worship of Dionysus.
Pericles, noted Greek statesman during the early part of the Peloponnsian War.
Perigune, chief executive of Sinn.
Periphetes Logistics Corp., mainframe computer manufacturer named for the one eyed monster that attacked travelers between Athens and Troezen.
Perseus, king of Mycenae who slew Medusa.
Persia, kingdom of Anatolia.
Phaeacians, inhabitants of Phaeacia who provided aid to Odysseus.
Phaeax, counsel to the creditors committee for Asterion.
Phalius, hedge fund manager.
Phaselis, coastal city in south Anatolia.
Philoctetes, skilled archer during the Trojan War.
Phoenicia, city of the east Mediteranean.
Phormion, director of Asterion.
Phylas, senior litigation associate.
Phylos, chief executive of software development and hosting business.
Piraeus, Athenian port.
Pirithous, loyal friend of Theseus and securities partner.
Pisander, Athenian statesman.
Pittheus, king of Troezen and Theseus' grandfather.
Plataea, Boeotian city and Athenian ally during the Peloponnesian War.
Ploutus, god of wealth.
Podarge Health Associates, Inc., developer of medical facilites named for a harpy known for stealing food.
Polymedes, Athenian citizen and father of Calliphon.
Polyphemus, cyclops that captured Odysseus and his crew.
Polyxena, friend of Iole from Rhodes.
Pontus, south coastal region of the Black Sea.
Poseidon, god of the sea.

Poulydamas, Trojan warrior.
Praxiteles, famous Athenian sculptor.
Prometheus, Titan that gave fire to man.
Proteus, king of Pharos, an island of Egypt.
Pylades, loyal companion to Orestes.
Pylos, city in Messenia.
Pyrrhos, Athenian citizen.
Radamanthos, director of Asterion.
Rhea, environmental partner.
Rhegium, city in Italy.
Rhesus, associate lawyer representing Nemean.
Rhodes, island in the southeast Aegean Sea.
Salamis, island off the coast of Attica.
Samos, island in the east Aegean Sea.
Sardis, city in Lydia.
Sargeus, director of Asterion.
Sarpedon, Trojan warrior.
Satyros, executive recruiter.
Scythia, region north of the Black Sea.
Seculus, pension partner.
Selegus, bankruptcy partner.
Selene, corporate paralegal.
Silenos, president of Asterion.
Silenus, satyr that attended Polyphemus.
Sinis, chairman of Sinn.
Sinn Consulting Co., marketing company named for a robber that killed travelers along the road from Attica to Troezen.
Sipylus, city in Lydia.
Smyrna, city in Aeolis.
Solon, famed lawgiver of Athens.
Sophos, first year associate.
Sostias, Athenian soothsayer.
Sparta, city in Laconia.
Spartoi, hotel in Thebes named for the progenitors of the first inhabitants.
Sthenelus, young Athenian citizen.
Stheno Distribution Corp., distibution company named for one of the Gorgons.
Stichius, securities commission attorney.

Stolos, investment banker at Typhon.

Straton, junior associate.

Stratus, city in Arcanania and site of Asterion's call center.

Strybele, junior investment banker at Typhon.

Stymphalae Flight Co., shell corportion formed by Minos named for man eating birds with metal beaks and feathers.

Syracuse, major city in Sicily attacked by Athens during the Peloponnesian War.

Talos Bank, Minos' personal bank named for a giant bronze man that lived in Crete.

Tantalus, tax partner and Athenian citizen.

Tartarus, the underworld.

Tegea, city in Arcadia in the central Peloponnese and site of Asterion's data center.

Telchines, technical university named for the early people of Rhodes.

Telemachos, son of Odysseus.

Tellus, Athenian citizen praised by Solon.

Termerus Corporation, producer of high density storage devices named for a robber slain by Heracles.

Teucer, first year associate.

Thanatos, first year associate.

Thargelion, month of the Greek calendar.

Thasos, island in the north Aegean Sea.

Thebes, city in Boeotia in central Greece.

Themis, goddess known for law and social order.

Theoclymenus, son of Proteus and wooer of Helen.

Thermodusa, young attorney and one of the Amazons.

Thero, hedge fund manager.

Thersites, Greek warrior in the Trojan War.

Theseus, Greek hero and corporate securities lawyer.

Thespia, city in Boeotia in central Greece.

Thrasycles, junior executive of Asterion.

Timais, law student and summer associate.

Timarchus, manager of hunting grounds in Aetolia.

Timocrates, Greek sophist.

Tiro, venture capitalist.

Tisias, regulatory partner and lobbyist.

Titanomachy, battle between the Titans and the gods for

Mount Olympus.
Tityos Bank, Nemean's bank named for the giant son of Zeus.
Toxeus, justice attorney.
Trakas, founder of Termerus.
Triton, firm business manager.
Troezen, city in the northeast Peloponnese.
Troy, city in northwest Anatolia.
Tydeus, finance executive at Podarge.
Typhon Securities Ltd., investment bank named for a giant with one hundred dragon heads.
Ucalegon, Asterion programmer.
Urania, girlfriend of Timarchus.
Xenos, securities partner.
Xerxes, king of Persia during the second invasion of Greece.
Zeus, ruler of the Olympian gods.
Zosimus, patent partner.

Made in the USA
Lexington, KY
16 April 2013